The Dark Prophet Saga: Book One

Sir Edge

A Bowl of Souls Novel
By Trevor H. Cooley

Trevor H. Cooley
Copyright 2017 by Trevor H. Cooley

Books by Trevor H. Cooley

Noose Jumpers:
Book One: Noose Jumpers
Book Two: (Upcoming)

The Bowl of Souls Series:
The Moonrat Saga
Book One: EYE of the MOONRAT
Book 1.5: HILT'S PRIDE
Book Two: MESSENGER of the DARK PROPHET
Book Three: HUNT of the BANDHAM
Book Four: THE WAR of STARDEON
Book Five: MOTHER of the MOONRAT

The Jharro Grove Saga
Book Six: TARAH WOODBLADE
Book Seven: PROTECTOR of the GROVE
Book Eight: THE OGRE APPRENTICE
Book Nine: THE TROLL KING
Book Ten: PRIESTESS of WAR
Book Eleven: BEHEMOTH

The Dark Prophet Saga
Book One: Sir Edge
Book Two: Halfbreeds (2019)

The Tallow Mysteries
Book One: Tallow Jones, Wizard Detective
Book Two: Tallow Jones, Blood Trail
Book Three: (Upcoming 2019)

Dedication

To my younger sister Megan, who often seems like an older sister. You are like the Jhonate of our family. Firm, stern at times, but willing to sacrifice everything for those you love and when you want something you don't stop until it gets done. Love you, Sis.

Acknowledgements

A special thanks to my Patreon supporters and alpha readers. Here are just a few of you that have helped to make my dream of writing full time a continued success: Stephen Quinlan, Vincent Miles, Randy Stiltner, Ethan Nicolle, Derek Morgan, Adam Masias, Aglaia Greenberg, Brian Layman, Brian Every, Michael R. Clay, Amanda, Alexander Arn, Zekeriah Jones, Keith E. Scott, Madisen Dunn, Rebecca Smith, Jay Williams, Elliott Williams, Dave King, Michael Schober, Honor Raconteur, Chris Robey, Kami and Jacob Jenkins, and Vern Pehl.

Also, thank you to all of my active supporters on Facebook, Discord, Twitter, and everyone who have left reviews for my books. Your support and encouragement got me through a lot of stressful times this last year. I love you all.

Table of Contents

Chapter One

Sir Edge – Memories

The child lay dying. She was sprawled on the ground, her red hair looking oddly clean fanned out on the muddy street. Her breaths were quick and shallow, her lungs constricted by the tremendous pressure across her waist. The lower half of her body disappeared beneath the collapsed roof of the building.

Every building in the village was in ruins now. The monsters had swept through, killing everyone, burning and looting. She didn't know why. She only knew pain and sorrow.

She shivered as she grew colder, tears flowing, her mouth opening and closing in soundless cries. The sky above, tainted by billowing clouds of smoke, flowed slowly above her, populated by sparkles in her vision. Then, as her eyesight began to dim, a shadow fell over her. Someone crouched beside the child and a nightmarish face looked into hers.

The creature was bald and covered with tiny greenish scales. It had no nose to speak of, just slits for nostrils. Its eyes, set under thickly-scaled brow ridges, were golden and calculating. It placed a clawed hand gently on her chest as it surveyed her situation. When it parted its thin lips to speak, she saw teeth like razors.

Its voice was a dry hiss, but it managed to enunciate perfectly. "This one lives, but barely." It turned its earless head to speak to someone out of view. "A beam is crushing her. I don't know if she can be saved, but if you hurry you may at least find out what she saw."

9

"Take care with what you say. You're going to scare her," chided a man's voice. She would have turned her head to look at this newcomer, but at the moment it was taking all her strength just to continue drawing breaths.

The creature turned its face back towards her, its brow ridges shifting in an apologetic look. "Sorry if I frightened you, dying child," it said and moved out of her line of sight.

The creature's lithe form was replaced in her vision as a man knelt beside her in the mud. He was a big man, broad of shoulder and heavily muscled. Brown hair, cut at chin-length, framed a face that was both young and weathered. At the left side of his face hung a single braid that was interwoven with a green ribbon. He looked down on her with kind eyes and smiled.

"It'll be alright," he said and reached out to cup her face with his left hand.

The moment his hand touched her skin, the child's pain fled as if sucked away by his fingertips. Her breathing eased, and her vision cleared. She was numbly aware of her grievous injuries, but there was no emotion to go along with this information.

She managed to speak a single word. "Who?"

"Don't speak, sweetie. Just breathe," he said, and with her mind free from pain she noticed that the man was well-armed. He wore a complex leather armor vest that was stitched together with silver thread and stamped with a myriad of runes. Rising over his shoulders, she could see the hilts of two strange swords as well as a quiver of arrows. "Deathclaw, give me a hand?"

The creature returned to her field of view and drew the sword that was sheathed over the man's right shoulder. Now that she saw the weapon fully, she wasn't so sure it was a sword. The weapon was three feet long and crescent-shaped, the sharp curved edge of the blade arcing past the hilt to end in a dagger-like point at the bottom. An intricate square rune was etched into the blade just above the hilt.

10

"Where should I pierce her?" the creature asked, pointing the unwieldy-looking weapon at the girl.

The man's smile twitched and he gave the creature a reproachful glance. "You didn't need to ask that aloud."

It arched a brow ridge at him. "She cannot feel fear at the moment. You are stealing it away."

The man frowned at the creature and as they locked gazes, something unspoken passed between them. He rolled his eyes and returned his attention to her. "Don't pay him any mind. I'm going to do my best to heal you. You won't feel any pain, but it'll be kind of strange. You might see and experience things that you don't understand. Don't worry. Those thoughts will fade."

The creature brought the pointed tip of the blade closer to her body. The child watched with lack of emotion as it pierced the flesh of her forearm. She felt the steel enter her, but the man was right. There was no pain to go along with it.

Later, she would not remember the man letting go of her face and grasping the hilt of his sword. Nor would she remember the creature lifting the beam off of her body or the man's magic knitting together her ruptured organs and fractured bones. Instead, her mind was whisked away.

No longer did she have the thoughts of a broken girl of nine. She saw the sights and thought the thoughts of a young boy. His name was Justan. His father was a famous and powerful warrior, a leader in the Dremaldrian Battle Academy. His mother was a beautiful and kind woman, a wizardess in hiding who fiercely commanded the community they lived in.

All this boy wanted was to be a warrior like his father. One day, he too would be respected and given a warrior's name. Only as he grew older, his body was gawky and clumsy, the body of a scholar, not a fighter. He was a stubborn lad and refused to accept this fact. He trained himself hard and when he was old enough he joined the training school, determined to pass the Academy's entrance exams.

He failed. But though his body was weak, his mind was sharp. He excelled in strategy and showed enough promise that he was given multiple chances. Finally, he was given one last chance. Justan's father hired a strange young warrior woman from a far-off land to be his teacher. Her name was Jhonate and for one long year, she trained him mercilessly. He hated and resented her at first, but over time he began to trust her and under her harsh tutelage his ungainly body began to improve.

The trust between Justan and Jhonate blossomed into a deep friendship. On his eighteenth birthday, she gave him the priceless gift of a Jharro bow, a powerful weapon that would link him with Jhonate and her people forever more. When the year of training ended, the time of testing came once again. Justan went into it with a renewed confidence, not knowing that schemes were in place to stop him from entering the Academy.

On the day of the stamina test, Justan was pushed down a steep embankment where he encountered a wicked ghost known as the Scralag. The creature scarred his chest with a frost-covered rune and vanished inside him. On the day of the final test a miraculous event happened, and he used a strange form of magic that gave him the skill and stamina he needed to win the day. Justan exulted, thinking his goal finally met, but it was not to be.

A wizard appeared with the Academy Council and it was decreed that before Justan could enter the Academy he had to go to the Mage School and learn to use this strange magic within him. Justan had no choice but to go and as he parted from Jhonate he realized that the friendship between them had deepened to love in his heart.

It was during the journey to the Mage School that the nature of Justan's magic began to be revealed. He became lost in the woods and was beset by evil moonrats. As he contended with the beasts, he was rescued by a magical creature that was a mix of horse and lizard. Her name was Gwyrtha and the magic within him forged a permanent mental bond between them. As a side effect of this bond, his stamina was increased.

Justan spent a year at the Mage School, frustrated that his dream of being a warrior was put to the side. He learned quickly, and on the day he was to graduate from cadet to apprentice, his life's course was changed once again.

During the apprenticeship ceremony, each cadet stood before the Bowl of Souls, a holy artifact that could see the true value of the person before it. The bowl was the ultimate arbiter of good and truth and as Justan stood before the bowl, its magic enveloped him. A new name burst from his lips and he was marked with runes on the back of his right hand and the palm of his left. Justan was named Sir Edge and marked as a warrior and master wizard.

Justan couldn't understand why the bowl had done this. He wasn't a great warrior. Nor could he use magic like a wizard. Justan looked at his naming runes and felt cheated. He hadn't been given the chance to earn his new name. He wouldn't feel comfortable using it for many years.

Over the ensuing months a war erupted in the land. A dark wizard by the name of Ewzad Vriil sought power and the destruction of both the Battle Academy and the Mage School.

Justan's magic expressed itself twice more. First, he forged a new mental bond with a tender-hearted ogre by the name of Fist. Fist gained intelligence from his bond with Justan and Justan gained strength from the ogre. His final bonded was Deathclaw. He was a raptoid, a type of dragon who had been captured by Ewzad Vriil and altered by his wicked magic.

Now with a humanoid form, Deathclaw had only revenge on his mind. Justan gained agility and control over his body from the raptoid. Through his bond with Justan, Deathclaw gained intelligence and human understanding.

During the war, Justan saw many of his friends and mentors killed. The Academy was destroyed, and the surviving forces gathered in the Mage School. It was here that Justan learned that the Scralag who lived inside his chest was bonded to him and was actually the corrupted spirit of his great grandfather, Artemus.

With the help of the combined might of the Mage School and Academy forces, Justan and his bonded were able to destroy Ewzad Vriil and his army of monsters. The Academy started the process of rebuilding and Justan was now free to marry Jhonate, the love of his life. The only thing standing in the way of their union was her father, the Protector of the Grove, leader of the Roo-Tan.

In the land of Malaroo, the Roo-Tan guarded the Jharro Grove, a holy forest of ancient trees that emitted a power that protected the land. Jhonate's father was not pleased that she had become betrothed to an outsider and he refused to allow their marriage until he had settled his countries problems.

An ancient witch known as Mellinda had returned from death seeking to destroy the Jharro Grove. She sought the help of the trollkin that lived in the swamps. Their goddess, a troll behemoth that lived beneath the swamps, was eager for the power of the grove. Mellinda used that eagerness to gain power and control over the trollkin.

During a treaty meeting, the behemoth attacked. It swallowed half of the Roo-Tan warriors, including several of Justan's friends and Jhonate's family members. The behemoth took away the memories of those it consumed and combined their flesh with the flesh of trolls to create more trollkin. They were led by the Troll King, who had once been Jhonate's oldest brother.

As the Roo-Tan fought against the trollkin, Justan led a force of his bonded and their friends to the heart of the swamps. There they fought Mellinda and the behemoth she controlled. Justan managed to use the power of his sword to rend the behemoth's mind asunder and finally destroy Mellinda for good.

Malaroo enjoyed its first true peace in a thousand years. Justan and Jhonate were finally able to wed.

In the sixteen years since their marriage, Justan and Jhonate had gone through many adventures together. During this time, Justan had grown into his name. He was Sir Edge now and his deeds were well-known. He had the fame and glory that he had dreamt of as a child, but those things meant nothing to him anymore.

He was now embroiled in a new conflict and driven by a deep pain within him, a pain fifteen years in the making . . .

Sir Edge knew that the little girl was searching through his memories. This was an unfortunate side effect of using his left sword to heal another person. While his sword was in their body, a temporary bond was created. This allowed Edge to use his magic to heal them from within, but it also connected their minds, leaving his thoughts open to intrusion.

Most people he healed this way didn't think to intrude this deeply, but the girl had been through a terrible tragedy. To flee from those horrors, she had taken refuge in his mind. He didn't stop her. While she was experiencing his past, Sir Edge experienced hers.

The child's name was Lillian and she was nine years old. She had spent her entire life in this small village. Her family was poor, but happy. They worked hard in the fields and spent their evenings together playing games and telling stories.

Lillian didn't know why her father had been frightened that morning. The other kids said that the town council had met and that something big was going on, but that was grownup stuff. Lillian's mind was focused on the coming harvest festival and the enormous melon that she knew was cooling in the creek.

Edge's lips twisted as he experienced her horror and fear as her family was slain. He saw the devastation of her village and he saw enough to know the identity of the monsters that had committed this atrocity. The vision ended and as he finished healing her, tears fell from his cheeks. He blinked and saw the child looking up at him.

"Don't cry for me, Sir Edge," she said, reaching one arm up towards him, her small brow wrinkled in concern.

"Sleep, Lillian," he said gently, and she did.

Edge slowly drew the tip of his sword from her forearm, healing the wound left by his blade as he went. When he sheathed his sword, only the shallowest of cuts remained in her skin. He bent down and picked her up carefully in his arms.

"You shouldn't have let her see so much," Deathclaw said in disapproval. The raptoid stood a short distance away, his arms folded over the bandoleer of throwing knives that crossed his chest. "Her small mind will be overwhelmed by so many memories. And now she knows your secrets. Our enemies could find out."

Edge pushed away the sorrow of her memories and let out a patient sigh. He rubbed the tears away from his face. "I didn't let her see anything that would put her in danger. The memories she did see will help to crowd out the things she experienced today."

Deathclaw shook his scaled head. "You have a weakness when it comes to children."

"And you don't?" Edge teased. "I know your mind. I've seen how gentle you are with small ones."

Deathclaw hissed in derision. "They are delicate and easy to harm." He gestured towards Lillian. "What would you have us do with this child, Edge?"

"There is a village not far from here," he said. "We will bring her there and find someone to care for her."

Deathclaw nodded in approval, relieved that Edge didn't intend to care for the child himself. "And then?"

Sir Edge set his jaw. "And then we hunt down the people who did this."

Chapter Two
Lucinder - Adventure

"Come, Cinder," said Nurse Deena, who was standing in the doorway of the prince's small library. The portly old woman gestured impatiently at him. "There is little time, child!"

Lucinder sighed at being called a child. He was fifteen after all and a prince, even if few people knew of him. He put a feather in his book to mark his place.

He had been reading the ancient exploits of Sar Gander, a female gnome warrior who had been named by the Bowl of Souls nearly 500 years ago. She had been the personal bodyguard of Regus Drelbach, first king of Khalpany and Lucinder's direct ancestor. He had read the book multiple times, but this was one of his favorite parts and he loathed to put it down.

"Can I bring my book?" he asked.

Lucinder knew that wherever the nurse planned to take him, he would just have to sit and wait again. His days were often spent being dragged around from one place in the palace to the next, always with urgency, but most often just to sit around and wait for whatever purpose was laid out for him.

"If you must. Now come!" she said and Lucinder realized that her gestures weren't just impatient, they were panicked. She turned her head away from him to look down the hallway, her eyes full of fear.

He put the book down and stood from the cushioned couch. He came to her side, intrigued. What could have his normally stoic nurse so flustered? He looked in the direction she was peering but could see no one in the long hallway outside the room. "Is father calling for me or something?"

"Undoubtedly," she said. "Let me see your hands."

Obediently, he held out his hand and let her inspect them. Nurse Deena often did this. She looked at his palms and the backs of his hands, then carefully examined his fingernails. Seemingly satisfied, Deena stepped into the library with him. She shut the door behind her and locked it with her master key.

"If father wants me, then why lock the only door? There's no other way out of this room," he said, his puzzlement increasing.

She returned her attention to him and her frightened eyes softened. She reached up and cupped his chin with one wrinkled hand. "Cinder, do you trust me?"

"Of course, Nurse Deena," he replied, and it was true. The irascible old woman had been at his side since he could remember. She had even raised his father before him. In a way, he was closer to her than his own mother who, for some reason he couldn't fathom, could scarcely stand to be near him for more than a few minutes at a time.

"Then will you promise to stay at my side and follow my instructions without question?" Deena asked, her tone as serious as he had ever heard.

Lucinder blinked. "Uh . . . okay."

With a firm nod, she then fished a small vial of clear liquid out of her apron pocket. She pulled the stopper from the vial. Carefully, she bent and poured the liquid into the library door's keyhole.

The keyhole smoked and hissed. The hole was soon filled with a black sludge that quickly solidified.

Lucinder blinked again. His mind was suddenly full of questions, but he forced them away. "You've sealed us in."

18

"I've bought us time," Deena corrected, then hurried across the modest library to the edge of the rearmost bookcase. She reached behind it and pulled on something. Lucinder heard a dull clank and the nurse pulled on the edge of the bookcase. It rotated smoothly away from the wall, revealing an opening and a descending stairwell beyond.

"A secret passage!" he said, his worry turning to excitement. How many countless hours had he spent in this small room throughout the years, often locked inside? Yet this exit had been here all along.

"Secret to most," Deena said and motioned for him to go inside. "We can only hope it remains so for a while longer."

Lucinder stepped inside and his nanny joined him. She pulled on a chain affixed to the back of the bookcase. It swung shut and there was another clank as an iron bar connected with a latch on the back of the bookcase to hold it in place. The stairwell was dark for a few long seconds. Then it brightened as Deena touched a small light orb in a wall sconce. She picked the orb up with her hand and started down the twisting stone steps.

"Uh, I know I promised not to ask questions . . ." Lucinder began.

"Then keep that promise," she replied, holding the orb in front of her. "Shh. We must be as silent as possible until we are free of this place."

A smile spread across the teenager's face as he followed his old nanny down the stairwell. He knew vaguely that he should be alarmed by the situation, but the only feeling in his heart was the sudden thrill of adventure. This was something the sheltered prince had rarely experienced outside of books.

The walls of the stairway were uniform and in the glow of the orb it was hard to tell for certain just how far they were descending. The winding stair seemed to continue for several minutes before they reached the bottom. At the base of the stairs was a short hallway that ended at a wall that was plain but for a single iron ring that was set in the center of it.

Nurse Deena placed the glowing orb in a sconce on the wall and gripped the ring with both hands. With a grunt, she pulled the ring and twisted. With a click, the wall swung inward and Lucinder found himself looking into a narrow walkway between curving stone walls.

Deena closed the door behind her and it was dark again until she grasped another orb out of a wall sconce. It glowed to life in her grasp and she continued forward. The air in this place was musty and damp and there was a thick layer of dust on the ground marred only occasionally by depressions left by past footprints.

They walked forward through a space that was just wide enough for Lucinder to pass through without scraping his shoulders on either wall. Every so often there was a small crack in the mortar between rocks that let a small beam of light cross the walkway. Lucinder paused briefly to peer through one such crack. He couldn't make anything out, but when he placed his ear against it he could hear a low rumble of traffic and muffled voices.

It took the prince a moment to figure out where they were, but he soon understood. They were within the outer walls of the palace. He had always assumed the six-foot-thick walls to be solid and he wondered if they were hollow all along the base. That seemed like a weakness if the palace were ever besieged.

Deena continued ahead, and he hurried to catch up with her. They continued through the narrow curving passage until they reached a point where it ended at a wall of solid rock. Just before the end there was an iron door. Like she had before, the nurse placed the orb in a sconce. She lifted a steel bar that was set across the door and pushed it inward.

They stepped into the room beyond. Light streamed in from small openings in the tops of the walls of the room revealing that it was full of sealed barrels and casks. Deena shut the door behind them and opened one of the barrels. She reached inside and withdrew two dirty blue cloaks.

She donned one of them and pulled the hood up. She handed the other one to Lucinder. "Put this on. We don't need people taking notice of your finery."

The prince wrinkled his nose at the filthy cloak. His clothes weren't all that fine. They were just for lying about. Not for ceremony or anything. Still, he was too intrigued to argue the fact. He threw the cloak around his shoulders and pulled the musty smelling hood up over his head.

They passed through a narrow aisle between casks and through another door. The sound of rough voices and laughter greeted them as they entered a kitchen area. There was one long countertop covered in stacked plates and the remnants of meal preparation. Pots and pans hung from hooks on the ceiling next to two cookstoves that radiated heat. A stoop-shouldered half-orc was mopping the floor between the two stoves and ignored them as they passed by.

Deena pushed open another door and they stepped into the common room of an inn. It was midday, but the place was packed with men and women of various races drinking or gambling. Tattooed slaves wearing steel collars passed between the tables, handing out mugs of ale or collecting empty plates.

Lucinder took in the place with wide eyes. This must be one of the many buildings that had been built against the base of the palace wall. He had never been so close to so many commoners before. They all looked so rough and uncultured.

Deena didn't pause to let him enjoy the scene but forged ahead to the front door. The prince was jostled along the way, but no one paid him any particular attention and he stepped outside into the open air. The street outside was made of cobblestone and was packed with carts and carriages and passersby.

Lucinder's smile widened. He was outside of the palace walls for the first time he could remember. He stepped away from the inn and turned to look up at the palace wall that rose twenty feet above the roof of the inn. In the distance he could just see the tops of the spires of the palace proper and the unending cliff face that rose above it.

Khalpany's royal palace was set into the base of the Khalpan cliffs and the Capitol city of Hagenton sprawled away from its walls, covering the foothills beyond. From Lucinder's rooms in the palace he had been able to see far out to the furthest edges of the city. He had often dreamed of walking the streets with all these people.

Nurse Deena gripped his forearm and pulled him out of the street and into the shadows between the inn and a blacksmith's shop. "Stay still. They should be along any moment."

He didn't get the chance to ask who "they" were. No sooner had she finished speaking than a carriage pulled up in the street before them. A woman in a black cloak looked down at them with sharp eyes from the driver's seat above the carriage. A long staff was laid across her lap. She nodded at Deena.

The carriage door opened, and a man stepped out. He wore a woolen tunic over a chainmail shirt and he carried an oval shield strapped to his left forearm. A sword with an ornate hilt was sheathed at his side. A crooked grin parted his weathered face.

"There you are! We've ridden by several times," he said in a friendly voice. He gestured into the open door with a gloved hand. "Milady. Sir."

"Come," said Nurse Deena and she stepped up into the carriage.

Lucinder began to feel the first stirrings of fear within him as he followed her inside. As thrilling as this all was, what was he getting himself into? Was this being done on his father's orders or was he going to be in trouble when this was all over?

The interior of the carriage wasn't as fine as the few carriages Lucinder had been in before, but the seats were cushioned. Deena sat down and pulled back the hood of her cloak and Lucinder followed suit as he sat next to her.

"Can I ask a question now?" he asked.

The man stepped into the carriage with them and shut the door. The woman driver snapped the reins and the carriage jolted as the horses moved forward. The man settled down in the seat across from them. His hair was brown and curly, his eyes cornered by laugh lines. The windows at either side of the box were covered by curtains, but enough light was let in that Lucinder could plainly see that the crooked grin hadn't left the man's face. His eyes were taking Lucinder in.

"Well, here he is," said the man with a pleasant chuckle. He glanced at Deena. "Did you check his hands?"

"And fingernails," she said.

He returned his attention to Lucinder. "The hidden prince. Did you know that some people don't think you're real? There are rumors that the king made your existence up just so that he could claim to have an heir."

Lucinder frowned at being called the "hidden prince." This wasn't the first time he had heard himself referred to by that name. Sometimes servants whispered it as he was led past them.

"My name is Lucinder," he said. "And I'm only kept hidden because mother and father worry for my safety."

"They would tell you that, wouldn't they?" The man cocked his head. "Yeah, well Lucinder won't do anymore. You look more like a . . . Shea." He nodded. "Yeah, Shea is a nice trustworthy farm boy name. Nice to meet you."

Lucinder's frown turned to a scowl, but before he could say more, the man pulled off his glove and stuck out his hand. Lucinder's eyes widened. There was a square tattoo on the back of the man's hand. "Y-you're a named warrior."

The man's smile widened. "Sir Bertrom." He shook the prince's hand. "I know. It's not as impressive sounding a name as most of us get. The woman you met outside is Mistress Dagger."

"She's a named wizardess?" Lucinder whispered in awe. A shiver passed through the prince. Here he was, in the presence of two heroes like those in the books. This must be a rescue. What was it that they thought they were rescuing him from?

"I know what you're thinking!" Sir Bertrom said. "Dagger is a great name. But it's not very wizardy. I've offered to trade with her, but she won't do it. She just says, 'The Bowl wills what it wills.'"

"Even if the Bowl would let you, why would you want to trade?" Lucinder wondered. "Do you use a dagger?"

Sir Bertrom scratched his head. "Well, no. I'm a sword wielder," he admitted, gesturing at the sword belted at his waist. "But I have a dagger. Everybody has one, right? The point is it's a good warrior name."

"That's true. But Sir Bertrom isn't a bad name," Lucinder replied, thinking back to some of the more adventurous histories he had read. "Not like 'Sir Stump' or 'Sir Lizzy.'"

Bertrom laughed. "Wow. You must read a lot. Those are some obscure ones. I met Sir Lizzy's daughter once. She was studying at the Academy. Hard-nosed woman. Boy could she swing an axe."

The sound of the carriage changed as the wheels left the cobblestone and traveled across dirt road. They must have exited the older part of the city and entered the outer city. Lucinder swallowed. This had all gotten far too real. "Why are the two of you here? Where are you taking me?"

"Sir Bertrom and Mistress Dagger have agreed to take you far away from Hagenton to a place where you will be safe," said Nurse Deena.

24

"Safe from who?" Lucinder asked. He had been in his rooms in an isolated part of the palace. There were at least a hundred guards between there and any threat. The only way he could have been in danger is from someone inside the palace.

Deena gave him an apologetic look. "Cinder-."

"Shea," Sir Bertrom corrected. "Might as well start using it now, Deena. He'll need to get used to it. In fact, we should flesh it out a bit to make it more convincing . . ." He snapped his fingers. "Shea, son of Ralf. That'll do it. I have some proper clothes for you to change into once we get out of the city so you can look the part."

"I don't want to change my name or my clothes. I just want to know what's going on!" the prince said. The novelty of the situation was starting to wear off. As fun as this was, every moment that passed he was being taken farther away from his parents.

Before Deena could respond, the carriage was jolted. There was a loud crack and the sound of splintering wood. The carriage slowed and there was a sharp rapping as Mistress Dagger beat on the roof with her staff.

Sir Bertrom swore and grasped the door handle. "Stay inside unless I call for you."

Bertrom opened the door just as they came to a stop. Lucinder caught a glimpse of squat buildings and a dusty road before the named warrior shut the door behind him. There were shouts of alarm and he could hear a rush of people running past the carriage. Lucinder moved closer to the door and pulled back the curtains, hoping to see what was going on, but whatever it was seemed to be happening in front of the carriage.

Nurse Deena grabbed his arm, but he pulled away from her and opened the door. He pushed it open just in time for a bright flash to fill his vision. A lightning bolt struck nearby with an impact that he could feel in his bones.

Lucinder fell forward out of the carriage and stumbled onto the street, blinking away the glowing residue of the flash.

Standing in the street before the carriage, electricity crackling and popping all around her, was a woman he recognized right away. It was Priestess Sren.

The priestess was as beautiful as she was fearsome, with long flowing blond hair and luscious lips painted black. She wore an intricate suit of leather armor and a red cape, but her real protection came from the multitude of runes tattooed on her skin. The runes were glowing a soft green as they repelled the energy from Mistress Dagger's lightning attack.

Sren's lips parted in a contemptuous sneer as she pointed her black scepter at the wizardess that stood atop the carriage. A lance of fire shot from the tip. Mistress Dagger jumped down from the driver's seat just in time to dodge it. The blazing lance of fire continued its arc through the air and stabbed through a building on the street beyond.

Sir Bertrom was a short distance away contending with a hulking figure that Lucinder also recognized. Standing at nearly seven feet tall, Warwielder Ghat was the captain of the Royal Guard. The orc's massive form was covered in blood red platemail and he moved far more quickly than an orc his size should have been able to. The battle axe he swung at the named warrior was a huge and wicked thing, double sided and tipped with a dagger-like blade.

Sir Bertrom danced in front of the orc captain, deflecting a swing of the axe with his shield and stabbing the tip of his shining sword into the gaps in the orc's armor. If his strikes wounded Ghat, the Warwielder didn't show it. He spun and swung his axe again.

Priestess Sren was now walking toward Mistress Dagger. The wizardess raised her arms and the ground on either side of the priestess erupted. Two slabs of rock rose from the ground and slammed together in an attempt to pulp the priestess between them.

The rock simply crumbled and the priestess continued, her strides unbroken. She pointed her scepter at the wizardess and another lance of fire shot from it, but Mistress Dagger met the blast with her staff and the fire spell disintegrated into smoke.

While the wizardess' vision was blocked by the smoke, Priestess Sren's off hand moved quickly throwing a small dart. Mistress Dagger gasped, and her legs buckled. She held tightly to her staff to keep from falling to the ground.

Sir Bertrom had been fighting toe-to-toe with Warwielder Ghat and seemed to have gained the upper hand. The orc captain was moving with a slight limp, his right leg bloodied. But when the named warrior saw Mistress Dagger's predicament, his concentration faltered.

"Dagger, flee!" he cried.

Ghat smashed Bertrom's shield aside with a backhand blow and when he spun to strike again, the named warrior raised his sword a fraction too high. The orc saw this and swung low, aiming for the named warrior's forearm.

The orc's axe sunk into the flesh of Sir Bertrom's sword arm, but it didn't cut through. A named warrior's right arm couldn't be broken or severed. His rune protected it. Nonetheless, the impact of the strike spun the man around and the orc kicked out with a spiked boot.

The spike caught Sir Bertrom in the side and pierced his mail shirt. As he staggered away, blood poured from the wound. Warwielder Ghat followed after him, swinging his axe back once more.

"No!" shouted Lucinder. "Stop fighting. I'll go with you!"

Priestess Sren, who was now standing over Mistress Dagger's unconscious form, turned her menacing gaze his way. "Silence, boy," she said and threw something at him.

Lucinder felt a sting in his shoulder and he lost feeling in his limbs. He crumpled to the ground and as his vision faded, he saw Nurse Deena rushing to his side.

When Lucinder woke, he was standing in a room made of polished black marble. Every surface was dark with only small swirls of green and gray. He knew this place. His parents had brought him here once a month every year of his life since he could remember.

The room was lit by a chandelier of burning candles that reflected off of every polished surface. In the middle of the room was a slight depression and at the center of it was a pedestal that held up a wide bowl of purest silver. His parents stood next to the pedestal, watching him with stony expressions. Lying on the floor in front of them, stripped naked, were the still and bloodied bodies of Mistress Dagger and Nurse Deena.

A sob caught in his throat. Those poor women. He shouldn't have gone with Deena. This was all his fault.

"Father! Mother!" Lucinder said and tried to move towards them but rough hands held him still.

Priestess Sren spoke from behind his ear. "Quiet, boy!"

"Let go of me!" he said, struggling in her grip.

"She said quiet!" shouted Lucinder's father.

King Karl Drelbach was entering the sixteenth year of his reign and his once black hair and goatee were streaked grey. A dark and solemn look was etched into his angular face. Lucinder noticed that both his father's gloves were off. The king never removed the glove on his right hand because it exposed his blackened and withered ring finger.

He raised that hand and pointed at the prince. His voice was strained and furious. "You may not have taken part in the planning of today's treachery, but you are not without blame!"

Lucinder's mother's face was just as solemn, but her eyes were tinged red and filled with sorrow. Her lips quivered, but she said nothing.

Priestess Sren propelled him towards the pedestal. Lucinder struggled, but it didn't matter. He soon found himself standing before the silver bowl. The interior of the bowl was

28

polished silver, but the underside was carved with the shapes of tortured faces. Sitting in the center of the bowl, floating atop clear water, was a shriveled black orb.

"You know what to do," Sren said.

Lucinder did know. As he had done every month that he could remember, he reached into the bowl and picked up the black orb. At least the voice would understand. He repeated the words he had been taught to say. "I . . . stand ready."

The Dark Voice rose in his mind. **Is that so, Lucinder? Has the time come?**

He cried out in pain as an all-powerful force searched forcefully through his mind. The Dark Voice had never treated him this way before. It had always spoken to him as a friend in the past. When the search was over, Lucinder's head throbbed and the voice spoke to him again. **You very nearly are.**

"Is he ready, David?" asked Priestess Sren eagerly.

When the Dark Voice spoke again, it filled the minds of everyone in the room. Its tone was exultant. **The time is close. I have set plans in motion to retrieve the necessary tools. In just a few short weeks he will be ripe, and I will return!**

Priestess Sren cried out in joyous prayer to her god. King Drelbach nodded grimly. Lucinder's mother, Queen Elise Drelbach, once Queen Elise Muldroomon, looked away, tears streaming down her cheeks.

Chapter Three

Sir Edge - Elemental

Fall came early in the northern reaches of Dremaldria and though the sun had only just begun its westward descent a chill had risen in the air. Edge carried the sleeping child back through the ruined and burning town to their horses. He then wrapped her in a blanket and mounted the horse, sitting her small form in front of him.

As Deathclaw moved to the side of his own horse, the animal shied away. He let out a low hiss of disgust and grasped its reins. Though the raptoid understood the practicality of using such a beast for transportation, and had often done so as situations merited it, he would much rather be afoot. His own feet were something he could depend on while even Academy-trained horses such as this one resisted being ridden by a rider with his particular predatory scent.

"You miss Gwyrtha, don't you?" Edge teased, sensing the raptoid's discomfort through the bond.

Deathclaw didn't bother to deny it. "She could grow large enough to carry us both," he replied. "She is faster than these horses, and the energy she gives us is invaluable."

Edge smiled at him fondly, knowing that the raptoid's desire to have the rogue horse around wasn't just practical. The two of them had grown as close as siblings. "I miss her too."

"Don't look at me like that," Deathclaw growled as he mounted his horse. "You do realize that this mission we have undertaken brings us no closer to finding her or the Prophet."

"You don't know that," Edge replied. "We are here because we were guided by the Creator's will. John could show up at any time."

"So you have been saying," Deathclaw grumbled. "But it has been two years since he 'borrowed' Gwyrtha and nothing you have done has helped us find them yet."

Edge couldn't argue with the raptoid's logic. When the Prophet had appeared that day, the horse he was riding had been nearly dead with exhaustion. He had asked Gwyrtha to go with him and since she had been willing to go, Edge hadn't thought it necessary to ask many questions. After all, John had given no indication that their absence would be a long one.

Edge also hadn't expected that her thoughts would be cut off from their bond. He couldn't even tell what direction she was in. The only reason he knew that she was alive and well was because his bond with her was still strong. It was just blocked off.

"We both knew it was a long shot when we set out," Edge reminded Deathclaw. "All we can do is trust in him to bring her safely back to us."

"I don't dispute his trustworthiness," Deathclaw replied. "It's his sense of time."

"True," Edge said. As far as he could tell, John had been around since the world had been created. He worked on his own schedule and had a definite tendency to show up only at the precise moment he needed to.

Deathclaw wheeled his horse around in the opposite direction Edge was facing. "While you find the child someplace to stay, I will track down our prey and discover just how formidable they may be."

"Very well," said Edge and as the raptoid galloped off, he set off on the road towards the next village.

The foothills of the Trafalgan mountains were a dangerous place to live. There was always the possibility of monster raids and only the constant patrolling of the Academy and Dremaldrian soldiers kept the roads clear of bandits. Nevertheless, the soil in this part of the land was fertile and the relative freedom that came from rural life made the risk worth it to hardy frontier folk.

Those benefits were appealing enough that the region was booming. People staked out land and clustered together forming villages that dotted the countryside, even extending up into the more dangerous areas of the mountains. Generally, the villages were no more than a day's ride apart. A traveler could ride along these roads and never have to spend a night under the stars.

While Edge rode, he sent a tendril of thought through the network of spirit magic connections that composed the place within himself that he knew as "the bond." He searched out one connection in particular; the bond between himself and the naming runes on his hands. This connection was different from his others. It had been created by the Bowl of Souls itself. This made it his closest connection to the Bowl and thus, the Creator's will.

Every named warrior or wizard had this connection. It was the source of the odd promptings that led them to the places the Bowl needed them to be. Over the years, Edge had learned to open himself up to this place. It took a great deal of concentration, but sometimes if he communicated his desires and listened closely, he would receive promptings. They usually weren't specific, just a general positive feeling when he was going in the right direction. But every once in a great while he would receive a direct impression of what he needed to do.

He and Deathclaw had set out from the Mage School in an attempt to use this connection to lead them to the Prophet. The logic was that since the Prophet used a similar method to decide where to go, they might be able to find him. So far, the method had seemed to work, but not in the way they had intended.

All this connection had done was lead them from one person in need to another. They had spent the last two months traveling across the country of Dremaldria doing a lot of good, but mostly in small ways, slaying the odd monster or escorting people through dangerous areas. Edge found satisfaction in this work, but as far as he could tell, it hadn't brought him any closer to his goal.

This time, as he listened to his connection to the Bowl, he focused his mind on another question. Where would be the best place to take this child? No sooner had he asked the question than he felt a strong desire to travel in a specific direction. He immersed his thoughts in this feeling and let it guide him off of the main road and down a small but well-worn trail.

It was dusk when he topped a rise in the trail and saw the torchlights of a village in the valley below. He didn't continue to the village proper though. He turned his horse down a side path that led him along a section of fenced in pasture and up to a rather large farmhouse.

The family that lived here seemed well to do. As he approached, two farmhands armed with axes came out to greet him. He expected that he would need to explain himself, but they took one look at the sleeping child in the saddle before him and led him up to the door of the house. One of them ran inside and by the time Edge dismounted, a woman appeared at the door. She was middle-aged and a cluster of children peeked out from behind her.

"By the gods!" she gasped and hurried down the steps to take the child from him. "Lillian?"

The child stirred at the sound of the woman's voice and opened her eyes. "Auntie Jane," she mumbled before falling asleep again.

"She is alright physically," Edge said. "But she's seen some horrible things."

"What happened?" the woman asked. "Who are you?"

He showed her the naming rune on the back of his right hand. "I am Sir Edge," he began.

She lifted one hand to her chest. "Sir Edge, himself, here at my home." She swallowed. "It must be bad, then. Lillian's parents?"

"The village was razed to the ground," he told her. "She was the only survivor."

The woman squeezed her eyes shut, then nodded and turned towards the house. She called a few older children out and had them carry Lillian inside. She turned back to face him. "And the people who did this?"

"They will be dealt with," he promised.

"It's getting dark," she said. "I have a stew in the pot. Please, eat with us and stay the night. We have a spare bunk. You can sleep with the farmhands."

Edge's immediate instinct was to refuse her offer, but it had been a long day and he needed at least a few hours sleep if he was to do battle the next day. If he'd had Gwyrtha around, he could have just pulled the energy from the rogue horse's limitless stores, but that was a luxury he didn't have.

He accepted her offer. He ate quickly at the long farm table, uncomfortable with the room full of stares directed his way. The people were kind enough not to ply him with too many questions, but as soon as he could, he excused himself and escaped to the bunkhouse.

Troubled by the day's events, he laid down, twisting the Jharro wood ring on his finger. The living wood was warm between his fingers and he could faintly sense Jhonate's presence far to the south where she was at the Mage School, helping train the new Academy recruits. Seeing the child's memories had made him miss her desperately. He wished he could reach her through the ring and speak with her. Unfortunately, the connection that the ring provided wasn't strong enough to communicate at this distance.

In their sixteen years of marriage, they had rarely been apart this long. He normally wouldn't have left her side to undertake a quest this nebulous. It was just that she had work to do, while he didn't. It also hadn't helped that the curse she was under had made her distant lately, but he wouldn't admit that fact to himself.

Sighing, he closed his eyes and sent his consciousness into the cloudy whiteness of the bond. He reached through his bond with Fist, but the ogre was already asleep, and he saw no need to wake him just yet. Instead, he approached his link with Artemus.

His hand moved down to the hilt of his great grandfather's dagger that he kept sheathed at his waist. The cracked naming rune at the base of the pommel was sealed with ice.

When Edge had first discovered the bond between himself and the ghostly elemental that inhabited the scar on his chest, there had been an icy blockage in the bond that kept them from communicating. He had helped his great grandfather overcome the creature that his magic had become and gradually the two of them were able to break down the barriers between them.

Now, instead of a blockage in the bond, there was a door. It was made of solid ice, but carved with a wood-like grain. In order to interact with it, Edge had to visualize a physical representation of himself within the bond. Soon, he was standing before the door and was able to grasp the handle and push it open. The neutral warmth of the bond was hit by a cool blast of air as Edge stepped into the Scralag's world.

The construct formed by Edge's own stolen magic was represented as an enormous open cavern. The ceiling far above was covered in icy stalactites. The ground at the entrance to this place appeared to be smooth rock covered in a layer of frost.

When he had first come to this place it had been taken up by a huge maze of ice. Where those towering walls had once stood was now a grove of leafless trees. Their branches were made of icicles, and the multifaced fruit that grew on them was blood red. Standing in the middle of this forest, towering above the trees was the Scralag.

Gaunt, with long pale limbs and long black talons, it stood motionless, passively watching him through beady red eyes deeply set in skeletal sockets. A chill mist radiated from it, giving the grove a ghostly aura. Its jaw hung open and he could just see the pointed blue tip of its tongue through its razor-sharp teeth.

At one time he had been terrified of the spectral creature. The knowledge that such a horrible being was living in his chest had given him nightmares. But that had been years ago. Edge gave the elemental a casual wave as he walked past the trees.

He headed down a paved walkway towards a small cottage that stood in the middle of a field of pale yellow grass. It was a quaint building that looked out of place in this frozen construct. Its walls were made of stone and it had a thick thatch roof. Smoke rose in a lazy trail from the cottage's single chimney.

Edge walked up to the wooden door and knocked twice before stepping inside. The interior of the cottage was a cozy place, a single large room with a fire in the hearth. In one corner was a plush, empty bed. Along one wall was a tall bookcase packed with books. In front of the hearth, in an overstuffed chair, snoozed Artemus.

The old wizard was dressed in a light blue robe embroidered with a series of circular and crescent runes and a knitted blanket lay across his legs. He seemed to have embraced his age. His wrinkled hands were folded over his belly, his fingernails a well-trimmed gray. His hair was brittle and white. He wore an odd beard that stretched from ear-to-ear across his chin but did not touch his lips.

Edge reached out and grasped his shoulder. "Great grandfather Artemus? I need you."

36

The wizard's eyes fluttered open and he snorted awake. "Already? Why how long has it been?"

"A few weeks," Edge said. "Not since we had to put out that forest fire near Dremald."

"Is that so?" Artemus said. He stood and dusted himself off, then peered through the cabin's solitary window, gazing at the Scralag standing in its frozen forest. He stuck out his hand and a small tea cup appeared in his fingers. Steam wafted from the cup and he took a sip. "Well, dear boy, the elemental dozes so I suppose it has been long enough."

Whenever Artemus expended a great deal of the elemental's magical energy, the wizard had to undergo a long period of sleep afterwards. If he didn't, the Scralag's wild nature began to take over his mind and there was always the danger that it could break free and wreak havoc. It had happened a few times in the past and it was always difficult to get it back under control.

"I assume that you aren't here simply to talk?" Artemus said. "Have you found John? Is Gwyrtha back?"

"No," Edge replied. "Unfortunately. We have another problem."

He sent Artemus a series of memories, showing the old wizard what had happened. "Deathclaw is already tracking the raiders, but from Lillian's memories I think there will be a great number of them to deal with."

"Filthy monsters," the wizard said and as he took another sip, Edge noticed that his fingernails had blackened and had sharpened to talons. His eyes had grown hard. "I shall go to the elemental and prepare. We shall be ready when you call."

"Thank you, Great Grandfather," Edge said.

"You know, it is a pity we find ourselves in this rut," Artemus said. "My life has become a series of battles and long sleeps . . . I very much miss the time we used to spend together conversing. You, me, and the others."

"And Sarine?" Edge said. His great grandmother was a bonding wizardess and despite her advanced age was still going strong. She was the Mage School's official historian and was currently off on a trip to the gnome libraries in Alberri to do research.

Artemus smiled wistfully. "Ah yes. Her too."

"I promise, I'll do my best to make sure you get that time," Edge promised.

"Oh, that's okay, my boy! No need to promise something out of your control. We move as the Bowl wills. That's the curse of being named." He let go of the cup and it disappeared before it hit the ground. "Now go along while I prepare."

Artemus waved his hand and Edge found himself once more standing in front of the icy door in the bond. He couldn't help but feel guilt at his great grandfather's predicament, but there was little he could do about it at the moment. Shrugging, he let his mental construct dissolve and left the bond, letting his mind succumb to sleep.

When Edge woke, it was still a few hours before dawn. He reached through the bond and found Deathclaw many miles to the north, at the base of the mountains. He was sitting high in a tree, in a trance-like state, his body resting as he watched a series of campfires in the far distance through slitted eyes.

What did you find? he asked

A challenge, the raptoid replied, and sent Edge a series of memories and images, telling him what he had discovered about the raiders that had ransacked Lillian's village. Their numbers were overwhelming. *Do you wish to call in help? Perhaps Fist and Rufus could come.*

Edge considered it briefly. It would take the ogre several days to arrive, even on his rogue horse. He didn't feel like waiting. The little girl's memories were still vivid in his mind. *I woke Artemus. He's ready to join us.*

It will still be a challenge, Deathclaw said, though he let out a mental chuckle as he considered the strategies they might employ. *A challenge I will enjoy.*

Edge found the raptoid's enthusiasm infectious. He rose from the bunk and pulled his equipment back on, then went back out to retrieve his horse. He re-saddled her and was about to mount up when a small voice called out behind him.

"Justan?"

Sir Edge froze and turned to find Lillian standing in the doorway to the farmhouse, sleepy-eyed.

"I'm sorry," she said. "I mean, Sir Edge?"

"Yes?" he asked.

"I know you can't stay," Lillian said, and her lip quivered. She rushed forward and embraced him. "I just wanted you to know that . . ."

Edge patted her head and gently pried her arms away. He took a step back and gave her shoulders a soft squeeze. "It's okay, Lillian. You'll be safe here with your family."

"It's not that. It's-." She hesitated again, frowning. "Are you and Deathclaw going to kill those monsters?"

"We won't let them hurt anyone else," he promised her.

She nodded quickly, but the frown didn't leave her face. "You would have been a great daddy. You know that?"

Edge patted her head again and urged her back inside the house before mounting his horse. As he rode off into the darkness, there was a lump in his throat he couldn't quite swallow back.

Chapter Four

Nod - Zeston

"I'm sorry, sir. You shouldn't be in this part of the tower. The line for supplicants begins at the bridge outside," said a young woman with the officious air of someone given a responsibility they felt was beneath them.

Nod quickly assessed her. From the cut of her robes, this girl was an apprentice. She looked to be in her mid-teens, so she'd probably only been at the Mage School for a couple years. Not much of a looker, though maybe she could have been if she tried harder. Her ruffled hair and the circles under her eyes told him she was more interested in study than socializing.

More importantly, the silver and white runes on her robes told him that this particular apprentice was a spirit magic user with a talent for binding magic. This made her a possible threat. Not that she had any magical ability to worry about, but if she used spirit sight and saw the black rune on the back of his left hand, she would know he was named at the Dark Bowl. Things had been so much easier before spirit magic had been taught at the school.

He was wearing fingerless gloves to cover up that rune, but wizards sometimes made people remove their gloves to check for black runes. If she did demand he take the gloves off, he'd have to kill her. That would be messy. He'd have to hide the body and hope it wasn't discovered long enough for him to complete his tasks. Fortunately, she didn't seem all that worried to find an unfamiliar man in this section of the Rune Tower.

Nod bowed obsequiously. "My apologies, Love. I've already been in the line. A friend o' mine is holding my spot while I run to find the privy," he lied in an exaggerated accent. It was something he had made up for this particular persona, a mix of east Khalpan and southern Razbeckian dialects. "Your directions would be much appreciated."

The apprentice let out a tired sigh. This must happen fairly often during naming days. The Mage School set aside two days a month for supplicant warriors to approach the Bowl of Souls in the hope of being named.

Ever since the school had announced that warriors would be allowed to try once a year, would-be heroes made the journey from every corner of the Known Lands. The waiting line stretched nearly to the school's main gate at times. Armed Battle Academy guards watched over the supplicants to make sure that none of them got out of hand.

Most of these supplicants came for the fame and glory that naming would bring. Little did they know that naming came with a lifetime of responsibilities. They thought that the Bowl was simply searching for the most skilled warriors. In reality, it searched their souls and only chose those rare few that it knew would make the right choices at the right time.

Of course, Nod had no intention of going anywhere near the Bowl of Souls. He had been named at the Dark Bowl decades ago. The way it worked was the polar opposite of the Bowl of Souls. It didn't matter how skilled he had been, only how he could best be used. In Nod's case, it had branded his soul with the name Zeston, which was also his job title. It meant that he was the Dark Prophet's retrieval specialist.

The Dark Bowl hadn't stopped with giving him a new name. It had bound itself to his soul, then shoved the memories and skills of past Zestons into his mind. One day, he would die and his memories would join the others to be given to the next

Zeston. Nod was determined that it would be a very long time before that happened.

Sometimes these predecessors of his spoke to him, but Nod had learned to filter their opinions out. Their knowledge was all he needed. Today he was using that knowledge to lead him to the items he was here to steal.

The apprentice pointed down the hallway Nod had just come from. "There are closets for disposal of waste outside of the Rune tower near the center square." She saw the grimace that appeared on his face and sighed again. "If you don't think you can make it that far, there is a 'privy' across the corridor from the main library entrance. It is for students, but the wizards do let outsiders use it in case of emergency."

Nod bowed again. "Many thanks, Love."

"Don't call me that," she said and gave him an impatient gesture.

His smile fading, he turned and walked back the way he had come but kept his thief's eye trained on her. The thief's eye was one of the abilities granted to him by his title. He could use it to see in any direction regardless of the way his natural eyes were looking. It only saw in black and white, but he could see vividly regardless of the light.

He walked forward with purposeful strides until he saw the apprentice shake her head to herself and enter a side room. Nod turned and slid into a shadowy alcove. This place was full of such nooks and crannies.

The Rune Tower was a mind-numbingly enormous structure. The base of it was a quarter of a mile in diameter and the exact number of floors was unknown. The top of the tower was so high that it disappeared into the clouds above on most days and the number of subterranean levels was a subject of debate. Even the memories of Nod's predecessors contradicted each other.

The one thing his memories agreed upon was the route to the Bowl of Souls and the directions to the vault where Nod's first goal lay. He just had to get there without being noticed. That an apprentice had stepped out of a room and surprised him wasn't a good start. He could cloak himself in darkness, another skill given by the Dark Bowl, but that wouldn't keep him from being seen in these well-lit corridors.

He waited a few moments, extending his senses to make sure that no one else was approaching. When he was reasonably certain that the corridor was empty, he left the shadows and rushed forward on silent feet. He darted past the door that the apprentice had entered and turned down another corridor that led to a stone stairwell that led both up and down.

Nod paused at the entrance to the stairs. He didn't sense anyone descending from above, but he could hear distant footsteps far below. He crept upward, knowing that his goal was a full twenty floors up from his current location.

As he climbed he kept his senses extended, employing every trick in his arsenal to make certain that he wouldn't be surprised again. His lithe body moved tirelessly and as he reached the tenth floor, his senses warned him that a powerful magical presence was somewhere ahead. He climbed two more flights of stairs, the presence growing, and then he stopped and pressed his ear up against the stone wall. He was certain that the Hall of Majesty was on the other side. There was no entrance to it from this stairwell, but he knew the Bowl of Souls was only yards away.

Nod's dark rune vibrated against the back of his hand and he briefly considered what would happen if someone like him did approach the Bowl of Souls and dip their weapon in its waters. Would the Bowl burn him to cinders with its holy power or simply alert the local wizards that an enemy was in their midst? Would it sever his connection to the Dark Bowl? There was one other possibility. What if it named him?

The thought made Nod chuckle. His skills would be useful to the Bowl's cause, but he was not the type of person the holy artifact was looking for. Besides, even if it did decide he could be turned to the side of good, he didn't think he'd like the punishments that would come his way for betraying the Dark Voice.

Nod pushed away from the wall and continued his climb. He passed the openings to several corridors. One time he saw a wizard walking in the distance, but he managed to slip by unnoticed. At the eighteenth floor, he paused once again.

His memories told him that the entranceway to the vault would be protected. There would be a series of traps for him to overcome. As expected, the next set of stairs was different from the previous ones.

The stairwell narrowed and became an upward spiral and the rock used in its construction was a slightly different hue. He bent to get a closer look and noticed a tiny set of runes carved in the corner of each step. Access to this particular vault was scheduled in advance and any unauthorized pressure on these steps would trigger an alert.

Easy enough, Nod thought.

He placed his hands against the inner wall and jumped up to plant his feet against the outside wall, suspending himself above the steps. Nod's body was just long enough to manage this particular maneuver in the narrow twisting stairwell. His muscles strained as he edged his way upward, moving one foothold or handhold at a time. He was grateful that he only had to continue this awkward climb for a short time before the runed steps ended and he arrived at the vault door.

The door was solid iron and covered in protective runes. It was impervious to magical attack. Each stone in every wall surrounding the vault was inscribed with similar protections. In order to open the door, a wizard had to touch a series of runes on the door using each of the magical elements. The pattern was secret and changed monthly.

This was where Nod could only trust in the Dark Prophet's other servant in the Mage School. Nod didn't know the wizard's identity, only that they were highly respected and too well-placed for the Dark Prophet to risk having them steal this item themselves. Nod, on the other hand, was a bit more expendable. If he was caught, the Dark Bowl could always bind another Zeston.

Wincing slightly, he reached out and grasped the door handle. He pulled and it swung open soundlessly. He looked at the door jamb and smiled.

It's always the oldest tricks that work, he thought. A small rock had been placed in the lock plate to prevent the door from latching. All he had to do was remove it on his way out and none would be the wiser.

The moment Nod stepped inside the vault he knew that this place was dangerous. Powerful magical artifacts of every kind lined the walls, most of them in protective chests. Most of this power was neutral, but some of them radiated malevolent energies from violent, bound spirits. A few of them pulsed black in his sight and Nod knew that his master would love to possess every item in this room.

Unfortunately, he couldn't carry it all and Nod had been sent for one item in particular. That didn't stop his fingers from itching as he passed shelf upon shelf filled with legendary items. He let out a low whistle as he saw the black mace of Cassandra, the Dark Prophet's previous Priestess of War. It was leaning against one wall, its aura thick with menace. He had seen her use that thing to destroy magical armor and weapons on several occasions.

He finally found the item he sought a nearby shelf. It was a long slender box of black wood. This was also an item that had been in Cassandra's possession when she had been killed. The surface of it was carved in intricate runes of bewitching magic and Nod's inner eye showed him glowing bands of white and black spirit magic crisscrossing it to contain the presence of the item within. In the center of the lid was a single jade stone.

He grabbed it and as he lifted it, he hesitated. It felt a little light. What if the item wasn't inside? Should he open it and check? He feared to do so. If the box was opened, and the

Prophet was anywhere nearby, he might sense its presence and come to destroy it. Yet, if the dagger wasn't in the box he would be wasting his time.

Even as he considered that dangerous action, the rune on his hand pulsed with recognition and he relaxed. Inside that box was Celos, the Jade Dagger, the last remaining of the Dark Prophet's ceremonial daggers. He slid the box into the inner pocket of his jacket.

His goal in hand, he turned to leave, but his eyes fell on a nearby shelf. There was a small leather pouch sitting there. It wasn't anything special in and of itself. There weren't any magical protections on it or anything. But the items inside glowed with every type of magic imaginable. The intensity of it, even among the rest of these artifacts, gave Nod a chill.

"Hello, what's this?" he whispered to himself and carefully opened the pouch to peer inside. A gasp escaped his lips as he recognized what it was. Even his master's wizard contact hadn't known this was in here. This was an item that could change the tide of the coming war. He tucked it away in another pocket and left the room, removing the small rock so that the vault door would lock behind him. Chuckling, he made his way back down the staircase, certain that he would be rewarded for this.

When he left the Rune Tower a short time later, he blended in with the disappointed warriors on their way out. The sun was on a downward path. Shadows were lengthening and soon the last of the warrior supplicants would be politely ejected from the Mage School grounds.

Nod still had one more assignment to complete before he could leave, so he quickened his pace. He sought the guest houses near the front gates of the school. These weren't for mere supplicants, but housed important visitors to the school. As he neared the school's enormous outer wall, he overheard guards say a name that made him stop cold.

"Did you hear? The Daughter of Xedrion went up to stand before the Bowl," one of them, a wide-shouldered dwarf, said.

"Sir Edge's wife? The Hell-Trainer?" said the other one, a young female. "When was this?"

"About an hour ago," the dwarf replied. "She was standing in line with the rabble before one of the wizards recognized her and brought her inside."

Nod forced himself to keep walking. Jhonate bin Leeths was going before the Bowl? Why would she do such a thing? She was a member of the Roo-Tan. Her allegiance was to the Jharro Grove. Her husband may have split his allegiance and served both the Bowl and the Grove, but Nod's sources claimed that she would never do such a thing.

Her weapon was a Jharro wood staff. Could the Bowl of Souls even use a living Jharro wood weapon in the naming ceremony? How would the Jharro tree react to the permanent binding nature of a naming rune? It was an intriguing question. Would the power of such a weapon be strengthened or lessened?

Nod told himself that it didn't matter. In fact, it was to his advantage that Jhonate was inside the Rune Tower. With Sir Edge and his bonded away on some errand, this meant that her home was unguarded. He could enter their home, take the second item he had come for, and leave before she returned.

Not far to the left of the Mage School's main gate, in the shadow of its 50-foot-high walls were a dozen small homes. These guest houses were little more than tidy cottages, but the Mage School didn't see their size or distance from the tower as the insult that Nod knew it was. In Nod's mind, these homes were the wizards' way of telling their guests that they were begrudgingly allowed to stay within the walls, but not trusted enough to let them stay inside the school grounds proper.

Several of the houses were occupied, but Nod was happy to see that no one stood around outside to witness his approach. He found the house that he was looking for right away. Jhonate's house had a small stable next to it where Sir Edge's rogue horse slept when he was around.

Nod made certain that no one was looking his way before he made his approach. The lock on the door was no challenge. Nod picked it easily and slipped inside. He reached out with his senses, probing for the pure blaze of spirit magic that he had been told would be somewhere nearby.

His senses betrayed him. He searched quickly and efficiently with practiced hands, careful to go through every hiding place in the small house without leaving a trace. Surely, the information he had been given wasn't wrong.

The item he was searching for was Tulos, the Ruby Dagger. It had once been one of the Dark Prophet's ceremonial daggers like the one he had just retrieved from the vault. The Prophet had found Tulos and purified it, turning its power against its master. The once black blade was now the purest white and the rubies in its hilt held the power to destroy darkness. Nod had to retrieve this artifact in order to complete his next assignment.

The information his informant had sent him told Nod that the Prophet had given the dagger to Jhonate during Ewzad Vriil's attempt to conquer the land. She had used it to sever the power of the Mother of the Moonrats. It was still in her possession, but Nod had been told that she didn't carry it on her person.

Nod continued his fruitless search for several long minutes before giving up. He stood in the center of the house's small dining area with fists clenched, knowing that he had somehow been thwarted. His source had claimed they had seen the dagger among her belongings here at the school. Either she had hidden it away or she had decided to go against habit and carry it with her for some reason.

He had no choice but to lie in wait for her to return. Even if Jhonate appeared freshly named at the Bowl of Souls, he was confident that he could take her. If she had the dagger with her, he would kill her and retrieve it. If not, he would interrogate her. He had ways of making even the most stubborn of victims talk.

As he considered the best place in which to stage his attack, his eyes fell on a letter lying on the table. Its wax seal had been broken. Curious, he picked it up.

Nod read it, his eyebrows rising. So that was why she went before the Bowl. She didn't know it, but she was heading for the same destination he was. Perhaps there was an alternative way to retrieve what his master wanted . . .

Chapter Five
Deathclaw - Horde

Deathclaw sat high in a fir tree overlooking the raider camp, his body anchored to the trunk with his claws. He was confident that he would not be detected. He stayed absolutely still, and the color of his scales had changed to match the wood and needles.

All dragons, even lesser species like the raptoids Deathclaw had once been part of, had adaptive magic in their blood that allowed them to survive in the most rugged of conditions. Raptoids lived in predatory packs that roamed the deadly Whitebridge Desert. Other dragons had adapted to live in icy snowbound peaks or deep in the ocean or within live volcanoes. The process of adaptation within their bodies was normally a slow one, taking weeks or even months. Deathclaw, however, was different from other dragons.

Ewzad Vriil had captured Deathclaw and made changes to his body with a powerful artifact called the Rings of Stardeon. The rings had left a remnant of their magic behind, leaving his cells bound together by intricate and unstable energies. His dragon heritage, along with Deathclaw's unique control over his body, let the raptoid use that instability to his advantage. He could alter his body in many small ways, such as lengthening his claws or the sharp barb on the end of his tail.

The ability to shift his color was something he had only learned in the last decade, but he had spent the intervening years perfecting the process. He now did so almost without thinking. The only downside to making changes was that the process left him ravenously hungry, something that the large owl who had previously occupied this tree had learned. Deathclaw could still taste it on his tongue.

Can you tell me anything more about these monsters? asked Edge through the bond.

Sir Edge was riding through the darkness of early morning, his hands clenched around the horse's reins. Deathclaw could feel the emotions warring within him. Edge felt sorrow for the girl who had lost so much, he felt pain from his own wounds that her words had reopened, and he felt rage towards the evil beasts that had destroyed that town.

Calm yourself, Deathclaw advised. *As much as you want your emotions to fuel you for the coming battle, all they are doing is distracting your mind. Use your sword if you must.*

I've been relying on it too much lately, Edge replied. *I can't let Peace's power become a crutch.*

Deathclaw hissed in irritation. Edge had always been worried he would become lost in his powers. The raptoid understood his leader's fears, though he didn't agree with them. Edge was too self-aware to let himself lose control and even if he did, the rest of their tribe would be there to correct him.

There is nothing wrong with using a crutch if your leg is broken. It is the proper tool for the job, the raptoid sent. *Your swords are tools for battle. We face a battle.*

Edge shook his head. *When did you become wise? That's usually Fist's job.*

This is not wisdom, Deathclaw replied. *It's strategy.*

Very well, Edge acquiesced and Deathclaw felt him embrace the power of his left sword. Peace's magic eagerly sucked the emotions from Edge's mind and converted them to pure energy. Edge felt Rage, his right sword, vibrating with the need to release it.

When Edge spoke again his thoughts were clear and calculating. *I'm ready. Show me what you see.*

Deathclaw opened his senses to the bond, letting Edge see through his eyes. *This group of raiders should not exist.*

The camp below was populated by as motley a crew of raiders as Deathclaw had ever seen. Four bulky female orcs shared a campfire with two human men, a ten-foot-tall giant, and an elf. Perhaps most strange of all were the beasts that accompanied them. A huge mountain treecat lay stretched out on the ground not far from the fire and gnawed on a bone. Next to it were the piled coils of a massive fur-covered rock python. It's slitted eyes gleamed in the firelight.

The two animals seem to ignore the others. Perhaps they are pets? Deathclaw suggested.

They'd have to be, Edge replied. He thought it likely that they belonged to the orcs. Orcs were known to train beasts for use in battle, though he had never heard of someone taming a rock python. *Has anyone said anything that tells you what is keeping this group together? Which one is the leader?*

Edge's focus was on the elf, though Deathclaw didn't think he looked like a leader. His hair was cut short and he wore leather armor with a bow and quiver slung across his back. He sat next to the giant and stared into the fire, an odd smile on his lips.

I cannot tell. They barely communicate, Deathclaw replied. Their mood seemed almost cheery despite the grim events of the day. There was a lot of rough laughter, but they did very little talking and none of the raiders seemed to defer to any other. *When they do speak, they mainly chant one phrase. 'Praise the Maw.'*

The Maw? said Edge. *Maybe that's the name of their leader. Could it be the giant's name?* It was a decent assumption. The giant's jaw was wide and toothy.

I don't think so. He chants it with the rest of them, said Deathclaw. *But that is not the only strange behavior. They have been at this campsite all night, yet they haven't slept and none of them have bothered to keep watch. Also . . .* He sent Edge the image of the wagon tethered just outside the camp. It was loaded with the bodies of dead villagers. *A few hours ago, they dragged the corpses of three villagers to the fireside and ate them.*

Deathclaw shuddered at the memory. All of them, including the elf and the humans, had partaken of the gruesome feast. The remnants of the meal were scattered all around the raiders.

Cannibalism? The power of his sword kept Edge's disgust at bay, allowing him to think of the situation objectively. Of the races represented around the fire, only giants and the two animals were known to eat men. Even orcs looked down on such a practice. *Why resort to that? The village was full of food.*

This was something that had bothered Edge ever since he had looked through Lillian's memories. The raiders had left most of the village's goods behind, only taking a few treasures. They had come in, killed everyone, loaded their bodies on the wagon, and rode off into the hills.

Perhaps this Maw is their evil god, said Deathclaw. *Eating the flesh of their enemies could be a ritual of worship.*

Edge considered the suggestion. It wouldn't be the first time they had come across some sort of wizard or powerful beast that claimed to be a god. This was a strange group of worshippers, though. *What kind of back country god could capture the imaginations of humans, elves, and orcs?*

Then they are under a spell? Deathclaw asked. He had already looked over the group with mage sight and spirit sight. The orcs' weapons glowed the dull red of fire magic and the elf's bow had the soft white glow of a bound spirit, but there was nothing strong enough to control minds.

I guess there is only one way to find out, Edge said.

Deathclaw nodded. *We kill them and search their bodies for evidence.*

Or, said Edge. *We kill most of them and I interrogate a few with Peace.*

I didn't think that needed saying, the raptoid replied.

There was a sudden stirring in the camp below. As if on cue, the raiders stood together and began kicking dirt over the fire.

"Hail the Maw!" cried one of the female orcs. "The Maw!" replied the others.

Edge saw the scene through Deathclaw's eyes. *It looks like they are getting ready to leave, but I'm still several hours ride from your position.*

Then I shall slow them down, said Deathclaw. He descended from the tree quickly but silently. The sky was just beginning to lighten, but the dark was cover enough for his darting form as he edged around the camp and headed for the wagon.

The wagon was a large sturdy affair. It was painted a garish red and the words, "Farmer Oak's Gourds and Honstule" were painted on the side in yellow paint. Not a likely raider wagon. Deathclaw could smell the corpses already beginning to turn. He examined the wheels. The spokes were thick and sturdy, not something he could disable with a single strike of his sword.

No one had bothered to tether the two horses. They were still hitched to the wagon. This made his job easy. He snuck up to the horses and pulled a throwing knife from the bandoleer that crossed his chest.

Quickly, he severed the harnesses. Deathclaw expected the horses to run, as most such animals did when catching his scent, but these horses seemed well-trained. They stood still. He spun and delivered a stinging slap across their rumps with his tail. He took care not to cut them open with his barb. There was no need to injure the beasts.

Instead of galloping away, both horses kicked at him. Deathclaw was so caught off guard that he didn't dodge in time. One of the horses' rear hooves caught him in the shoulder.

The force of the blow sent him colliding against the edge of the cart and he felt two of his ribs crack. Something was wrong with these animals. He backed away from the wagon, hissing at the inconvenience. His body's regenerative magic would soon heal both his bruised shoulder and ribs, but the wounds would hamper him for a while.

Shouts echoed from the camp, but before Deathclaw could run the horses turned on him and reared, their forelegs lashing out at him. The raptoid wasn't caught off guard by their aggression this time. He focused his senses, slowing the world around him, and dove under one of the horses.

Ignoring the pain of his injuries he rolled to his feet on the other side of the animal and lashed out with his tail again. This time his tail barb carved deeply into the beast's belly. It was likely a fatal wound, but if they wouldn't be run off, he felt no guilt in killing one of them to slow the enemy down.

What just happened? Edge asked through the bond.

Deathclaw replied while he ran. *I cut the horses free, but they turned on me. So I had to disable one of them.* He glanced behind himself and saw that the horses were galloping after him. *I think that this group is definitely under a spell of some kind.*

Wow, said Edge. *I've never been attacked by a horse before.*

Nor have I, but they are large and their hooves are shod with steel, Deathclaw replied. He could still feel the imprint of one horseshoe in his shoulder. *It is surprisingly intimidating.*

This was especially the case since he was running on foot through an open field and they were gaining on him. Deathclaw reached up with his good arm and grasped the hilt of his sword. It was a bit awkward trying to draw the weapon while running, but he managed to pull Star from its sheath just as the first horse caught up with him. It was the horse he had wounded.

The horse's eyes were wild, its lips drawn back from its teeth as it tried to bite him. Deathclaw ducked under the bite and twisted to lash out with his sword. Star's power wasn't at its full might during the early light of morning, but as the blade carved into the horse's throat, the wound sizzled. The animal stumbled to a stop and collapsed.

The attack slowed Deathclaw's stride and as the second horse caught up to him it screamed and reared up, its forelegs swiping at him. The raptoid spun to bring his weapon to bear, but before his sword could hit its mark, Deathclaw was struck from the side.

He was borne to the ground by the attacking treecat. The beast was twice his weight and pinned him with its claws while its jaws reached for his throat. Deathclaw managed to bring his wounded arm up and jammed his forearm into its mouth to hold it back.

While its teeth pierced his arm, Deathclaw kicked out repeatedly, slashing its belly with the talons on his feet. The cat let go of his arm and backed off, growling. Deathclaw wasted no time coming to his feet and lashed out with Star, gashing the treecat's nose open with the tip of his sword.

The wound sizzled, and the cat flinched and Deathclaw dove to the side again as the horse tried to trample him. The raptoid hissed in fury at being harried by mere animals.

Are you going to survive until I get there? Edge asked, unable to keep from needling him despite the danger of the situation. *They might have a cow with them.*

A hiss of laughter escaped Deathclaw's lips. *A cow would be preferable.*

The cat's bite had severed an artery in his arm and he had to pause a moment to will his arm to stop bleeding. His body's healing magic focused on the area and while the wound knit closed, the horse reared up at him again.

Deathclaw tired of the beast's madness. He slashed out with Star and lopped off the horse's leg at the knee. Then, as it came down he stabbed out with his tail and sent his barb through its eye.

As the horse collapsed to the ground, he spun to avoid the treecat's claws. A backhand swing of his sword slashed it across the nose a second time and the beast howled. It backed away, but Deathclaw didn't let up. He darted forward and stabbed, carving a steaming gash in the side of the cat's head.

His senses focused, Deathclaw saw its next lunge coming. He leapt into the air, jumping over the beast and as he stabbed down, his sword pierced its back. It howled again and thrashed and Deathclaw had to let go of the sword.

He backed away, fearing that it would run away and he would have to track the dying beast down to retrieve his weapon. But the cat turned to face him again despite the searing sword sticking out of its back.

It growled and Deathclaw pulled a throwing dagger from his bandoleer. This was one of his favorites, a gift from Hugh the Shadow, leader of the Academy's Assassin's Guild.

As the beast launched itself at him, he threw. The point of the dagger struck between the cat's eyes and the magic of the blade parted the thick bone of its skull as if it were made of clay. The great cat was dead before it came to rest at his feet.

Deathclaw bent to retrieve his blades and an arrow flashed by his face.

"The Maw!" shouted out a chorus of voices and he looked out across the field to see the raiders approaching. The elf was already nocking another arrow and the enormous furry python was slithering at the front of their charge.

The raptoid grabbed his sword and dagger and ran.

Close call, Edge said. *Are you able to outrun them?*

I can run, Deathclaw assured him. *Though my wounds may slow me.*

Suddenly, Deathclaw felt a surge of energy flood him through the bond. He picked up speed and he felt Edge's magic enter him, working to close his wounds even faster than the raptoid's own magic could.

Don't be so foolish! He admonished with a hiss. It was reckless for Edge to transfer his own life energy through the bond. The raptoid ducked a second arrow and darted through a thick stand of trees, putting more distance between himself and his pursuers. *You will need your energy for the battle ahead*!

I'm siphoning the energy from my sword, Edge explained. *Rage was full and you needed help. You never know. You may still face a cow in the coming battle.*

Then I'll let you fight it, Deathclaw replied. *I'll take the giant.*

Once Deathclaw was certain he had outdistanced his pursuers, he circled back around to the camp. By the time he got there, his wounds were fully healed. He watched as the raiders left the area. They hitched the wagon to the giant and the four orcs helped to push the cart from behind.

Where are they taking those bodies? Edge wondered.

I will find out, Deathclaw replied. *When you get here, stop to collect my horse.* He sent Edge the memory of where he had left the Academy-trained animal. *I will follow them by foot.*

The raiders continued their journey higher into the foothills, taking turns pushing the wagon, until they came to a mountain road. They stopped to rest and Deathclaw climbed the rocky cliffside to get a better vantage point.

When he reached the top, he heard a rattle. His approach had startled a viper that had been sunning on a nearby rock. Deathclaw reached for it and as the viper struck at him, he snatched it out of the air and wrung its neck. He ate the snake as he surveyed the raiders below.

The motley group sat around for a full hour before Deathclaw discovered what they were waiting for. *We have a problem*, he sent.

What is it? Edge asked. He had retrieved Deathclaw's horse and was less than a mile away.

The raptoid glared down at the new group of monsters that had arrived to join the raiders. He ground the viper's rattle under his foot. *They have received reinforcements.*

Chapter Six
Sir Edge - Reinforcements

Sir Edge left the two Academy horses tethered loosely in a copse of trees a fair distance from Deathclaw's position. The beasts were well-trained. If he or Deathclaw didn't return to them by morning the following day, they would head down out of the mountains and try to make their way back to the Academy. *Any more newcomers since we last spoke?*

Just a few goblins. replied the raptoid, sending him new mental images of the raider horde. They hadn't traveled any further up the mountainside, but had camped in the middle of the pass, building a fire in the center of the road. *Any more and we would be foolish to attack.*

"We're already foolish by any normal measure," Edge said aloud and then through the bond replied, *What do you think our best strategy of attack should be?*

Deathclaw watched the raider horde with calculating eyes, the scales on his body altered to take on the color of the rocks around him. He had already given the question a great deal of thought. The strange group of raiders that had committed the massacre in Lillian's village had been joined by even more oddities.

Two giant spiders had crawled down out of the pass. Clinging to the backs and legs of the hairy arachnids were a dozen goblins. The spiders didn't seem to acknowledge the goblins' presence and the small creatures weren't very good at hanging on. Several of them had lost their grip and fallen while the spiders were descending the steep cliffs at either side of the pass. One goblin had died as it struck the ground.

Two more creatures had approached from the road at the center of the pass. One of them was a tall, long limbed creature with a thick brown shell on its back and two smaller shells on each of its forearms. It had hairy paws tipped with massive claws and its head was narrow and rodent-like.

Deathclaw had seen a creature like this before, but only from Fist's memories. The ogre had called it a digger beast. The creature that rolled along the road next to it, however, was something he was completely unfamiliar with. At first glance, the thing was a large fleshy ball about six feet in diameter. Its skin was a mottled gray with occasional hints of purple and it glistened as though covered in a thin film of mucus. It wasn't until the thing had come much closer that Deathclaw saw that what propelled it along the road were a series of stubby flipper-like protuberances that pushed at the ground to maneuver it.

When these newcomers arrived, the goblins had climbed down from the spiders and let out tiny cries of "Praise the Maw!" The raiding horde had replied with an enthusiastic, "The Maw!"

There is much we still do not know about this group, and our numbers are small, Deathclaw sent. He decided to recommend an old raptoid custom. *Our best strategy would be to harry them, killing a few at a time before retreating. Eventually they will weaken, and we will reduce their number enough that we can manage a direct assault.*

Normally, I would agree with you, said Edge as he circled around to the far side of the raider horde. He wanted to get a different vantage point than the raptoid. *However, we can't take the time.*

Why not? Asked the raptoid. *There is always time for a wise decision. Is that not what Jhonate says?*

Edge pursed his lips. It was typical for Deathclaw to use one of his wife's more annoying sayings against him. As he neared the cliff on the opposite side of the pass from the raptoid he looked for a good spot to climb. His bond to Deathclaw gave him a nimbleness that few other humans had, but he didn't have the claws and unique sense of balance that the raptoid did.

He spied one section of the cliff face that had crumbled, leaving an ascent with good handholds. He explained his reasons as he climbed, careful not to make any noise that would give him away. *We may not know the exact purpose of these raiders, but they are camped right in the entrance of the pass. Any travelers that try to use it will likely be attacked.*

Then we will warn any travelers away, replied the raptoid. *Or perhaps they will join us in our attack.*

It's not like you to avoid a fierce fight, Edge replied, nearing the top. He had managed his ascent without knocking any rocks loose. *We have faced similar numbers before-. Wait, are there any more horses or cats lurking about that you forgot to mention?*

Deathclaw replied with a mental hiss. *The reason I suggest caution is the same reason you wish to act right away. You saw that child's memories. You are no longer holding your sword and you are letting your emotions guide you. This has become personal and when that happens you do not think clearly.*

The fleshy boulder creature below moved once more and Deathclaw paused in his thoughts. It approached the dead goblin at the base of the cliff and one of the stubby flippers that propelled the thing extended out of the glistening body on a cylindrical stalk. The strange tentacle moved as if it had a core of bone, bending in jointed sections to reach for the dead goblin. This limb gripped the small corpse and hoisted it into the air before curling back towards the thing's round body.

A small puckered hole in the side of the ball blossomed outward, revealing a thick pink tube covered in wicked curved teeth. The tube latched onto the head of the goblin and withdrew back into the fleshy ball, its teeth biting into the small creature and entombing it within. The jointed tentacle also withdrew into the central body, disappearing until only the small flippered end remained outside once more.

Deathclaw unconsciously grabbed the hilt of Star as he watched the gruesome feast. Instinctually, he sensed that this sort of thing was best killed with fire. The soul within his sword stirred as if in agreement.

That thing's called a trench worm, Edge said in recognition. He had crawled up to the edge of the pass across from the raptoid and was peering at it with his own eyes. *I've never seen one close up before, but I've seen it illustrated in one of the creature compendiums at the Mage School.*

That does not look like a worm, Deathclaw replied glancing across the pass at him in confusion.

I didn't name it, Edge replied with a shrug, though he also agreed that a worm shouldn't be ball-shaped. Scholars had odd reasons for naming things. *They're scavengers and live mostly underground. Supposedly, there are a few of them in the sewers in Dremald.*

Deathclaw hissed in disgust. *Why would humans allow such things to live underneath them?*

They eat the rats down there, Edge explained. *Also, old King Muldroomon used to order that the bodies of executed traitors be fed to them.*

Deathclaw nodded in understanding. *A practical use of such a creature. This would definitely dissuade treachery.*

The trench worm's feast wasn't the only interesting thing going on in the camp. The horde had unloaded the wagon and laid the bodies of the villagers in a line on the ground. The goblins were undressing the bodies and dragging them over to the giant spiders.

The enormous hairy spiders were grabbing each body and using their spinnerets and rear legs to cocoon them in thick webbing. The digger beast was stacking the cocoons to the side once the spiders were finished. They had already made it through half of the bodies.

If you are certain you wish to attack right away, then we should do so at a distance, Deathclaw recommended.

I agree, Edge said, and he pulled his Jharro bow off of his back.

He strung the weapon and ran his hand along its nearly featureless wooden surface. Its name was Ma'am and he had very nearly mastered his connection with it. There was only a thin runic line remaining in the wood and that too would disappear once his connection with its home tree was complete. Jhonate said that he would have done so by now if he would only take the time.

He looked across the pass to the place where Deathclaw perched, his camouflaged form blending with the rocks. *Are you sure you can manage a distance attack? Will Retriever help you?*

Deathclaw fingered the bandoleer that crossed his chest. He'd had it specially made by old friends of theirs based on the design of the quiver that Fist's wife Maryanne used. The Academy's half-orc forgemaster Bettie had made it and Listener Beth had used her magic to bind it with the spirit of a hawk that Deathclaw had killed.

The magic of the bandoleer was supposed to retrieve Deathclaw's weapons once he had thrown them and sometimes it worked as designed. Unfortunately, the particular hawk that Deathclaw killed had been a mother trying to protect its eggs. It had now imprinted on Deathclaw's weapons and did not like him throwing them away. Sometimes, instead of returning them to the bandoleer it would hide them from him.

I have been doing as Beth suggested, Deathclaw said. He tried to communicate with the bird's spirit daily, and he felt he was making some progress. *If Retriever knows we are in a battle she should work as designed.*

Alright. I'll call out to Artemus and see if he's ready, Edge sent. *Maybe he'll see something we don't.* He reached a tendril of thought through the bond. *Great grandfather? Are you ready to help?*

A chill breeze blew through the bond as the wizard's thoughts replied. *Is it time for me to act?*

Almost, but I want your opinion before we do, Edge replied and sent Artemus everything that he and Deathclaw had seen from the horde below. *Have you seen anything like this before?*

The wizard's cool thoughts surged up into Edge's mind and looked out of his eyes. *I haven't seen this exact behavior before, but their behavior does speak of spirit magic domination.*

Edge switched to spirit sight. *I thought the same thing, but I don't see any spirit magic in use.*

Nor do I, Artemus said, *but we are watching from a distance. If someone was the same distance away watching you and Deathclaw right now, it would be difficult for them to see the bond you have between each other.*

Maybe so, but I have trained my eyes to look for bonds. I should be able to see it if it were there, Edge said.

As should I, Deathclaw added.

Even so, there are ways to disguise such things. Remember the day you fought the Protector of the Grove?

Edge nodded slowly. It ended up that one of the Protector's wives had managed to bewitch him. She kept her magic from being detected by sending it under the earth. Jhonate had only discovered it because the Protector had lifted his foot, revealing the magic connected to his heel. *Do you think that the magic controlling them is under the ground?*

Maybe. Maybe not, but that is only one way of disguising it, said Artemus. *The connection could be extremely faint. Their master could be far away. Or he has shrunk the connection purposefully. It does not have to be a visible connection unless the evil wizard is currently instructing his servants.*

If it is just a wizard, said Deathclaw. *Making their servants eat human flesh? Having them cocoon the bodies? That is not the behavior of a human.*

Not a sane human maybe, Edge replied.

What are you suggesting? asked Artemus.

They could be under the thrall of a creature, said Deathclaw. *An ally of the Dark Prophet, perhaps.*

The ruins of his old palace are just on the other side of these mountains, Edge said. *Though after the last time we were there I don't see how it could be of any use to him.*

A decade prior, the Prophet had sought their help on a mission. John had claimed that the Dark Prophet's servants were planning something in his old palace. Edge and his bonded had gathered together a force to clear out the site, but when they had arrived they only met token resistance. The goblinoid force they destroyed had unearthed the palace and cleared it of rubble, but any artifacts remaining from the Dark Prophet's prior reign had been removed.

The Prophet had been furious that they had arrived too late. John called forth an earthquake to destroy the palace once and for all. The place had collapsed from within, leaving a crater in the mountainside. When they had left, nothing but a few outbuildings had remained standing.

I suppose there's only one way for us to know for sure, said Artemus and there was a chilling menace in his voice. *We destroy the majority of them and you can interrogate the rest.*

This was kind of what Edge wanted to hear, but the wizard's tone made him wary. *Are you alright, Artemus?*

Oh, I am perfectly fine, Artemus assured him, but his voice had risen in pitch. *But you know how the elemental gets when a fight is at hand. It is eager to begin and these particular foes . . .*

The frost-covered rune on Edge's chest crackled and a cold mist trickled from the seams in his armor. He touched the center of his breastplate and felt a film of ice on the surface.

Back away from the edge, Deathclaw warned. *They could see you.*

Edge realized that mist was beginning to coalesce in the air around him. As he backed up, he started to have second thoughts about this battle. Perhaps Deathclaw was right. Heading straight into a fight wasn't the best idea right now. *Artemus, I need you to regain control.*

Edge felt a weight settle on his shoulder and he looked back to see a pale hand resting there. The fingernails were pointed and black.

"This is odd," said Artemus aloud. The wizard stood two full feet taller than Edge. His beard was a mass of icicles, his eyes beady and red. When his lips pulled back from his teeth his mouth was full of razor teeth. "The elemental and I seem to be in full agreement at the moment."

Edge swallowed. This wasn't good. The wizard hadn't done anything like this in years. "Artemus-."

"We'll explain later," Artemus said, his form growing, his arms elongating. His voice had taken on a disconcerting duality. "I have a message to bring these beasts."

The wizard dissolved into a cloud of mist that flowed over the cliff's edge and into the pass below. Edge and Deathclaw both hurriedly readied their weapons as the mist poured across the ground towards the enemy.

The raiders didn't notice anything was amiss until the mist had covered their feet. Their backs suddenly straightened, and they looked around for the source. One of the orcs looked up at the cliff face and pointed as he saw Edge at the top.

Then a column of frost rose from the center of the group and exploded outwards. The Scralag stood among them, ten feet tall and skeletal. The only visible remnant of Artemus' presence was the icicle beard and a long flowing robe covered in frost runes. It let out an eerie laugh and when it spoke to them its voice came out in twin chilling tones.

"Horde of the Maw, your time of reckoning is at hand. On behalf of the Big and Little People Tribe, I bring your death!"

Chapter Seven
Sir Edge – The Fray

Why did the wizard do that? Deathclaw wondered as he pulled a throwing dagger out of his bandoleer.

I plan to ask him when this is over, Edge said, nocking an arrow on his bowstring. There was a lot about Artemus' sudden rush into the midst of the raider horde that didn't make sense to him.

When the Scralag had left its home within Edge's chest, Edge had assumed that the elemental had overcome the wizard. But its behavior afterwards seemed to indicate that Artemus was still at least partially in charge. For one thing, there had been aspects of the wizard's appearance in the Scralag. Also, it had stopped to talk to Edge in a reasoned tone. Whenever the Scralag had talked in the past, it had been a creature full of rage and menace.

Then it had charged into the midst of the enemy, which was something the Scralag was likely to do, but why announce the name of the Big and Little People Tribe? Why had it spoken to them at all?

The raider horde was definitely startled by the Scralag's sudden appearance in their midst. There were a few long seconds where none of them moved. But there was no fear in their faces or worry in their stances.

Then, in unison, the group shouted, "Praise the Maw!" and those closest to the Scralag attacked.

Several goblins drew crude daggers and ran at the elemental. They leapt onto its legs, their daggers chipping at its icy flesh. Two of the bulky female orcs were also nearby and swung axes. These heavier weapons had more effect, the thick blades sinking into Artemus' form.

Chuckling, the Scralag raised its arms and the cold that radiated from its body intensified. The very air around it crackled with its chill aura and the foes nearest to the Scralag were slowed. Frost gathered on their bodies and when the elemental brought its clawed fists down upon the orcs that had chopped at it, their skin shattered and cracked and they fell to the ground in frozen pieces.

The rest of the horde took hesitant steps back, brandishing weapons, their eyes watching the Scralag, who wasn't even trying to brush off the frozen forms of the three goblins that clung to its legs.

The Scralag's thin lips drew back to reveal a razor-filled smile. "You see, servants of the Maw? Your end is near!" it said with its chilling echoing voice. It pointed a black talon at the giant and the elf standing next to it. "Your master will be next."

The elf fired an arrow that darted into the elemental's open mouth. The giant hurled a huge rock and the Scralag took the blow in the chest. It staggered back, the front of its robes shattering and falling like snow beneath it. Then it staggered forward again as another rock struck it from behind, this one thrown by the lanky digger beast. Emboldened by the seeming success of these ranged attacks, the rest of the horde began throwing weapons or rocks.

Hold for now, Edge sent to Deathclaw. So far the enemy had become completely focused on the elemental. Even the orc that had pointed at him seemed to have forgotten he was there. Until it was necessary, it was best not to get involved. Edge wanted to see how many the Scralag could kill on its own.

The enemy's success was short-lived. The parts of the elemental's body that were crushed by the boulders simply reformed and the rest of the attacks were minor annoyances. Both the giant and digger beast found more rocks to throw.

The Scralag shook its head as it continued to take the blows. Then it reached its long fingers into its mouth and pulled out the arrow that the elf had fired. Ice formed around the arrow and grew until it resembled a pointed ice javelin that was six feet long.

With an eerie laugh, the Scralag threw the javelin. The giant saw the throw coming and raised its arm defensively, but the javelin pierced its arm and continued through its chest. With a choked sound, the giant fell dead.

The elemental pulled another arrow out of its chest and began to form another javelin.

"This isn't a creature that can be destroyed physically!" shouted one of the humans. His voice was intelligent for such a scruffy-looking man. "It's a mere simulacrum!" He cried and looked up the cliff face at Sir Edge. "We must kill that man. He is the source of its magic!"

Edge was taken aback by the accuracy of the man's statement. The Scralag would eventually tire as it rebuilt its body over and over again, but the only way to truly hurt it would be to attack the scar on Edge's chest. This scruffy man was dressed in humble road attire, but he had the knowledge of someone trained by wizards. Could he be the one controlling the others? Edge focused on the man as he pulled back an arrow.

The man saw him draw and tried to dive to the side, but the Jharro bow didn't fire the arrow at a normal speed. As Edge let go of the arrow, the wood changed. It stiffened and flexed, sending the arrow at twice the speed of a regular bow. The arrow pierced the man's ribcage mid-dive.

The Scralag was struck in the back by another boulder and turned to throw its second ice javelin. The digger beast hurriedly spun around to take the blow to the thick shell on its

71

back. The tip of the ice penetrated into the shell only a short distance before the javelin shattered, but the force of the blow sent the beast stumbling forward and crashing to the ground.

As Edge watched the situation develop he used a skill that he had gained from his connection with Deathclaw. His thoughts and reactions sped up and the world seemed to slow around him. His eyes darted around the pass, keeping track of what each enemy was doing. It was in this state that Edge saw the enemy elf turn his bow at him and fire.

He noticed that the bow glowed a soft white. That told him that a spirit was bound to it. This was potentially a problem, but he noticed that when it fired none of that energy was passed on to the arrow. The projectile arced towards him in a predictable speed. Edge slowed the world even further as he leaned to the side and reached out with his hand. His fingers started to close before the arrowhead reached his palm and he caught it mid-shaft.

Can I attack now? Deathclaw asked, his thoughts amused. The enemy still hadn't noticed his camouflaged form.

Yes, now! Edge said, taking the arrow he had just caught and nocking it to his bowstring. He prepared to fire it back at the elf.

Just as he was about to shoot the arrow, he was interrupted by the unpleasant feeling of his hair standing on end. He noticed that the last remaining human man was pointing at him, his face pinched with concentration. Edge acted instinctively, throwing up a domed mix of air and water magic above his head just as the lightning bolt struck.

Thanks to the nature of his connection to the Scralag, defensive magic was the only kind of magic Edge could cast outside of the bond. He had become quite good at it, but his shield had been hastily cast. The best defense against electric attack was to ground yourself and channel the energy away from you. The shield didn't completely reach the ground on either side of Edge and some of the electricity reached around the shield.

72

Edge was struck with a flash of pain and his body seized up. As he fell to the ground, his limbs twitching, he gasped aloud and through the bond. *"Kill the wizard!"*

The Scralag heard his command and began to form another javelin but was interrupted as a beast slithered forward. The furry giant rock python twined itself around the elemental's legs and climbed his body in a constricting embrace that crushed the frozen goblins that still clung to the elemental.

The Scralag flexed its magic, intending to freeze the creature. Frost formed outside the snake, but its movement didn't slow. This type of python was native to the high mountain crags and there was an innate magic in its body that warded off cold. It climbed higher and attempted to wrap itself around the elemental's arms.

In the moments before the lightning bolt struck, Deathclaw had already thrown four of his standard knives, killing four goblins. They were minor enemies, but the closest to his position and easily struck. The hawk spirit inside Retriever had already reached out to gather in the knives he had thrown, but it would take at least half a minute before the weapons rematerialized in his bandoleer.

Then, as the lightning bolt filled his vision with light, Deathclaw realized that Edge was in real trouble. The remaining goblins had leapt back on the giant spiders and were riding the arachnids toward the cliff face under Edge's position. In addition, the elf was preparing to fire again, and the human magic user had ducked behind the wagon to prepare another spell. All of these threats were just outside his normal throwing range.

Hissing, Deathclaw pulled a special throwing knife from his bandoleer. The knife was named Speedy and had been made for him by Lenny Firegobbler, his friend and master weaponsmith. When he threw this particular knife, he had to be careful because the moment it left his fingers, its magic took over. A blast of air magic propelled Speedy in the direction it was thrown as if fired by a crossbow. It would continue in that direction for hundreds of yards if unimpeded.

There had been times in the past when the knife had missed its target and been lost outside of Retriever's range. Throwing the knife down from this angle meant that wasn't a problem, but timing the release with the way the magic engaged was tricky. He focused his concentration and threw.

His aim was true. A blast of air hurtled the knife forward and it penetrated the elf's leather armor, piercing its heart. As the bowman fell, clutching his fatal wound, Deathclaw sent a warning thought. *Careful, Edge! You have spiders.*

Then the raptoid jumped off the cliff.

Deathclaw plummeted with his claws extended, aiming his fall. He landed atop one of the remaining orcs, digging into her armor and flesh with his rear talons. He caught her off-guard, but his weight wasn't enough to bear the strong creature to the ground. The surprised orc cried out and stumbled. The raptoid reached around and tore its throat open with his left hand, then rode it to the ground and rolled towards the wagon and the human hiding behind it.

The last orc stood in his path and swung her axe, but to Deathclaw's quickened mind, her movement was sluggish. He ducked under the weapon and dove between her legs, slashing her thighs with his claws as he went. He then continued to the wagon just as the human stood again, another spell ready to be released.

The man saw the raptoid's approach at the last second and with wide eyes, tried to turn the spell on him. Deathclaw smelled ozone and felt the air around him crackle just before he struck the man. His teeth gripped the man's throat and his claws ripped into the man's abdomen.

Edge heard Deathclaw's warning and caught the mental image of the two giant spiders climbing the cliff beneath him, goblins clinging to their hairy legs. Unfortunately, he was still recovering from the effects of the lightning spell. He commanded his twitching and cramping legs to come back under his control.

His bow was still clutched in his left hand, but he couldn't get his fingers to let go. He managed to raise his right arm and grasp the hilt of Rage, but the way he was lying he couldn't draw it all the way from its sheath. He saw the tip of one spider leg grip the top edge of the cliff.

He was alone and practically helpless. This kind of situation was exactly the kind he needed to avoid as a bonding wizard. All of his bonded were tied to his life force. If he were to die, they would all die too.

Edge still couldn't let go of his bow and grasp his left sword, but he reached mentally for the magic of Peace. His pain and worry were sucked away and he was finally able to force his stubborn legs under control. He climbed to his feet just as the first spider pulled itself over the top. Three goblins dropped down from the deadly creature and ran at him.

With a mental command, Edge's bow morphed into a different shape. The bow's name was Ma'am and like all Jharro weapons, the forms she could take were only limited by her wielder's understanding of her true nature. She became a sword in his hand, her shape similar to that of his other swords.

Ma'am's first swipe lopped off a goblin's head. He stabbed her through the second goblin and kicked the other one to the side. With his considerable strength, he lifted the squirming goblin in the air and threw it at the spider.

The spider flinched, giving him time to draw Rage completely. The sword buzzed, hungry to release the energy stored within it. The spider reared up, its fangs dripping with venom and Edge surged forward to meet it.

Its legs reached for him and he swung Rage at the center of the spider's eyes. The moment the blade touched its chitin-covered head, he released half of the sword's pent up energy. At the point of impact, the energy was converted to an explosive blast of pure air magic. The spider's head blew apart and its huge body tumbled backwards over the cliff's edge.

He had no moment to breathe though, for the next spider was already climbing over the lip. The four goblins clinging to its limbs leapt down as the others had and ran at him. Edge swiped Rage in front of him in a horizontal slash.

This time, he altered the nature of the magic before releasing it and a long blade of air magic extended from tip of his sword. Though the steel of his sword never touched them, the goblins' flesh gave no resistance as the impossibly thin blade of air cut through their midsections. The four goblins fell into eight pieces.

He stabbed Ma'am into the ground and drew Peace from its sheath. He faced the last giant spider with both naming weapons in his hands.

Deathclaw threw the dead magic user to the ground and spat out the man's blood. No matter how often he was forced to taste the blood of humans, he had never liked it. They tasted too strongly of iron.

He turned to survey the pass and saw that Artemus was still struggling with the enormous rock python. The digger beast had gotten back to its feet as well and was approaching the elemental, but Deathclaw was more worried about the spiders that were climbing the cliff face.

He needed to go and assist Edge. Only that last female orc stood in his way. Her thighs were bleeding but the wounds were superficial. Her hard eyes were focused on him and she had taken up one of the axes of her fallen sisters and was waving one in each hand.

Deathclaw did not want to waste time with her. He drew a throwing dagger from his bandoleer and threw it at her neck. The orc raised her arm and didn't even flinch when the dagger speared her forearm. She rushed at him, swinging both axes.

The world slowed around Deathclaw and he ducked under her blows once more. This time she anticipated the move and altered her swipe, bringing one axe down in a backhand. Deathclaw sensed the movement and twisted out of the way, but the tip of the axe cut a deep furrow across his left hand.

Hissing, Deathclaw rolled to the side and stabbed out with his tail, sending his barb into her kneecap. The orc howled and kicked out at him with her other foot, catching his tail and sending him off balance. Deathclaw struck a large soft boulder and rebounded to come at her again, but his hand was stuck.

The raptoid turned to see that the boulder he had struck was the trench worm. It's long tube-like pink mouth had gripped his wounded left hand and it was trying to pull him in as it had the small goblin before, its many rows of curved teeth piercing into the flesh of his arm. Two of the tentacle-like flippers on the trenchworm's side extended from its fleshy body in jointed arms and tried to encircle him and pull him in closer.

The Scralag struggled mightily against the powerful snake. The elemental felt no pain from its constricting coils, but it was being kept out of the battle. It had managed to grip the snake's neck with one hand and was trying to strangle the thing when another boulder struck its back.

With the snake wrapped around its legs, the Scralag nearly fell over. It whipped its head around and saw the digger beast ripping another large rock from the ground. The tip of the elemental's ice javelin still protruded from the shell on its back.

The digger lifted the rock and as it threw it, the Scralag turned its body and held out the snake's head. The boulder struck the snake a glancing blow, but it dazed the creature just enough that the Scralag was able to pull its other arm from the coils.

The elemental gripped the snake's head and forced its jaws open wide. Then, heedless of the python's curved fangs, it plunged one hand down the snake's throat. Whatever magic was in the snake to protect it from the cold could not withstand the full fury of the Scralag's power unleashed within its body.

The full front quarter of the python's body froze solid. With a twist of its arms, the Scralag broke that section of the snake free. The digger beast saw this and turned to flee, but the Scralag threw its grizzly prize.

The frozen head and neck of the snake struck the back of the digger beast with tremendous force and drove the tip of the javelin the rest of the way through its tough shell. The digger beast fell dying and the Scralag turned back to see Deathclaw's predicament.

The raptoid had managed to pull Star free from its sheath and cut one of the grasping flipper arms away, but the mouth had pulled his arm further into the trench-worm's body. He could already feel the powerful acids in its body attacking his wounded hand. To make things worse, the orc had managed to stay on her feet and was limping towards him. She had dropped one axe but was ready to swing at him with the other.

Deathclaw tore into the trench worm, kicking it with clawed feet, stabbing it with his tail barb, but the thing would not let go of his hand. He stabbed it with Star, and the magical sword stirred to life, its blade glowing red with heat. Steam burst from the wound and the giant fleshy ball quivered, but it continued to try to draw him in. The pain in his hand was excruciating now.

He glanced back at the orc and saw that she was standing absolutely still. The Scralag stood behind her, one clawed hand plunged into her back. Her body crackled as it froze solid and the elemental casually pushed her over. The orc hit the ground and shattered.

"Do you need help, Deathclaw?" it asked, amusement in its beady red eyes.

"No!" Deathclaw hissed. He twisted his red-hot sword in the trench worm's body, and ichor boiled from within it. The flipper arm that had been trying to grasp him before was flailing at the air. A high-pitched whistle came from somewhere within the thing and steam began to burst out of its mouth around his arm. The skin of the boulder grew taut and began to flush pink.

"Aren't you afraid of hurting yourself?" cautioned the Scralag, its voice sounding more like Artemus'.

Before Deathclaw could reply there was a loud pop. The insides of the trenchworm blew out of the backside of the thing, spraying against the cliff wall. Deathclaw and Artemus stared in surprise at the thing and Deathclaw finally managed to pull his arm free.

That was when they felt Edge being wounded through the bond.

This giant spider was larger than the other one and seemed more wary. It circled around him, getting away from the cliff's edge. Sir Edge's focus was absolute, his world slowed so that he could follow its every movement. He moved with the spider, making sure that it couldn't put his back to the cliff.

When it surged towards him, he was ready. He met it with a double thrust of his swords, prepared to fire off another blast of magic, but it backed away at the last moment. He didn't let up and he charged toward it, extending another blade of air from Rage. He swiped down with the sword and the air blade caught one of its legs, cutting it nearly in two.

The spider hissed and withdrew further, the stump of the leg drooling ichor while the rest of the limb dangled limply. Edge let it retreat and rotated around a large rock, trying to get its back towards the cliff again. He had used most of the magic Rage had stored. He had one more good attack left before he had to fight it with bare steel.

He readied himself to release it and when he came around the other side of the rock, the spider launched himself at him. He stabbed Rage straight ahead and sent an air blade out from the tip, skewering the creature. The attack wasn't instantly fatal, though. It continued its charge, letting Rage pierce through its thorax so that it could get close enough for its poisonous fangs to reach him.

Edge brought the flat of Peace's blade up under the fangs to keep them off of him. He could feel the poison dripping off of the blade and onto his skin. He strained to keep the weight of the dying creature from bearing him to the ground and this was when he felt the small crude dagger enter his lower back.

It was the goblin he had kicked aside earlier. He had been so preoccupied with the spider that he had let it slip out of his mind. The thing had snuck up behind him and slipped its blade under the bottom lip of his armor.

Peace sucked the pain and shock of the wound away, but Edge knew it was a deep one. Letting out a shout, he managed to push the spider aside just as the goblin withdrew the dagger and stabbed again.

Edge twisted and took this second stab to the hip. He kicked out at the goblin and it fell to the ground, leaving its weapon stuck in his flesh. He swung around with Peace and stabbed the goblin through the chest.

The moment that his blade pierced the goblin's flesh, Peace sucked away it's pain and emotion and, for a moment, their minds were joined. The thoughts within the creature's mind weren't the thoughts of a goblin.

As the goblin had stabbed him, another mind had taken control. It was an odd mind, alien and strange. Its thoughts were both ancient and new. It had powerful spirit magic and a clever method for controlling those in its thrall. This was the Maw.

This was all Edge was able to learn, because as his mind had recognized the thoughts of the Maw, its mind had recognized his. The Maw had done so eagerly at first, thinking that the connection forged by the magic of Edge's sword was a weakness it could plunder. But as it glimpsed Edge's powers and saw the nature of his mind, the Maw cut its connection with the goblin.

Edge stood over the body of the small dead creature and withdrew his sword. His mind was going over what he had learned when Deathclaw called out to him. The raptoid was standing at the bottom of the cliff, furious.

Edge! You are wounded! How could you let a goblin stab you?

Edge turned his attention to the raptoid and winced as he noticed the raptoid's own hideous wound. *Me? You're missing a hand.*

"My hand will grow back!" Deathclaw snapped aloud, his hissing voice carrying to Edge's ears from the pass below. *Your flesh will not heal so easily.*

Deathclaw had a good point. If his wound was severe, he had no way of healing himself. Artemus was no good to him as a healer either and Fist was too far away to reach until nightfall.

We have some elf potions in our saddlebags, he reminded him.

They heal you too slowly, Deathclaw replied.

There was a rush of icy mist and Artemus appeared at Edge's side. He had shrunk down until he was the same height as Edge and looked more like the old wizard he used to be. Until he opened his mouth and Edge saw that his teeth were still razor sharp.

The old wizard examined the wound in his lower back. "It is deep. It barely missed your kidney. We are lucky. But it could still get infected." He shifted his focus to Edge's hip. He pulled out the small dagger and tossed it aside. "This one was just a flesh wound, but the blade was filthy. Either of these could get infected."

"We'll treat them," Edge said. "It'll be fine until we can reach Fist tonight." He glanced at the setting sun. "It's almost dark anyway. Just an hour or so and we can try. Maybe he will be able to heal me through the bond."

The ancient wizard growled. "My own healing powers are gone. Useless!"

Artemus had difficulty explaining why he couldn't heal with the Scralag's powers. He had use of air and water magic only. Water worked best with earth magic when it came to healing, but there were ways around that. Some things could be done with water magic alone.

Artemus' healing ability wasn't on the forefront of Edge's mind at the moment, though. He had his own bone to pick with his great grandfather. *Why did you attack before my command?* he asked and even though Peace was draining his emotions, the question still came out as a demand. *Why did you rush down and announce the name of our tribe to the enemy?*

Artemus raised his eyebrows at Edge's sudden interrogation. *The master of this horde needed a name to fear,* he explained. *As for why the elemental and I attacked?* He looked down at the back of his pale hand and the black nails that tipped his fingers, then turned it over to peer at the naming rune on his palm. *There's something new stirring in the bond. Have you felt it?*

No, Edge replied. *Felt what?*

Artemus touched his naming rune, running his finger along the same line that matched the crack on his dagger. *We can feel it from the source on the other side of the rune. The time of the Dark Prophet's return is near. Our purpose will soon be fulfilled.*

You can feel his return coming? Edge said, and his hand fell to his hip where Artemus' dagger was sheathed. Ice encrusted the base of the blade, sealing the crack in the naming rune. *When is this going to happen?*

I don't know. But the time for me to use my powers solely to protect has passed. He let out a wide yawn, and Edge saw that his teeth were human once more. *The elemental and I will sleep now. I fear you will need our power again, and soon.* He reached out to touch Edge's chest and disappeared in a frosty mist.

Deathclaw let out a grunt and Edge turned to see him climb up over the cliff's edge. Somehow, he had managed to make the climb with one hand. His magic was working quickly. The half-melted stump on his left arm wasn't even bleeding anymore.

"Next time, do not call him out until we know it's time to fight," Deathclaw chided. There was a throwing knife sticking out of the meat of his left shoulder. It was the magic knife that Lenny had made him.

"How did Speedy end up there?" Edge asked.

Deathclaw pulled the knife out of his shoulder and stowed it in his bandoleer with the others. "Retriever was being mischievous while returning it."

"You need to spend more time communing with her," Edge said. "What if she had stabbed you with one of your magical daggers?"

"Do not change the subject," Deathclaw hissed. "Today's assault was reckless. We cannot depend on the wizard to follow orders."

Edge rubbed his hand over his chest and sighed. His great grandfather's words had left him troubled. The Dark Prophet's return was nigh? Wasn't John out there working to stop it?

Deathclaw put his hand and stump on his scaled hips. He had listened in to Edge's conversation with the wizard and had also heard Edge's unspoken mental question. "We can only leave that to John. If he needs us, he'll come and tell us. For now, what do we do about this 'Maw?'"

"The Maw is a threat that needs to be hunted down," Edge replied. "Though I'm still not quite sure about his nature. I . . ."

Edge paused and cocked his head. Something had changed and that feeling was coming from somewhere among his bonds. Peace sucked away the stab of worry that entered his mind at the thought. Had the Maw done something to him during their brief connection? He did a mental check through the bond, evaluating each connection. Nothing seemed to be wrong. Then he found it.

Edge's clutched the wooden ring on his finger. It was still warm to his touch, but that faint connection to Jhonate was gone. He couldn't sense her anywhere.

Chapter Eight
Sir Edge - Aftermath

"Jhonate's gone," Edge said, his eyes wide with shock.

Deathclaw came to his side, the urgency in Edge's thoughts clear to him through the bond. "Where has she gone?"

"I don't know," he replied, his will probing at the ring in an attempt to find her. The only thing preventing him from full on panic was the power of his sword which was draining his emotions.

His ring was a piece of Jharro wood that had been fashioned from Jhonate's staff. It was tied to her life force in a bond that was similar to his bonds with his own swords. For that connection to be cut off could only mean bad things. The only proof that she wasn't dead was that the wood was still alive. If she ever died, the wood's connection to the Jharro tree that had birthed it would be severed and it would become cold and dead. He twisted the ring on his finger and shook his hand as if that would jar the connection to his wife.

Deathclaw listened carefully to his thoughts through the bond. "Her connection to the ring is weaker than our bonds," he said. "Could she simply be far away? Perhaps she traveled somewhere."

"I don't know," Edge said again.

There had been many times over their sixteen years of marriage where he and Jhonate had needed to travel apart for whatever reason, but this had never happened before. He thought of how far apart they had been in the past and the distance between them had never been more than a month's travel at the most.

"Perhaps she has gone farther away than you have been before," the raptoid suggested.

"The Mage School is only two weeks away from here by horse. How far could she have gone?" He had spoken to Fist just two nights ago and the ogre hadn't mentioned her leaving the Mage School. He squared his jaw. "We've got to go. We must head back right now."

Deathclaw narrowed his eyes. He could feel the intensity of Edge's worry begin to crackle through the bond and he knew that the bonding wizard had altered the sword's magic. He was still allowing it to take away the pain from his wounds, but was forcing it to let him feel his emotions. "You're being remarkably self-indulgent right now."

Edge shot him a glare. "She deserves my emotions. Besides, sometimes I need my feelings in order to think clearly." He walked to the edge of the slope and searched for the path that he had used on the way up.

"We can't simply leave," the raptoid pointed out. "Your wounds need to be tended."

Deathclaw had a point. His injuries weren't life threatening at this point, but he could feel warm blood still dripping down his lower back. It was going to be hard climbing down the cliffside. "I'll drink an elf potion when we reach the horses and when I talk to Fist later tonight we'll see if he can heal me."

"And what of the Maw?" Deathclaw asked.

Edge's stopped just before beginning his descent. "A dark wizard. The Mage School's responsibility. We'll tell them to send some hunters."

"Maybe so, but wasn't it the will of the Bowl that brought us this way?" Deathclaw said.

Edge clenched his fists. He had no desire to follow the raptoid's logic. "We've defeated the Maw's forces as directed."

Deathclaw cocked his head. "Are you certain that's all we're supposed to do?"

"I won't have *you* be my conscience," Edge replied. "This is Jhonate we're talking about. I will not take the time to chase after a wizard when she could be in danger. She is far more important."

"I do not disagree. She is an invaluable member of our tribe," the raptoid said. He had move to peer down at the goblin Edge had killed. "I only suggest that we learn more before acting. Wait for a few hours, at least until you have spoken with Fist. There could be a simple explanation."

Of course Deathclaw made sense. He usually did. But Edge wasn't ready to concede his point. "A few hours won't be enough time to hunt down this wizard."

"No, but we can gather information to pass on to the Mage School," he replied, crouching next to the small corpse. "Let go of your emotions so that you can focus."

Deathclaw had grown much over the time since he and Edge had bonded. He had learned the ways and language of human kind and had shifted his behavior from being a pack leader to being a tribe member. He had even accepted Edge as the leader of the tribe. That didn't keep him from talking like he was the boss.

Edge let out a slow sigh and allowed the sword to take away his emotions once more. The irrational urgency in his mind faded. "What have you found?"

Deathclaw reached out and jerked something free from the goblin's neck. He held it out to Edge. "A dart."

Edge took the small item from the raptoid. The dart was a cruel barbed thing and seemed to be made of bone. He switched to spirit sight and focused in. There was only the tiniest trace of magic, but he saw it, a dark wisp of energy. "This could be how the Maw controls them."

Spirit magic could be used to influence people, making them excited or afraid for instance, but the spirits of intelligent beings resisted being controlled. The body that a spirit resided in was a natural barrier of protection from mental attack. The only way to truly control someone was to pierce through their defenses and that meant piercing the body.

Deathclaw had already moved to examine the corpses of the other goblins Edge had killed. Each of them were also pierced with a dart, though in different spots on their bodies.

"Okay," said Edge. He put three of the darts side by side on his palm. The magic in them was already fading. He was starting to regret killing the two men and the elf.

"There was no way around it," Deathclaw said.

"If we had known with a certainty that these people were being used against their will we could have gone about this differently," he pointed out.

The raptoid shook his head. "We couldn't have known."

Edge put the darts away in a pouch he kept on his belt. "Now we do. We'll have to tell the wizards about this when we get back. Maybe Locksher will get something more from these darts."

Deathclaw reached out with his good hand and touched the side of Edge's head. "Your temperature is high. We must see to your wounds now."

Now that the raptoid had pointed it out, Edge knew what he was talking about. The sword was taking away his discomfort, but the symptoms were there. The goblins knife had been dirty and infection was already setting in.

Careful not to further aggravate the injury, Edge made his way down the crumbled section of the cliff face. As they walked to the horses to retrieve the elf potions another thought occurred to him. "We can't just leave all those corpses lying there in the pass."

"Now you think of reasons we cannot leave?" said Deathclaw. He waved his stump dismissively. "The monsters can rot."

"It's the bodies of the villagers I was thinking of," said Edge. "Leaving them the way they are is disrespectful."

"We avenged their deaths already!" The raptoid let out a derisive chuckle. "The villagers are dead. Their spirits do not care that they rot."

"This isn't about dead. It's about the living. The other people that live here would care."

Deathclaw hissed. "I have one hand and you are feverish and cannot bend over. Would you have us digging graves?"

Edge stewed over the dilemma as they approached the horses. Deathclaw helped him out of his armor and washed out the wound as well as he could with one hand. It was all the more difficult because raptoid claws were terribly filthy. He then poured a bit of the potion into each wound and Edge drank the rest.

Edge could feel the life magic in the potion begin to work right away. His skin was already beginning to cool. The potion wouldn't heal the wound instantly, but it would bolster his body's natural healing. He thought about things while he helped Deathclaw apply bandages.

"I know what we have to do." Edge said.

"What?" the raptoid asked. "You're not still talking about those corpses and your human traditions are you?"

"We cut Artemus' nap short," he decided. "Let the Scralag do some labor for once."

*   *   *

Coalvin son of Tollivar, second year apprentice of the Mage School, ran into the library of the Rune Tower. He was careful to circle behind the main desk in the center of the floor so that Vincent, the gnome librarian, wouldn't see his hurried approach.

The Mage School library was an enormous place. Wide, open, and several stories tall with ladders and stairways to the different levels sprouting from multiple places on the floor. High above, a domed ceiling arced overhead, painted with fantastic murals. The place was packed with students and wizards and as Coalvin had hoped, Vincent was distracted by others. He bolted up a set of stairs to the second floor and saw the wizard he was looking for.

Fist was rather hard to miss. At eight feet tall and weighing at least 600 pounds of pure muscle, the ogre war wizard dwarfed the table he was hunched over. He wore richly embroidered robes of black and gold that were covered in protective runes. Over the robes, stretching diagonally across his back, was the leather sheath for his naming weapon, a huge mace whose head was spiked on one side. The chair Fist sat on looked grossly small for him. Coalvin almost felt sorry for it.

"Master Fist!" said the young apprentice, breathing heavily as he came to the ogre's side.

"Coalvin," Fist said in a deep rumbling voice, not looking up from the dusty tome he was reading. "There is no need for vociferousness in the library."

Coalvin pursed his lips at the named wizard as he puzzled out the meaning of the word.

"It means you were being loud," Fist said, smiling inwardly. He enjoyed stumping students with his vocabulary.

"Oh!" said Coalvin. "Sorry. It's just exciting news!"

Fist put one thick finger on the page and looked over at the 17-year-old. As usual, Coalvin wasn't alone. Standing silently just a few feet behind the apprentice was a gaunt hooded figure, its features as always in shadow. It appeared to be unarmed, but radiated menace and danger. Coalvin found it hard to gain friends at the school with that thing following him around.

"What could be so exciting that you're willing to risk the ire of Librarian Vincent?" the ogre asked.

"It's about Sir Edge's wife," Coalvin said, his grin returning. "Have you heard the news?"

Fist looked back to his book. "She would prefer you to call her Daughter of Xedrion."

Coalvin rolled his eyes. "Why won't she just let me call her by her real name? She's known me since I was little. Is it just 'cause I'm a student? She lets your kids call her Jhonate."

"That's her business," said Fist reprovingly. "She'll tell you when she decides you've earned the right."

"Hmph," he said and shrugged. "I guess it don't matter so much after today."

"Use proper language. You're no longer on the farm," Fist replied. Then he frowned and looked at the apprentice again. "What do you mean, 'after today?'"

Coalvin grinned. "She's gone and got herself named."

Fist's jaw dropped. "Surely you're mistaken." Jhonate had refused to stand before the Bowl for years. Not even a direct invitation from the Prophet had swayed her.

"I'm not," Coalvin declared. "I heard it from Jack. He was stationed at the petitioner line and he saw her come out and she had a naming rune on the back of her hand."

Squirrel, did you hear that? Fist asked through the bond.

I told you it was only a matter of time, Squirrel replied from inside his pouch.

Fist wasn't just the only ogre to ever be named at the Bowl of Souls. He was also the only ogre bonding wizard. His bonding magic wasn't all that strong, though. He only had two bonded. One of whom was Squirrel, who was getting old and tended to spend most of his time curled up in the fur-lined pouch that Fist kept under his bulky robes.

Fist shut the book he had been reading and stood. He held the book out to Coalvin. "Thank you for telling me. Would you put this away for me? It goes in aisle 341c fourth shelf. In the section on Khalpan thaumaturgy."

Coalvin grunted with the weight of the tome. "Uh, sure, Master Fist."

"Good boy," Fist said and patted the apprentice on the head. He spared Coalvin's unpleasant follower a glance before heading down the stairs. *Rufus*, he called through the bond.

Fist's other bonded responded enthusiastically, his thoughts staccato. *Ooh! You done reading?*

I am. Meet me at the moat? Fist asked.

Yes! Rufus exclaimed, and Fist knew that he was rushing down off of the wall. Rufus liked to prowl the top of the wall. It made the guards that patrolled it nervous, but most of them were used to his presence by now.

Fist made his way out of the library, managing to weave his bulk through the press of students and out of the doors. He told Rufus what he had just learned and by the time the ogre crossed the moat Rufus was standing in the darkness waiting for him.

"Ooh! Jhonate named?" Rufus said, carefully pronouncing each syllable. He found it difficult to communicate in the common tongue, resulting in his breathy staccato way of speaking.

Rufus was a rogue horse, a rare magical creature that had been created by a powerful wizard named Stardeon long ago for the purpose of bonding to a bonding wizard. There were very few of his kind left and they all looked different. Each one was made of a bunch of different animals fused together by magic.

Rufus didn't look much like a horse at all. His front half was that of a massive gorilla with black fur and dark gray

92

skin. His eyes were wide and intelligent and his teeth were the size of dinner plates. His rear end was that of a great cat, with a tufted tail and clawed paws. The only things obviously horse-like about him were his ears and the mane that ran from his head down his broad back.

"That's the rumor I heard," Fist replied. "Do you want to take me to her house so we can find out for ourselves?"

"Yes!" the rogue horse replied.

Rufus' natural height was the same as Fist's, but one benefit of being a rogue horse was that Rufus' body was malleable. His soul was like an enormous battery full of magical energy and he could use it to increase or decrease his size as he saw fit. Depending on what was needed, he could become the size of a small dog or the height of a towering giant. As soon as he knew the ogre wished to ride him, his body swelled proportionately.

When Rufus had grown large enough to accommodate Fist's huge body, the ogre climbed on his back and they started off into the night. An ogre riding a giant ape-like beast was a fearsome sight and, although most people at the Mage School were used to them by now, they stayed off of the main paths and rode across the manicured lawns of the grounds towards the guest housing.

Rufus' gallop was an odd-looking thing in action. He ran on the knuckles of his hands, but his gait was smooth and he was surprisingly agile. With his powerful hands in front and the claws on his cat-like rear legs, he was able to climb over any obstacles in his path with ease.

They quickly arrived at the guest house where Jhonate and Edge lived and Fist dismounted to approach the door. No light came from the window, but it wasn't that late. It had only been dark for an hour or so. He knocked. "Jhonate?"

"She not in there," said Rufus. The rogue horse had shrunk down until he was back to Fist's height. He was sniffing at the air and had put his ear up against the side of the house.

It was Jhonate's habit to retire early. She liked to be up before dawn putting the Academy students through a grueling training regimen. "She could be off visiting with someone. Maybe at the guards' mess hall?" Fist could faintly hear the raucous laughter of the guards and students on the other side of the main road.

"Ooh! I check," Rufus exclaimed and ran off towards the sounds.

Fist stood next to the house and stroked his chin. What could have convinced Jhonate to go before the Bowl? She was already pledged to the Jharro Grove.

Nope! Came Rufus' mental announcement and he relayed to Fist what the guard commander had told him. Jhonate had resigned her training post and left the Mage School grounds.

Squirrel stirred at that bit of information. He exited his pouch and climbed up on Fist's shoulder. He was a rock squirrel and his bond with Fist had made him as large as a house cat. He had brown fur and a thick fluffy tail, and he wore a leather vest made from dragon skin. His bond with Fist had extended his lifespan, but twenty years was still very old for a squirrel. There was gray in that fur and he moved much more carefully than he once had.

He folded his small arms. *Jhonate wouldn't leave without telling us.*

"I wouldn't think so either," Fist said. "Maybe she left a message?" He reached up and pushed on the door, but it seemed to be locked.

You pull, remember? Squirrel said.

"Right," Fist said, his cheeks coloring as he pulled on the handle. The door opened easily. "I knew that. It's just that I usually knock and they open it for me."

Fist stepped into the house, hunching over and sidling through the doorway as was his custom. The house was embarrassingly small for heroes of Edge's and Jhonate's stature. The Mage School really needed to give them a permanent home on the grounds. They were here often enough. Fist made a mental note to bring it up to Wizard Beehn again. The wizards had offered them apartments in the Rune tower but Jhonate preferred to stay out near the guards.

Fist reached out and palmed a sconce on the wall and a glow orb lit the room. Jhonate always kept the place tidy, but this seemed empty. Fist checked the bedroom and Jhonate's equipment was gone, as was her bedroll. Where had she gone?

When he turned around and headed back into the small kitchen area, Rufus was there. He had shrunk down to half his regular size and was sniffing around the place. *A man was here with her.*

Fist felt a sensation from the bond, faint but insistent. Edge wanted to talk. He reached a tendril of thought through their connection. *Just a moment.*

Squirrel pointed, and Fist saw two folded letters on top of the table. One of them said "Fist" in large neat lettering. He picked it up and read the message under his name.

Fist,

Read these letters to Edge, but no matter what he tells you do NOT come after me.

He frowned and opened the letter. He felt another urgent prod from Edge through the bond, but he ignored it as he read.

Dearest Husband,

I have much to tell you, but little time to write before I must leave. First of all, I was named today. I know this will shock you considering how long I have resisted the idea, but you will understand once you read the letter I received from Seer Rahan.

Secondly, I have found a way to rid myself of this curse, but I must do it without my companions. This means that neither you nor any of our other tribe members can accompany me. Seer Rahan's letter explains this partially. Do not worry, I am not completely alone in my journey. Another person who seeks the seer is joining me. He knows where to find him.

I know that you will refuse to accept these conditions, so to be certain that you cannot follow, I have cut off communication with my ring. Please forgive me for these measures I have taken. I will contact you as soon as the curse is lifted.

I am sorry, my love.

Your wife, Sar Zahara

"Sar Zahara?" Fist said considering the meaning. Of course, Sar was the feminine version of Sir, the title for any named warrior. Her new name was a mystery, though. He would have to look up the meaning of it later.

Edge is not going to like this, Squirrel observed.

Fist grimaced. As happy as he would be to learn of her naming, Edge would not like the way this letter was worded. Nor would he like the thought of her going on such a mission alone. "That is undoubtedly true."

The ogre picked up the next letter. It was written on a different type of paper, more yellowed and stained by travel. The blue wax that had sealed it was broken. He opened it and saw that it was the letter from Seer Rahan that she had been referring to.

As he read it, the worried frown on his face deepened.

"Ooh!" huffed Rufus, who was still snuffling around the room. *I don't like this man.*

"What do you mean?" asked Fist. "Her visitor? The other person seeking the seer?"

"Stinks," Rufus replied, and he sent the ogre the impression he had gotten from the man's scent. He had carried with him a faint odor that reminded the rogue horse of the Black Lake, a foul place of great evil.

"How could the man smell of the Black Lake? We destroyed it years ago." It had been the summer before Edge's wedding, in fact.

Rufus shrugged. "He stinks."

Squirrel sniffed a few times. *I don't smell it*, he declared. Fist didn't dare tell him that his sense of smell wasn't what it used to be.

Fist felt Edge's insistent nudge in the bond once again. The ogre sighed. "I suppose I'd better tell him."

Chapter Nine

Sir Edge - Letters

Edge and Deathclaw waited impatiently for Fist's response. Edge was lying in his bedroll in a trance-like state, while Deathclaw sat in a tree above the small camp. The raptoid was keeping his senses alert, letting his subconscious mind stand watch.

While their bodies were in this semi-awake condition, their thoughts remained deep within the bond. Both of them had formed mental representations of their physical forms and waited within a chamber that Edge had created. The room was wide and square with walls and ceilings made of white cloud.

Edge paced the chamber worriedly, his form fidgeting. Deathclaw leaned against one wall, his body partially translucent. His arms were folded and his eyes were focused on the other member of their tribe in the room.

In the center of the room was a polished wooden table surrounded by four plush chairs. At one of them, slumped forward onto the table and snoring softly, was Artemus. The ancient wizard still retained aspects of the Scralag in his form. His skin was light blue and his beard was made of icicles. The fingernails on his hands were long, black, and pointed and covered in mud.

It hadn't been easy for Edge to rouse him enough to send the Scralag back out and dig a mass grave for the dead villagers, but he had managed to do so. The mud clinging to this mental representation of Artemus was clear proof that the elemental was still sulking about it.

Edge walked to one wall and stuck his hand through it as he reached into his connection with the ogre. "Come on, Fist! Answer me!"

"He is most likely just getting ready for bed," said Deathclaw. "First he must change into his nightgown and clean his teeth. Then he must tuck Squirrel in and think about what big words he's going to use tomorrow. Then he may deign to speak with us."

Edge looked over at the raptoid, but in his current mood he felt no compulsion to smile at Deathclaw's accurate depiction of Fist's habits. "He keeps telling me, 'Just a moment' like he can't tell how urgent this is. If he doesn't-."

I'm here, sent Fist and Edge felt a large hand grasp his own.

Edge pulled with all his mental might and as he backed away from the wall, the hole he had made opened wider and the ogre's huge arm followed his own. Fist slid out of the wall and into the room with the rest of them. The gravity of the place didn't seem to affect him at first. He didn't fall to the ground, but floated forward a short distance before pulling his feet under him.

Fist soon stood, towering over him. He reached out to grasp Edge's shoulders, and concern etched in his features. "Edge, you're wounded!"

"We had a battle today. But we can talk about that later," Edge replied. He lifted his hand to show Fist the ring. "Something is wrong with Jhonate! I can't feel her presence."

"Does the wood still live?" Fist asked.

"Yes, but I can't even tell what direction she's in."

Fist nodded. "She's doing that on purpose."

"Why would she cut off her connection to me?" Edge asked and as secure as he had always felt with their relationship, a small jolt of fear came unbidden to his mind. He had been gone a long time. Had she met someone else?

"Of course not," said Fist. "The point is she's not hurt. I'll explain everything I know, but after you let me heal you."

"Can you do it from this distance?" asked Deathclaw.

"I should be able to. Rufus is back at the Mage School boosting me with his energy. That's why he isn't in here with me," said Fist he returned his focus to Edge. "I learned that trick from you. You've done it with Gwyrtha often enough."

"Right," said Edge. After spending two years away from his own rogue horse, he had momentarily forgotten that Fist wasn't as impaired. "Where is Squirrel?"

"He's on your shoulder," said Deathclaw.

Edge turned his head and found himself being proffered a nut from a scaly outstretched hand.

When inside mental confines of the bond, Squirrel's appearance wasn't limited by his physical form. Instead of an old graying squirrel, he had taken a form very similar to Deathclaw's. He looked like a miniature raptoid, covered in scales, his hands and feet tipped with talons. The one remnant of his true self that remained was a thick bushy tail that curved up his back.

His appearance wasn't the only thing he could alter in this place. He shook the nut at Edge. "Eat this," Squirrel said in a hissing voice similar to Deathclaw's. "It will help strengthen the connection."

"What has Fist been teaching you lately?" Edge asked as he opened his mouth.

Squirrel placed the nut on Edge's tongue, then reached a hand under his chin and shut his mouth. "Not all things are learned from others. This is something I discovered on my own."

Edge chewed the nut and found that Squirrel was right. Though nothing had changed physically, it felt like the distance between himself and the ogre had halved. Almost immediately, he felt Fist's magic enter his physical body. His lower back tingled as his flesh began to knit together. Within less than a minute, his wound had closed.

Fist gave him a warm smile and clapped his shoulder. "All done. The elf magic that currently proliferates your body should ensure that the healing doesn't fatigue you." He shifted his gaze to Deathclaw and raised a thick eyebrow. "You're missing a hand."

The raptoid shrugged. "It's not the first time."

"True," Fist replied. He gestured curiously towards Artemus' sleeping form. There was a frozen puddle of drool on the table under the old wizard's head.

"He helped with the fight," said Edge. "Now . . . Thank you for healing me, but please tell me what is going on with Jhonate?"

Fist reached up and scratched his head. "First, you should know that she decided to go before the Bowl."

Edge's eyes widened. "Jhonate? When? Why?"

"Today. Coalvin heard about it and told me. As for why?" A folded letter appeared in Fist's hand and he held it out. "I found this on the table in your house."

Edge first read the note to Fist that she had scribbled on the outside of the letter, then opened it and read the message inside. His concern increased as he read. After all these years, she decides to go before the Bowl because of a letter received from a stranger?

Edge knew of Seer Rahan by reputation. Listener Beth was the one who had recommended they find him. He had once specialized in breaking curses and was supposedly one of the few living people who had the ability to see future events. Edge and Jhonate had been seeking him for over a decade, but until now he had remained hidden.

While Edge read, the rest of his bonded followed his thoughts. Deathclaw's response was different than his own.

"Sar Zahara?" the raptoid said. "What does it mean?"

"Zahara . . ? In the days of the first gnome warlord there was a general by that name. She was a brilliant teacher and . . . commander . . ." said Artemus. He had done a lot of research on naming back in his living days and evidently the discussion had stirred his mind. The ancient wizard didn't move from his spot or even open his eyes, but his lips moved all the same, his voice echoing in a lazy whisper. "In one ancient dialect it could be translated to mean . . . 'trainer of men.'"

"That fits her," said Squirrel.

Edge couldn't help but agree and normally he would be ecstatic over Jhonate's decision, but that was the only part of the letter he did like. "But why does she think she has to find him alone?"

Fist held out another letter. This one was old and worn and had once been sealed with wax. "This is the letter she referred to."

Edge snatched it from his thick fingers and read the salutation.

*To Jhonate bin Leeths of the Big and Little
People Tribe, Defender of the Grove, Daughter
of Xedrion Bin Leeths, Wife of Sir Edge,
Academy Graduate, Mother of Arriana and
possible mother of many more,*

Edge froze, his fingers gripping the pages tightly. He and Jhonate had not told anyone the name they had picked for the daughter they had lost in childbirth. Her people didn't believe in giving a name to a child that had never drawn breath. Only his bonded knew.

By writing her name, the Seer had given proof of his power and identity. But Edge did not like reading her name written in this stranger's hand. It felt disrespectful and

102

manipulative, especially the last part. 'Possible mother of many more'? He read on.

I know of the curse upon you and I have long known that you seek me. You wish to have this curse removed, but I warn you that doing so will not come without cost. There will be conditions and there will be sacrifices. They will not be easy to bear, and you will feel the weight of most of it alone.

Before you undertake this quest, you should consider something very important. You are already a mother. That your child was taken from you does not change that fact and this curse upon you does not keep you from fulfilling your purpose in this world. If you can find peace in this knowledge, you need not sacrifice more. In fact, I would not have sent you this letter except for the fact that the knowledge I have been given is not for me alone. If I refused to tell you, I would be taking away your choice.

If that assurance is not enough and you still wish to break the curse, you must seek me out and I will tell you more. I will be at the holy site of Alsarobeth at the outer edge of the Known Lands.

In order to reach me you will need to make your first sacrifice and that is of your pride. Only those with holy names and bearing certain types of holy artifacts can gain entrance to Alsarobeth. You know the meaning of this.

One last caution. I have foreseen many futures and the possibility of our meeting is a slim one. In the only eventuality where it happens, neither your husband nor any of your friends will be at your side.

I await your decision, whatever it be. Time is a
factor. My life is nearing its end. If you decide
to seek me, you must begin your journey within
a week after you read this letter.

May you be blessed,

Rahan

Edge reread the letter twice more, trying to digest its every meaning. "He says that neither I or any of our friends will be there if she meets him. It doesn't say that we can't accompany her on her journey."

"She is strong," said Squirrel, this time without a reptilian hiss in his tiny voice.

Edge didn't doubt her strength. She was every bit his equal as a warrior and in some ways more equipped to survive on her own. But this was a journey to an ancient holy site and such journeys were always fraught with danger.

He looked to Fist. "Did she leave any other hint as to where she was going?"

Fist hesitated. "No. She just took what she needed for travel."

Deathclaw approached Artemus and grabbed a handful of the wizard's frosty hair. He lifted the wizard's head from the table. "Do you know where to find this Alsarobeth?"

Artemus' eyes fluttered open. They were beady and red. Frost covered the raptoid's hand and Deathclaw let go with a hiss.

Artemus replied to Edge. "I do not. But the seer is right that she would need to bring a holy artifact. Otherwise the guardians of the holy site would not let her pass. It is likely that she has Tulos with her. Since the Prophet cleansed it, the dagger is a powerful artifact indeed."

"I was thinking the same thing," said Fist. "She may even have used it as her naming weapon."

Edge nodded. One of the things that had stopped her from standing in front of the Bowl was fear of what would happen if she tried to dip her Jharro staff into its waters. The staff already belonged to the Grove. The trees might not like it if she bound it to another holy power.

He glanced at the ogre. "In her letter, Jhonate mentioned another person she had met. Someone who was also seeking the seer. Do you know anything about this person?"

"I haven't heard of anyone like that, but I reached out to you immediately after I read the letters. I will do what I can to find out." He hesitated again. "There is one other thing I should mention."

"Yes?" asked Edge.

"Rufus smelled traces of a visitor in your house," Fist said. "He didn't like the way the man smelled. He sensed traces of rot on the man."

"Rot?" said Deathclaw.

"Rufus said he smelled faintly like the evil stench of the Black Lake," Fist said. "But I can't see how that could be. It makes no sense how he could smell this on a person so many years after the Black Lake's destruction."

Edge's lips pulled back from his teeth in a snarl. "It doesn't matter. If there is any chance that smell came from the man she is travelling with we have to go after her."

Fist nodded. "Then I shall send Rufus to come and get you. While I wait for your return I will do research on the holy site of Alsarobeth. I'll also look into the identity of this visitor."

Artemus rose from his chair. "Might I offer a word of caution?"

A word of caution was the last thing Edge wanted to hear at the moment, but he waved the wizard on.

"Jhonate chose to undertake this mission on her own and she specifically said she did not want us coming after her," Artemus said. "She must have her reasons for believing this and for trusting the visitor that came to her. Shouldn't we trust her judgement?"

Edge forced himself to give the wizard's words some thought before he responded. "I trust Jhonate's judgement in most things. But when it comes to this curse . . ." He shook his head. "Because the curse is on her body, she lets it weigh upon her like she did something wrong. She is desperate to cure it and that does affect her judgement. She forgets that I also share this burden. We should fix this together."

"I don't disagree with what you are saying, but I must point out that this letter was not addressed to you," Artemus said. The more he spoke, the more the elemental's influence over his appearance diminished. His eyes were no longer red and his nails weren't quite so long. "This message and the instructions within it seem to apply to her alone."

Edge let out a slow breath. "But can we trust the authenticity of this letter after the way this was worded?" He gritted his teeth. "Every phrase was perfectly formed to manipulate her feelings! I know Jhonate and I know exactly how she felt as she read it!"

"Ah, so it's the letter's tone that bothers you," Artemus said. Then, with a regretful smile, he added, "But is that not also how the Prophet talks?"

Edge's lips twisted in frustration. There was truth in his great grandfather's words. John did seem to know exactly what to say to make you do what he wanted.

Fist tried to come to his aid. "But we know to trust John. For centuries he has proven himself. This Rahan is a complete stranger. How can we know to trust him?"

"This is a valid point," Artemus admitted. "But can you explain how he knew Arriana's name? Such hidden things are revealed to servants that know how to listen to the Creator's will."

"That's not the only way hidden things can be discovered," Edge said. "How many times have the Dark

Prophet's minions gotten away from us because they found a way to learn hidden things?"

"I could take the letter to the Head Wizard Valtrek," Fist suggested. "He might be able to verify its authenticity."

Edge didn't like the idea of sharing so personal a letter with Valtrek. That crafty wizard had burned him in the past. But he had little choice. His arguments were falling apart. "Go ahead and take it to him," Edge said softly.

Artemus frowned. "Edge, son, I didn't say those things because I wished to discourage you."

"I know," said Edge, giving the wizard a mollifying smile. "I appreciate you speaking up and making me face the flaws in my thinking."

Deathclaw hissed. "I heard nothing to keep us from our current course of action. We should still go to the Mage School while Fist looks into the letter and that other man that was in your house. You can decide what to do after we know everything."

"That is indeed my plan," said Edge. He took a deep breath. "We will set out right away. Fist, have Rufus leave right away and meet us at the Academy outpost near Oldbriar Village. We can make it there in two days. I have some instructions to give the patrols along the way. Also, there are some things I need you to pass on to Valtrek when you speak with him. There is a new dark wizard threat in the mountains here."

Edge passed on everything that they had discovered about the Maw. Then they ended their communication and broke camp. He and Deathclaw mounted their horses and rode down the main road towards the nearest Academy outpost.

They traveled throughout the night and arrived just before dawn. This particular outpost was a small one, basically a few buildings and a stable surrounded by a wall of pine logs. Edge woke the outpost captain and told him about the threat. He requested that guards be posted at the villages near the pass in case the Maw sent more raiders. Then he and Deathclaw managed to sleep for a few hours before traveling on.

When they finally arrived at the Oldbriar outpost, Rufus was there excited and waiting. Like all rogue horses, Rufus could move at tremendous speeds and do so tirelessly. He had traveled through the portal that led from the Mage School to the Academy. This cut their distance by half and he had run without stopping from there.

He barely waited for Edge to dismount from his horse before wrapping him up in an enormous hug. He would have done the same thing to Deathclaw if the raptoid hadn't drawn his sword.

"Ooh! Fist wants talk to you!" Rufus huffed.

"Tonight?" he asked.

"Yes!" said the rogue horse. "While we run."

Rufus then grew, increasing his overall size and lengthening his back just enough for Edge and Deathclaw to tie their gear onto him and climb aboard together. They left their horses at the outpost and rode away.

The rogue horse ran all day and continued into the night, giving Edge time to delve into the bond and contact Fist. He didn't bother to try and build a room in the bond this time. That would take too much concentration to attempt while riding, so they just spoke mind to mind instead. The ogre had important new information.

When I showed Head Wizard Valtrek the letter, he said that it did look to be authentic as far as he could tell. The paper he used is from a tree that only grows in Alberri where Rahan is from. The wax seal had been stamped with an ancient holy symbol. Also, he says the cadence of the letter fits that of a seer.

I guess that's as close as we could expect him to get, said Edge, but there was a frightened tone to the ogre's thoughts that told him Fist wasn't finished. *What else?*

*I asked him about the visitor at your house. Neither he
or any of the guards knew of anyone seeking information about
Rahan or looking for Jhonate, but it was a pilgrimage day.
Hundreds of warriors were in line to stand in front of the Bowl.*

That's a heavy pilgrimage day, said Edge, his concern
growing. *If someone was going to get in without being noticed
that would be the time to do it.*

Yes, Fist replied. *And when I told him about the smell
that Rufus sensed in your house he grew worried. He told me
to wait for him in the library and rushed away. When he came
back, his face was white.*

What did he find? Edge asked.

*Something was missing from one of the tower vaults. It
was an item of power that was recovered from the Priestess of
War's belongings after we defeated her at the Black Lake. If
Jhonate's visitor had smelled of the Black Lake . . .*

Edge's blood ran cold. *What was it?*

*A long slender box covered in protective runes and with
a jade stone on top. When I asked him what was in the box, he
said that it had radiated such menace that he had never opened
it.* Fist paused. *Does that sound familiar to you?*

Edge swallowed. *I think you have the same theory that
I do.*

Celos, the jade dagger, Fist said.

The last of the Dark Prophet's original sacrificial
daggers. They had known it was out there somewhere. They
had even searched for it a few times. He found it frustrating
that it could have been in a Mage School vault the whole time.
Jhonate was in terrible danger if the person with her had that
evil thing in his possession. *How could the wizards have
missed it?*

*There was a lot going on and there were a whole lot of
artifacts brought back that day.* Fist said.

Edge remembered. Artemus' dagger had been one of
the many things retrieved from amongst the Priestess of War's

trophies. *Then we have not choice. We have to track Jhonate down.*

I'm still looking into the holy site of Alsarobeth, Fist said. *Valtrek had heard of it, but didn't know where it was. Librarian Vincent has promised to help me search the records for mention of it.*

Alright, said Edge. *One other thing. Is Tarah Woodblade's daughter still stationed at the school?*

Sukie? Yes, I talked to her yesterday, said Fist. *She's expecting to be transferred back to the Academy in a couple weeks.*

See if she knows if her mother is around. We are going to need to track Jhonate down and there is no one better than Tarah. With her skills they'd know for certain if the man who was with Jhonate had stolen the dagger.

Oh, said Fist. *Sorry. Tarah and Djeri are in Malaroo right now. They're doing some work for the trollkin.*

Edge sighed. *We'll have to make do then. Make preparations. At the speed Rufus is making, we'll see you tomorrow night.*

His prediction was spot-on. They arrived at the city of Reneul as twilight hit the following day. Despite the urgency of the situation, Edge couldn't help but smile as the city of his birth came into view.

Since the rebuild, Reneul had grown larger than ever, sprawling over the nearby hillsides. Rising high above the city was the towering wall of the Academy. With the Mage School's help, the Dremaldrian Battle Academy was bigger and more impressive than ever.

The new Academy covered twice as much ground as the old Academy and the walls towered 40 feet into the air. Every stone was runed to withstand attacks both physical and magical. The battlements bristled with ballistae and other weaponry. Should they ever be under siege again, they were prepared.

Edge wished that he had time to stop in and visit his parents or Lenny and Bettie and their family, but there was no time. He had Rufus skirt around the city and approach the portal site directly.

The three-mile road that led from the portal cave to the Academy was now a busy thoroughfare lined with shops and inns and taverns. Though Rufus was known in the area, the sight of the huge rogue horse with Edge and Deathclaw riding him was enough to cause a stir. Luckily when they arrived at the portal gatehouse, they were recognized right away.

The guards and mages stationed at the gates gave Edge salutes as they waved him through. The portal between the Academy and Mage School was an integral part of the relationship between the two schools as it shaved off two weeks of travel time by horseback. The level of security around the portal showed just how important it was.

The hillside around the cave had become a fortress in and of itself. High walls and guard stations watched over the entrance. They had to pass through two checkpoints before coming in full view of the cave. Once inside they had a surprise waiting for them.

Standing in front of the portal was a five-foot-tall dwarf that was massively muscled. He wore a suit of leather armor in plate style that left his arms bare. The armor was a masterwork and covered in protective runes that glowed heavily to Edge's mage sight. A large forge-blackened hammer hung at his side and under a thick red handlebar mustache, was a familiar gap-toothed grin.

"Len-wee!" said Rufus excitedly and ran up to the dwarf.

Lenui Firegobbler, Master Weaponsmith, Wobble Representative on the Academy Council, and long time member of the Big and Little People Tribe shook his head. "Calm it, monkeyface. I'm wantin' to talk to Edge first."

"Lenny!" said Edge, climbing down from Rufus' back. When he had first met the dwarf nearly two decades before, he

111

had said Lenui's name wrong and though it started as a running joke, the pronunciation had stuck. Nearly everyone in the tribe called him Lenny now. "What are you doing here?"

The dwarf's grin slipped, his handlebar mustache drooping. "What am I doin' here? Is that any way to talk to yer dag-gum best friend?"

Edge blinked at the sudden outburst. Lenny was indeed one of his best friends. They had been in countless adventures together over the years. He gave the dwarf a teasing smile. "Well, you're definitely one of my oldest friends. I don't know about 'best'-."

Lenny scowled. "Yer gonna doubt it? Would anybody else but yer best friend make you two of the most powerful swords in the Known Lands and not even charge you?"

"That wasn't without compensation-," Edge began.

Lenny didn't pause to listen. "Would anybody else but yer dag-blasted best friend hoof his way all the way to Malaroo to help him kill a garl-friggin' god?"

"The behemoth wasn't a god," said Deathclaw.

And at the same time Edge said, "You weren't there for me. You were there for Jerry."

Lenny poked his thumb at his chest. "Would anyone else but yer best friend go hoofin' all the way back to Malaroo again for yer wedding after you didn't bother to go to his own wedding?"

This was probably the least fair part of the dwarf's diatribe, but this time Edge kept his mouth shut and waited for Lenny to finish.

"Would anyone else but yer best friend join you in dangerous missions time-after-time over the years, takin' wounds and getting' a dressin' down from his wife every time? Even makin' her name a son after you?" Lenny said.

"I was honored," Edge said sincerely, placing a hand against his chest. His namesake, Lenny's youngest son, was almost five now. He had been a husky little boy the last time

112

Edge had seen him, though that was to be expected with a child whose parents were a dwarf and a half orc. "How is Justanathan doing? I would have stopped in to see him but-."

Lenny stopped him by raising an outraged finger into the air. "And then, after you ain't spoken to him fer a year and a half, would anyone but yer own bestest friend in the whole durn world, come runnin' to help the minute he learnt yer wife was in trouble?"

"I . . . you heard that?" Edge asked.

"I knew somethin' was wrong when Rufus came through the portal by hisself and run off towards the mountains like his tail was on fire. So I went to the Mage School and made Fist talk," said Lenny.

"Of course the ogre talked." Deathclaw hissed with a roll of his reptilian eyes. "You are wrong about who Edge's best friend is." It pained the raptoid to admit the next part. "Fist would be first. Then me. Then Gwyrtha-."

"His bonded don't count!" Lenny protested. He folded his bulky arms. "Yer too close a part of him. That'd be like me sayin' my own arse was my best friend."

Edge sighed. "The only reason I didn't agree with you right away was because of Jhonate."

"Wifes don't count neither, dag-blast it! A man's gotta say that," Lenny grumped, and it seemed he was legitimately getting upset. "Startin' to wonder why I even came here."

Edge placed a calming hand on the dwarf's broad shoulder. "Okay, best friend. How do you plan to help?"

"I'm comin' with you, of course," said Lenny.

Edge straightened. "You are?"

"'Course I am!" said Lenny. "Ain't gonna let you go off after Jhonate without my hammer and my cookin'!"

"She's called Sar Zahara now," Deathclaw pointed out. He folded his arms. "And as much as your 'cooking' helps, we must move swiftly. Your presence would only slow us."

"Why you ungrateful, scale-faced, bird-lickin',
noseless, baby-handed . . !" Lenny began and Deathclaw
tucked his regenerating hand under his other arm. ". . . tree-
climbin', slimy, no-good, dirt-dragon! This ain't the first time
you've said somethin' like that and you've always been wrong
before. The only one slowin' you down is you by hissin'
complaints when we could be on the road already!"

"We will be riding Rufus," Deathclaw said patiently.
"It will be uncomfortable enough with Fist, Edge, and I."

The dwarf jerked a thumb at the large warhorse that
stood not far behind him. "I got my own ride. He's already
loaded up with everything we need fer a long journey."

Edge's eyebrows rose as he noticed the burn scars on
the horse's neck and realized who it was. "Is that Albert?"
Albert was an Academy-trained warhorse that Edge had known
as long as he had known Lenny. He had thought Albert had
been retired. He walked up to the horse and gave him an
affectionate rub. "Isn't he old for this kind of journey?"

"Old? I think you mean experienced," said Lenny.
"Don't worry 'bout his age. Me and Bettie been feedin' him
elf-grown hay and with that saddle we made him, he runs as
fast as any racin' horse. Does that ease yer mind, Deathclaw?"

The raptoid had no rebuttal this time.

"Is Bettie okay with this?" Edge asked.

"Don't matter if she is!" Lenny barked. Then he
shrugged. "But yeah. Soon as I told her it was Jhonate, she
gave her blessin'. 'Sides, she knows I ain't been on the road fer
a long time. My feets have been itchin' fer a while now."

"Fine," said Deathclaw and the raptoid headed into the
cave.

Lenny scowled after him, but Edge gave the dwarf a
comforting smile. "You know he's just putting up a front.
Deathclaw likes you, but he's never been comfortable
expressing the way he feels."

Don't speak for me, Deathclaw hissed through the bond.

"I, for one am happy to have you along," Edge promised, patting the dwarf on the back.

"Ooh! Me too!" huffed Rufus smacking the dwarf on the back with his much larger hand.

Lenny stumbled and grunted, his gap-toothed grin returning. He grabbed Albert's reins. "Let's go, then."

Chapter Ten
Lucinder - Knight

The rooms that housed Khalpany's hidden prince were luxurious as one would expect. Each room was spacious with high ceilings, and brightly lit by a series of glowing orbs. The walls were made of stone and mortar, but there was nary a bare wall to be found. Some walls were covered by tapestries and paintings of Khalpany's past princes. Others were hidden by bookcases.

Some of these bookcases were new to his rooms. They had been moved in over the last few days now that Lucinder was no longer allowed in the small library. Every shelf was overflowing with old tomes. Most of them were histories, but there were a good number of fanciful stories as well, allegories and fables designed to keep his young imagination lively. For all his parents' attempts to keep Lucinder away from any true life experience, they seemed to want him to have an active mind.

Lucinder couldn't see the luxury around him. He was aware that a commoner would think his life beyond lavish, but in Lucinder's mind these were the trappings of bondage and servitude. Even the silken sheets on his huge downy bed were little more than shackles and these shackles chafed more of late.

Ever since Nurse Deena's unfortunate attempt to free him from this place, a vague certainty had arisen in Lucinder's mind. He was being groomed for something other than an eventual kinghood. As for what that something was, none of the possibilities he could think of were good.

Along with this certainty had come a brooding melancholy and with this melancholy came an unending headache. At night, the ache was a constant dull throb that he could feel even in his dreams. During the day it was worse. Sometimes it brought sparkles to the edges of his vision.

On this bright morning, his open window was letting in brain-piercing light. Lucinder was slouched in a chair with his back to the window. He stared at the pages of the book before him, but didn't register the meaning of the words. Not even the bold adventures of Sar Gander could keep his attention.

The room's sullen silence was broken when a small rock soared past his shoulder and clattered across the stone floor. Blinking in surprise, Lucinder braved the morning sunlight long enough to turn and look towards the window.

A man was crouching on the window ledge. His tunic was emblazoned with the emblem of House Drelbach and tied around his waist was the long yellow sash that identified him as a member of the palace staff. He was motioning at Lucinder.

The servant's appearance in this place made no sense. There was a sheer drop of at least forty feet beyond that ledge. Despite the sparkles that flared in his vision, the prince squinted in an attempt to make out the man's features. Slowly, the man's crooked grin came into view.

"Sir Bertrom!" Lucinder said, bolting out of his chair.

The named warrior made a shushing motion and pointed to a small metal cube that was sitting on the windowsill next to him. It was emitting a soft glow that Lucinder could somehow see despite the brightness of the morning sun. Sir Bertrom beckoned him closer, his mouth moving soundlessly.

Lucinder stepped closer, his curiosity piqued. When he was just a few feet away, he could suddenly hear what the man was saying.

117

" . . . yes, I'm still talking. Still talking. Wave if you can hear me."

The teenager blinked. "What?"

Sir Bertrom's grin broadened. "You can hear me now?"

"Yes," said the prince hesitantly.

"Good! I've been crouching here for a good five minutes trying to get your attention. I finally had to chip a chunk of stone free and throw it at you," said Bertrom.

"Why didn't you just come in?" Lucinder asked.

"Because the floors in this place are monitored. Deena told us about it. If anyone comes in here that isn't familiar to the spells, the guards are alerted," he explained. "They sometimes listen in too, which is why I brought this little cube with me."

Lucinder had momentarily forgotten about his headache. "It's casting a spell of silence."

Bertrom nodded. "Exactly. By the way, it would be good if you don't step any further away. The spell this thing casts only works in a very small radius, which is a good thing really because that means Sren or any other wizards won't notice it unless they're really close."

Lucinder blinked at the smiling man. This was all so strange that he began to wonder if he hadn't somehow made him up in his mind. "But . . . what are you doing here? What about your wounds? I saw Warwielder Ghat hit you."

"Yeah, that was not my most shining moment," Bertrom said with a bit of embarrassment. "He very nearly killed me. I managed to escape, but just barely." He showed Lucinder his right forearm and the red scar that had come from the orc's axe. "Luckily, I have some friends in this city. Have you seen Ghat since then by any chance? I'd love to hear if he managed to get his hand put back on."

Lucinder grinned. "You cut his hand off?"

"I did. That's how I got away. Lopped it off and kicked it into a cesspit." He shrugged. "He lunged for it and I ran."

The teenage prince couldn't help but laugh at the visual. Enormous Ghat in his blood red armor sprawling onto the ground and pawing through sewage looking for his lost hand. The exertion caused his headache to flare again and Lucinder winced.

Sir Bertrom's expression turned somber. "Now that I've answered your questions, I have some for you. I wasn't able to catch what happened after I fled, but I heard that Mistress Dagger and your nanny were captured. Do you know what happened to them?"

Lucinder hesitated to answer. "I . . . Priestess Sren threw something at me and I blacked out. When I woke, I saw their bodies, bloody and . . ." His face turned red. "N-naked on the ground."

Bertrom's brow furrowed and he pressed, "They were dead?"

Lucinder grimaced. "I'm not sure. They weren't moving when I first saw them, but then some men came in and carried them away and I-I thought I saw Nurse Deena move. Maybe?"

The named warrior chewed his lip in thought. "Where were they when you saw them?"

"Underground. Deep in the mountain behind the palace. It's that room where I-." He clamped his mouth shut. "I don't think I'm supposed to talk about it."

"Well, I know that the royal family has their own dungeon in the mountainside," Bertrom said. "But I need to know more if I'm going to find them, Lucinder."

The prince took a half step back. "You'll only get killed too."

Bertrom put a hand to his ear and motioned him closer again.

Lucinder returned to the field cast by Bertrom's cube. "If I tell you more, you might get killed."

Sir Bertrom sighed and shifted his weight gingerly as he stopped crouching and moved to sit on the window ledge. He let his feet dangle into the room, careful not to touch the ground. As he did so, some of the servant's livery he was wearing moved stiffly and Lucinder realized that it wasn't what it appeared to be.

The sash that was tied around his waist and dangling at his side was actually a belt and sword sheath. Some sort of illusory magic was hiding it. And the way his tunic bunched up in back when he sat told Lucinder that he most likely had something strapped to his back, probably his shield.

"I know you don't know me," said Bertrom. He slid the glove off of his right hand. "And I know that the only proof you have that you can trust me is the rune on this hand. And I also know that the only time you saw me in action was when you saw Mistress Dagger and I fail to help you. But listen, I'm a lot better at this kind of thing than I have shown you. Right now I'm the one who needs your help. Mistress Dagger and I have worked together for a long time and I . . . I can't leave her in that dark dungeon knowing she could still be alive."

Lucinder sucked in a deep breath. This man really was like one of the heroes in the stories. "The place where I saw her isn't near any of the cells."

"Describe it to me anyway," he said. "If I can find my way there I might have a way to track where she was taken."

"It's a room carved from polished black stone. The center of the room sinks down a bit and in the middle of the depression is a pedestal. A . . . large silver bowl sits on top of it."

Bertrom's eyes widened. "Describe this bowl."

The prince swallowed. The throbbing in his head was increasing. "It's-. The inside of it is clean like a mirror, but the underside of it is carved with faces in pain and misery."

"So the Dark Bowl is here." He rubbed his hand over his face. "We hadn't thought that the Dark Prophet would be so brazen as to bring it to the seat of power in Khalpany. This makes things even more dire than I had feared."

"It's been here as long as I can remember." Lucinder looked down and he told Sir Bertrom his secret shame. "Every month, the guards come and take me down there. My parents make me approach the bowl and there is a black orb in the water. I pick it up and I hear a voice in my head. It tells me things."

The named warrior's expression was unreadable. "What does it say?"

"Wh-when I was little it was nice to me. It said that one day we would meet each other, and it would be my friend," he said. "But now it sounds scary and last time . . . it said that there were only a few short weeks left and I would be 'ripe.'" He swallowed again, but his mouth was dry. He looked up at the named warrior and saw pity in the man's eyes. "What does it mean? What are they going to do to me?"

Sir Bertrom didn't say anything right away.

"Are they going to kill me?" He asked, his lip trembling as he told the man the thing he most feared. "Did my parents raise me this long just to sacrifice me to the Dark Prophet?"

Bertrom's eyes remained focused on Lucinder and he rubbed his chin. Finally, he beckoned the prince closer. Lucinder moved right to the window and Bertrom placed his hands on his shoulders.

"Whatever they have planned, we're not gonna let it happen. Okay?" Bertrom gave him a comforting smile and waited for the prince to nod. "Now tell me about this black orb. What does it look like?"

"It's uh, round and kind of wrinkled. I don't know what it's made of but it feels kind of slimy when I pull it out of the water. I think it might have once been an organ of some kind because some of the wrinkles on it might be veins." He looked closely for Bertrom's reaction. "Do you know what it is?"

"No, but I'll look into it," Bertrom promised. He sighed again and leaned out of the window to look down. "Can you leave your rooms?"

"They have me locked in most of the day," the prince replied. "They come and get me when I'm allowed to leave."

Bertrom nodded thoughtfully. "Show me your hands."

He did so, and the named warrior looked at his palms and the backs of his hands, then checked his nails. Lucinder cocked his head. "What are you looking for? Nurse Deena used to do that all the time, but I just thought she wanted to make sure I had washed for supper."

"It's an old Khalpan trick that the Dark Prophet's priestesses like to use. They can place a small rune of spirit magic on your hands or under your nails and use it to track you." He let go of Lucinder's hands. "Let's check your feet just in case. Take off your shoe and stick your foot up here on the windowsill next to me."

Lucinder took off his shoe and put up his right foot. The named warrior checked it and shook his head and the prince lifted his left foot.

"There it is. Under the nail on your middle toe." Bertrom pursed his lips. "That's how they found us on our way out of the city."

Lucinder peered at the toe, but he could see nothing. "I can't remember Priestess Sren ever touching my foot."

"It doesn't do them as much good if you know about it," Bertrom said. "Alright. I can't get you out of here today, but at least we have a timeline to work with."

"All the voice said is a 'few short weeks'," Lucinder said worriedly.

"So, at least two. Probably three or more," Bertrom said and gave him a confident look. "Plenty of time. It's going to be a big job, so I need to gather some help and make sure we have a better plan than last time."

"But-," said Lucinder.

"Don't worry," Bertrom chided. "Just be ready. And . . . when you start to doubt, I want you to know something. The reason that Dagger and I are here is because the Prophet sent us. He didn't know exactly why at the time, but he sent us."

"He did?" said Lucinder in awe.

"And not just that, but when we got to Hagenton and met with some of our friends, they put us in contact with Nurse Deena. You should know that she didn't just come to us on her own volition. Someone high up in the palace sent her."

"Who?" Lucinder asked.

Bertrom wrinkled his nose apologetically, "I'm afraid I can't tell you that. This person is in grave danger if they are caught. But I want you to know that I'm not the only person on your side. Okay?"

Lucinder nodded.

"Alright. Before I go, I need you to tell me everything you can about the dungeons in the mountain," Bertrom said.

The named warrior grilled the prince for several minutes asking him for details ranging from the route he took when going to the Dark Bowl to the guards' schedules. Once he had seemed to exhaust the prince's knowledge, he said he would be back when he could and stood back up on the window ledge. He picked up the small cube and turned away.

"Wait. Sir Bertrom?" said Lucinder. "Remember when we first met and you said that your name wasn't impressive?"

He paused and looked back into the room. "I'm okay with it, really. The Bowl named me what it wanted. I was just trying to make you feel at ease."

"Well, it pricked something in my mind. I knew I heard it somewhere before and yesterday I looked it up and found it in one of the old Khalpan histories," Lucinder told him. "Back in the early days of the kingdom, there was a special person on the king's staff. He was called 'the Knight Bertrom' and he was basically the king's personal problem solver. He would send him out whenever he couldn't get things done through official channels. The Knight Bertrom was very well respected, and it was said that he never failed the king."

"Hmph!" Bertrom said, his crooked grin returning at full force. "Well, that's certainly how John uses me. Hopefully it rings true this time. Thanks, kid," he said and dove off of the ledge.

Lucinder's breath caught in his throat and he bent over the edge to see what happened to the man. Sir Bertrom fell all 40 feet, spread-eagled, but just before he hit the ground he seemed to slow just a bit, and he landed like a cat. Then he looked around to make sure he hadn't been seen and ran out of view.

Chapter Eleven
Sir Edge – Generations

The portal was large and square in shape and shimmered with a soft blue light that illuminated the cave. A steady stream of mist pooled out from the bottom of it. On either side of the portal were two lodestones; triangular gray stones set in rectangular runes made of silver. These were the keys that held the portal open. If there was ever an emergency, the lodestones could be removed and the portal would close.

As Edge and the others stepped into the light, there was a brief flash and a disorienting lurch in their bellies. Then they walked out into a large ornate hall. The floors were made of polished marble, the walls painted white with gold filigree. Enormous pillars rose to the ceiling, each one covered in colorful murals.

This entrance area was on the ground floor of the Rune Tower not far from the library. Signs were posted to direct visitors and Mages were stationed nearby to give assistance, but they recognized Sir Edge and his friends right away and didn't bother approaching.

Fist ran into the hall. "Good! You're here. I have something to . . . Lenny!" exclaimed the ogre in surprise. He did a decent job with his intonation and facial expression, but it was obvious through the bond that he was faking it. "What a coincidence! I was going to recommend that we come and see you."

"Don't bother, Fist," said Deathclaw with a derisive hiss. "The dwarf already told us of your flapping lips."

"Lenny," said Fist with deep disappointment.

"Sorry, Son," said Lenny abashedly. "These dag-gum crab-snatchers drug it outta me."

"It was the first thing he blurted," said the raptoid.

Lenny frowned. "Not the first thing!"

"I'm sorry, Edge," said Fist. "He came at me with questions and superlatives and I wasn't on my guard at the time."

"He came at you with 'superlatives?'" said Deathclaw in confusion and Edge sent him the meaning of the word through the bond.

"I didn't say he was 'super' anythin'!" said Lenny. "Just told him how proud I was of how his daughter was doin'."

"It's okay, Fist," said Edge, raising a mollifying hand. "I am perfectly happy to have Lenny along with us. Now what was it you wanted to say when you came in here?"

The ogre's anxiety didn't lessen all that much. "Well, I know that you want to leave right away, and I have everything packed for the journey." He glanced at the mages that were posted nearby and kept this next part mental. *But we need to talk to Head Wizard Valtrek before we leave. He has things he wants to talk to you about.*

Edge sighed. His relationship with Valtrek was complicated to say the least. He respected the man, and thought he had good intentions for the most part, but he wasn't fond of his tactics.

Valtrek had been the spymaster for the school for many years and the habits he had developed while in that position had carried over. He kept far too many secrets close to his vest and Edge wasn't so certain that he liked the man being in charge. Valtrek was the first head wizard in a very long time who hadn't been named by the Bowl of Souls. There had to be a reason for that.

"It's fine, Fist." *I needed to talk to either him or Locksher before I left anyway*, Edge said. "Where does he want me to meet him?"

Fist gestured towards the exit. *He wanted to keep your meeting secret, so he's waiting at your house.*

"Right," said Edge. "Let's go then."

The party left the chamber and exited down a short corridor before arriving at the main hallway. They left the tower and cut across the grass in the darkness, not exactly slinking through the night, but they took the most inconspicuous route possible.

When they arrived at the guest houses, Edge saw that his house was lit from inside. He walked up to the door and thought to Fist, *Did you have to leave him in my house alone?* Not that he had anything to hide in there, but he didn't like the idea of the old spymaster looking through his things.

"I didn't!" Fist said. "Not exactly."

Edge opened the door to see Wizard Valtrek sitting at his small dinner table, a steaming cup of tea in his hands. He wore fine white robes trimmed with blue and black and a multicolored sash that indicated his office. His hair was shoulder length and white and his beard, which had been black when Edge first met him, had some streaks of gray in it.

Valtrek wasn't who drew Edge's eyes though. Sitting next to the head wizard, fiercely examining Seer Rahan's letter, was Edge's mother.

She looked resplendent in a red and black robe that was embroidered with golden thread. Her dark hair, tinged with gray, was tied back and her fine featured face was only mildly wrinkled. To the casual observer she appeared to be in her late 40s. No one that looked at her could tell she was nearly 200 years old. Habitual use of elf-grown food had kept her young.

In her youth, she had been known as Wizardess Sherl, one of the greatest dark wizard hunters the Mage School had ever seen. After a century of such work she had gone into hiding intending to live a quiet life. Edge had been her only child and had grown up knowing his mother as Darlan, a fierce leader in the local community. But just before the battle at the Black Lake she had finally gone before the Bowl of Souls and had been renamed Mistress Dianne. Now she was the Mage School Representative to the Academy Council. She was supposed to be in Reneul.

Edge sent an irritated thought through the bond. *Fist!*

I couldn't help it, sent Fist with a grimace. *Jhonate sent in her resignation to the Academy and when Dianne found out that Jhonate had been named and then left the school, she came through the portal and found me and mandated that I tell her what I knew.*

You didn't have to show her the letter! Edge didn't let his consternation reach his face. He calmly stepped inside and said aloud, "Mother."

She looked up from the letter and her eyes were red-rimmed. "Her name was Arriana?"

Edge bit his lip. She had known about Jhonate's miscarriage and the curse that had caused it, but they hadn't told her everything. "We kept that part to ourselves."

She put the letter down on the table. "Why didn't Jhonate come to me when she got this?"

"Probably because she knew you would demand to go with her," Edge said.

"Of course I would have." Mistress Dianne pointed at the page. "It doesn't say that she has to travel alone. Only that she would meet with him alone."

Edge nodded. "I agree with you. I've been giving it some thought and I think that she may have decided that this meant that anyone who went with her on the journey could be killed."

She grunted. "That's reading a lot between the lines."

"It is also possible," said Valtrek, speaking up for the first time. "That the thief who posed himself to her as someone also seeking the seer convinced her that she could not bring anyone."

"Jhonate is a very bright woman," Dianne said. "How could a strange man have convinced her of something like that?"

"We should remember that her name is Sar Zahara now," Valtrek chastised gently as he placed his teacup down on the table.

Dianne frowned. "She's my daughter-in-law. I'm sure she wouldn't mind."

"Really?" said the wizard with an eyebrow raised. He glanced at Edge. "I rather thought that she was precisely the kind of person who would mind."

"She would," said Deathclaw from just outside the door.

Edge realized that he was still standing in the doorway and stepped aside so that his friends could join them. "Actually, Mother, he's right. You know how proper she is about names."

"Oh," said Dianne, nodding to herself. "True. I never could get her to call me anything else but Dianne."

"To answer your earlier question," said Valtrek. "I imagine that our robber knew how to manipulate her into believing him because he had snuck into the house and read this letter before he spoke to her."

Anger surged within Edge at the thought. "How do you know this?"

Valtrek gestured towards Rufus. The ape-like rogue horse had shrunk down to the size of a dog and was sitting on the floor next to Lenny. "Rufus smelled traces of the man's scent in your home. Would Sar Zahara have let a strange man into her home?"

Edge gave it some thought. Jhonate wouldn't have feared to let anyone in, but it was her habit to step outside to talk to people. Only close friends were invited inside. "I don't think she would."

"Also, Rufus smelled a trace of the man's scent on the letter," said Fist.

Rufus came up to the table and stood on his cat-like rear legs so that he could point at the letter. "Stinks," he said in a small voice.

"She wouldn't have let him read something as private as this," Dianne said.

"Alright," said Edge. "We know that the man who stole the Dark Prophet's last remaining ritual dagger convinced Jhonate to go with him. Why would he do that? What could he want from her?"

Valtrek leaned forward and steepled his fingers. "You read the letter. Only someone who is named by the Bowl and carries a holy artifact can get to Seer Rahan. Sar Zahara now fits both of those qualifications."

"Then he is using her to get to the seer?" said Deathclaw. "Is this just to set up an assassination?"

"It makes sense," said Edge. "If the thief came here to steal the dagger he has to be working for the Dark Prophet. We know that the Dark Prophet fears seers. Anyone who might see his plans in advance is a threat."

"Perhaps," Deathclaw said skeptically, his arms folded. "But I think it is more personal than that."

"In what way?" said Edge.

"A chance to get at you," said Fist, knowing exactly where the raptoid's thoughts were taking him. "This could be part of an elaborate trap."

A chill went up Edge's spine at the thought that Jhonate's predicament could be his fault. The Dark Prophet had a particular animosity towards him because of his bond with Artemus.

Back when Artemus had been alive, there had been a prophecy stating that he would be crucial to the Dark Prophet's destruction. When the Priestess of War killed Artemus, the Dark Prophet had assumed the prophecy void. But ever since he had learned that the old wizard was bound to Edge, he had been sending a series of assassins after him.

"I dunno," said Lenny. "That dark bastard's a tricky egg-licker, but don't you think this is a bit too elaborate? Why go through all that when he could just kill you from a distance with an arrow? Or have some assassin stab you in a crowd?"

"He's tried those things," said Deathclaw.

"Yeah. And it's almost worked before," Lenny pointed out.

Edge's mother bared her teeth. "I don't like the sound of any of it."

"It doesn't matter what his motivations are," Edge decided. "We'll consider all of the options and prepare for them as best as we can, but what it comes down to is that we are going to track them down, retrieve the dagger, and escort Jhonate safely to the seer."

"I agree," said Deathclaw. He looked to Fist. "Did you discover where this Alsarobeth is?"

"This is the main reason I wanted to meet with you," said Valtrek and he reached in his robes to withdraw a leather tube. "I discovered this in one of the ancient vaults. It tells of Alsarobeth and its location. Take care not to touch it."

He placed it on the table and raised his hand over it. Gentle threads of air and earth magic pulled a yellowed scroll out of the tube and unrolled it, then held it open. The top half of the scroll was covered in tight script that was written in faded ink and hard to read. The bottom half was a map of the northern half of the Known Lands.

Valtrek waved his hand over the scroll and a duplicate of the map appeared in the air above the table. He pointed to the top, where an altar-like symbol was drawn. "Here lies Alsarobeth, in the mountain peaks at the very edge of the Known Lands."

"Right next to the barrier?" said Lenny.

"It touches the barrier," Valtrek replied.

Lenny whistled. "I been to the barrier a couple times. In my younger days. When I was full of piss and vinegar."

"I don't think that's changed," said Edge.

Lenny grinned. "Maybe not. At least the piss part. I think Bettie might've wrung all the vinegar out of me. Anyways, it ain't a place you want to stay long. It makes yer limbs cold and yer teeth feel funny. I tried to walk into it just to see what would happen. Bounced right off of the dag-blamed thing."

The barrier that surrounded the Known Lands was impenetrable. It was said that the barrier was there to protect the Known Lands. What it protected them from was widely speculated. The Known Lands were so vast and the barrier was so far away that Sir Edge had given it little thought.

"Do you think that this holy site has something to do with the barrier itself?" Edge asked.

Each of the different holy sites in the world had a different purpose, some of which were guessed at by scholars, but most of them were kept hidden. The Bowl of Souls was the lone site that had a stated purpose. The Jharro Grove was the only other holy site that Edge had visited and even the elves that guarded it weren't sure of its purpose, only that its power held back a vast evil.

"I don't know," Valtrek said. "But it must be a very important one because it is protected by two different sets of guardians."

Lenny whistled again. "Don't want to mess with them things."

"Do you know the nature of these guardians?" asked Fist.

While the Bowl of Souls had the entire Mage School guarding it and the Jharro Grove had the ancient elves and the Roo-Tan people, the other holy sites had guardians of a wilder and more unpredictable nature. Edge's mentor Sir Hilt had once told him of a bizarre and endlessly regenerating series of guardians that he had faced near a holy site.

"The text speaks of one kind of merciless guardian that bites, stings, and kills with unending thirst," said Valtrek. "And another type with fierce mental cries and unending hunger."

"Like I said," said Lenny. "That's probly why Jhonateer, Sar Zenara has to go up there alone."

"It's Sar Zahara," said Fist.

"Right," said Lenny.

Deathclaw had stepped closer to the image of the map and Edge could feel a reluctant fear coming through the bond. "We will have to cross the Whitebridge Desert."

"Yes, the mountain where Alsarobeth lies is on the far side of the Whitebridge," said Valtrek.

Deathclaw hissed. "It will be dangerous."

"It's a good thing we have you with us, then," said Fist. The ogre could sense that same fear coming through the bond and was trying to encourage him. "You can show us your old home."

"You will not like it," said Deathclaw, though his interest had risen enough to overcome the fear. "But very well. We will test our tribe against the desert packs."

"Or," said Lenny, who didn't like the thought of battling a pack of vicious desert raptoids. "We'll do our best to avoid the blasted things."

Deathclaw's shoulders slumped slightly. "That would be wise."

"Thank you for the information, Head Wizard Valtrek," Edge said. He gazed at the map, absorbing every detail. "This is most helpful."

"It is in the best interest of all of us that you retrieve that dagger," said Valtrek, a bitter tinge to his voice. "Had I known it was there, I would have asked John to destroy it years ago." He watched until Edge stepped back from the map. "Have you seen what you need to see?"

"I have it committed to memory," Edge said.

One benefit of the bond was that he could delve into past memories and share them with his bonded. He had discovered that this process brought his original thoughts and sights back in clear focus. He never truly forgot anything anymore.

Valtrek gestured and the scroll rolled back up and slid into the leather tube. "Now, I understand that you have something for me? Something to do with this dark wizard known as the Maw?"

"Yes. He will need to be dealt with," Edge said. He pulled out a pouch and emptied it on the table in front of the wizard. Ten tiny darts clattered onto the table. "We retrieved these from the bodies of the raiders we killed. These darts are how he controls his horde. When we first pulled them from the bodies there was a small amount of black spirit magic attached to them but it has since faded."

Valtrek bent to peer at the darts with interest. "They are organic in nature. Not carved, but grown." He glanced at Dianne "Have you seen anything like this before in your huntress days?"

Mistress Dianne picked a dart up to look at it closer. She raised her other hand over it and sent energies into it. "No . . . there are tiny pathways in the bone specifically grown to house spirit magic energy." She placed it back on the table and wiped her hand on her robe as if a residue had been left behind. "Whatever these spines are, they came from an animal. If this dark wizard needs a separate dart for each creature he commands, he'll need a ready supply."

"Good point," said Valtrek. "I shall see if I can't find an expert to help me identify the beast."

"Ain't Locksher around?" Lenny asked. "He's usually all over this kinda stuff."

"He is in the mountains not far from here doing some kind of research," Valtrek said. "I have ways to contact him. Hopefully I can pique his interest enough to get him to return."

"Good luck with that," said Edge. "As for us, we need to get going." He glanced at Dianne. "Well, Mother? Are you determined to come with us?"

She gave him a conflicted look and sighed. "When I heard what happened, I was determined to come along, but . . . You have a strong party already and I really am needed here. Especially with a dark wizard in the mountains. The Academy Council will need my help to deal with it."

Both of Edge's eyebrows rose. "Really?"

"Yes, dear," she said. "Just promise me that you will bring my only daughter home."

"You know I won't come back without her," he said.

Dianne stood and came around the table to embrace him. "Of course I know. But a mother is supposed to say these kinds of things. I love you."

"I love you too, Mother," he said and then he turned and left.

The party stopped by the small stable next to Edge's house and geared up with everything Fist had prepared. The ogre tied it all onto a special saddle that Bettie had made for Rufus. It was oddly shaped to fit his body and was runed and designed to grow and contract when Rufus did, but it was a real pain to tie together, so Fist rarely bothered with it unless there was a long journey ahead.

Now that they were finally ready, they set off for the front gates of the school. The walls that surrounded the Mage School grounds were a monstrous 50 feet tall, black, and made of solid magically-reinforced rock. As they neared the gate, familiar voices called down to them.

"Hey!"

"Hoy! Halt!"

"Blast it," Lenny grumbled. "I was hopin' we'd slip by unseen."

There was a loud sound of jangling armor and heavy feet on the stairs and three large forms loomed before them. The biggest one of them, just over seven feet tall walked right up to Fist. The hilt of a huge greatsword rose over one shoulder.

"Were you gonna leave without saying bye, papa?" she asked in a low alto voice.

"I already said goodbye to you earlier, Sweet One," Fist said. "I didn't think you would want me to do it again and embarrass you in front of the other students."

"Bah, they're too scared of me to poke fun," she said and stepped up to give the ogre a huge hug. The pats they gave each other's backs were loud in the night air.

"Hello, Golden," said Edge. He stuck out his arms. "What about me? I haven't seen you in months and I'm already having to leave."

Golden stepped back from her father and allowed Fist to plant a wet kiss on her cheek before she approached Edge. "Missed you, Uncle Edge."

Golden was one of only two ogre/gnome halfbreeds in existence, the other one being her younger brother. At 16 years old, her frame was somewhere halfway between her father's monstrous musculature and her mother's slender form. She had been given her name because of her lustrous golden locks. She had her father's kind eyes, but the pointed nose and floppy ears of her mother's gnomish heritage.

She had to bend a bit to embrace Sir Edge and he gave her a tight squeeze despite the bulky breastplate she wore. Golden was probably the closest thing Edge had to a child of his own and he doted on her whenever he could. He had been very proud of her when she had passed Training School at age fifteen. She was now well into her second year in the Academy and the only other students excelling as much as her were the other two guards with her.

"Ooh! Me too!" said Rufus and when he rushed up to hug her, she was engulfed in his huge arms.

"Well, you ain't getting a hug from me," grumbled Jacques Firegobbler, better known by his friends as Jack. Lenny's oldest son, now seventeen, had the height of his half-orc mother and the width of his dwarven father. Even though at six-foot-six he was a foot shorter than Golden, he was a good half foot wider, making him a truly formidable figure. The slight greenish tone of his skin was barely noticeable in the torchlight

"Nobody was askin' fer one, you corn-farmin' layabout!" Lenny growled.

"If I hadn't said something, you would've run over and grabbed me in front of everybody, you knee-high, forge-blackened, gap-toothed, blowhard!" Jack growled back.

Lenny laughed. "Keep practicin' and you'll curse like a Firegobbler yet."

"We wanna come with you," said the third member of the group. Sukie Woodblade was nearly as tall as Jack and with her own mixed heritage was just as wide at the shoulders. She was more soft spoken than the others and preferred a bow to the up-close fighting style of her friends, but she was every bit as talented.

The three of them were known among Academy circles as the Halfbreeds. What had started out as a derogatory term had evolved into a respected moniker as they out fought and out endured the rest. The three students were skilled beyond their years and it was expected that they would graduate early.

"No," Edge said. "If you left, you'd be breaking the terms of your contract. They don't let deserters back in. You are sticking with the Academy until you graduate."

"That's fer damn sure," said Lenny.

"But this is about Aunt Jhonate," Jack argued. "She's the best dag-gum trainer in the school. She's the only one who knows how to get the best out of us. We could help you."

"The answer's no and her name ain't just Jhonate anymore," Lenny reminded them.

"Oh, right," said Jack, looking afraid as if she might have heard him. "What is her name now?"

"Sar Zahara," said Deathclaw.

"Zahara," said Jack with an awed smile.

"Ohh, melty!" said Golden in approval.

"Way melty," said Sukie. "When I get named one day, I hope my name is as melty as that."

Fist grimaced at the slang of this new generation. "Don't you think you three could come up with better descriptive terms than that?"

"C'mon, Uncle Fist," said Jack with a roll of his eyes. "You don't need to get so dag-gum pickled over it."

The ogre groaned.

"Papa?" said Golden hesitantly. "You don't know anything more about when Mama and Grandma Sarine are coming back, do you?"

"I'm sorry, Sweet One," said Fist. "The last message I received was two weeks ago, same as you."

Fist's wife, Maryanne was bonded to Edge's great grandmother. Mistress Sarine was well over 200 years old. As the Mage School's historian, she was currently on a mission to Alberri to study at the libraries in the Gnome Homeland. Maryanne had gone with her hoping to train with the gnome warriors and had taken their son along for the journey. They were set to return in a few months' time.

Fist placed a hand on her shoulder. "Don't worry. I'm sure we'll hear something soon. She might even be back before me."

"See!" said Lenny loudly. "This blasted slobberin' cry fest is the reason I wanted to sneak on by! Are you three warriors or whanny babies?"

"Warriors!" the three students announced.

"Then get back to yer dag-blasted guard duties and let us by!"

"Yes, Sir!" said Sukie and the others repeated her. They turned to leave.

"Bye, Sweet One," said Fist with a wave.

"Bye Papa," Golden replied and the three of them ran back up the stairs.

Their heavy steps echoed through the darkness and as the party walked through the gate and began their journey, Lenny shook his head and grinned. "Dag-gum kids."

Chapter Twelve
Sar Zahara – Pilgrimage

Jhonate sat still next to the fire. Her legs were crossed and her eyes closed, her mind in a meditative state. The backs of her hands rested on her knees and her Jharro staff lay across her palms. In her mind's eye, she floated in soft white emptiness, focused on her senses of hearing, smell, and touch.

Though it was late at night, she was still dressed for battle. The runes on her hardened leather breastplate reflected the firelight and her hair was braided and pulled up in the traditional style of the Roo-Tan people. Two braids hung down at either side of her face, interwoven with green braids that matched the color of her eyes.

It was difficult to differentiate the sounds of the night so close to the rushing sounds of the Wide River. She almost didn't hear the approaching creep of the attacker. If she hadn't already known it would come, she might have mistimed her attack.

When the moment was right, the smooth tip of her staff narrowed to a spear-like point. In one smooth motion, Jhonate twisted and thrust the point into the eye of the gorc that was standing next to her, its dagger raised. She rose to her feet, her eyes opening and taking in the rest of the attackers. They were all goblinoids, that beastly triumvirate of goblins, gorcs, and orcs.

"Nod! Now!" she cried and pulled her staff out of the eye of the convulsing gorc as she rolled to avoid the slash of an axe that was aimed at her back. A crossbow twanged in the night and an iron bolt pierced the head of the orc whose ax she had dodged. Its eyes lost focus and looked in opposite directions as it let out a wheezing sigh as it fell over.

Once more, Nod had proved himself not to be entirely worthless. They had stuffed his bedroll with sticks and leaves to look like it was occupied, and the man had hidden in the bushes to await the attack. Despite his crippling deformity, the man had a surprising range of skills. It was too bad his personality wasn't more pleasant to be around.

Three more beefy orcs charged into the firelight and stabbed their spears into Nod's empty bedroll. Two more gorcs and three goblins encircled the camp, waiting for their own opportunity to attack. It was a minor raiding party. Their armor was of a bedraggled sort, cobbled together from the armor of people they had waylaid. Their weapons, chipped and rusty as they were, were still deadly enough.

Jhonate darted at the orcs and changed the tips of her staff, making them thick and dense. She spun as she approached and ended up behind one of them, a thick brute with a light green complexion and multiple facial piercings. She swung her staff into the back of his head with skull cracking force.

She didn't stop, but continued her movement, spinning again. As she did so one tip of the staff changed again, becoming a blade. The second orc saw her blow fell the first one and was in the process of raising its spear in a motion that protected its throat and head.

Jhonate slashed the staff across his abdomen and the blade-like tip of her staff cut through the leather armor it was wearing. Fluids poured immediately from the wound and its belly bulged in an unpleasant way. She followed up that strike with the weighted end, bashing the side of his knee and causing it to buckle inward. The orc squealed in pain and surprise and nearly fell over, but it managed to use its spear like a staff to support its weight.

Jhonate dodged to avoid the thrust of the third orc's spear. She knocked the spear aside with her staff and used that motion to follow through with another strike on the wounded second orc. It was clutching its belly and couldn't defend its throat. The blade tip of her staff flashed in a gray blur and opened its jugular.

As it toppled to fall upon its unconscious companion, the remaining orc took a fearful step back and assumed a defensive stance. This orc had a darker skin color than the other two, but it was more brown than green. Its features were less bestial than the others as well.

Perhaps it wasn't a full-blooded orc. One of its parents could have been a half-orc. This wasn't too uncommon. Sometimes orcs kept half-orcs in their camps to use as bedslaves. Resulting offspring were raised for manual labor or as fodder in their armies.

She allowed herself a brief second to feel pity for the poor beast's wretched existence before she attacked. The kindest thing she could do would be to kill it quickly. She came at the orc, swinging her staff in alternating strikes. The orc fended off the blows with expert parries, swinging its spear like it was a quarterstaff.

A grudging respect for the unfortunate creature's skill grew in her mind. The orc must have been a veteran of many battles. She didn't let this respect alter her intentions, though. Jhonate took a step back, then shifted her grip to the bottom half of the staff and caused the end to swell into a sphere and sprout spikes like a morning star.

Jhonate stepped forward again and swung the staff downwards in a two-handed overhead strike. The orc made the proper counter, raising its spear over its head with both hands to absorb the blow. In mid-swing, Jhonate commanded the wood in the center of her staff to go limp like a rope. The staff hit the upraised haft of the orc's spear and bent. The hardened spiky ball swung into the top of its head.

The orc cried out and tried to back away, but the spikes had embedded themselves in its skull. Grimly, Jhonate caused the spikes to grow into the orc's head, seeking out its brain. While the orc trembled and jittered, she glanced behind her and saw the incoming rush of a gorc with a curved sword.

Jhonate didn't have the time to withdraw the wood from the orc. She let go of her staff with her right hand and grabbed the hilt of the jeweled white dagger sheathed at her waist. She drew the dagger just in time to parry the gorc's clumsy thrust.

This gorc was of a similar height as Jhonate, though its build was slightly heavier. Its face was a pale yellow and its eyes were wide and panicked. Jhonate realized that it was quivering with fear even as it attacked. She noted this information as she stabbed out with her dagger, piercing its chest and heart.

The moment that the white metal of her blade entered its flesh, Jhonate's mind caught a brief glimpse of a hungry mind. She grew certain that this gorc had been compelled by a mind other than its own. Then her blade flashed brightly with light and the connection ended. The gorc slid off of the dagger and fell with a dying gurgle.

She stared down at the dagger and watched as the gorc's blood beaded and fell away as if repelled by the blade's very nature. It was a cruelly shaped weapon, but there was a beautiful purity about the white metal. The rubies set in its hilt and pommel glittered even in the dimmest light. At the base of the blade, just above the hilt, was a square naming rune that shone in silver on the white blade.

The rune on the dagger matched the rune on the back of her right hand. The square was filled with tiny symbols, both elemental and spiritual. When looked at from a distance, the intricate symbols in the rune combined to form a swirled pinwheel-like pattern. Many of her travelling hours had been spent pondering the meaning of it. Why had the Bowl chosen the rune and the name that it had given her? *Sar Zahara . . .*

She knew the name was correct, yet it still felt foreign in her mind.

When Jhonate had stood before the Bowl of Souls on the day she had received the seer's letter, she had been filled with indecision. Was this truly the right thing to do? Like it had every time she had been in the Bowl's presence, she could feel it calling out to her; beckoning. Yet, the Jharro staff that had filled her hands had resisted the idea. It was as if her tree was telling her no. She had pledged herself to the Grove.

Seer Rahan's letter had been specific, though. She needed to be named and even though she had refused time after time in the past, Edge's arguments that she should do it suddenly seemed more valid. After all, the Bowl of Souls and the Jharro Grove both served the Creator. And she already did the Bowl's bidding every time she went out on missions with her husband.

Despite her self-assurances, her hands had tightened on her Jharro staff and she knew it wasn't right to use it. Reluctantly, she had put the staff aside and withdrew the white dagger that the Prophet had left in her care. This was a holy artifact like the seer had specified, but was it right for her to use it as her naming weapon?

Jhonate stood before the Bowl as a warrior, yet she had never killed a creature with the dagger before. The only time she had wielded it before was when she had used it to sever the Moonrat Mother's connection to this world. But as she had held the dagger before her, the Bowl had called out to her again, more insistent than ever and this time she had stepped forward.

As she did so, a chant had built within her mind. The words were foreign to her, yet without knowing it, her lips had moved along with the chant. Soon the words had poured from her lips. Jhonate had raised her dagger into the air and as the chant reached a crescendo, she had plunged it into the water, her new name bursting from her mouth in a shout.

"Well, that didn't go so bad now did it?" said Nod in his odd lilting accent.

Jhonate started and shook her head, realizing that she had become entranced in the middle of battle. She whipped her head around and saw that there were no foes standing. Those that she hadn't killed herself were sprawled on the ground, either pierced by a crossbow bolt or lying in a pool of blood from Nod's short sword.

"You alright, Sar?" asked the pilgrim.

He picked up his small crossbow off of the ground and collapsed it. It was an ingenious device, designed to be folded up and worn on a warrior's belt, but putting it away seemed a laborious task. It looked all the more complicated because of the man's disfigurement.

His left forearm was permanently drawn up, the fingers of his gloved hand twisted into a rigid claw. He managed well despite the disfigurement and told her that it was because he'd had it for years. It was the result of a curse put on him by a dark wizard. Evidently, in addition to the state of his arm, the curse had rendered him infertile.

His previous life as a minor Khalpan noble had been ruined. His house had taken away his birthright since he could never produce an heir and his wife had left him. Nod had become a pilgrim, traveling to holy sites and searching for a cure to his curse.

The man clipped the collapsed crossbow to his belt and drew his sword. It was a fine weapon and she could believe that it had belonged to a nobleman. The hilt was golden and smattered with tiny runes. It glowed blue and black to her mage sight, a sign that it was enhanced with earth and water magic. This was the second time they had been attacked on their journey and each time he had acquitted himself admirably.

Jhonate put the dagger away in its sheath. "There was something wrong about this attack."

"Is that so, Sar?" Nod said, and he walked around to each body, stabbing it with his sword to make sure the goblinoid was dead.

"They came after us as if compelled to do so," she explained. "When I killed this gorc with my naming weapon it felt like there was another presence in its mind forcing it to fight." She looked around the campsite and shook her head. "Their order of attack was strange as well. Normally, orcs force their smaller brethren to attack first as fodder." She pointed. "These three orcs ran in at our decoy and let the goblins prowl the perimeter."

Nod crouched down next to the orcs and grunted, then plunged his sword through the neck of the first orc she had downed. Evidently it had only been knocked unconscious because blood gushed from the wound.

"I noticed the same 'fing," he said. "Not that I saw any vision about it or nofin'." He pulled something that looked like a crooked thorn from the orc's neck and tossed it aside. He then sheathed his sword and began rummaging through the orc's armor. "But one 'fing I've found in me years of pilgrimin' is whenever you're on the trail of a new holy site, 'fings tend to come at you."

"What kinds of things?" she asked doubtfully.

He pulled a couple of rusty throwing knives out of the orc's beltloops and tossed them aside, then opened a pouch and shook it to discover it was empty. "Oh, brigands, goblinoids, monsters. You name it, anyfing with a dark side gets drawn towards you when you're on the path of goodness."

He moved on to the next goblinoid and started going through its belongings.

Jhonate pondered what he had said. She had noticed that when doing the Bowl's business, her husband seemed to be drawn to dark beasts. Did the reverse work as well? Could a holy mission really bring evil upon you? Was the Dark Prophet's will strong enough to compel his minions even at such great distance?

She cocked her head, distracted by Nod's movements. "What are you doing, Pilgrim Nod?"

"Oh, it's just Nod, Sar. No need for honorifics wif' me," said the ex-nobleman as he pulled meager pouches from the belts of the dead goblinoids. "But as a man of little means I find it's always a good idea to check any bodies I run across. You never know what treasures even filthy beasts like these might hold."

One of the pouches held some flint and steel. Another was full of broken arrowheads and a few small pieces of unrecognizable jerky that Nod casually tossed into the fire. But the third pouch he opened contained a single gold piece and two small gems. He showed them to her proudly before stowing them away. "Everyfing adds up."

Jhonate gave him a stony look. Her people would never stoop to looting foul beasts. If you hunted down and killed a thief it was fair and right to reclaim stolen goods, but otherwise it was disrespectful to yourself and your fallen foe to steal their things. This wasn't an uncommon behavior for uncouth warriors and mercenaries, but seemed beneath a man on a holy pilgrimage.

"Are you going to check their teeth for gold fillings while you are at it?" she asked, her voice steeped in disapproval.

"Bah," he said with an unashamed grin. "Grunts like these wouldn't bother with fillings." When she didn't smile in return, his back straightened. "Now, don't you be judgin' me too harshly, Sar. The curse what's on me is what drove me to this lowly state. Ain't like I could work for my food, now is it?"

Jhonate placed her hands on her hips and wondered why she was stuck with this particular man. Even his introduction to her had been uncouth.

When she had returned to her house after being named, he had stepped out of the shadows of her stable and called out to her as "Jhonate, wife of Sir Edge." After she had reprimanded him for using her name without permission, he had apologized and introduced himself.

Nod had told her of his curse and that he had been searching for Seer Rahan, just as she was. Then he had produced his own letter from the seer. In the letter, Rahan had told him that his curse could be lifted, but that he could not do it alone.

He told Nod to travel to the Mage School and seek out a woman who had also been cursed. It said that she was also looking to find the seer and that she would know the location where he was. They would only succeed on their journey if they traveled together and alone. It then ended with the warning that Seer Rahan's life would soon end and they needed to leave right away.

Jhonate had read over it several times, at first unbelieving that these events would come together so quickly after her naming. But the letter seemed to be genuine. The paper it had been written on was slightly different, but the handwriting and cadence of speech was the same.

When she had told Nod that the location he sought was Alsarobeth, the pilgrim had been excited. He knew exactly where it was. After years of searching for Rahan, Jhonate finally had a course of action to follow. She had written her letter of resignation to the Academy right away and they had left that night.

Nod walked over to his bedroll and sighed at the multiple cuts the orcs had made in his blankets. He shook the leaves and sticks out of it. "It's gonna take me hours to sew up this mess!"

Jhonate sighed. "I do not wish to sleep here tonight."

"Yeah. Me neither," he said. "You want to ride on?"

"Yes," she said and started kicking dirt over the fire. "Let us continue along the river."

They quickly dismantled their camp and climbed back on their horses. It had not been necessary for Jhonate to arrange for her steed upon leaving the Mage School. Nod had brought two well behaved animals with him, knowing that they would need to travel together.

They rode through the night and into the morning hours before they stopped to eat and stretch their legs. Jhonate ate quickly and as she put the rest of the rations away she felt a shiver and glanced back at Nod to find the man leering at her.

The way he was watching made her sure that he was imagining foul things. It wasn't the first time she had caught his eyes on her in this way, but she certainly wasn't going to put up with it any longer. She sent him a steely glare. "Do not look at me like that, Pilgrim."

The leer fell from his face and he raised an eyebrow. "Like what, Sar?"

"You know what I mean," she snapped. "Do not make me clout you over the head until you admit it."

"Oh that," he said and glanced down embarrassedly. "I'm sorry, Sar. I can't help that you're a feast for a man's eyes. That dark skin, those green eyes. Your slender-."

"Enough!" she snarled.

He flinched away, raising his crippled hand defensively. "Please don't worry about me, Sar! It's just a harmless observance. I'm no threat to you. After all, you know that the curse crippled more than just me arm."

He had told her that vulgar detail when they first met. "So the curse is what makes your attention harmless? How would you be acting if the curse had not taken your virility?"

"Then we would'a never met," he said, looking genuinely hurt. "I'd still be in Khalpany. Me wife would'a never scampered off and I might even have a clutch of kids of me own."

Jhonate frowned, feeling a slight surge of guilt. Perhaps she was being a bit hard on the unfortunate man. "Nevertheless, keep those leering eyes away. If you would look at me do so with the eyes of a traveling companion. If you cannot do this I shall leave you behind, no matter what your letter says. I am not without means of finding Alsarobeth by myself."

He sighed and gave her a reluctant nod. "It'll be hard, Sar. I am just a lowly man, after all. But outta respect for you, I'll do it. Every time I glance your way, I'll just remind meself that you're naught but a friend and married woman."

"Who carries no compunctions about beating you senseless and leaving you for the buzzards," she added.

He laughed good naturedly. "Oh yes, I'm well aware of that, Sar. Don't you worry."

"Good," she said and spurred her horse to ride ahead of him for a while. It would be good to give him time to think on his actions.

She didn't see his smile turn to a glower. Nod stared daggers at her as he flexed his suddenly uncrippled hand.

East Filgren came into sight just after noontime. The city was the prime crossing point for the Wide River and it seemed to grow every year. Its current size rivaled the Dremaldrian capitol city of Dremald. Its sister city on the Razbeck side of the river, West Filgren, was almost as large.

The docks of West Filgren were nearly as wide as the city itself and hung out over the river as anchoring points for three enormous loops of chain that extended across the vast body of water. Each chain was connected to multiple barges that ferried people and goods from Dremaldria to Razbeck and back again. The chains were moved by gears that were powered by large water wheels spaced out along the docks. The undertaking was a huge feat of engineering and was owned and run by a powerful noble family.

Jhonate didn't particularly like the idea of crossing the river at Filgren. She felt that they would be better served crossing at the shallows several miles further up the coast where they were less likely to be noticed. If Edge did as she suspected he might, and decided to chase after her, this was an obvious crossing point. She was known well enough that people might recognize her.

When she told Nod her concerns, he agreed. "Oh yes, Sar. No doubt we want to avoid your bein' seen." He reached into his saddlebags and withdrew a thick woolen cloak. "You can hide yourself with this and shrink your staff down into, well . . . somefin' else, right?"

Jhonate frowned and took the cloak from him. It smelled of dust and mildew. She held it back out to him. "I would still rather we cross at the shallows."

"It's bleedin' cold this time of year, Sar! I dunno if you've noticed, but there's icy bits floatin' in the river out there. These horses might not make it and even if they do, I might not," he said. "So please, Sar. Put this on and wait at the outskirts. Let me go into the city proper by meself. I've got connections in town and I'll get us a good berth on a ferry nice and private-like."

"You have connections here in Dremaldria? In Filgren?" she said.

He smiled. "I may be from Khalpany, but I am a pilgrim, ain't I? I've been travellin' from site to site hopin' to find old Rahan. Made the crossin' here a dozen times and, well, I'm sure you don't approve of a man drinkin', but I've made meself some friends. You know, other pilgrims what knows what it's like."

"Very well," Jhonate replied with a sigh. She took off her own cloak and replaced it with the smelly brown one. It wasn't runed with magic, but at least it would ward off the chill while she waited.

"Good!" he said and started to climb down from his horse. "Now hold on while I go have a wee. Be a jiff."

While the man ran up to the nearest bush, Jhonate edged her horse up next to his. She turned a section of her staff soft and pulled a small pinch of wood away. She formed the wood into a ball and dropped it into one of his saddlebags. She pulled her horse away before he turned back around.

Nod remounted and they travelled down to the city outskirts. The pilgrim indicated that she should stay put and urged his horse into the traffic-heavy main road.

Jhonate waited for a few minutes, then rode slowly after him. She could feel her connection to the wood in his saddlebags and was sure to stay back just enough to remain out of his sight.

She wasn't completely sure why she had felt the sudden compulsion to follow him. Though she didn't particularly like some of the man's behaviors, that was something that could be fixed. In all her years as a trainer, she had molded rougher men into shape. She didn't have a reason to distrust him either. Rahan wouldn't have sent him to her if he was a true scoundrel. Nevertheless, there was something about his recent behavior as they had neared the river, a shiftiness that told her that he was up to something.

Jhonate continued to keep her distance and let the crowds hide her until she sensed that the piece of wood had stopped moving. She decided it was time to see what he was up to and urged her horse forward. She drew closer to the wood she had planted on the man and got down from her horse. She led the animal around several carts that were parked outside of different establishments until Nod came into view.

The man was standing under the shade of an awning and was talking to two figures. One was a grim-faced man. The other one had a hood up, but from his height and build she was certain he was a dwarf. While she watched, he went to his horse's side and withdrew two items from his saddlebags. One of them was a pouch and the other was a long and slender item wrapped in black cloth. He walked back to the figures, the cloth-wrapped item tucked in the crook of his crippled arm.

He handed the items over to the man and gestured commandingly at the dwarf. They nodded and gave him a brief bow, then turned and went through the door and into the building.

Jhonate pursed her lips. She felt that she had seen enough to know that some sort of shady dealing had just happened. She strode towards him dragging her horse behind her. "Pilgrim!"

Nod turned around and saw her approach and he shook his head, a smile appearing on his face. He trotted over to her. "Why Sar Zahara, couldn't wait, eh? I was just about to come back out and tell you the plan."

"Who were those men you were talking to?" she demanded, gesturing towards the door that the two men had entered. "What did you give them?"

He blinked in surprise and placed his uncrippled hand on his chest. "Why that was me brokerin' our passage. It weren't easy, but I convinced me friends to get us our very own ferry for the trip. It's the smallest boat, used mainly by employees of the town. It's also got a covered top so's no one will see us standin' in the open. Leaves tonight. Right after dark."

"What did you pay them with?" she wondered. After all, the man had been scrounging from dead goblinoids just the previous night.

"That there was what we call pilgrim's wages, 'fings we collect on the way. A couple dusty scrolls, a bag full of rocks gathered at holy sites," he shrugged and looked regretfully towards the door. "'Fings that ain't worth nofin' to nobody but the likes of us. I really hated to let it all go." He hesitated a moment, then frowned. "Are we okay, Sar? You've been awful rough with me the past day."

Jhonate opened her mouth to tell him how strange he had been acting, but as she did so she realized that he had already explained away all of her issues. The only thing she had were nagging unsubstantiated doubts. If only Edge were with her. He would have had some good ideas.

Oh how she missed her husband. They had been apart for far too long already. At least before this journey she had been able to feel his presence through the ring she had given him.

"I think I am just missing my . . . tribe. It has made me irritable. I-." She forced the words out. "I apologize."

"Aw, that's fine. I'll tell you what. You can make it up to me." He grabbed the reins of his horse and gestured towards the river. "I know a good tavern close to the docks where we can wait 'till it's time for us to make our move. You can buy us both a good meal while we wait."

Jhonate couldn't deny the appeal of a properly cooked dinner, even if it was likely to be a liquor-soaked dimly-lit den. She offered him a conciliatory smile. "Very well. But I am not buying you hard drink."

He grinned widely. "Grand."

Chapter Thirteen
Sir Edge – Tracking

Edge and his tribe were at a disadvantage from the start. Jhonate and the mysterious thief she was with had a full day's head start. To make things worse, they didn't know whether the two of them were on foot or on horseback. Edge felt that it was more likely that they would travel by horse.

Even though Jhonate preferred traveling on foot, she had become a decent rider over the years. The guards said she hadn't taken any horses from the stables, but it was a very long journey to Alsarobeth. Besides, despite her requests, she probably knew that Edge would be coming after her.

Their one advantage was the two fantastic trackers in their group. Rufus had keen eyesight and sense of smell and Deathclaw was one of the best trackers in the Known Lands. His senses were almost as keen as the rogue horse's and Edge had never known anyone other than Tarah Woodblade that could learn more from a track.

Rufus had caused his body to grow to a size large enough for both Fist and Edge to ride his back comfortably together. The conical top of his head nearly reached the treetops. Lenny rode on old Albert, sitting on a saddle specially built for his short legs. The saddle glowed multiple colors to Edge's mage sight. He wasn't quite sure how it worked, but the warhorse certainly acted nimble enough for his age.

Not knowing whether Jhonate had taken the road or had cut across land, Deathclaw stayed off the road. The raptoid took a parallel course east through the woods on foot, looking for recent signs that someone may have traveled off the path. Edge, Fist, and Lenny kept to the road, Rufus snuffling at the dirt.

Edge was bothered by how much the tracking process was slowing them down. The trip to Sampo, the first major city on the road, usually took around six hours. It was going to take them much longer while trying to track their quarry at night. He wasn't the only one bothered by the pace.

"We oughtta forget 'bout trackin' 'em," Lenny argued. The dwarf was wearing a pair of runed spectacles that he claimed helped him see well in the dark. "We should just run on straight to this dag-gum holy site fast as we can. "We can try to get there first and cut 'em off. If'n we come across the two of 'em along the way, hell, that's even better!"

Edge had already considered that option. It was the fastest course of action and that appealed to his sense of urgency, but he and his bonded had already discussed it through the bond and there were problems. "We're assuming they're heading to Alsarobeth, but what if they're not?"

"Why wouldn't they be?" Lenny asked with a frown.

"Seer Rahan's letter told Jhonate to go to Alsarobeth, but it didn't say where the site was," Fist explained. "According to Jhonate's own letter, she is depending on her companion to take her to the correct place."

"We don't know his intentions yet," said Edge. "We assume he's taking her to the holy site so that he can use her to get close enough to kill the seer, but what if that's not his plan?"

Fist nodded in agreement. "If this is all just a ruse to lure Edge into a trap, he could be taking her anywhere really."

"We can't afford to gamble," Edge added. "Right now, their trail is still relatively fresh. Imagine if we travelled all the way to this holy site and waited and Jhonate never arrived. By the time we were able to come back here and try to pick up the trail anything could have happened."

Lenny cocked his head and gestured up at the two of them irritably. "Y'all already done talked about this in yer heads, didn't you?"

"Yes," said Fist.

Lenny's hand tightened on Albert's reins. "Dag-blasted bondeds! How's I 'posed to know? Use yer gall-durn mouths when yer talkin'!"

"Sorry, Lenny," Edge said. "We get so used to talking this way that we sometimes forget everyone can't just hear us."

"That's a dumb-arsed thing to forget!" the dwarf griped. "'Course nobody else can hear what's in yer brains. That's normal. Y'all are the weird ones."

"Ooh! I heard," Rufus offered, turning his head to grin at the dwarf without breaking stride. His enormous eyes were level with Lenny's head.

"That's 'Cause yer one of 'em," Lenny said, pointing at the rogue horse. "You just keep yer nose on the road and keep sniffin'!" He shifted his gaze back to Edge. "Anyways, I see yer point. That rug-licker could be takin' her anyplace. But this Alsarobeth is the only clue we got. Jhonate's a first-rate Academy veteran. She knows her stuff. If'n she's tryin' hard to hide her tracks, we ain't gonna find nothin'!"

I found something! sent Deathclaw from the trail ahead.

"Deathclaw found something!" both Edge and Fist said at the same time and Rufus bounded ahead towards the raptoid's position.

"Dag-gum bondeds," Lenny grumbled. He fumbled in his pocket and pulled out a pair of spectacles, then spurred his horse after them.

The undergrowth was thick in parts of these woods, though this wasn't much of a problem for Rufus. Albert, on the other hand, balked at traveling through such treacherous foliage in the dark. Lenny was forced to pull out a special device to place over Albert's eyes. They were basically a version of the same spectacles the dwarf was wearing, but made for horses.

The raptoid had stopped at the edge of a small clearing and Edge arrived at his side within minutes. They could hear Lenny cursing in the forest behind them, but didn't bother to wait.

Edge slid down from the rogue horse's back. "What is it?"

"I found the tracks of two people on horseback that had left the road to cut through the woods," Deathclaw replied. "They stopped here for a short time." He walked a short distance into the trees and gestured. "Jhonate urinated behind that bush."

"You recognized her scent from that?" Fist asked, wrinkling his nose.

Deathclaw hissed. "When I know someone well, yes, I can smell their scent even in their urine. Besides, she left a few faint boot marks in the soil. Her scent was with them."

He pointed to the far side of the clearing. "The male that is with her urinated way over there."

Edge knew exactly how the situation would have gone. Jhonate would have forced the man to do his business as far away from her as possible. She was very modest when it came to things like this.

"Did you learn anything about the man?" Edge asked.

"From his stance and bootprints I can guess that he is just under six feet tall," Deathclaw said. "His weight is somewhat close to my own. Also, he doesn't drink enough water."

Fist patted Rufus' head. "Go see if you can sniff anything out."

The rogue horse moved across the clearing just as Lenny arrived. His hair was mussed and his glasses askew. His face was twisted in a scowl. The dwarf had been battered in the face by branches all along the way.

"Alright, dag-blast it! What'd you find?" Lenny asked.

"Stinks!" Rufus declared.

"We found their tracks," Edge said. "They are on horseback and stopped here briefly. Rufus smells the stink of the Black Lake on the man."

"I thought the smell of that place was long behind me," Lenny said, his lip curled. "I can still remember it. The water was thick as puddin' and filled with maggots and its shores was piled high with the leg-draggin' corpses of movin' dead things."

"I have seen Fist's memories of it," Deathclaw said, his expression mirroring the dwarf's.

"Don't worry, it is long behind you," Edge assured Lenny. "Rufus is the only one that can smell the traces of the stench on that dagger."

They set out again, Deathclaw leading the way with his senses focused on the trail. Sometime just before dawn they reached the outer edge of the forest. Jhonate and her thieving companion had avoided travelling through Sampo. Edge could just make out the city far to the northeast.

They followed the trail westward into vast rolling plains. It seemed as though Jhonate was still heading in the right direction for a journey to Alsarobeth. The distance would be shorter if she had traveled directly northwest, but the route she was taking was best in order to avoid villages along the way.

They traveled throughout the morning and Edge felt weariness overtake him. He had traveled for two straight days with only a couple hours of sleep. Fist noticed his discomfort and pulled energy from Rufus' stores, then fed it through to Edge's body through the bond.

Edge immediately felt more alert, his tiredness evaporating. This was one huge benefit to being bonded with a rogue horse, however it wasn't wise to fend off true sleep for long. The body might be rejuvenated by borrowed energy, but the mind needed sleep as well. Edge knew it well. He had gone a full week without sleep during one mission and by the end of it, he had been plagued by hallucinations. He needed his mind to be sharp at the journey's end.

"Thank you, Fist," Edge said.

The ogre looked over to the dwarf. "How are you doing, Lenny? Tired?"

The dwarf snorted and blinked. "What? Huh?"

"I asked if you were tired after riding all night," Fist said.

Lenny yawned. "Don't worry 'bout me. I know how to sleep in the saddle a bit at a time. Albert knows to follow y'all."

"What about Albert?" Edge asked.

"The saddle gives him some extra juice. We do plan on stoppin' fer real sleep eventually, right?" Lenny asked.

"Uh, yeah," Edge replied.

"He'll be fine," the dwarf said, patting the horse's neck. Albert snorted.

The trail wasn't too difficult for Deathclaw to follow through the plains. There hadn't been any rain for about a week, but the cool air and thick grasses had kept the ground damp enough for good hoofprints. Jhonate and the thief seemed to be making a beeline for the shores of the Wide River.

It was mid-afternoon when they found evidence of the first attack their quarry had fended off. From what Deathclaw was able to puzzle out, five men had hidden behind a hillock waiting for the two travelers. The particulars of the initial confrontation were unclear. Perhaps the men had jumped out with bows and swords and demanded money.

At any rate, Jhonate and the thief had dismounted and then the would-be bandits had learned that they had underestimated their prey. Three men lay dead in the grass with the various wounds consistent with Jhonate's shifting staff style. One dead man had been disemboweled with a sword. The fifth man had run away.

Deathclaw examined the bodies, but could find nothing particularly special about them. These weren't veterans of battle or mercenaries. Perhaps they were just locals who thought they could make some money on the side, or roaming thugs new to the business.

"The man travelling with Jhonate carries a peculiar sword," Deathclaw said upon examining the disemboweled man.

Edge came over to the body and crouched next to the raptoid. "I see traces of earth and water magic in the wound."

Deathclaw pulled back some of the flesh and Edge saw damage radiating beyond the slices made by the blade. The wound was a mess. He wished that he had external healing magic so that he could examine it with more detail. "Fist? Can you give this a look?"

The ogre came over to them and held his hands out over the body. He sent energies into the corpse and winced. "It is as if the structures of the tissues around the wound have burst from within. I can't necessarily tell the mechanism in which the magic of the sword did this, but a wound like this would be extremely difficult to heal."

Edge grunted. "When we meet this man, remind me not to get stabbed by this blade."

"I will trust you to remember," Deathclaw said.

They travelled on, keeping to Jhonate's trail until dusk and Edge finally made the call for them to rest. He planned for everyone to sleep for six hours and get right back up again. Deathclaw felt that they had made up a few hours' ground on their quarry and he didn't want to lose any of that time.

They found a hollowed-out hillside that would protect their campsite from being seen across the plains and dismounted. While they laid out their bedrolls, Edge told them

161

his plan. Fist and Deathclaw thought it was reasonable, but Lenny disagreed.

"Give us seven hours," Lenny suggested.

"Why?" Edge asked.

"You want six hours sleep, which ain't much with how much you been runnin' 'round the past few days-," Lenny began.

"And with the energy given by Rufus that should be plenty," Edge said. "Don't worry about us."

"I wasn't finished, gall-durn it," the dwarf grumped. "Six hours is fine fer sleep as far as I care. But that don't give me time to fix a proper supper."

"Oh," said Edge, understanding. Lenny had always been particular about his trail food. It made him a good cooky. "We can make do with trail rations for now."

The dwarf folded his thick arms. "Is that so? Well tell me somethin'. When's the last proper meal you et?"

Edge thought back. He looked to Deathclaw.

The raptoid shrugged. "I hunt along the way. A bird or rodent here and there. As for you . . ."

Edge snapped his fingers. "I ate at Lillian's aunt's house. It was . . . I can't quite remember what it was, but it was a full meal."

"Three days ago," said Deathclaw.

"I've had jerky and . . . dried berries while we rode," he replied.

Edge felt the heavy weight of Fist's hand on his shoulder. "I agree with Lenny. We should take time to eat."

Before Edge could give in, Lenny was already unpacking his pots and seasonings. "Get a fire started. I'll have a pot of stew ready in a half hour." He looked to Deathclaw. "Any rabbits or birds nearby you could wrangle?"

"Perhaps," the raptoid said. He drew a throwing knife from his bandoleer and slunk into the grass.

"Me too!" Rufus said excitedly, and he bounded off on a hunt of his own.

Edge sighed and busied himself breaking off branches of a dead tree for use in the fire. As he did so, he felt a light presence appear on his shoulder. He snapped a branch over his knee and smiled. "Squirrel."

He felt a shifting in his connection with Fist as Squirrel's thoughts entered his side of the bond. Squirrel's mind was much more complex than it had been when Edge first bonded with Fist. As he had aged physically, Squirrel had somehow developed a sophistication of his own. He had learned to manipulate the bond in ways Edge found difficult to duplicate.

Tell me, Edge, said Squirrel while he expertly shelled a nut. He was wearing a knitted orange vest that Mistress Sarine had made for him. He had a wardrobe of the things in his pouch. *Do you think you will ever bond again?*

Edge was surprised by his sudden curiosity. "Why do you ask?"

I was watching your magic with spirit sight, said Squirrel, watching the white tendrils that constantly extended from Edge's body. They waved through the air, reaching for any living thing that came within range. No creature seemed too insignificant. Be it bird or insect, the tendrils touched them before moving on. *In the years we have known each other it has never stopped searching.*

"True," Edge said. The last time he had bonded had been with Deathclaw and that had been nearly 18 years ago. He had become so used to the way his bonding magic acted that he rarely noticed. "To tell you the truth, I don't know what it's searching for. The only thing I know is that there has to be a mutual need."

What constituted a mutual need was rather broadly defined. Usually, the bonding wizard and his bonded had weaknesses that could be made strong by the talents of the other. Edge's bond with Fist had given him strength. His bond with Deathclaw had enhanced his senses and given him control. But sometimes the benefit was more nebulous than that. One of Edge's former mentors, Master Coal, had bonded with a goblin because he was too innocent and trusting and needed to learn the darker side of human nature.

There are many stupid creatures out there that need to be smarter, Squirrel observed. *What do you think you need?*

"I . . . I'm not sure," he said and bent to pick up the branches. Certainly, he wasn't perfect. He had much to learn and physically, his skills weren't quite where he wanted them to be yet, but he was happy with the benefits his bonds had given him. There was no hole in his life that another bond could fill. His problems weren't of a physical sort. "What has you so curious?"

It's about Fist. Squirrel glanced over to the center of the camp where Fist had used earth magic to open up a fire pit and pulled rocks out of the ground to pile around the edge. *I think his bonding magic is growing.*

Edge raised an eyebrow and turned to look at the ogre. Fist's bonding magic had always been faint. This was why his first bond had been to a small creature like Squirrel. One benefit Fist had gained from his bond to Edge was an increase in his magic ability to go along with an increase of intelligence. Even then, the increase in his bonding magic had been slight. He had barely enough magic to bond with Rufus and rogue horses were designed to be like magnets for bonding wizards.

Lately, if I watch closely, I see a rope of the bond leave him and touch something else, Squirrel said. *When you return to the fire, you'll see.*

Edge did as Squirrel suggested and returned to lay the branches next to the pit. He looked at Fist so intently that the ogre could feel it through the bond.

"What?" said Fist, turning to stare back at him. "What are the two of you looking at?"

Then Lenny walked past Fist to build the cookfire and Edge saw it. It was just a flicker, but a lethargic tendril of magic reached out from the ogre to touch the dwarf. It didn't gain purchase, but Fist's magic was definitely searching for something.

Chapter Fourteen
Sir Edge – Messages Received

Deathclaw soon returned to the campsite with his kill. He walked into the camp with the small creature hanging from the barb on the end of his tail. It was a black and white speckled wild pig, bristling with hair and weighing perhaps twenty pounds.

Lenny was just getting the water in his pot boiling when the raptoid whipped his tail forward and slung it at the dwarf. Lenny swore, but managed to catch it without knocking the pot over.

"Dag-blast it, you garl-friggin' viper spawn!" The dwarf's scowl turned into an impressed nod as he looked over the carcass in his hands. "Good catch, though. Better than the trash monsters Fist usually brings in."

Fist rolled his eyes. "You are never satisfied."

The ogre had been known to hunt bears, snakes, or even giant insects. His philosophy was that as long as it couldn't talk back, it was good meat. Lenny's discerning tongue disagreed.

Lenny shook the pig at him. "I'm friggin satisfied with this!" He took out his belt knife and expertly skinned and gutted it, setting the heart and liver aside. Then he cut it into chunks and added it to the pot. Whistling a tune to himself he dug into the dried spices and vegetables he had brought and began building a soup.

A few moments later, Rufus returned, emerging from the darkness with a wide grin on his huge head and his own

166

kills tucked under one arm. "I'm back!" he declared and held out his trophies.

Hanging from his enormous hand were the remains of two large groundhogs. He had smashed them so flat with his fists that they were barely recognizable. Their bones were crushed and their entrails bulged from their ruptured hides. He brought them to Lenny. "Ooh-ooh. Cook!"

The dwarf grimaced and waved him away, "No! Ain't no way I'm gonna try and separate the meat from that mess. We're fine with the pig meat"

"But . . . I hunt," Rufus complained, waving the dripping rodent carcasses at him.

"I said hell no!" Lenny barked. "Take them disgustin' things away from my pot!"

"This isn't the first time this has happened," Fist said with a sigh. "He gets too excited about the catch." He looked at Rufus and placed his hands on his hips. "We've talked about this before, Rufus. You need to practice self-restraint while hunting. No one wants to eat something that had been crushed beyond recognition."

"B-but . . ." The rogue horse hung his huge ape-like head in rejection.

"Think of the positive side," encouraged Edge. "Now you can eat them both yourself."

Rufus lifted the kills in front of his face and wrinkled his nose. "They . . . raw."

"Since when does that matter to him?" Edge asked. Rogue horses were omnivores. Gwyrtha loved eating raw game even more than she liked grass or grain.

Lately, Rufus has become picky, sent Squirrel, who was still standing on Edge's shoulder.

"I think it's all the treats that the students keep feeding him," said Fist. "I keep asking them not to do it, but all he has to do is shrink to the size of a puppy and they can't deny him anything."

"I not want raw!" Rufus pouted.

Hissing, Deathclaw approached Rufus. "I will eat one if you eat the other."

Rufus' smile returned, and he handed one of the crushed animals to the raptoid. Then he looked back at the remaining carcass and his smile faded. He stuck out his tongue. "Ick!"

"Do not waste it. That is the law of the hunt," Deathclaw warned him. He lifted the flattened groundhog and scraped some dirt off of it, then took a bite out of the side of it."

"Don't do that in front of me!" Lenny said. "Take yer nasty arse into the grass and eat it where I don't gotta see."

Arching one scaly eye ridge, Deathclaw took another bite and let gore dangle from his jaw as he chewed. Then, since it was what he wanted to do anyway, he slunk into the grass to finish his meal.

Rufus looked once more at the glistening hairy disk in his hand and edged closer to Lenny. "Please?"

"Dag-blast it, Monkeyface!" barked Lenny, as he stirred his bubbling pot. "If'n you have to cook the durn thing, you'cn put it on the coals. Just do it on the other side of the fire so's it don't stink up our food."

"Not monkey face," Rufus mumbled, but he lumbered over to the fire and laid the flattened groundhog directly on the coals at the fire's edge. It instantly started to smoke and hiss in the heat. He inhaled the fumes and smiled.

The flavor won't be much improved, Fist said to Edge through the bond.

It seems to make him happy, though, Edge replied.

Squirrel sighed and shook his small head as he began shelling another large seed. *1000-years-old and he's still just a big child.*

Edge nodded in agreement. He had noticed the same odd thing with Gwyrtha. Fist and Deathclaw still continued to grow in their intelligence and understanding all these years after bonding with him, but Gwyrtha had seemed to reach a certain point and stopped in her progression.

I think Stardeon made them this way, Fist sent. *I doubt he wanted his rogue horse companions to be very intelligent. It is harder to keep a smart person docile and eager to please.*

A half hour later, they ate Lenny's stew. The meat hadn't cooked as long as the dwarf preferred, but it was still tender and the spices were flavorful as were the dried bits of vegetables that he had added to the pot. Edge and Fist were happy to see that the dwarf hadn't made it as spicy as he usually did. Lenny said that was because he was saving his dried pepperbeans for colder nights.

Rufus pulled his rodent out of the coals proudly. He still had a lot to learn about cooking. It was half burnt and half raw, but he seemed satisfied. The huge rogue horse shrank himself down until the flattened groundhog seemed like a decent-sized meal. Then he pulled up several large handfuls of grass and wrapped it around the carcass and ate it like a sandwich. He smiled in contentment, crunching the grass and bones.

"Only a rogue horse," said Lenny with a grimace.

When everyone had finished their meals, Lenny refilled the pot with the rest of the meat and left it on the coals to simmer and stay warm until morning. While everyone else laid down for the night, Squirrel stayed up to keep watch. After all, he had been in his pouch all day and was the only one that had gotten any sleep during the journey.

Edge's sleep was deep and dreamless. When Deathclaw woke him six hours later, he felt like he could have used six more, but Fist sent him some energy and he was up and ready to go. The party ate quickly and dismantled the camp, then set off on Jhonate's trail before the sun cleared the horizon.

At about mid-morning, Deathclaw sent Edge a message through the bond. *I found a camp site. There was a battle here.* He followed that statement with a series of mental images,

169

showing him the state of the site. Dead goblins lay all around the area.

How old is it? Edge asked.

More than a day. Less than two, Deathclaw replied.

When the group caught up with the raptoid, he had more details for them. It appeared that Jhonate had slain four of the beasts, three of them with her staff and one with her dagger. Her mysterious companion had killed six of them, two with crossbow bolts and the rest with his horrifically wounding blade.

Edge frowned at the numbers. "What were so many goblinoids doing this close to the river?"

Deathclaw held out his hand and Edge saw multiple tiny bone darts lying in his palm. "The Maw's reach is farther than expected."

"That doesn't make sense," Edge said. "If his influence has spread this far from the mountains, why did we only just hear of him?"

Fist grunted, his thick brow furrowed. "If this companion of Jhonate's is indeed one of the Dark Prophet's servants, as we suspect, then perhaps the Maw is as well."

"That's a definite possibility," Edge said. Most dark wizards weren't interested in getting involved with the struggle between the prophets. They were in the business of collecting power for themselves. But at the height of the Dark Prophet's influence, he had swayed a number to his side. It made sense that he was recruiting them again.

"If the Maw serves the Dark Prophet, why attack one of his servants?" Deathclaw asked.

"What would you say is the biggest challenge that this thief faces on the way to Alsarobeth?" Fist asked in reply.

"Keeping Jhonate from discovering that he is a fraud and killing him," Edge said.

The ogre smiled. "What better way to gain her trust than to prove himself in battle?"

170

"Then this fight was arranged," Deathclaw said in understanding. "This explains the goblinoids' approach. They tracked Jhonate and her companion through these plains for several miles before the attack, and yet their pattern of attack made little sense." He bent and picked up a crude bow from the grass. "Several of them had ranged weapons but they did not use them. The Maw must have made them charge in, a ridiculous strategy for goblinoid raiders."

Edge agreed. The minions of the Maw that he and Deathclaw had faced had used much better strategy during battle.

Lenny had walked to the center of the campsite and was standing next to a small pile of leather bags and purses. "Looks like Jhonate and her pal took the time to loot the bodies before leavin'," he observed.

"That doesn't sound like something Jhonate would approve of," said Fist.

"No, she wouldn't," Edge agreed. His wife was very particular when it came to spoils of war. Even after all these years, the traditions of her people still ran deep in her veins.

Shrugging, Lenny upended a few of the bags. A folded scrap of paper fell out of one of them. "Huh. What's this?" said the dwarf. He opened it and as he read what was written inside, his bushy eyebrows rose. "Uh, Edge. I think thisun's fer you."

"For me?" Edge walked over and took the paper from the dwarf. The note was brief and unsigned. Edge bared his teeth.

> *Don't worry, I will deliver her to the site*
> *unharmed. I suggest you stay in Dremaldria*
> *where you are needed. If you insist on*
> *following, know this: If you catch up to us I will*
> *be forced to kill her.*

Fist immediately felt Edge's fury through the bond and came to his side. "May I see it?"

Edge handed it over wordlessly. Fist read it over, then frowned and took Jhonate's letter from Seer Rahan out of his robes. He compared it to the note Lenny had found. "Like I thought . . . Edge, this note is in the same handwriting as Seer Rahan's letter. It's identical. The paper is different, and so is the ink, but-."

"Holy hell," said Lenny. "You think that the seer's letter is a fraud?"

Edge swallowed, his anger rising as he considered it. If the original letter from Seer Rahan was a fake, then everything that had happened was just a ruse to get Jhonate to follow this man. But if this was the case, why convince her to get named first? How could that help the Dark Prophet? And why leave a note behind for him to find in the seer's handwriting? If the entire journey was a fraud, surely it was in the thief's interest to keep Edge thinking that Jhonate was acting under holy instructions.

"I don't think so, Lenny," said Fist. The ogre was rubbing the paper of Rahan's letter in his fingers. "If anyone knows subterfuge, it's Valtrek and he confirmed its veracity. And Edge, the letter just . . . feels right." He held it out to him. "Touch it."

Edge reached out and took the letter from him. "I don't feel anything."

"That's because you're full of anger," Fist said. "Let go of it and listen to the bond."

Reluctantly, Edge opened himself to the power of Peace and let the sword drain his anger away. Then he closed his eyes and let go of the weapon's power. He reached his senses out towards the letter and this time he felt something. It was faint, but it was there. Something within the bond resonated with the intent of the letter. "I think I see what you mean."

"Well, true or not, this dag-gum nose-farmer's messin' with us," said Lenny with a scowl. "Tryin' to put all sorts of doubts in our heads. It pisses me off!"

"Does it matter?" Deathclaw asked, having seen the thoughts unfold in Edge's mind. "True or not, our only goal should be to slay this thief. We will need to plan our attack carefully so that he cannot hurt her."

"He won't get the chance to try," Edge promised. "The moment they come in sight, I am putting an arrow through his head."

Their fury stoked, the party followed Jhonate's trail away from the camp and were frustrated to see that Jhonate and her companion had decided not to stop for the night, but had continued their journey northwestward, parallel to the Wide River.

"We shouldn't have stopped to sleep. They gained on us," Edge said in bitter frustration.

"It's a long trip," Lenny reminded him. "We got plenty time fer catchin' up."

They travelled throughout the day and it appeared that they were headed towards the city of Filgren. Edge hadn't thought they would cross the river there. The city was full of possible witnesses. It was more likely that they would continue up the coast and cross at the shallows. The water was cold this time of year, but Edge and Jhonate had done it before. Yet, when evening came and the lights of the city came into view, it looked like Jhonate and her companion had indeed gone into the city.

"I don't understand why they would cross here," said Fist.

Deathclaw hissed in irritation. "This could actually be to the thief's advantage. Their tracks will be impossible for me to follow in that busy place."

"Then we'll take the advantage it gives us and see if anyone saw them cross. Jhonate is well known and the Roo-Tan are rarely seen this far north of Malaroo," Edge said.

"So we waste hours searching for witnesses?" Deathclaw said, folding his arms, and though he didn't mention it, Edge knew that part of the raptoid's reluctance was that he hated being in these kinds of crowds. "Even if they were seen crossing the river, that will only confirm what we already know. When we cross the river, their tracks will be just as well hidden by the city on the far side."

"Let's not borrow trouble," said Edge, though he was just as concerned with this development as Deathclaw. "We do what we can and worry about the problem of finding their trail again once we are on the other side."

Edge and Fist dismounted from Rufus and they traveled into the city. Even at night, stares followed them from the moment they entered the streets and people kept their distance. Dremaldria was a melting pot of races and cultures, but that didn't usually include 8-foot-tall ogres and enormous gorilla-like beasts and humanoid dragons.

Several times, members of the city guard rushed up having been called by worried citizens. Fortunately, Edge was able to diffuse each situation by showing them his naming runes. Even though they hadn't met him before, the guards had heard of the famous Sir Edge and the unusual members of his tribe.

Lenny made discreet stops into taverns along the way inquiring about travelers meeting Jhonate's description, but these stops proved unfruitful. It wasn't until hours later as most of the taverns were closing down and shoving patrons out the door that the dwarf had success.

One loose lipped tavern patron overheard Lenny questioning the barkeep and claimed to have seen a strange and beautiful woman wearing green ribbons in a tavern by the docks. When the patron asked for money, Lenny dragged the witness out into the street so that Edge could interrogate him.

The man was slovenly and reeked of cheap ale and the stained tunic he wore was embroidered with the emblem of House Roma.

"Do you work for the Roma's?" Edge asked.

The man looked him up and down and decided it was best to be polite. "Oh, uh thankee, Sir. I uh, repair things for my lords and ladies as they need it . . . and on odd days, I work the docks."

"And you saw a woman with green ribbons in her hair in a tavern by the docks?" Edge asked.

The man scratched his head. "Well, uh, my memory's a bit fuzzy at the mo. You, uh, got some coin to loosen my thoughts?"

"You already said it, you dag-burned, biscuit-eater!" Lenny said as he shook the man, but Edge gestured to the dwarf and he let the man go.

Edge drew his sword. The man gasped and yammered as Edge placed the flat of Peace's blade against his cheek. He forced the blade's magic to take the man's emotion and clear his thoughts. "Tell me the truth and tell it quick."

"Uh, yeah," he said, momentarily confused, his body growing still. His eyes fell on the ogre and the rogue horse standing behind Edge and he didn't feel the compulsion to turn and run.

The blade didn't create a deep connection with someone unless Edge pierced them with it, but just by touching them with it he could learn a lot. Edge could feel the man's fear being sucked away and when the man spoke again, he could feel the truth of his words.

"I saw the lady in 'The Wayward Wastrel'. It's on the dock right by the center wheel. She was a fine wench, dark skin and hair braided all up strange, and her eyes were a kind of green a man don't soon forget."

Edge caught a brief glimpse of Jhonate's visage in the man's thoughts and for a moment he was tempted to stab him and wring out every last detail, but he held himself back. This man hadn't wronged her. He didn't deserve to have his mind violated.

"Can you describe the man who was with her?" Edge demanded.

The man blinked. "He was pretty plain. Just a man in a cloak and hood. A traveler. He and the lady didn't look too close, if you know what I mean. He laughed and talked and she just sat there with a slight frown on her face."

The man's memory of the thief was blurry, tainted by liquor, and Edge could learn little more. He took the sword away from the man's cheek and held out a gold coin. Lenny frowned at the amount, but Edge didn't care. "How long did they stay?"

The man winced as his drunkenness returned and his mind began to cloud back over, but he was eager for that gold. "Uh, they left late in the night. I dunno. They were gone when I had to leave."

Edge put his sword away and flipped the coin to the man. They hurried to the docks, hoping to find the Wayward Wastrel before it closed. Luckily, it wasn't hard to find.

The Wayward Wastrel was a combination tavern and inn. The facade of the building was well lit with oil lanterns. The sign outside featured a shirtless child carrying a small bag of belongings over one shoulder, his lips puckered in a whistle. They were one of few taverns that stayed open all night to cater to the ferry workers.

Edge accompanied Lenny inside. The common room was fairly clean for a dockside tavern. It smelled of pipe smoke and roasted fish. Since many of their patrons were men on breaks from their nighttime labors, the tables were just as likely to be loaded with food as liquor.

They approached the cheery-faced barwoman behind the counter. She didn't seem surprised when they asked about the two travelers they were seeking.

She remembered Jhonate right away, though her memories were hazy when it came to describing the man Jhonate had been with. The woman had something more interesting to give them than just his description. She told them that the man had left a note in case anyone came around asking for him. She searched under the bar for a moment, then handed it over to Edge.

The message was written on a small folded square of paper. There was no salutation.

I don't know if you saw my first warning, but just in case you didn't I'll tell you again. I'm taking her where she wants to go. She'll arrive there safely unless you interfere. If you continue, I'll make your life much harder. And if I see you, she dies. Please, let her rid herself of this curse in peace.

-N-

Edge frowned. This message wasn't in the same flowing handwriting as the seer. Also, there was that initial. 'N'. "Did you happen to catch the name of the man who left this?"

"No," the woman said with a shrug. "But he and the lady left late. I heard somethin' about the house ferry."

Edge left the tavern feeling just as anxious as he had when he'd entered it. Lenny approached the ferry ticket office and was able to get passage on the next boat. The group walked past the enormous water wheel that worked the gears and stepped onto the pier.

Up close the ferry system was even more impressive. The huge links of the chain rattled and clanked constantly as they moved through the gears pulling the ferry boats along. The boats were broad and flat bottomed and were anchored to the chain at their tips so that they were pulled through the river's current all the way across.

Each one was surrounded by waist high railings and had hitching posts in the center for horses. Lanterns mounted at the front of the boat illuminated the deck and projected light onto the water. Two ferrymen were assigned to each boat and sat perched on the forward railings, prepared to use long poles to maneuver the boats or push away debris in the river if needed.

Workers pulled a lever to stop movement as the next ferry arrived so that passengers coming from the Razbeck side of the river could disembark. There weren't many of them this time of night, so it wasn't long before Edge and his companions could climb aboard.

The boat bobbed slightly with the weight of Fist and Rufus as they stepped onto the deck. Deathclaw looked even greener than usual. He had never liked boats. He wasn't fond of large bodies of water in general.

When the chain started back up again and the ferry moved out into the water, the boat rocked with the current. It was an unpleasant sensation. Albert neighed, Rufus and Fist chose to sit down, Edge put a hand on the railing to steady himself, and Deathclaw crouched on all fours.

"Was it this rough the last time?" the raptoid asked.

"You ask that every time we travel this way. It's just a bit rough when we start out of the dock," Edge replied.

Lenny barked out a laugh. He was standing proudly, his hands on his hips. "Look at you, Deathclaw. A-scared of a little rockin'?"

Deathclaw merely hissed in reply.

The journey passed quietly, the night sounds muffled by the low whisper of the water, only occasionally punctured by the splash of a nearby fish. Once they had grown used to the movement of the ferry, the group gathered in the center of the boat and spoke about the day's findings.

"What do you think the thief's tryin' to tell us by usin' different handwritin' on the two notes?" Lenny asked.

"I'm not sure," said Edge. "I don't even know why he's bothering to send these messages. Does he really think he could scare us away with these kinds of threats?"

"How could he be certain that we would find them?" Deathclaw asked. "If Lenny had not opened that pouch or we had not found that tavern, we wouldn't have either note."

"It's a gamble. He's taking risks even by trying to leave messages while traveling with Jhonate," Edge said. "If she discovered either one of them she would kill him."

"I think it goes back to what Lenny said earlier," Fist said. He was still sitting down on the deck, his long thick legs stretching out in front of him as he leaned back and supported his weight on his hands. "This is done to unnerve us. To make us doubt and argue. The more discombobulated we become, the more likely it is that we will do something foolish that he can take advantage of."

"Well you know what I think?" said Lenny. "I think that foul-arsed, no-good, corn-jiggin', hoop-skirtin', cheek-squeeaki-!"

The dwarf's tirade cut off with a gurgle and Edge looked at the dwarf in shock. An arrow had plunged into Lenny's neck.

Chapter Fifteen
Sir Edge – Archer

Lenny staggered, his hand reaching for the red feather fletchings of the arrow that protruded from his neck. There was a look of surprise and confusion on his face and blood bubbled at the corners of his mouth.

Edge sent out mental orders. Deathclaw moved to the railings, his mind speeding up and his senses focusing as he watched for more arrows. Fist rolled to his knees and grabbed Lenny. He pulled the dwarf close to him and began sending healing energies into the wound.

Lenny tried to say something, but no words were coming out. He gripped the arrow and gave it an experimental tug, but it didn't budge.

"Don't touch it!" Fist said with a grimace. He told Edge, "It's difficult to see inside him. His blood magic is interfering."

All dwarves' flesh was infused with magic that toughened their bodies, lengthened their lifespan, and made them resistant to magic. This was useful when they were fighting against wizards. It was not so useful when a wizard was trying to heal them.

Edge stood in front of Lenny and the kneeling ogre and, like Deathclaw, used his mind to slow the world around him as he searched for another incoming missile. *What kind of arrow is it?* he asked Fist. *What kind of arrowhead? Can it be pulled out?*

Fist's concentration increased. He was beginning to sweat. *It's too fuzzy for me to tell, but he tried to pull it out and it won't budge. I think it's pronged.* Lenny gurgled and coughed, sending a gout of blood across Fist's arm. The ogre glanced back at Edge. *It's obstructing his airway and his lungs are filling with blood.*

"Damn it!" said Edge. If another arrow came in right now he would be too distracted to catch it. He forced his worry for his friend aside. Fist was a good healer. He needed to let him care for Lenny and focus on the attacker.

One of the ferrymen had seen the arrow hit the dwarf. He hurried over to them with bandages. "I-I don't know how this happened. The shore is still a half mile away."

"Just set them down," said Fist absently, his brow furrowed. Bandages would be little help if he couldn't get the arrow out.

"Is there anything I can do?" he asked, and it was obvious that he knew the identities of his passengers. An incident like this could make both the city of Filgren and the Roma family look bad.

"You and your friend extinguish the lanterns!" Edge ordered.

The ferryman hesitated. "We're not supposed to do that. Without the lights we won't be able to see any debris coming towards us."

"They're hampering our night vision," Edge said. "And they're making us easy targets to whoever's out there in the darkness."

The ferryman nodded, and he and his coworker put out the lights. For several long moments the boat was silent, the only sound being Lenny's gurgling attempts to breathe.

Deathclaw sensed the second arrow coming before it struck. He heard it whistling through the air. He focused in, slowing the world within his mind as much as he could. This arrow had been fired from a slightly different position in the darkness than the first and it was being propelled at a faster speed than most arrows. His eyes, altered to see well in the darkness despite the moonless night, caught a flash of movement and he reached out to catch the arrow.

The raptoid miscalculated slightly, and the arrow buried itself in the meat of his left hand. It would have passed through completely had it not lodged itself in the crook of his thumb. Deathclaw hissed in pain and anger. *I just grew that hand back!*

With his teeth bared, he grasped the shaft of the arrow and leveraged it away from the bone, then shoved the barbed arrowhead through. It was a wicked-looking thing, with curved hooks on the edges. He broke off the head and pulled the shaft of the arrow out of his hand. Ignoring the blood that pattered onto the deck, the raptoid concentrated his body's regenerative magic on the wound and returned his attention to the direction the arrow had come from.

"This was not fired from the shore," Deathclaw declared. He pointed. "I think there's a boat out there."

"North of us?" said the ferryman, who had watched the raptoid attempt to catch the arrow in shocked awe. He rushed back to the rail and leaned out over the water, a hand to his ear. "I don't hear any oars."

I know where it is, said Squirrel, projecting his thoughts to the others from Fist's side of the bond. He had left his pouch and was perched on the domed top of Rufus' gorilla-like head. *I can see it through Rufus' eyes.*

"Ooh! There!" said the rogue horse, pointing with one massive arm. He sent Fist a mental image of what he saw and Fist passed it to the others.

Out on the river to their northwest was a small water craft. It was the size of a one-person rowboat, but there were no oars to be seen. Somehow it managed to maintain its position without floating downstream towards them. Standing in the center of the boat was a man wearing a hooded cloak.

Very little of his form could be made out in the darkness, but he had a longbow and had pulled another arrow back. He was lining up his shot.

Deathclaw, watch for that next shot. Edge pulled his bow off of his back and quickly strung it. *He must have some sort of magic in his bow to hit us from that distance.*

Before he could grab an arrow from his quiver, he heard the next arrow coming. It was headed for the dwarf in Fist's arms. Deathclaw had moved too far down the railing to catch it.

Edge focused his eyes, intensifying his vision. It was a trick Deathclaw had taught him that went beyond a simple slowing of the world. His irises widened, taking in more of the ambient light. For a few moments he could see as well as if there had been a full moon out. He couldn't have his senses ratcheted up this high for more than a few seconds. In this state bright lights were painful, and he had discovered that keeping it up was a heavy strain on his eyes and gave him horrible headaches.

His enhanced sight was barely enough for him to see the arrow coming in. As he had suspected, the arrow passed just out of Deathclaw's reach. When it passed the raptoid's outstretched claws, Edge's hand was already closing. In the silvery light of the stars he saw the wicked head of the arrow pass between his fingers. Then his hand closed onto the shaft. When his senses rushed back to normal, he held the arrow by its fletching.

He lifted his Jharro bow, prepared to send the cruel arrow right back at its shooter. He just had to be able to see him and unfortunately, he wouldn't be able to refocus his vision for a while. "Rufus, keep your eyes on that boat. Fist, feed what he sees through to me. I'm going to try and fire back."

Edge, wait! sent Fist, panic rising in his thoughts. *I need your help.*

Edge hurried to his side. Lenny was gasping, his lungs mostly full of blood. He was pale, and he was mouthing something. He reached out to Edge and pointed at the arrow. He made a shoving motion.

"He's saying we have to push it the rest of the way through," Edge said.

Fist grimaced and shook his head. "It's going to do a lot of damage and he'll lose blood even faster." He looked at Edge. "My magic isn't working. You're going to need to stab him. Maybe healing will work better from the inside."

Edge pulled Peace from its sheath. He had never tried to use his sword on a dwarf before, but Fist had a point. The sword created a temporary bond and healing through the bond had advantages over regular healing. It allowed the wizard to see the body from the inside and get a better perspective on the wound. The only downside to using the sword in this situation was the intimate nature of the bond. He didn't know what would happen when their minds were connected.

Lenny's eyes were wide, and he was shaking his head.

"Sorry, Lenny," he said, knowing how private the dwarf was about his innermost thoughts. "But this is the only way," he said and stabbed the tip of the sword into the dwarf's arm.

Deathclaw felt a wave of emotion overtake Edge, but pushed those feelings away. "This archer is going to keep firing at us until it has finished its purpose," he said. "I could swim out there if I wasn't trying to catch these arrows!"

This wasn't entirely true. Even if the archer wasn't firing at them, the water was frigid, and the boat was too far away. Also, he didn't like to swim. He had forced himself to learn and had become proficient at propelling himself through the water, but he had bad memories of the last time he had swam across the Wide River.

184

"Ooh! Ooh. I can see it. I can throw . . ." Rufus looked around the ferry for something heavy enough to sink the small boat in the distance.

Deathclaw thought that wasn't such a bad idea. Rufus knew how to throw at great distances and he had proven his accuracy many times over the years.

"Do you think you could throw me at it?" Deathclaw asked.

"Ooh! Okay," Rufus agreed and eyed the distant boat, his tongue sticking out of the side of his mouth as he did some internal calculations. He began to swell in size, his arms lengthening and the muscles in his torso bulging as he altered himself to make the perfect throw. Squirrel wisely scampered down from his perch on the rogue horse's head.

Deathclaw tried to determine the best way to go about this. He had seen the rogue horse pick up boulders and launch them at foes hundreds of feet away. He pulled his sword sheath off his back and set it on the deck, not wanting Star to become dislodged and lose it at the bottom of the river. Perhaps he could crouch in Rufus' hand and at the precise moment that the rogue horse threw, he could-.

Rufus grabbed Deathclaw's tail in both hands. He lifted the raptoid of the deck and began to swing him.

Not by the tail! Deathclaw cried mentally, but Rufus was already spinning, gaining momentum as he prepared for the throw. Hissing, the raptoid drew in his legs and wrapped his arms around them, ducking his head in an attempt to provide the least amount of resistance possible.

Rufus' spin quickened, and his muscles bunched in preparation. The ferry rocked with his increased weight and momentum. With a wood-cracking stomp and a roar, the rogue horse slung Deathclaw high into the air.

The raptoid hurtled through the dark night sky and quickly overcame his fear and discomfort to look down at the river passing beneath him. To his quickened mind, he wasn't moving that fast at all. There was something exhilarating about soaring through the air. Maybe one day he'd see about having Edge help him grow wings. But at the moment he had hit the peak of his upward momentum and was starting a downward path.

He set his eyes on the small boat he was falling towards. It was a curious craft, shallow and leaf-shaped. The figure that stood in the center of the boat was aiming an arrow up at him. He saw a flash under its hood just before it fired.

Deathclaw spread his arms and legs wide, trying to contort his body out of the arrow's path. The arrow that was meant for his heart struck two inches below the mark. The arrowhead sunk into his chest and through his left lung to exit his back. The raptoid accepted the hit and reached towards the archer intending to land on it claws first.

Without making any move that the raptoid could see, the archer somehow caused the boat to shift five feet to the south. Deathclaw plunged into the icy water.

His body seized up, his muscles clenching in response to the cold. But that reaction was momentary. He knew that the current would soon drag him away from his enemy. Ignoring the cold and his wounds, he swam up under the craft. With swift kicks and a whip of his tail, he burst out of the water and grabbed the lip of the boat.

The boat rocked and came dangerously near to tipping as he scrambled aboard. The archer let out a startled yelp and staggered, but it was light on its feet and recovered quickly. It drew a knife and thrust it at the raptoid. A flick of Deathclaw's tail gashed the hand holding the knife and the weapon fell into the water.

Deathclaw rose to his feet, slightly unsteady on the boat. His body was hampered by the cold and his punctured lung. The shaft of the arrow was still stuck in his chest. He closed off the use of that lung and just used the right one for now. He lunged at the archer, slashing with his claws.

The archer leapt nimbly backwards and perched on the pointed prow of the small craft, then swept off its cloak and threw it over the raptoid. Deathclaw caught a brief glimpse of the archer's face. It was a female and appeared to be human. Her hair was tied behind her head and she wore a strange apparatus on her face. It was like a pair of spectacles with multiple lenses stacked in front of each other causing a telescoping effect.

He spun, sweeping out with his tail to knock the cloak aside and saw the archer dive into the water. Immediately, the boat started to move away from her as if commanded by her mind. Hissing, Deathclaw dove in after her.

He swam after the woman. She was several yards ahead of him and seemed to be a competent swimmer. Deathclaw used his powerful tail to propel him through the water and he gained on her.

She gasped when Deathclaw's claws latched onto her foot. He yanked her towards him and she cried out, swinging her arm at him, another knife in her hand.

The blade stabbed him in the shoulder, but Deathclaw grabbed her arm and wrenched it, breaking the archer's wrist.

He wrapped his arms around the woman, his feet kicking to keep their heads above water. "Do you wish to live, archer?" he hissed. "Tell me! Why did you attack us?"

She sneered back at him. "I don't wish to die, monster, but I will tell you nothing!"

Deathclaw took no pleasure in causing pain, but he was prepared to do so for the sake of his tribe. He bared his mouthful of pointed teeth. "Are you certain? Your death will not be pleasant."

"Oh, I'm sure," she said, and her sneer turned into a confident smile.

She ducked to the side just as the leaf-shaped boat struck the back of Deathclaw's head. The raptoid's eyes glazed over and his grip around her loosened. She kicked him away and swam back to the boat.

Deathclaw shook his head, sparks flaring in his vision. He was having a hard time recovering from the blow. Lack of oxygen and loss of blood were slowing him. The woman was climbing back into the boat. He didn't understand how she propelled the boat, but if he didn't act soon she would get away.

Numbly, he grabbed his bandoleer and drew Speedy, the throwing knife Lenny had made him. It was a ridiculously complicated throw to make while treading water and with his head spinning, but Deathclaw took command of his weakened body. Focusing his will, he whipped his tail to raise him out of the water and swung his arm forward. With a flick of the wrist, the knife was away.

There wasn't much force behind his throw, but his aim was accurate. Speedy took over from there. A blast of air propelled the knife forward and just as the woman came to her feet, the weapon plunged into her side. She turned to look at him with uncomprehending eyes and collapsed into the bottom of the boat.

Deathclaw somehow managed to swim his tired body to the boat. He pulled himself in just as the woman let out her last ragged breath and died. The leaf-shaped craft began to spin out of control.

In the disorienting first few seconds after Edge pierced Lenny's flesh, his mind surged through the dwarf's memories. Before he could take control of the magic, he experienced the dwarf's early childhood.

Lenui Firegobbler had been born to Jimbeau Firegobbler, his proud blacksmith father, and Maggie Cragstalker, a mother who had run away from her smuggling past to marry Jimbeau. His early years had been happy ones. His parents were loving and early on his father brought him into the forge to train him. But his mother began to chafe under the laidback lifestyle of a blacksmith's wife and one day she ran away and went back to join her smuggler kin.

Edge had already known these things about his friend, but much more was coming at him and without intending to, he skimmed along the dwarf's memories, catching glimpses here and there. In his 268 years of life Lenui had done about everything there was for a dwarf to do. In his youth he had joined his mother in her smuggling trade. Then he had farmed the land for a few years before rejoining his father and discovering he had a true talent for smithing.

In the culture Lenui was from, being a blacksmith was about the noblest trade for a dwarf to aspire to. He received praise from all around for his work, but like his mother had, he chafed under the structured lifestyle that being a blacksmith demanded. He left the forge and spent years adventuring. He saw just about every corner of the Known Lands. He fought everything from dark wizards and dragons to monsters of legend.

Eventually, he decided to quit the adventuring life and returned to the forge, where his fame grew even more. But that restless spirit that came from his mother's side of the family still burned within him. He was never able to stay in one place for too long. He would build a forge and a reputation, then after a few years move on to another adventure.

Then he had met Edge and his life had taken a new direction. He had met his wife Bettie and became a father, then a leader, something he had never aspired to. Now he was in a crucial role for his people, the head of the Wobble Smithing Conglomerate with a seat on the Academy Council. His wife was the Academy Forgemaster and he had four children, each of whom he loved dearly.

Lenui had never been happier and yet he had never chafed under his responsibilities more. The call of the road and adventure tugged on him more than ever and it was tearing him apart. Lenui feared that he would one day become like his mother, shirking his responsibilities and running away from everyone he loved. He was certain that Bettie had come to fear it too which was why she had let him come on this journey with Edge.

Now, as much as he was enjoying his time on the road with his friends and being a member of the Big and Little People Tribe instead of the leader of hundreds of dwarves, he felt a deep sense of guilt. He didn't deserve his people's trust. He didn't deserve the loyalty of his wife and children. One day he might let them all down.

Edge pulled himself away from his friend's memories, feeling his own sense of guilt for letting his thoughts linger while Lenny was so close to death. The blending of memories had taken very little time at all, but every second counted. He left the dwarf's mind and plunged his thoughts into Lenny's body.

Immediately, he felt the fuzziness that Fist had talked about. The dwarf's blood magic resisted his presence, but Edge's experience navigating the bond was able to overcome this resistance. He brought his mind to the site of the injury. At first it was like peering through muddy water, but through sheer force of will he was able to push that sensation aside and the injury came into view.

He brought his magic to bear on the problem and used air magic to cut through the arrow puncturing Lenny trachea. It was oddly hollow. He cut open a pathway for the pronged arrowhead and guided it around the dwarf's jugular and out the side of his neck. Once he had removed the arrow pieces out of his friend's neck, he set to repairing the major blood vessels that had been damaged. Then he closed the wounds and forced the blood out of the dwarf's lungs.

Next, he sent water magic through Lenny's veins to help replenish his plasma and got his bones working extra hard to make more blood to replace what was lost. Finally, he backed out through the connection and removed the sword slowly, healing the cut in the dwarf's flesh as he went.

Edge opened his eyes and felt a wave of weakness. He realized that he had put a lot more energy into the task than he had thought and as he pulled the blade away, he noticed something strange. His connection with Lenny hadn't closed completely. A thin silvery cord of spirit magic remained linking his body with the dwarf. His bonding magic was more active than ever before. Dozens of tiny tendrils lashed out at the dwarf as if trying to grab on.

"Death-Claw!" shouted Rufus loudly. The rogue horse had both hands held up to his mouth.

Edge realized that Deathclaw was badly wounded and disoriented. The raptoid was in a small craft that was spinning out of control and rushing downstream but not directly towards them. He was careening to the east of the ferry and would be swept past them, possibly colliding with the chains.

"Go get him, Rufus!" Fist said.

The rogue horse surged forward and leapt off of the ferry boat and into the water. He grew as he went, and the force of his departure caused the boat to buck wildly, knocking everyone off of their feet and causing the wood to creak.

Rufus splashed into the water and luckily this section of the river wasn't too deep. His legs and arms grew until they were ten feet long and he stood solidly on the riverbed, the flowing water lapping against his chest. Very near the limit of his size and power, the rogue horse forced his way through the current and reached out to grasp the spinning leaf-shaped boat.

"Ooh! Got it!" Rufus said with a booming voice and he picked the craft up and carried it slowly back to the ferry.

He placed the boat on the deck and struggled to climb aboard while shrinking back down. Fist rushed to the side and gripped onto Rufus's mane, holding the gorilla-like rogue horse steady until he was small enough to pull onto the deck. Rufus lay there panting and shivering. "Co-old!"

"Good boy, Rufus," Fist said fondly and sent warming magic through his body.

Edge went to the side of the small boat where Deathclaw lay next to a dead woman. The raptoid was breathing shallowly and Edge sent his magic through the bond to discover that he was only using one lung. The other one was collapsed. Deathclaw's magic was working to repair the wounds, but it was slowed by hypothermia.

Hold on, he sent as he first set to warming Deathclaw's body, then began to work on the wounds. In addition to the major damage to his chest, he still had a wounded hand as well as a stab wound in his shoulder and a cracked skull.

Deathclaw's regenerative magic would heal most injuries, but it usually wasn't this heavily taxed. Edge pulled the arrow the rest of the way through the raptoid's back and healed his lung, then gave his regenerative magic a boost.

That's enough, Deathclaw warned. *You're using too much your own energy.*

When Edge pulled back from the bond, he fell to the seat of his pants and realized that the raptoid was right. His vision swam and he felt exhausted. Once again, he mentally cursed the Prophet for taking Gwyrtha away. This didn't happen when she was around.

"Let me help," said Fist, and the ogre fed some energy through to him. He helped Edge to his feet. "Even Rufus' reserves are low. I think we're all going to need to rest soon."

Thank you, Edge said through the bond and returned his attention to Deathclaw. "What did you find out about the archer."

"Too little," the raptoid said irritably and sent Edge his memories of what had happened.

The raptoid reached into the boat and dragged the archer's body out and onto the deck of the ferry. As he did so, he grunted in pain. His knife Speedy was now sticking out of the flesh of his previously undamaged shoulder.

"I was just about to return it!" he snarled and pulled it out of his shoulder to put it away.

"You really do need to do have a conversation with that bandoleer," Edge said and crouched to examine the body.

There was something familiar about the woman, though Edge was having a hard time trying to place what it was. Then he noticed a scar on her chin and he remembered who she was. "This is Lana Sure Strike! She went into the Academy a few years before I started Training School." He stroked his chin. "She went missing while out on her first assignment. Everyone assumed she was dead."

"Now we know what happened to her," said Deathclaw. He had removed the fingerless gloves she was wearing and on the back of her left hand was a charred rune. "She joined the other side."

When someone was named by the Dark Bowl, it left a black rune on their hand that could only be seen by spirit sight. But when they died, the Dark Bowl took back the memories and skills it had given them and took a piece of their soul along with it. The rune that had been invisible in life became seared into their flesh as it exacted its price.

"Edge," said a gruff voice behind him. Lenny was standing there, a confused look on his face. "You didn't have to do that," he said softly. "I would'a survived. Firegobblers are tough."

"No, you wouldn't have," said Fist. "You were very near death before he intervened."

"I would'a survived, dag-blast it," Lenny repeated, but there was no anger in his voice. "But, thanks fer what you did. And thank you too, Fist, fer tryin'."

"Of course," Edge said.

"And, uh, I don't know what you saw while you was rummaging 'round in my noggin, but . . . keep it to yerself, huh?" he said.

Edge gave him an embarrassed smile. "I-I will. I'm sorry about that. It just happened. I didn't mean to pry."

"I know that," Lenny said, patting him on the chest. "I know what kind a man you are, Edge. In fact, it's kinda stuck in my brain like a part of you's still in there somehow."

Edge switched to spirit sight and was surprised to find that the faint cord of spirit magic was still connected to the dwarf's arm where the sword had pierced him. His bonding magic was just as active as ever. It was like it was trying to make a more solid connection but failing to find purchase. "Uh, Lenny?"

"Hey," said the dwarf, gesturing to Deathclaw. "What you got there?"

The raptoid had pulled the archer's bow out of the boat. It was made of steel and covered in a red lacquer. Runes ran up the length of it. He handed it over to the dwarf.

Lenny hefted the weapon. "I'll be dag-gummed if this ain't familiar."

You should look at this, Squirrel said through the bond. He was standing on the deck holding the back half of the arrow that had been in Lenny's neck. As Edge had thought, it was hollow. Squirrel had pulled out a rolled-up piece of paper.

Edge took it from him and asked the ferrymen to light the lamps again. Once he had enough light, he read it with confusion. The piece of paper said "Firegobbler" in thick red letters and there was a line drawn diagonally through the name.

The dwarf dropped the bow to the ground and read the note and his features rippled with rage. Some of his old energy returned to him as he crumpled the piece of paper in his fist. "Vern!"

Chapter Sixteen

Sir Edge – Nemesis

"You think the archer's name is Vern?" said Fist with a frown. "Are you certain? Edge thinks her name was Lana."

"Not the gall-durn archer," said Lenny. His teeth were bared and his eyes were narrowed with loathing. "Vern is the yellow-bellied cheek-sneaker who hired her. Dag-blasted idjit's been out to get me fer years."

This pricked Edge's mind and he recalled catching glimpses of this rivalry in the dwarf's memories. "Vern . . . Earthpeeler? The Earthpeelers are from an old mining town, right?"

Lenny gave him a curious look. "That's right. Them dag-blamed dirt-diggers were some of the best miners in the region. Us Firegobblers respected 'em fer it. Only then they got uppity and thought they'd become smithies too. To make things worse, they thought they could just snatch contracts out from under us!" He cocked his head. "How'd you know that?"

"It was still left over in my head after I healed you," said Edge, unsure how the dwarf would react.

Lenny blinked at him, then looked away. "Yeah, well, Vern's the worst of his family. He's done gone off on his own. That crabsnatcher will make a weapon fer anybody, good or bad. He's also a purty good fighter and he's got an adventurin' streak in him. Folks say he hires himself out."

"A dwarf mercenary?" Deathclaw asked.

"When he feels like it," Lenny said with disdain. "Other times he's just cheatin' folks by chargin' way too much fer half-arsed smithin'!"

"This weapon was pretty effective," Deathclaw observed, gesturing at the dead archer's bow.

"I ain't sayin' he ain't good," the dwarf replied. "He just overcharges."

"He's like an evil version of Lenny," said Fist and a smile began to spread on his face.

Lenny scowled at that remark. "Don't you say nothin' like that. I ain't nothin' like Vern and he ain't nothin' like me!" He cocked his head at the ogre. "What're you smiling at? Ain't nothin' funny here."

Fist's shoulders had relaxed. "Because if this attack was just an assassin sent after you by an old enemy, it was personal. That means it doesn't have anything to do with our mission."

"And why is that better?" Lenny barked.

"Because that means it's over with. At least for now," Fist explained. He yawned and sat cross-legged on the deck. "My worry was that this was set up by the Dark Prophet or one of his servants to keep us from catching up to Jhonate. I wasn't looking forward to being harried all the way to the border of the Known Lands."

Lenny walked up to Fist and with the ogre sitting down they were looking nose-to-nose. The dwarf poked a thick finger at Fist's shoulder. "Lemme tell you somethin', dag-gum it! Just 'cause he's made it personal don't mean it's unrelated. I ain't seen nor dealt with that corn-jigger in 20 years! And in all our run-ins this is the first time he ever tried to kill me. Why would he start now unless it's somethin' to do with Jhonate?"

"That's a good point," Edge agreed. It was far too big a coincidence that Lenny should be attacked by a Dark Bowl-named assassin while they were tracking one of the Dark Prophet's thieves. "Our thief likes sending messages. Maybe the arrow that hit Lenny wasn't the only one with a note inside."

He bent and picked up the arrow that he had snatched out of the air earlier. It was well-crafted and perfectly balanced. The shaft wasn't thick enough for it to be carrying a message. "Were any of those other arrows hollow, Deathclaw?"

Deathclaw picked up the broken arrow that had pierced his hand and the arrow that Edge had pulled from his chest. He looked them over briefly, then cast them into the water. "No messages."

Edge frowned, and he approached the body of the slain archer. "Let's see what else we can discover about her."

They searched the assassin's belongings. She had an empty quiver clipped to her belt. Perhaps she had lost her other arrows to the water during Deathclaw's pursuit of her. Other than that, she had some pouches on her belt. There were a few vials of clear liquid in one pouch, a handful of coin in another.

"She doesn't have much of worth on her," said Deathclaw, though he did take the two vials from Edge and was eying them curiously.

"And other than the black rune, nothing to identify herself," Edge observed. This was a pattern he had noticed before. In the many times he had been attacked by the Dark Prophet's assassins over the years it was always this way. Nameless foes holding nothing to track them back to their origin. "It's only because I remembered her from her Academy days that we know anything about her."

"Is there anything about this boat that can tell us more?" Deathclaw asked grasping the edge of the leaf-shaped vessel and lifting the edge of it. "What about these runes?"

Edge joined him and crouched down to peer at the boat's underside. "These are binding runes." He reached out to touch them. They were half filled with a red sort of paste. It looked as if the water had been washing it away. "I see. There was a soul bound to this boat and it was tied to the archer.

Whatever her deal with it was, it was a temporary one, broken upon her death. The soul is now free."

"So we still know nothin' 'bout her. 'Cept she used to be good, but then she went to the Dark Bowl, so . . ." Lenny scowled. "So basically, we still got nothin'. Hold on."

The dwarf stepped carefully over Rufus' arm. The rogue horse had fallen asleep on the deck, his wide mouth was hanging open. Once past that obstacle, Lenny stomped over to talk to the ferrymen. The ferry was drawing near enough to the western docks that Edge could see a light blinking at them furiously from the guard tower. The ferrymen were using a shade on the side of their lantern to respond.

"There been any other attacks on the river lately?" Lenny asked.

The ferryman who was communicating with the lights at the shore simply shook his head. The man who had been the most helpful to them so far stepped away from the lantern and addressed Lenny.

"Sorry, master dwarf, sir," he said with an embarrassed grimace. "There's been the occasional fight between passengers, but nothing serious. Before tonight, we hadn't seen an actual attack on one of our ferries in years."

The group continued to puzzle over what had happened as the ferry arrived at the dock in West Filgren. The Wide River was the dividing line between Dremaldria and Razbeck and the Razbeck side of the city looked similar to the Dremaldrian side, but the Roma family had little sway here. House Torbald was the family in charge of Western Filgren. They were the Razbeckian nobles closest to their king.

The moment that Edge and his friends debarked from the ferry, a small force of guards boarded and took possession of the archer's body and her leaf-shaped boat. A short balding man with an aristocratic air stepped forward to meet them. He wore finery in the Razbeckian style with lace bulging from around his collar and hanging from the cuffs of his jacket. The silver insignia of House Torbald was pinned on his breast.

"Sirs," he said, then hesitated and bowed deeply, forcing a grin. "I mean, of course, Sir Edge and Master Fist and . . . other honored friends. I am Gerval, managing head of the central branch of the Torbald Ferry Company. Uh, we of West Filgren feel terrible about the ordeal you went through while using our ferry system this evening. House Torbald would like to make amends if we can. Perhaps you will stay awhile and partake of our hospitality?"

"How do you already know so much about what happened?" Edge wondered. "We only just arrived."

"Oh! Your guides signaled us with their lanterns when they were close enough. I'll admit I'm not sure of all the details yet, but we'll work it out," he declared. "I'm quite certain that we'll find the people behind this attack."

"Right," said Edge with a sigh. "Well, thank you for your offer, but we must be moving o-."

"That sounds wonderful!" said Fist loudly, stepping forward to engulf the representative hand in his. *We need the rest Edge.* "But we are short for time. We can only stay the night. Do you have beds for us to sleep in?"

The small man was obviously unnerved by having an enormous ogre shaking his hand, no matter how famous it was, but he managed to keep his composure. "Of course! That is the least we can do. Come. Follow me and I shall take you to our finest inn."

Edge pursed his lips at the ogre. He didn't like the idea of wasting time sleeping when Jhonate and the thief were already so far ahead of them. However, Fist's reasoning was true. Every one of them, except perhaps Squirrel, had expended a tremendous amount of energy during the crossing. Even Deathclaw looked bleary-eyed.

Fine, he replied mentally to everyone through the bond. *But it will be morning in a few hours. We only sleep until light. Then we go.* He turned to Lenny to update him on what they were doing, but the dwarf nodded and waved him on.

"Good. I can use a few hours," the dwarf said.

The ferry manager led them past the docks and water wheels into a wealthier section of the city. The streets here were completely quiet and well lit. They passed closed businesses that catered to wealthy clientele before stopping at the door of a four-story building made of white brick. The sign out front read: "The Torbaldian."

Gerval knocked and a bleary-eyed old man answered with a yawn. Edge found himself yawning in response. Gerval gave the man brief instructions and a boy came out to take Albert back to the stables. Rufus, who normally would have argued about sleeping with the horses, followed after Albert without complaint. The boy kept staring back at the rogue horse with wide eyes.

Even Deathclaw, who loathed sleeping indoors, followed everyone in. He sensed Edge's surprise. *In a building of this size I cannot watch over you from the roof*, the raptoid explained.

"Sure," Edge said with a smile.

Gerval bid them good night and left them in the hands of the old man, who took them upstairs. Fist didn't think there was any chance they would have a bed to fit him, but he was surprised when the old man led him to a room with an enormous curtained bed designed for the most extravagant of nobles. It wasn't quite long enough for his legs, but he was able to climb inside and fell asleep on top of an abundance of pillows, his feet just hanging off the bottom of the feather mattress.

Edge was taken to the room next door. His bed was just as large and comfortably outfitted as Fist's. He stripped off his leather armor and shoved a pile of pillows onto the floor before climbing into the bed and lying face down on top of the blankets.

Deathclaw, who had followed him inside, snorted at the extravagance. He had never understood the human desire to sleep on manufactured softness. He laid down on the floor under the room's large window and placed his hands behind his head. His left hand, newly grown and recently healed, twinged. He took that hand out from under his head. Then, after a few moments' consideration, he grabbed one of the pillows and placed it under his head instead. It smelled faintly of human sweat, but felt surprisingly comfortable. He placed his hands on his belly and ignored the muffled chuckle that came from Edge's bed. Moments later they were both asleep.

When Deathclaw woke him five hours later, Edge groaned. His body felt so heavy. He was still lying on his stomach and realized that he hadn't moved an inch since falling asleep. "I think sleeping was a mistake."

"It was a necessity," Deathclaw said. His body didn't need as much sleep as a human's and it had taken full advantage of the time it had been given. He had almost fully recovered from his injuries and felt no morning discomfort at all.

Groaning, Edge forced himself to roll over to his back. That felt nice. Sleeping more would be nice.

Fist, sent Deathclaw through the bond. *Edge needs help waking up.*

Sure, said Fist and Edge got the distinct sensation that the ogre was eating something wonderful. It was such a strong feeling that he could taste it. Eggs covered in cheese and butter.

His mouth watered and he sat up. He still felt miserable, but now he was hungry too. *You're mean.*

Oh? Is this what you were hoping for? Fist replied in amusement, and he reached out to Rufus.

Suddenly, Edge was flooded with energy. He stood and donned his armor and pulled on his boots. Then he strapped on his swords and sent Fist a mental thanks as he headed down the stairs to the common room.

The smell of the morning repast was heavenly. The tables were loaded with fresh bread and bacon and eggs and honstule. Wow, there was a lot of honstule. It was prepared in multiple ways; baked, or steamed, or fried with minced potato and ham.

The yellow vegetable had a texture that was a mix between a squash and a tomato. It grew quickly and had a faint amount of elf magic in it which made the plant hearty and gave people a feeling of general wellness as they ate it. Over recent years it had begun to populate every garden. It was a major part of daily meals for nobles and peasants alike. Edge wondered how they would all feel if they knew that honstule was created by and named after a goblin gardener.

Edge joined Fist at the table and ate until he couldn't possibly eat another bite. Deathclaw joined them, but wasn't interested in the well-cooked food. Edge talked to one of the servers and they went into the kitchen and returned with a dozen raw eggs which the raptoid ate shell and all.

The other patrons of the inn were likely merchants or nobles from the way they were dressed. Though some of them seemed genuinely excited to be sharing their morning meal with famous heroes, others eyed the ogre and raptoid with distaste and decided to go elsewhere to eat. That kind of behavior would have angered Edge in the past, but Fist and Deathclaw weren't bothered by such petty things and so Edge let it go.

Lenny came down a short time later, but he didn't eat very much. There seemed to be a lot on his mind. Edge decided not to press him about it. There was a long journey ahead and that meant there were plenty of opportunities to discuss whatever was bothering him.

Fist talked to the cook and they gathered all the leftovers and table scraps to bring out to Rufus. The rogue horse devoured it all happily while everyone readied themselves to leave. After thanking the innkeeper, they headed for the outskirts of the city.

As they navigated the busy streets of West Filgren, they were already pondering the next stage of the journey. Their first obstacle would be finding Jhonate's trail once more.

Assuming that Jhonate's companion was truly leading her to Alsarobeth, they had a general idea what direction their quarry would take.

Edge was feeling optimistic since there had not been any rain to muddy the tracks. That optimism faded after they spent half the day searching to the northwest of the city. This part of Razbeck was all farmland and the roads were fairly well traveled. It wasn't until mid-afternoon that they caught their first break.

Deathclaw found a spot just off of one of the country side roads where a small cookfire had been built. Two people had slept in this place and he had found Jhonate's scent. It appeared that, just over two days ago, Jhonate and the thief had taken this road in a westerly direction.

They kept to the road, Deathclaw and Rufus searching the edges of the path as they went just in case their quarry changed their mind and cut through some farmer's field. But as they traveled, the farms became more and more sparse and eventually they entered a forest of oak trees.

Lenny recognized the area. The road they were on cut through the edges of the Fasdark Forest and from this point out there was much less traffic. Rufus picked up the scent of the horse that Jhonate was riding and was able to follow its tracks uninterrupted for several miles.

At one point during this stretch Lenny rode Albert next to Edge. "Uh, can you tell me somethin, Son?"

"Certainly," Edge replied.

"It's about yesterday and when you . . . healed my neck and all," the dwarf said hesitantly.

"Yes?" Edge said and when Lenny didn't continue immediately, he asked, "Are you worried about what I saw in your memories?"

"No. At least I don't think so." He frowned. "Why? Did you see anythin' I should be embarrassed about?"

"Oh, no. Not at all," Edge assured him. That wasn't exactly true, but there was no need to bring up anything that would make Lenny more uncomfortable. "So, what's bothering you?"

Lenny scratched his head. "Well, ever since you . . . did that. I feel-. I mean, do *you* feel any different?"

"In what way?" Edge wondered. He looked at the dwarf and switched his vision to spirit sight. That faint cord connecting from him to the site of Lenny's wound was still there and ropes of his magic were still trying to add to the connection. "Lenny. Do you feel different? Because even though I don't feel anything, I see something that wasn't there before."

Lenny's eyes widened. "What is it?" Edge told him about the faint line and the dwarf nodded. "Dag-gum . . . So, what it is, is that ever since then I can sorta feel what yer . . . feelin'."

"Can you hear my thoughts?" Edge asked and as he did so, he felt through the bond looking for that connection. Where could it be?

"No. I just feel general feelin's. Like I knew when you was tired yesterday and this mornin' I knew you was eatin' and that you liked it," Lenny said.

"That is strange, Lenny," Edge said. "This has never happened before." Was it possible that while focusing so hard on penetrating the dwarf's blood magic, he had somehow created something more permanent?

"And I can kind a tell where yer at. Like just where you are in relation to me," he said. "You got any idear why?"

Actually, Edge had been giving that connection some thought. But before he could voice those thoughts, Deathclaw stopped in front of them and held out a warning hand.

Wait. I smell something.

As he said that, Rufus sniffed at the air and huffed and took on an offensive posture. *He says there's someone hiding nearby*, Fist told Edge through the bond.

They were all peering at the road ahead just as a glittering sphere rolled up the road from somewhere behind them and stopped at Rufus' feet. A buzzing sound filled the air and a powerful paralyzing spell hit the party, immobilizing everyone.

A hearty laugh echoed from the tree line beside the road and a spell of invisibility was dropped. Stepping out from the side of the road appeared a dwarf. He was about four and a half feet tall and he wore a suit of plate armor that was padded to reduce sound. It was inscribed with protective runes and glowed a dull blue to mage sight. He held a helmet under one arm and carried a large double-bladed axe in the other.

He laid the axe over one shoulder and smiled under a thick black handlebar mustache, exposing a mouthful of gold-capped teeth. He glanced at the tree line. "Looked like they noticed us 'fore we sprung the trap."

A withered old man stepped out of the trees. He leaned on an intricately-carved staff and wore robes that were a dull red and gold. His voice sounded more youthful than he looked. "They shouldn't have. I had us well hidden from regular sight as well as mage sight. I blame Belfae. He was supposed to cover our scent."

An irritated snarl came from behind a nearby tree and another figure stepped out to join the others. This individual was a foot taller than the dwarf and wore a peculiar red armor covered in spikes. His skin was pure white and his head was topped with a shock of black hair. The imp focused a scowl on the wizard. "I did hide our scent. But it's hard when someone eats garlic bulbs like they're apples!"

"Enough, you two," said the dwarf. "We got 'em froze up like I wanted. Just don't screw up again."

A set of footsteps sounded behind everyone announcing a fourth member to the dwarf's band. In addition, there was a shifting in the trees and, even though Edge couldn't turn his head to look, he could make out three huge shadows.

"Well-well. Lookee here. My old buddy Lenui done survived." The dwarf walked over to Albert and as he looked up at Lenny sitting astride the warhorse, his smile turned into a sneer. I still cain't believe it." He gave Lenny a mocking shake of his head. "I dunno how Lana managed to miss yer big fat-."

His words were cut off as Lenny kicked him in the face.

Chapter Seventeen
Lenui Firegobbler – Ambush

The moment that the paralyzing spell hit the party, Lenui knew what had happened. He broke free of the spell within seconds and was waiting for the right opportunity when Vern stepped within range. He put all the force he could muster into that boot to the face. There was a satisfying crunch as his heel connected to Vern's nose. The dwarf mercenary's head snapped back, and he staggered two steps.

"I'm dag-gum insulted!" Lenui barked. "First you send a lone archer after me? Try an assassination from long range? Then you use smugglers' tricks to get the drop on me? What've you become Vern? Some kind of a sugar-bellied, wobble-kneed, mud- crawler?"

"He's free!" cried the imp. He unsheathed a sword with a blade that was the color of open flames. Lenui had seen swords like it before. Imp smiths were flamboyant like that.

"'Course I'm free, you bloated white pincushion!" Lenui shouted. "My mama taught me how to break free of a freeze orb when I was ten!"

The imp pointed the sword at him and fire blossomed from the tip. The wizard raised his staff and prepared to unleash a spell. The three large shapes in the trees surged towards the road. Lenui ignored them, his gaze focused on Vern.

"Stand down!" Vern ordered and the shapes stopped just at the tree line. Vern had placed his helmet under his axe-wielding arm and was feeling his nose. A slow stream of blood had begun to pour from both nostrils. "Dag-blast you, Lenui! And yer filthy Cragstalker mother."

"Say whatever you want about Maggie. It don't bother me none. What bothers me is yer complete lack of honor! Sneak attacks? Is that the Earthpeeler way? Is forgettin' yer heritage the only way you think you can get the better of me?"

"It ain't just about you, Lenui," Vern said. "I got a job to do and I aim to do it. Getting' to kill you is just a nice perk."

"Horse-puckey!" Lenui growled. "I challenge you to a Corntown Hoedown!"

"A fight just you and me?" Vern guffawed. "I ain't stupid. Yer just trying to buy time fer the spell to wear off so yer friends can get free."

"They're already free, you garl-friggin' idjit!" said Lenui and he shouted out to his friends. "Y'all can kill ever'body else. Vern's mine." As the words left his mouth, Fist disappeared from Rufus' back.

Lenui had known not to worry about them the moment the spell hit. Edge and Fist knew how to free themselves from these spells. They had learned it early on since paralyzing spells had been one of Ewzad Vriil's specialties. And once they were free, it would be easy for them to free their bonded as well.

Besides, Lenui had felt it through that strange new connection with Edge. The man had been startled at first, but then that emotion had been replaced with confidence. Vern and his little crew had made a big mistake.

Fist reappeared behind the bent old wizard. His eight-foot frame towered over the tiny man, his mace held high over his head.

When the paralyzing spell hit, Fist had been more irritated than worried. He quickly dismantled the threads of the smuggler-standard spell and would have acted right away, had Edge not sent out mental instructions.

Wait. Pretend their spell worked, Edge said. *Let's see what their plan is first.*

While Vern walked up to confront Lenny, Fist went through the bond and cut Rufus loose from the spell. When he tried to do the same with Squirrel, he discovered that the old rodent had already freed himself.

Shall I kill them all? Squirrel asked.

Save your energy, the ogre replied. *We don't know what they can do yet.*

Ever since Squirrel had learned that he could use the bond to steal Fist's magic and cast spells on his own, he had developed his skills in unexpected and sometimes vicious ways. He was always eager to use these abilities, something that was a constant source of worry for Fist. Even in his old age, Squirrel seemed ever ignorant of how small and frail his body was.

Ooh! What about me? Can I go? Rufus begged. He was excited at the prospect of a brawl. He had only been freed for a couple seconds but it was taking all of the rogue horse's will to hold still.

Don't move yet, Fist sent as he analyzed the ambushers. *Just a few seconds longer.*

There appeared to be seven enemies. Vern, the wizard, and the imp were clearly in view. Without turning his head, Fist couldn't make out the identities of the brutes in the trees, but from their size and the fact that they didn't seem to be moving very quickly, they were likely ogres or some type of shorter giants. The only figure that he had no clue about was the person that had rolled the paralyzing orb into their midst. Whoever it was stood on the road behind Rufus.

Smells like a woman, Rufus said. *Half-elf.*

She's moving, said Edge. *Approaching Deathclaw.*

I see her, said the raptoid.

Deathclaw had been frozen while glancing to the side of the road and without moving, he was able to see the woman's approach. She wore black leather armor and a cloak similar to the cloak the archer assassin had worn. She had thrown back the hood to expose a head that was shaven bald. Her ears were slightly pointed and the delicate features that had come from the elven side of her heritage were twisted with hatred. In one hand she held a sword, in the other hand a dagger.

Then Lenny kicked Vern in the face and Fist new that there were only seconds before they had to act. *I'll go for the wizard and the imp*, he told Edge. *Catch them off guard.*

I agree that they're the biggest threats, said Edge. *Are you certain you wish to handle both of them?*

I'll be fast, Fist said. *Rufus will help you with the big brutes in the trees.*

Ooh! Okay! said Rufus excitedly.

Squirrel let out an irritated sigh. *You want me to stay out of the fight again? Fine, Fist. Just leave me on the side of the road. I'll come in and save you when you need me.*

Alright, Edge sent. *Be ready to move any moment now.*

That was when Lenny shouted out, "They're already free, you garl-friggin' idjit!"

Fist took that as his cue. He enveloped himself in a cloak of air magic, causing himself to disappear from normal sight, and reached up to grab his mace. Its name was Quickening and it was runed to enhance the speed of its wielder. Since becoming named, Fist had learned to control the intensity of its magic and at this moment, he used it to become inhumanly fast.

He dropped down from Rufus' back and to his suddenly-enhanced reflexes it seemed as if everyone else was standing still. He could only keep up this intensity of speed for a short period of time before he would run out of energy and need to pull more from Rufus. Keeping this in mind, he rushed to the side of the road away from the enemy and hung Squirrel's pouch on a branch, then ran to stand over the wizard and raised his mace to strike the old man down.

As he did so, a spell came in from the side and disrupted his cloak of air. He brought down his mace, but before it connected, his blow was stopped by an upraised sword as suddenly the armored imp was standing in front of him. Somehow the imp had the speed to get between him and the wizard and the strength to catch his heavy blow without being blasted to the earth.

The wizard was startled by the imp's abrupt movements and when he looked up and saw the eight-foot-tall 600-pound ogre standing over him, he yelped and fell to the ground. "We miscalculated!"

Fist pulled in more of Quickening's magic and brought the mace back down with two blurringly quick blows. The imp moved his sword just as quickly and parried each one.

Fist was dumbfounded. It was frustrating enough that the imp had disrupted his cloaking spell, something that was difficult for even a well-trained magic user. But this was the first time he had come up against someone that could match his speed and strength.

"Strong imp," he said.

"Master Fist, named ogre wizard," said the imp with a sharp-toothed grin. "I am Belfae of house Yen. You're my chore for the day."

Deathclaw waited until Fist acted before he turned to face the half-elf advancing on him with her sword and dagger. He drew Star from its sheath. At this time of day, its powers were low, but each cut would still sting. "You smell like the archer that attacked us on the river. Are you as unwise as her?"

"I watched the whole thing from the shore!" she said and Deathclaw realized that this woman had a vision device similar to the one that the archer had worn clipped to her belt. "You hunted her down and mauled her like an animal!"

She came at him, swinging her sword with her dominant hand. Deathclaw parried her swing and leapt back to avoid the thrust of her dagger.

Deathclaw came back at her with multiple thrusts of his own sword, that she expertly parried aside. "Yes. Your friend shot at us and I was forced to kill her. Do you wish to die as well?"

"Lana was my sister!" she shouted and went into a frenzied series of strikes, mainly using her sword to tie up his weapon so that she could get in close and bring her dagger to bear.

Her aggression kept Deathclaw on the defensive, forcing him to contort his body to avoid being skewered. She backed him towards the edge of the road and the trees. He waited until he had the proper opening and parried her sword aside, then spun and avoided a thrust of her dagger as he brought his tail around. The barb tore a long gash in her leather armor, but did not pierce the mail shirt she wore beneath it.

Deathclaw felt no guilt for killing this woman's sibling, but he understood the nature of her pain. "If you do not wish to die like she did, tell me who hired you," he hissed.

"Silence, monster," she growled and came back at him.

She was good. Deathclaw had not been so harried by a single combatant in quite some time. The raptoid smiled.

Lenui hopped down from Albert's back and the warhorse smartly trotted away from the fighting as the old dwarf faced his old foe. He hefted his favorite hammer in his hand. It had a long handle and its head was shaped for use at the forge, with two fire-blackened and blunt sides. The hammer was covered in runes that gave it the power to impact with double the force of any blow. "You remember Buster, Vern?"

It had been decades since his last run-in with Vern and Lenui had proven himself the better fighter that day. Their battle had been over the rights to a blacksmith shop in Dremald. Lenui's hammer had knocked Vern unconscious and he had been dragged away by friends and put on a wagon headed out of town.

Vern snorted as if the reminder meant nothing to him. But he placed his helmet on his head. It was an open-faced helmet with the crest of the Earthpeeler family embossed over his forehead. The crest was square and in the center were the crossed forms of two pickaxes over an anvil.

He pointed his axe at Lenui. "Yer gonna put your forge hammer up against Cutter? 'Specially when all yer wearin' is leather armor?"

"'Course you named yer axe 'Cutter'," Lenui said and spat with disgust. "You ain't got no gad-flamed imagination, Vern. There's a thousand axes and swords named Cutter out there in the Known Lands."

Both dwarves paused briefly in their confrontation as Rufus bounded past them and into the trees with Sir Edge on his back. They collided with the three brutes and were met with loud shouts and the sounds of heavy blows and snapping branches.

"Our advantage is broken!" shouted the wizard from the ground as Fist and the imp struggled over him. "We should retreat."

"Shaddup, Ghazardblast, you yellow-livered nose-dripper! We ain't goin' nowhere!" Vern yelled back. His lips twisted as he focused back on Lenui. "Well, this Cutter is gonna be the one that takes off yer ugly tin-sniffin' head!"

"Ha! Go ahead'n try, you brick-arsed, belly-baster!" Lenui said and came at him.

Vern had been right thinking that Lenui's hammer fighting style was at a bit of a disadvantage against a fighter with a double-bladed battle axe. Normally, he'd want a shield in his off hand. Lenui settled for grabbing one of the smaller throwing hammers off of his belt. He called them his 'Buster Juniors' and each one of them had the same kind of enchantment that Buster did.

Lenui rushed at Vern and met the dwarf's axe swing with Buster. The head of the hammer struck the blade of Vern's axe with an ear-splitting ring as the weapon's magic doubled the force of the impact. It was a testament to Vern's skill at enchanting his weapon that the blade didn't crack.

The weapons rebounded from each other and Lenui brought his other weapon across. The head of Buster Junior struck Vern's helmet with a ringing force that sent the dwarf staggering and knocked his helmet askew.

"Am I getting' through to you, you tar-eared, limp-whistled, fraud?" Lenui barked.

Vern adjusted his helmet and shook his head as he regained his balance. "I ain't the fraud, you numb-brained, lack-whit who forgot how to forge years ago. I bet yer daddy won't even look at you!"

"He just came by to see his grandkids last year, you droolin' cheek-sneaker who dyes his mustache!" Lenui charged at him and Vern swung his axe to meet him.

Lenui brought Buster down again, but this time Vern angled the blade so that the hammer just knocked the axe aside. He then reversed the motion, swinging with the other side of the blade. Lenui tried to parry it with Buster Junior, but he didn't get enough force behind the blow. The axe knocked the smaller hammer aside and struck Lenui in the side, doubling the dwarf over. Lenui grunted and dropped Buster Junior.

"And that's how I kill you, Firegobbler!" Vern said with a laugh. "You and yer sissified leather armor."

Lenui wheezed. "Damn." Then he chuckled and grabbed Vern's wrist with his freed hand. "Didn't you know that my wife's the best dag-gum leather-runer in the blasted Known Lands? This stuff's as good as plate, idjit!"

He head-butted Vern in the face, knocking the dwarf a step back, then brought Buster down on top of his helmet. The hammer hit with another loud ring and Lenui let go of Vern's axe. He pushed the stunned dwarf back and swung Buster again, this time striking Vern in the side of the helmet.

The dwarf's head was rocked violently to the side and he dropped to his knees and collapsed.

The fearful wizard that Vern had called 'Ghazardblast' saw his boss fall and shouted, "Belfae, we're leaving!"

The old man pulled something out of his robes that looked like a gray brick inscribed with intricate runes. He threw it on the ground and began to send elemental energies into it.

The brick shook and rose about six feet into the air. As it did so, another set of bricks appeared at either side of it, and then another and another, joining together and curving towards the ground to form an archway. The runes on the brick glowed and the air inside the archway shimmered and turned black.

"Now, Belfae!" the wizard shouted.

"What about the others?" the imp said, but the wizard simply leapt into the blackness of the archway.

Cursing, the imp barreled his shoulder into Fist to knock the ogre back, then used his speed to dart away. He ran to Vern's unconscious form and, as easily as if the bulky dwarf was a child, threw him over his shoulder and bolted for the wizard's impromptu portal.

Fist rushed towards him and swung his mace in a mighty blow, but the imp dodged to the side. Quickening missed Belfae and struck Vern's back, denting in the dwarf's magically reinforced platemail. The imp staggered under the weight of the blow, but made it to the archway.

Lenui refused to let him get away so easily. He pulled another one of his Buster Juniors off of his belt and threw it.

The hammer spun, and a burst of air rocketed it towards the imp. The imp and Vern passed into the darkness just before it struck. The hammer disappeared, but Lenui was certain he heard a distant thud.

"Bastards!" shouted the assassin that Deathclaw was fighting. She tried to break away from the fight and follow them, but couldn't. She knew that the moment she tried to run, Deathclaw would run her through. "Don't you leave me!"

No sooner had the words left her lips than the portal trembled. The glowing runes on the keystone brick flickered and died. The archway collapsed to the ground and the runed brick broke upon impact.

"WHAAT?" shouted a trio of voices from the trees and there was a heavy thud.

Rufus hurtled out of the trees as if thrown and Lenui caught a glimpse of his surprised and bloodied face as the rogue horse struck the ground and tumbled. Deathclaw and the assassin had to jump apart to avoid being struck.

"Ready yourselves!" shouted Sir Edge as he backed out of the trees. He was only clutching his right sword.

Walking out of the trees towards him came three of the largest orcs Lenui had ever seen. Each of them was nearly eight feet tall. One of them had Edge's left sword sticking out of its chest. It didn't seem to notice.

"They left us behind?" the three of them said in unison.

Chapter Eighteen

Sir Edge –Negotiations

They're warwielders! Edge sent through the bond as he backed out of the trees and onto the road. *Big ones with magic clubs*!

Warwielders were the highest form of the goblinoid races. It was widely known that one out of every ten goblin births produced a gorc and one out of every ten gorc births produced an orc. But few people knew that after many generations of purebred orc offspring came a new type of orc. Warwielders were bigger and stronger than their already formidable brethren, but they were rarely seen outside of the orc city of Khulbath in Khalpany.

Edge had faced and killed several of their kind over the years, but these were special. Their bodies were covered in tattooed runes that enhanced their bodies in various ways and there was some kind of spirit magic connection between them. The moment that he and Rufus had attacked them, they had acted in perfect coordination, fending off Edge's strikes.

He still couldn't believe how easily they had handled Rufus, beating him senseless and throwing him through the trees like that. Not only that, but Peace was still stuck in one of them. It had seemed immune to the sword's magic. Edge had felt nothing when stabbing that particular orc. The blade had penetrated its body and spirit but it was as if the soul inside the creature hadn't been an orc at all.

"Ready yourselves!" he yelled aloud and transmitted to Fist and Deathclaw all he knew about these monsters.

The three huge orcs pushed their way through the trees and followed Edge onto the road. They were the height of ogres, each of them almost as tall as Fist, and though they weren't as muscular as he was, their forms were impressive. They wore little in the way of armor, just chainmail breeches and boots.

"They left us behind?" the three of them asked in unison. Their voices sounded hurt.

The warwielder on the right, a bald pinch-faced orc with dark green mottled skin, hefted a huge runed club onto his shoulder and looked at the others. "What do we do, brothers?"

"I don't know, Chester," the other two said together.

The one in the middle placed the head of his matching club onto the ground and leaned on the handle. He was slightly shorter than the others, had braided black hair, and wore a yellow vest. "We were hired to fight, but Ghazard did leave us. That's against the terms of our deal. Never leave a living member of the party behind."

"And I got stabbed," said the rightmost one of them, a light green-skinned brute with gold rings piercing his nose, lips and ears. He gestured to the sword that was protruding from his chest. Blood was dribbling down the blade and dripping onto the ground. "This weird sword actually got through my skin." It spoke oddly, pronouncing sword with a hard w. "It's a real bad wound."

While the warwielders spoke, Fist rushed to Rufus's side and began healing him. *It's not too bad,* he told Edge with relief. *He's just concussed and a little bruised up.*

Rufus got to his feet and shook his head. He focused a determined look on the three orcs. "Ooh. Ouch."

"Just pull the sword out, Delvin," said the orc that the others had called Chester. "Your chest will heal, and you can stab him back with it."

"But if I pull the sword out I might bleed to death before it heals," Delvin argued.

The centermost warwielder disagreed. "You can't just leave the sword in there."

"What are you fools arguing about?" shouted the half-elf assassin. Her continued battle with Deathclaw was a fierce one. Her face was twisted with rage as she fended off the raptoid's sword blows and pressed forward with attacks of her own. "Fight! Kill 'em all! That's what we hired you for!"

"The lady's got a point, Evastus," said Delvin and Chester to the centermost warwielder.

"What she says don't matter because she's not the one that hired us," said Evastus.

Fist and Rufus spread out to either side of Edge. Fist sent electricity arcing across his mace. Rufus grew until he was ten feet tall at the shoulders. They were ready to attack on his signal.

The three orcs each held out a hand. "Hold on. We don't know if we're fighting yet," they said in unison.

"Yes, you do! Fight!" cried the female assassin.

"Hey, I think I know who these three are," said Lenny. The dwarf had walked away from the crumbled remains of the brick archway and now stood at Edge's side. He called out to the warwielders. "You folks the Bash Brothers?"

"Yes," they replied.

Lenny raised a bushy eyebrow and leaned in closer to Edge. He tried to lower his voice, but the dwarf never had been good at whispering. "Big time mercenaries in Khalpany. A merchant I know hired 'em once to guard an ore shipment. I thought he was exaggerating when he described them, but he said they was worth every gold piece. I didn't think they was still in business, though. I heard that two of the brothers died."

The warwielders overheard the not so quiet dwarf and sent frowns his way. "People keep telling us that," said Chester. "But we're still alive, see?"

"Yeah," said Delvin, moving his hand under Edge's sword to poke a thumb at his chest. "Still tickin' away."

Edge was pretty sure they were lying. At least partially. A theory about their natures had already formed in his mind, but he chose not to voice it just yet. There might be an opportunity to talk the orcs down.

"Excuse me. Bash Brothers?" he said, and they looked his way. "We'll fight you if that's what you want, but I'd rather not. How about we make a deal?"

"What kind of deal?" they asked.

"If you answer a few questions, my ogre friend will heal your wound and we'll let you go free," Edge offered. He couldn't do it himself. Peace wasn't making a connection he could use.

"Hmm," said the three orcs.

"An ogre's gonna heal Delvin?" said Chester, cracking a smile.

Evastus elbowed him, "Ghazard did say he was a master wizard, remember?"

Are you sure that letting them roam free is a good idea? Fist asked through the bond. *What if they leave here and go terrorize a farm or something?*

One problem at a time, Edge replied.

"I don't know," said Delvin, looking to his two brothers. "We don't have to make this deal. Ghazard will fix this wound for me when he comes back for us."

"Are you certain he's coming back for you?" Edge asked. "After all, he did leave you behind for dead." He held out his left hand and showed them the rune on his palm. "I've been named at the Bowl of Souls and so has Fist. You can trust our word over that wizard's."

Evastus nodded. "The man's got a point. Even if Ghazard is comin' back for us, who knows how long it'll take him to set up another of his portals way out this way?"

"What are you talking to them for?" shouted the half elf. She was bleeding from several shallow wounds but was still holding Deathclaw back. "Just fight already!"

"Fist," Edge said, and the ogre pointed at the woman. Thick cords of air magic formed around the assassin and wrapped around her limbs, binding her tightly. She cried out in anger and fell to the ground. Fist forced a gag of air into her mouth.

Deathclaw's shoulders slumped and he put his sword away. He nudged the squirming attacker with his foot. "I was enjoying that fight."

The Bash Brothers didn't seem concerned about her defeat. "What questions do you got?" asked Evastus.

"First of all, who hired you to attack us?" Edge asked.

They looked at each other, then looked back at him. "Not sure," they said together.

Then Chester nudged Evastus and the orc with the braided hair added, "I guess Ghazard's the one who hired us. We've done each other favors in the past and we work with him a lot. He showed up earlier today and said he had a job for us. Didn't say who hired him, but Ghazard let that dwarf Vern boss him around all day, so we think it's probably the dwarf."

"What about the half-elf?" Edge asked, gesturing at the magically bound woman who was squirming on the ground and grunting angrily, her eyes focused on the orcs.

The three orcs shrugged. "Don't really know her. She was there when Ghazard brought us to this place. He said she was a good swordsman, but all she's done is whine about her dead sister."

"We felt bad for her at first since her sister just died," Chester added. "But then she just got annoying."

"Why did you guys kill her sister anyway?" Delvin asked.

"She attacked us out of nowhere. We had no choice," said Edge. "When Ghazardblast gave you the job, what did he tell you to do?"

"He told us to wait in the trees and attack once he signaled," Evastus said. He and his brothers gave Edge an embarrassed grimace. "But then they decided to use that freeze spell and that's not our usual kind of job. We don't like to kill someone that can't fight back. I told Ghazard that and he said we only had to kill you if you broke free of the spell."

Edge noted the way that the other two orcs moved when Evastus talked, their expressions matching his as he spoke. He was growing more certain about his theory with every passing moment. "Did he say anything else about his plans?"

"Naw. Ghazard's the kind of boss that only tells you what you need to know. He was pretty nervous about this job, though. Said he'd been given very little time to prepare," Evastus said. He frowned. "Have I told you enough? Can you heal up my brother now and let us on our way?"

"One last question," Edge said. "When we let you leave, where will you go?"

Evastus blinked. "Huh." He scratched his head and looked at his brothers who just shrugged back at him. "That depends. Where are we? Ghazard brought us here through a portal thingy."

"Razbeck," said Lenny. "Just northwest of Filgren."

"Razbeck? Ughhh," groaned the three brothers in unison.

"That's a long ways from Khalpany," said Chester.

Delvin pouted along with him. "Very far."

Evastus sighed. "Can't believe he'd bring us all the way out here and leave us behind."

"So what will you do?" Edge pressed.

"Walk home, I guess," said Chester.

"Long walk," all three said.

"Maybe we'll find a merchant heading to Khalpany and hire on with him, make some money on the way," Evastus said, rubbing his chin.

"I guess," said the other two.

Fist send Edge a thought through the bond. *What if we were to hire them to join us on our journey?*

I've been considering the idea, Edge said. *But there is much we don't know about them.*

"Ooh! No!" said Rufus, who was listening through Fist's side of the bond. The rogue horse was fully healed, but memory of the beating was still fresh in his mind.

I do not like it either, hissed Deathclaw. *I doubt they could be trusted.*

They could slow us down, said Squirrel, who had suddenly appeared on Fist's shoulder. *They don't have horses. Also, two of them are already dead.*

Something isn't right with them, I agree with that, said Edge. *But if they're loose roaming the countryside, they might hurt someone. At least if they're with us, they aren't a threat to anyone else.*

Edge realized that Lenny was frowning at him suspiciously. The dwarf couldn't hear their mental discussion, but the tenuous new bond he had with Edge let him feel the emotions behind it. Edge was certain he would have plenty of opinions if he decided to go through with his plan.

We should just kill them, said Deathclaw. *Then they will be a threat to no one.*

I'll do it, Squirrel offered.

We can't do that now. Not while we're having a peaceful conversation, he told them. *Besides, killing them won't be an easy task. The protections tattooed on their skin is like armor. I had to hit a precise spot in order for Peace's blade to sink in.*

The three orcs had their heads cocked and were watching the party's silent conversation. "Uh, hello?" asked Delvin. "You gonna heal me now?"

I'll feel it out before I make a decision, Edge promised and focused his attention back on the orcs. "Yes. Go ahead, Fist."

As the ogre approached the wounded orc, Delvin pulled the sword out of his chest and held it out to Edge. The sword left his flesh with a soft sucking sound and blood spurted from the wound. Edge took Peace from him and wiped the blade before sheathing it on his back.

Fist held out his hand over the orc's wound and began pouring magic into him. He started on the major arteries that Edge had severed, and the bleeding slowed right away. *Edge, I think you and Squirrel may be right about these orcs. This body is technically alive, but it's overly stable and the whole thing's coursing with magic. It reminds me of the soulless bodies the wizards had us practice healing on at the Mage School.*

Edge remembered those healing lessons from his time as a student. He hadn't been able to use his magic to heal back then but it had been a fascinating and unsettling experience being brought to a room full of mindless living corpses. It was looking more and more like his hypothesis about the orc brothers was right.

While the ogre finished up, Edge stepped closer to Evastus. "I have a proposition for you."

"Oh?" Evastus asked, his eyebrows raised.

Edge stepped closer and put his left hand on Evastus' arm. "What if we were to hire you to guard us on our journey?"

All three orcs stared down at him in surprise. "You would hire us after we had been hired to attack you?"

"What the hell're you thinkin?" Lenny whispered loudly.

"It depends on a few factors," Edge said, ignoring the dwarf. "First, if we were to hire you, what would you do if Ghazardblast returned and ordered you to turn against us?"

Keeping his naming rune pressed against the orc's arm, Edge reached through the bond and pulled Peace's magic into the rune. He didn't allow it to pull away Evastus' emotions, but instead used the sword's magic to listen to his emotions. Touching him with the rune didn't let him see the orc's thoughts like it would if he stabbed them with the sword, but in many ways this was preferable. He could still tell if someone was lying or not and this method didn't leave him vulnerable to spiritual attack.

Immediately he learned that, unlike Delvin's body, Evastus' was as full of thoughts and feelings as anyone else. They were very busy feelings, but the orc was sincere as he replied.

"We're professionals," Evastus said, taking slight offence to the idea that he might double cross a client. "If you were to hire us, we would continue to protect you until the contract was over."

"And the fact that yer friends with this Guzzleblast won't change that?" pressed Lenny.

"No," the three orcs said.

"But his name's Guzzardblast," Evastus said, then blinked. "I mean, Ghazardblast."

"And he's not our friend. He abandoned us," said Chester. "So we ain't very fond of him at the moment."

"That's right. He broke our contract," added Delvin just as Fist finished his healing and stepped back. The orc felt at his chest and the faint new scar where the wound had been. "Thank you, ogre. You heal good."

Edge could feel the truthfulness of Evastus' statements. The brothers did seem to have a code of honor about this sort of thing. He let his hand drop from the orc's arm. "Alright, second question. How much?"

"How long would you be hiring us for?" Evastus asked. "Are we talking days?"

"We have a long journey ahead of us. It could be months," he said. "And it's possible that your wizard friend will attack us again on the way."

The three orcs looked at each other, or more accurately, they pretended to look at each other while Evastus gave it some thought. "Five hundred gold," he said.

"Five hundred!" Lenny exclaimed. "That's a garl-friggin' outrage!"

Edge was just as staggered by the price. He was expecting something more along the lines of Academy rates. This was triple what graduates would be paid for this kind of work. He and Jhonate had saved up a tidy sum over the years, but paying that would just about drain them.

"That's for two months," said Chester, folding his arms.

"One hundred each additional month," added Delvin. "And that includes our food and any healing we need."

"We'll fight for you, even against Ghazard," said Evastus.

"Screw 'em!" Lenny scoffed. "I'd make a full suit of indestructible plate armor for that kind of gold. And I hate makin' plate armor!"

All three orcs had their arms folded now. "That's our rate," they said firmly.

"Let me discuss this with my tribe," Edge said and grasped the dwarf's arm. He pulled Lenny to the side and Deathclaw and Fist moved closer to him. "I have the money. Barely."

Lenny knew Edge's situation well enough to understand just how big of a sacrifice this would be. "Yer gonna waste years of savin's on these three wagon-pullers?" the dwarf whispered loudly.

"Your friend vouched for them," Edge reminded the dwarf. "Does the price seem right for mercenaries of their caliber?"

The dwarf scowled. "If you was a prince hirin' bodyguards maybe."

"I'll pitch in," said Fist. The ogre had saved up more money than Edge had, actually. He and Maryanne were paid handsomely for their work.

"No!" said Rufus.

You'd give away our horde for one orc and two dead orcs? said Squirrel.

He's got a point, Fist, Edge replied through the bond. *I'm being stupid for considering it. You don't have to join me.*

I want to help, Fist replied, then said aloud. "By hiring them, we make sure they can't be used against us later on." The ogre smiled. "I doubt that wizard will be happy that we turned his own fighters against him."

"Exactly," Edge said. "Besides, this is only the start of a long journey and I have a feeling that it will only get more dangerous from here."

"They will slow us down," Deathclaw said.

"I don't think so," Edge said. "You didn't see how fast they moved when we fought. I don't think they will make us any slower than we already are while you're tracking."

The raptoid hissed. *I still do not like this.*

"Dag-blast it," Lenny swore. "Look here. Sounds like yer set on doin' this. Just don't accept their first offer. Mercenaries expect their clients to haggle. Let me talk with 'em and get us the best deal."

Edge nodded and the dwarf stomped over to stand in front of the trio. The three warwielders towered over his five-foot frame, but Lenny placed his hands on his hips and rebuked them like a father lecturing unreasonable children.

"Yer prices're dag-blamed ridiculous. We'll pay 300 for the first two months, fifty fer each month after, and you have to help hunt and do chores along the way!" he barked.

The three orcs blinked. "Our rates are standard."

"Bull-puckey!" Lenny said. "We both know that there's no such thing as standard rates fer mercenary work! 'Sides, you owe Edge a discount. You attacked us and beat up our rogue horse and he didn't like that much."

Rufus bared his teeth at them and reared up on his back legs as he cracked his huge knuckles menacingly. The effect was somewhat reduced by the words he said along with the gesture. "Yeah! Ow!"

The orcs didn't look cowed at all, but Delvin and Chester leaned in to whisper something in Evastus' ear. He grunted. "Fine. A small discount: 450 for the first two months, 100 for each month after."

Lenny let out a rough laugh. "Are yer ears clogged, you big dag-gum lump-heads? 350 and 55!"

The process went on for several long minutes until they reached a cost of 410 for the first two months and 75 for each additional month. Evastus looked positively angered by the amount at this point and Lenny threw up his hands in frustration. He swung around and gave Edge a wink.

"It's up to you, Son. These orcs won't see reason!"

Edge approached them and held out his left hand once more. "I think we've reached a fair sum. What do you say, Bash Brothers? Do we have a deal?"

Evastus hesitated, but engulfed the man's hand in his. "We'll work for you, but you can't tell anybody about the price break."

"You'll fight for us no matter who we're up against?" Edge asked.

"We'll fight anything that's threatening you," Evastus revised. "As long as you don't betray us."

"I can agree to those terms," Edge said.

"Deal," they said in unison.

With the power of Peace coursing through the naming rune on his hand, he knew that their promise was sincere. "Then welcome to our party."

Chapter Nineteen

Sir Edge - Interrogation

Sir Edge stepped away from the three orc warwielders and approached the half-elf assassin. Though her arms and legs had been bound with Fist's air magic she had managed to squirm off of the road and into the trees. He could hear her grunting and forcing her way through leaflitter and underbrush.

She heard his approach and redoubled her efforts to get away. Just as he neared her, she wormed her way over the edge of a trench in the forest floor. She slid into the trench face first and lurched to a stop in a tangle of briars.

Is she getting away from you? Deathclaw asked. *Do you need my help to retrieve her?*

Edge smiled wryly as he watched the assassin's legs sticking up out of the briars, her feet kicking weakly. The intermeshed tangle of dry briar bushes must have been uprooted and washed into the trench during a rain storm earlier in the season. He crouched at the edge of the trench and grasped her feet in his hands.

With the enhanced strength given him by his bond with Fist, Edge stood and yanked the half-elf out of the briars. He swung her over his shoulders and let her dangle behind him as he walked back out to the road. One of the smaller briar bushes came up with her and was tangled in the hood of her cloak. The assassin struggled against the magical bindings, grunting in rageful protest.

"She's determined. I can't deny her that," he said and dropped her in the dirt amongst his friends.

The bald half-elf woman was covered in dirt and leaves and her face and scalp were crisscrossed with tiny cuts from the brambles. She squinted up at them through eyes that were dazed. She must have struck a rock when landing at the bottom of the trench because a purplish knot was swelling on her forehead.

Edge looked her over carefully to see what he could glean from her appearance. Her black leather armor was well-made but nonmagical. She wasn't wearing gloves and a quick glance with spirit sight told him that she didn't have a black rune on her hand like the archer.

"Black rune or not, she is skilled," Deathclaw told him.

Edge called over to the orc warwielders he had hired. "Evastus, what can you tell me about this assassin?"

The three huge orcs joined the rest of the party in peering down at her. "We don't know her very well," they said in unison.

"Just met her today. But the dwarf called her, Felyan," said Delvin, his multiple facial piercings glinting in the afternoon light.

Evastus grunted. "She and Vern were together when Ghazard brought us and Belfae through his brick portal."

"Oh!" added Chester, who was scratching his bald head. "And she hates all of you for killing her sister."

Felyan blinked in surprise at their betrayal and fixed a glare on the orcs.

Lenny frowned down at her. "Fist, can you plug her ears?"

"I can." The ogre sent magic into the earth beneath her head and tendrils of mud rose up and forced their way into her ear canals.

"So what do we do with her?" the dwarf asked.

"First we need to talk to her," Edge replied. "She could be able to tell us more about what we're up against."

"Oh yeah? Why the hell would she talk to us?" Lenny asked. "You gonna risk stabbin' her with Peace?"

The dwarf knew well that there was a danger in using Edge's sword to probe an enemy's mind. The more he focused on accessing their memories, the more his mind was vulnerable to intrusion. Edge had ways to protect himself, but he knew nothing about this assassin. If she was skilled in mental warfare, she could find a way past his defenses. But that wasn't the sole reason he didn't want to try it.

Invading the mind of any unwilling person was something he tried to avoid if there was any way around it. The experience was intimate in a way that no one could understand if they hadn't been through it themselves. Not only would the experience be traumatic to the person his mind violated, the memories he plumbed from them would be a part of him forever.

"I have another way," Edge decided. He crouched next to the half-elf. "Fist, I'm ready to talk to her now."

With a gesture, the ogre withdrew the mud from Felyan's ears and the air gag in her mouth dissipated. The moment that her mouth was freed she tried to spit at Edge, but her mouth was too dry. So she settled on yelling at the three warwielders that were peering down at her.

"You filth!" Her voice was filled with venom. "You broke our contract!"

The three of them frowned back at her. "The Bash Brother's never break contracts!"

"Bull-puckey!" she shouted back at them.

"Our contract was with Ghaster, not you," Evastus said. "The wizard broke his end of the deal, so we're working for these guys now."

"I like them better than him already," added Delvin.

Edge reached out with his left hand and clutched her arm. The moment that the rune on his palm touched her, he let the power of his sword suck away all of her physical discomfort and emotion. As the sword did so, he mined those emotions for information. Her feelings were overwhelmingly fear and rage, but they were intermingled with sorrow. All tension left her features.

He let some compassion enter his voice. "Felyan, we weren't properly introduced. I am Sir Edge."

"What are you doing to me?" she asked. Her voice was dull, but through the emotions he pulled from her, Edge knew that she was shocked by the sudden effects of his magic.

"Your emotions were clouding your mind," he told her. "I'm allowing you to think clearly."

Felyan let out a slow breath and Edge could tell that the sword was now pulling away new types of feelings. She was glad for the relief from the pain of her bruised and bound body, but more important was enjoying sensation of emptiness that the sword's power left within her. This was a person whose mind hadn't been at peace in a long time.

"I won't tell you anything," she said automatically.

"I'm hoping that's not true," he told her. "I know you have reasons to hate us, but I also think you understand that your sister's death wasn't our fault. She attacked and we acted in self-defense. For what it's worth, I'm sorry that it had to end that way."

She looked to Deathclaw. The raptoid stood at her feet and stared at her with assessing eyes, his scaled arms folded. He didn't look sorry.

The sword sucked away the bitterness and rage that wanted to well within her. She would have rejected the truth and focused on her compulsion for vengeance, but Felyan was left with only logic to rule her thoughts. There was no escaping the truth of Edge's words.

She returned her gaze to him. "You are still the enemy," she said.

"I don't think we are," Edge replied. "Not really. Tell me something, Felyan. Where did you get the elf side of your blood? Your sister was human."

With her emotions pulled away she could think of no reason to withhold this particular bit of information. "We shared a mother."

"Are you the oldest? What happened with your father?" Edge asked.

Felyan didn't understand why he was following this line of questioning. What was he hoping to gain? She kept her mouth shut.

When he sensed her unwillingness to continue talking, he gave her a disappointed look. "You don't wish to answer? I could let go. Are you sure you want me to return that pain to you already? These are the easy questions."

She hesitated for a moment, but responded. "Yes, I am the oldest. In her youth, my mother became lost in the forest and spent some time with the Pruball elves," she said. "They made her leave when they saw that my father had grown fond of her. They didn't know that she was pregnant when they sent her away."

"I see." The Pruball elves were a large and influential sect. Their homeland was in the foothills of the Trafalgan Mountains on the Khalpany side. They did trade with other races but only rarely let humans stay within their borders. "So you are from Khalpany?"

"Why are you asking me about these things?" she asked. "What do you have to gain?"

"That's a good question," said the Bash Brothers. The looks on their faces were a mixture of confusion and boredom.

"You do not have to listen," Deathclaw told them.

They looked at each other and shrugged, but didn't move away.

Edge smiled at her and replied honestly. "I'm trying to get to know you so that I can have a better idea of what questions to ask next."

She blinked. "Yes, I'm from Khalpany."

"And how much older are you than Lana?" he asked.

"Ten years," she said. "Mother moved from village to village when I was small, but then she met my stepfather and Lana was born."

"I never had a brother or sister," Edge said. "You two must have been close."

Felyan was caught off-guard by the compassion in his eyes. "We were. Our mother died when Lana was young and our step father was taken by slavers. All we had was each other. We learned to take care of ourselves."

"And you felt responsibility for her?" he pressed.

"Of course, I did. I spent my life watching over her," she said. Her eyes fell back on Deathclaw and Edge felt that she was trying to dredge that anger back up. The sword didn't let her feel it.

Edge squeezed his hand tighter on her arm. "Then why is it that she was named by the Dark Bowl and you are not?"

"I don't know what you're talking about," she said. "It isn't possible."

Edge could tell that her statement wasn't completely true. There was a mix of frustration and disappointment being pulled away by the sword. She hadn't known for sure but she had at least suspected.

"There must have been some period of time when you weren't together," he suggested. "She was gone for a while and when she came back, she was different. More secretive. More skilled." He felt her emotions confirm his theory. "That's what happens when people go to the Dark Bowl. It forces skill into them and gives them new memories. The voices of ancient servants of the Dark Prophet become part of their minds."

She took several moments to digest that information. "Despite what you say, she was still my sister."

"Only now she had sudden access to a whole new group of friends?" he suggested. "People with more unsavory jobs? Or were you always assassins for hire?"

"In Khalpany you do what you have to do to make a living," she said, but Edge knew his words were sinking in. She was starting to have doubts. He chose to let that particular emotion stay in her mind.

"Do you know why my friends and I are out on this road?" he asked. "My wife is missing. One of the Dark Prophet's servants deceived her and took her this way. We're trying to track them down."

Felyan had no response for this.

"I think that servant hired you to attack us to keep us from catching up to him," Edge said. "Am I right?"

The sword sucked away her reluctance, leaving only doubt. Still, he could tell she wasn't telling the complete truth. "I don't know all the details. All I know is that Vern set it up. We work with him a lot and he told Lana he had an easy job. She was to go out on the river and take out as many of you as possible before the ferry reached the shore." Her eyes shifted to Lenny. "Starting with that dwarf. But the main thing was that we slow you down. Actually, killing you was just one way to dissuade you."

"Why go after Lenny first?" Edge asked.

Felyan shrugged as much as she could while lying with her arms bound. "Vern hated him. Called it a bonus kill. He gave Lana a special arrow to do it with." Her doubts increased, and Edge let her feel the regret that came along with it. "I would have gone out on the water with her, but she was the one with range. I just waited with Vern at the shore and watched."

"You never met the man that hired Vern?" he pressed.

"No," she said. "Vern went to meet him without us. He just returned to us with bags of gold and gave us the job."

236

"I got a question," said Lenny, his eyes tight with disgust. "Has that no-good, dirt-licker Vern also been to the Dark Bowl?"

"How am I supposed to know that?" Felyan said. "I didn't even know my own sister had been there."

Edge nodded slowly. He was disappointed that she didn't have more information on the mysterious thief. "What happened next? After Vern saw that his plan had failed."

"After my sister's death, I just wanted all of you dead," she said matter-of-factly. "But Vern saw that we needed more help, so he contacted the Specialist."

"The Specialist?" said Lenny.

Evastus spoke up. "That's what people call Ghazard. He knows how to put together the right group of mercenaries for the right job. He pays real good too. It's why we worked with him so much. Usually, he just wants us there to bust heads if something goes wrong."

"Vern had to pay Ghazardblast extra because we needed him to work fast," she said. "The wizard was able to use those portal bricks to bring in the people he wanted. Only . . . he scampered away before I could get my revenge."

Edge began to gain new respect for the wizard that had fled the scene. In only a few short hours after they had arrived on the Razbeck side of the river, he had somehow put together a crew specifically designed to fight their party. If his plan with the paralyzing orb had worked, they might have all been killed.

"And how do you feel about things now?" Edge asked her. "If I was to free you, would you still attack us?"

Her eyes narrowed slightly. "I don't know how you're doing this to me, but the minute you let me feel my emotions again I am going to want to kill that scaly fiend. I don't care about the rest of you and I'll probably never work with Vern again." She gestured at Deathclaw with her chin. "But that thing is dead."

Edge nodded and sent a message to Fist through the bond. The ogre gagged her with air again, but this time he didn't clog her ears. Edge let go of her arm and her eyes went wide as her emotions rushed back into her mind. He stood and turned away from her.

"So what do you think we should do with her?" Edge asked his friends.

"You could just cave her skull in and toss her into the trees," Delvin suggested.

Evastus punched his larger sibling in the arm. "Brother! That's not how a named warrior acts."

Unfortunately, the orc was right. While she was in the process of attacking them, Edge would have had no qualms about killing her. But now that she was bound and his prisoner and he had gotten to know her, he couldn't do it. "We could drop her off at an Academy outpost along the way and have them send her to the Dremald dungeons."

"Sorry, Son. There's no outposts along this road that I know of," said Lenny. He stopped in the road and bent to pick up the spent paralyzing orb. He stowed it in a pouch at his waist. "Closest one to us is out by Coal's keep, but that's durn near a full day's journey from here. We could maybe swing by Castle Razbeck and hand her off to the king. I'm sure he'd imprison her on your word."

Edge shook his head. "Either of those options requires us to veer too far away from Jhonate's trail. We can't afford to lose that much time."

"If you won't kill her while she's a prisoner, free her," suggested Deathclaw. "Let she and I continue our fight. I will kill her in battle."

Edge sighed. "I think you have the kernel of a good idea there, Deathclaw," he said and gestured to Fist. *Let her speak and when I signal you, remove her bindings.* The ogre once again removed the gag of air and Edge pulled her roughly to her feet. "Alright, Felyan. I can't take any more time with you. It's time to decide. What are you going to do if I let you go?"

"I already told you," she said, her teeth bared. She glared at Deathclaw with open hatred. "It doesn't matter that we were in the wrong. I'll never be able to forget that thing attacking my sister. I like its suggestion. Let me loose and I'll settle this with it right now. You can do whatever you want with me after I kill it. With Lana gone I have nothing left to live for."

Edge nodded slowly. "You're wrong, Felyan, but I see that you can't believe that right now. Unfortunately, I can't afford to have the two of you fight at the moment. What I care about right now is finding my wife. I'll need Deathclaw's help to do that."

Deathclaw hissed and was about to protest, but Edge sent him a message through the bond asking him to hold back.

"You have two options," Edge told the half-elf. "The most efficient one is the option Delvin gave me. It's true that I won't kill you in cold blood myself, but if you won't cooperate, I'll let Deathclaw drag you out into the woods and do it."

The raptoid gave her a grim hiss.

"And your second option?" she said, her eyes never leaving Deathclaw's.

"The second option is that I set you loose and you promise to leave us alone to complete our task," Edge told her. "I know you'll still want your revenge, but you'll have to wait until after I have my wife back."

"I prefer this idea," Deathclaw said. "I can always kill you in honest battle at a later date."

She glowered. "Fine."

Edge gripped her arm, making sure his rune was touching her skin. "I'll be able to tell if you lie to me. Do you swear to leave us for now?"

Felyan turned her gaze onto him. "I'll give you a month to find your wife, but I will come for him after that."

Edge could feel her sincerity. "Okay, Fist. Let her go."

The magic bindings fell away, and Edge waited until she was steady on her feet before he let go. She turned on her heels and picked up the weapons she had dropped when Fist had bound her. Then she stood still as if about to say something else. Shaking her bald head, she strode away.

Lenny stepped up next to Edge and put a hand on his shoulder. "You sure this was the right thing to do?"

Edge watched her disappear into the trees. "No," he said, already doubting his decision. "I just hope that over time she'll come to terms with her sorrow and understand that seeking revenge won't help anything."

"I think she'll show back up more dangerous than before," Deathclaw said. He smiled. "I will be ready."

Chapter Twenty
Sar Zahara – Wildlands

"Camel hump?" asked a shriveled man with very few teeth. He was gesturing at the largest cut of meat on his table. It looked like a huge lump of fat and meat, sitting on severed bits of spine and ribcage. He seemed quite proud to have it for sale.

The man wore the plain gray garb of a western pilgrim and the wide-brimmed hat on his head had a blue band across it to identify him as a merchant. He stood behind a table just inside his tent, where a number of different cuts of meat were laid out for sale. His sleeves were rolled back, and he wore a long blood-stained apron.

Jhonate had first seen camels several years back while traveling with Edge to Alberri. She had been curious about the nature of the large humps on the beast's backs, but this was the first time she had seen one offered as food. She wondered how it would taste but had no need for a cut so large.

"No," she said and pointed past the man to the floor of the butcher's tent where a canvas tarp had been laid out. Many different cuts of meat were on display including some decent-sized roasts. "Is that all camel meat?"

"Oh yes. All from the same beast," the man assured her. "It was a young camel. The meat is very tender and very fresh."

She believed that the meat was fresh, but she had doubts about the camel being young. In this part of the world, camels were usually too useful to slaughter unless there was something wrong with them. This animal was likely either very old or injured and in need of being put down. She had a feeling that most of the cuts would be tough and take a lot of cooking before they were edible.

Jhonate pointed to a fatty roast. "I shall take that one."

"Very good choice, madam! Four copper pieces." The butcher picked up the meat she had pointed to and set it onto the table next to the hump. "Are you taking this to cook for your husband?"

Her upper lip curled unconsciously at both the high price and the man's assumption. She pulled out the coins and let them clatter onto the table in front of her. "No."

"Travel companions, then?" he asked as he wrapped the meat in a bit of waxed paper.

"Yes," she said, though even admitting that made her tongue feel leaden in her mouth.

Nodding and grinning, the man tied the package with twine and left a long loop for her to carry it with. "Do you need spices? My friend Laseer is just two tents down. In my most humble opinion, camel is best flavored with turmeric and coriander."

She stuck the tip of her staff through the loop of twine and lifted the package off of the table. "I shall keep that in mind. Good day to you."

Jhonate turned to leave and let the wood of her staff form around the string to hold it in place, then rested the staff over her shoulder as she walked into the narrow street. She was wearing a gray pilgrim's robe over the top of her leather breastplate and a hooded gray cloak covered her braided hair. The disguise was useful for more than just hiding her identity. It also helped to keep her cool in this place. The Wildlands were terribly hot all year round.

The area known as the Wildlands was a stretch of unclaimed land north of Razbeck. It reached all the way westward to Corntown and northward to the Whitebridge Desert and beyond, continuing up to the barrier at the outer edge of the Known Lands. The area was rocky and barren, unfit for farming or ranching. It had been long known as a place of refuge for bandits and other undesirables. This made it a perfect place for a pilgrim tent city.

The tent city, known locally as Hoolahan Crossing, had formed at this crossroads nearly five years ago. The size of the city shifted and evolved as pilgrims came and went on their various journeys. At the moment there were a thousand tents spread across a quarter mile of flat scrub-brush laden land.

Jhonate had been surprised by the sheer number of pilgrims she and Nod had passed on the road to this place. The only pilgrims she had seen before meeting Nod had been the ones that came to the Mage School to see the Bowl of Souls, but they were mostly fighters. These people were part of something else, a new religious movement.

The Pilgrimage Movement had begun in Khalpany years ago and had spread across the Known Lands as people travelled from holy site to holy site. The way Nod explained it, there was no central dogma that was part of the movement. They didn't seem to be worshippers of the Creator or the Prophet. Each individual had their own reasons to undertake a pilgrimage, be it a life they wished to escape, or a curse they wished to break. There was a sense of community among them though. Every pilgrim Nod and Jhonate had met along the way had been kind and willing to share their fire for a night.

The tents that lined the central street of Hoolahan Crossing were large merchant's affairs, each one with brightly colored entrances and signs proclaiming services. These merchants had spread like leeches among the pilgrims, each one proclaiming to be a devout person, pausing in the middle of a journey of their own.

Jhonate paused at the spice tent that the butcher had recommended and took one look at the trays full of multicolored powders before shaking her head and moving on.

She had no idea which spices were the ones the butcher had mentioned and even if she did, she had no idea what quantity to buy or what amount to put on the meat. And she had little desire to draw attention asking foolish questions about it.

Jhonate was already regretting trying to save money by buying the raw camel meat instead of purchasing pre-cooked food at one of the tent stalls. She had never been much of a cook. Growing up at the palace in Roo-Tan'lan, her focus had been on training. Food was always provided. Her experience at the Battle Academy was much the same. Her years traveling at Edge's side had taught her little more. Edge was a serviceable trailside cook and they often traveled with someone that was better than either one of them.

This journey with Nod had made her regret her lack of knowledge in this area. She knew how to skin and clean any animals she caught, of course, but other than that, all she could do was cook meat on a stick or boil it in a pot. Nod seemed to know less than she did. The few times she had made him cook the food, he had managed to burn it and one time he had thrown in leaves that she was fairly certain were inedible.

Perhaps she would ask Lenny for cooking advice the next time she saw him. The dwarf cooked his food spicier than she liked, but he still was the best trail cook she had ever met.

She considered what to do with the meat as she walked towards the northern edge of the city where she and Nod had camped. Maybe if she cut the roast into small enough pieces and boiled it long enough it would be edible. Maybe one of the tents would be selling potatoes or carrots to add to it. She paused and considered going back to the spice tent just to purchase some salt.

Jhonate shrugged the thought away. She had travelled for three flavorless weeks with the man. One more night of mediocre food wouldn't harm her. She had a bunch of hardtack that was too hard to eat on its own. She could break some of it it up and toss in with the meat. It wouldn't add much flavor to the soup, but it would at least give it some texture.

As she approached their small campsite, she saw Nod talking to two figures in gray attire. One of them was a bent old man who was leaning on a staff and the other one was wearing a hooded cloak. The conversation looked to be heated and Nod ended it with a sharp word that she couldn't make out, but it sounded like an order.

The two figures turned away and walked in her direction. When they passed her, she got a better look at the old man's staff. It was made of gnarled wood that was carved in intricate runes. A quick shift to mage sight told her that this man's staff was an item of great power. She also caught a glimpse under the other figure's hood. The person had skin that was pure white and his lips were drawn back, exposing pointed teeth.

Jhonate continued to the campsite. Nod was pacing, an irritated look on his face. He reached into his cloak to massage his crippled left hand. It was something he often did while deep in thought.

"Who is that man you spoke with?" Jhonate asked.

She was fairly certain that he was aware of her approach, but Nod jumped as if startled, and swung around to face her with a look of surprise. "Ah, there you are, Sar! Is that our dinner hangin' on your staff? I'm famished!"

"I asked you about the people you were speaking to," she repeated firmly.

"Oh, them? No one, Sar. Just pilgrim friends of mine," he said and stepped closer to get a better look at her wrapped package.

Jhonate pulled her staff away from his reach. "A pilgrim wizard and a pilgrim imp?" Nowadays demons were a more common sight out in the world than when she had been growing up, but imps were still a rare sighting.

He cocked his head at her. "Got a good look at 'em did ya? Don't know why you'd 'fink it strange. Don't matter none if a person's wizard or warrior or imp or gnome. We pilgrims take in everybody."

245

She frowned. His explanation actually made sense. For some reason she could not fathom, this movement did attract all kinds. "Yet, for an imp and wizard to join and travel together seems an odd thing."

Or more specifically, a suspicious thing. Imps weren't evil as a rule. They were a people with a broad range of personalities like every humanoid race. But they were known for their underhanded dealings. Even the good ones had a tendency towards trickery.

"True, Sar. An odd pairing, that," Nod said with a shrug. "Which is why I sought 'em out. I heard they'd been near to Alsarobeth, see, and I asked 'em for a safe route through the desert. If anyone was gonna pass 'frough the Whitebridge unscathed it'd be a team with their magical power."

"It looked as though they said something you did not like."

The look of puzzlement left his features and he gave her a disarming smile. "I'd hoped for better news is all."

"Then they did not know a safe way through?" she asked.

Nod shrugged exaggeratedly. "They had a map what they found somewheres, but they can't promise it'll work. Like most folks, they turned back a'fore they make it through the Whitebridge. Just kept a jar of sand as a souvenir and called it good."

She chewed her lip for a moment, her eyes narrowed. He had managed to come up with logical answers to all of her questions while still leaving her feeling that he was lying to her.

Many of her conversations with Nod left her feeling this way. They had developed an odd sort of companionship over their long journey. She trusted him to a certain point, but they hadn't become friends. She didn't even like him, and for some strange reason, she thought he preferred it this way. It was like he enjoyed finding ways to keep her from getting too close.

Begrudgingly, she swung her staff over and released the package into his arms. He held it clumsily against his chest with his crippled arm and untied it with his other hand. He looked blandly at the large piece of meat she had bought.

"So you're cookin' again tonight? It's a fatty cut at least. What kind of meat is it, Sar?" he asked, adding a hopeful smile.

"Camel," she said.

His smile fell. "They didn't have any beef? Not a leg of lamb? Even a chicken? I wouldn't even look askance at a rabbit at this point."

"This is a pilgrim camp. We take what we can get. Why? Does camel taste bad?" she asked, disappointed.

A dark look passed briefly over his features, but he laughed it off. "I dunno! I ain't had it a'fore! Let's consider it an adventure. Me'n Sar Zahara eatin' camel. Why not?" He paused. "Did you happen to pick up any spices to go along wif it?"

Her back straightened. "If I had would you know what to do with them?"

Nod shook his head. "Well, you got me there, Sar. It's another culinary adventure for us."

Jhonate felt abashed about the whole situation and as she prepared the soup she did her best. The meat was tougher even than she had expected. She got the pot boiling and added the hardtack, which soon turned to mush, and even put in some pungent cheese that she had been saving. The resulting soup was greasy. The meat somehow managed to be both tough and blubbery. The cheese kept it from being flavorless, but that didn't mean it was a good flavor.

Nod forced his bowl down without comment. He didn't need to say anything. His facial expression told the story. Jhonate's experience was little better, but she had better control over her own reactions. She ate hers in stony silence. Nevertheless, the sound of his occasional gagging made her stomach turn a few times.

Knowing how tough the last leg of their journey was going to be, they made themselves eat as much as they could keep down and bedded for the night. Jhonate slept in her bedroll opposite the fire from her companion. She didn't like sleeping next to him when she could avoid it.

Ever since she had yelled at him at the beginning of their journey, Nod seemed to be on his best behavior. She had never caught him leering at her again, but sometimes she still wondered. Jhonate couldn't explain the feeling, but even when he was facing away from her it was like his eyes were still on her. She scowled at herself. There was no need to make things up just to spite the man.

The next morning, she awoke to Nod yelling at a group of pilgrims. There were four of them, large bulky figures in hooded cloaks that were standing not far from the campsite. They were just staring in Jhonate's direction.

"Go on! Move along a'fore I have to draw me sword!" The pilgrims shuffled their feet, but turned and headed into the tent city. "That's right. We don't need no gawkers!"

Jhonate climbed out of her bedroll and pulled on her boots. "What was that about?"

He shrugged. "Dunno. I woke up and saw 'em starin'. But they were harmless. Like I said last night, we pilgrims take in all types."

They quickly packed up and rode their horses northward. As they rode, those large pilgrims wouldn't leave her mind. Something about them tickled her memory, but Jhonate didn't know what it was. She really missed Edge right then. He would have been able to help her discover what she was missing.

Her thoughts took a gloomy turn at that point as she wondered what her husband was up to without her. Was he mad at her for leaving? Had he tried to follow?

Jhonate's mood darkened as the heat rose and by noon she was miserable. To make things worse, she saw a dark cloud system passing to their south. Those clouds were full of rain, but they weren't headed their way. The people in the tent city were going to get some relief, though.

Nod was usually a loquacious traveler, something that often got on her nerves. But today, he was either just as miserable as she was or he seemed to sense the intensity of her mood. The man wisely kept his inane prattle to himself.

A few hours later something happened to change her temper. The road took them up a sharp incline and when they reached the top, she caught her first glimpse of their destination. Far in the distance, beyond a wavering white horizon, she saw the snow-capped peak where Alsarobeth lay.

Nod reined in his horse and placed his hand to his brow. He smiled. "It's a lovely sight, ain't it, Sar? To have our destination in view?"

"Yes it is, Nod," she said.

They continued on their journey, the mountain peak growing slowly in the distance. Two days later they came to a stream. On either side of the water was a narrow strip of green and beyond that was their next great obstacle.

Stretching between them and their mountain was an ocean of sand. Heat rose from the dunes, distorting their view of the horizon.

"The Whitebridge," Nod said with a hint of fear in his voice. "A land of hot death and monsters."

A shiver passed up her spine despite the heat. This was Deathclaw's homeland.

Chapter Twenty One

Lucinder – Plans

Lucinder's head throbbed worse with every day that passed. He complained about it and one morning Priestess Sren came to him. The dangerous blond beauty made him strip down to his small clothes and then she walked around him in her leather armor. He blushed under her calculating gaze. Finally, she seized his head in both of her hands and kissed him with her black painted lips.

Her elemental power surged through his head, and the ache was greatly reduced. She pulled back and sneered at the shocked expression on his face. "You aren't eating enough," she had declared and turned to leave. She paused at the door. "Call for me if it worsens."

The door shut behind her and he dressed hurriedly, feeling like he had narrowly avoided something worse than headache pain. His headache returned a few hours later with a vengeance, but Lucinder knew better than to call for her again.

After that, his meal portions increased to a ridiculous degree and yet every day he was certain that the pain was worsening. Even worse, Sir Bertrom didn't return. He worried that something had happened to the named warrior and every hour that passed seemed an hour closer to his death. Lucinder's only respites were reading and sleeping. He spent most of his days in bed with the curtains drawn around him. He began refusing to eat.

One morning, as he sat in the dim light of his shade-drawn room, Lucinder was hungry enough that he picked at the extravagant breakfast the servants had brought him. A pile of bacon sat on a wide platter next to toast that was smothered with gravy and tender chunks of beef. Next to it lay a row of sliced honstule covered in cheese. A glass of fruit juice had been placed to the side.

None of it looked good to him, but he considered eating the honstule. The vegetable was the only part of the meal that ever made him feel any better. He cut a piece with his fork and was bringing it to his mouth when a tiny rock bounced off of the platter.

He looked to the window and saw Sir Bertrom's face peering at him from between the curtains. The warrior's expression was grim as he reached an arm into the room and beckoned the prince over to him.

Lucinder grinned widely and ignored the extra throbbing that came from standing quickly. He rushed over to the curtains and threw them open despite the way the sunlight stabbed his eyes. Bertrom crouched on the window ledge and placed his silencing cube on the ledge next to him.

"You came!" Lucinder exclaimed. "I worried that something happened to you."

The warrior's gaze didn't meet his. "I'm afraid I received some bad news." His face looked haggard, haunted even. "We aren't going to have all the help we hoped for."

Lucinder swallowed. "What does that mean?"

"It means were in a tight spot," Bertrom said. "Our numbers are few in this city and time is running out." He looked down. "That means we have some tough choices to make."

"A-are you saying you have to leave me behind?" Lucinder asked. "Please . . . I don't want to be sacrificed to the Dark Prophet."

Bertrom's eyes finally rose to his. "Lucinder, I'm going to be honest with you. It's worse than that."

His gaze was dark and this time Lucinder was the one to look away. "I know. I've read about how the priestesses sacrificed people to him. It's said that their daggers had the power to tear a piece of a person's soul away as they died. He used those pieces to increase his power."

"You're well-read, kid," said Bertrom with respect. "We've destroyed all but one of the priestesses' daggers, but . . . Look, that doesn't matter. What I need to tell you is that they have other plans for you."

Lucinder's jaw drooped and a feeling of dread overtook him. "What plans?"

Bertrom sighed and he sat down on the ledge. "A few decades back, a powerful seer had a prophecy. It spoke of the Dark Prophet's return." He rubbed his face with a tired hand. "Unfortunately, the wrong people got wind of it and they have been trying to bring him back ever since."

"What does that have to do with me?" Lucinder asked.

"The prophecy said that when the Dark Prophet rose again, he would return to this world as a king. He's been trying ever since. The Prophet has been working us ragged foiling the Dark Prophet's schemes as fast as he comes up with them. But one of his plans snuck past us." He gave the prince a firm look. "Until Nurse Deena reached out to us."

"He's coming back as my father? Or . . ." Lucinder blinked back at him. "Me? But I'm not king."

"Not yet," Bertrom said. "But you are the heir to Khalpany. And since your mother is a Muldroomon, you would also have a claim on Dremaldria's throne. You know that shriveled black orb you told me about? We think it's actually a moonrat eye. One of them, an artifact powerful enough to contain the entirety of the Dark Prophet's soul, went missing a year before you were born. All they have to do is cut you open and place this moonrat eye inside you. He'll be able to take over your body, toss your mind aside, and fulfill the prophecy."

Lucinder now realized why Bertrom had been so grim when he arrived. This wasn't a rescue. "I guess we can't let him do that. I . . ." He felt tears come up, but he forced them away and squared his chin. "I suppose you should kill me then."

Bertrom's eyebrows rose, but he didn't brush the idea aside. "Are you serious about that, Lucinder?"

The prince swallowed as he wavered. He wanted to live, but . . . this is what his life had become. One way or the other he would be led to slaughter.

"It's what you came here for, isn't it?" He straightened his back. "Don't feel bad for me, Sir. I understand that it needs to be done. A-and if it will keep the Dark Prophet from returning, then it's worth it."

Sir Bertrom put a hand on the prince's collar and gripped his shirt tight, his expression resigned. "Brave boy."

The named warrior leaned forward and Lucinder was certain that Bertrom was preparing to pull him out of the window and hurl him to the distant ground below. A jolt of fear passed through the young man and he almost pulled away, but he managed to regain his courage and stood still, closing his eyes. It was better this way. In mere seconds, the Dark Prophet's plan would be foiled. At least his headache would be gone.

"Dammit," said Bertrom gruffly, and he gave the prince a slight shake before letting go of his collar. "Maybe the Bowl was wrong to choose me."

"It's okay, Sir," Lucinder assured him and opened his eyes. "I'm not worth the . . ." His voice trailed away as he saw tears in the warrior's eyes.

"I won't do it," Bertrom said with a brusque shake of his head. "We won't do it." He placed his hand on Lucinder's shoulder. "We're going to do something much more difficult." He nodded, and a grin spread on his lips. "We're going to do something that will really put a thumb in the Dark Prophet's eye."

Lucinder smiled back at him. "Really? What is it?"

"Well, part of it's already planned," said Bertrom. "Even though we didn't receive all the aid we hoped for, we're going to stage a raid on the dungeon. We'll rescue Mistress Dagger and Nurse Deena. Only we're going to do it louder."

"Are you going after the Dark Bowl?" Lucinder asked.

"Unfortunately, we're not quite set up to do that. Even if we managed to reach the Dark Bowl, we have no way to destroy it or even move it." He lifted a finger. "But your father and the Dark Prophet's other servants don't know that."

Lucinder suppressed a wince at his father's name openly being tied to the Dark Prophet. He had already known the truth of the statement, but hearing it spoken aloud made it feel more real.

"We'll attack quickly and make it seem like we're going for the Bowl," Bertrom continued. "But while the enemy converges on the location, we'll get our friends out and come for you."

"You have enough men for that?" Lucinder asked. Bertrom had been so dour before.

"If we time things right . . . yes." Bertrom said with a nod and though there was confidence in his voice, Lucinder sensed that the man was trying to convince himself. "We'll just have to lean more heavily on our friend here in the palace. It'll be dangerous, but there is no better option and you are worth the risk."

Lucinder didn't know what to say to that.

"We'll have to cut off your toe with the spell on it, though. Can't have them tracking us." Bertrom chuckled apologetically. "You're not too fond of that toe, are you?"

Lucinder was surprised by how little he cared about his toes at the moment. He laughed. "I can do without it."

The warrior released his shoulder and tousled his hair, then picked up the glowing cube and stood on the window ledge. "I go now to tell the others. In a few days I'll get back to you with instructions."

"Thank you, Sir Bertrom. But I-." Lucinder spun around as he heard a knock on the door. His door opened, and a servant stepped inside. When he looked back, the named warrior was gone.

The servant walked to the prince's breakfast platter and let out a worried grunt. Likely, he had been commanded to make sure that Lucinder ate. "You haven't touched your food, my prince." He turned his head and looked out of the open window. "Is the sun too bright for your headache? Would you like me to draw your curtains?"

Lucinder rushed to the platter and sat back down. "No, it's fine. I was just waiting for it to cool down." He ate several bites of the cheese-covered honstule and the servant gave him an encouraging nod.

"Very good, my prince," he said and waited and watched while Lucinder finished every bite.

Lucinder now had a pained stomach to go along with his headache, but the servant went away happy. He waited for the door to shut behind the man, then rushed to his window to peer out and make sure that Bertrom was truly gone.

Sighing, but filled with determination, he shut the window and drew the curtains. He went back to his bed, intending to lay in the darkness and try to ease his pains, but his mind was too restless. After a few agonizing minutes, he left his bed and approached his bookcases, looking for any volumes of history that he hadn't yet read.

Over the next several agonizing days while he waited for Bertrom's return, Lucinder pushed his headache aside and focused on his studies. He went through several previously untouched histories and thumbed back through volumes he had read before, looking for any and all mentions of the Dark Prophet.

What he learned did little to calm his fears. He didn't find any mention of the prophecy Bertrom had spoken of, but he did read about the horrors perpetrated under the Dark Prophet's reign. More importantly, he learned about the man that the Dark Prophet had been. His name had been David and he was one of three prophets that the Creator had placed in charge of the races of the Known Lands.

Matthew was the prophet placed in charge of the demon and blood magic races. John was the prophet in charge of the human race and was made the caretaker of all holy sites. David had been placed over the goblinoid races. Each of these prophets watched over their charges in their own ways.

John walked among the humans and guided them in small ways, teaching those who he felt would make the most difference in humanity's development. He organized the Mage Schools and set powerful guardians to protect each holy site from destruction. He was widely respected and was to this day referred to by most everyone only as the Prophet.

The races in Matthew's care were born with powerful magics and he chose to rule them from a distance. He set them in enmity against each other and managed their populations with magic to keep any one of the races from growing too strong. This method of rule caused bitterness among his races and they began to call him the Stranger.

David was given the most troublesome of races. The goblinoids were fierce and unruly and had a tendency towards violence. He felt that the only way he could protect the world from them was to subjugate them to his will. He ruled over them with a brutality that matched theirs. For many years, he kept them leashed and they began to worship him as a god. David resented them for this. He resented Matthew and John for being given the easier races. He became used to being worshipped, though.

In some of the histories Lucinder read, David had learned through holy prophecy that he was the rightful god of this world. The Creator had abandoned it to him. In other histories, David simply grew mad with power and desired to have more than mere goblinoids at his beck and call.

Whichever tale was true, David felt he had the resources to claim the world as his own. Since the goblinoids bred as fiercely as they fought, he had vast hordes at his command. He began to spread his grasp, reaching out to those of other races and conquering those that would not join him. People began to call him the Dark Prophet.

Centuries of wars came from his thirst for power. John fought back against him time after time and finally, two hundred years ago, he led a group of warriors and wizards to David's palace and slew him. They returned to their lands triumphant and it seemed that they had been successful. To most of the world the Dark Prophet was gone forever.

The voice that had spoken in his mind since he was a small child had been the source of so much evil in the world. Lucinder shivered in realization that his parents had known the Dark Prophet's plans for him before he was even born. The thought that his parents had raised him simply so that his mind might be hollowed out so that the Dark Prophet could return to power left him sobbing. No wonder his mother couldn't even look at him.

As more days passed, he began to fear that Bertrom's rescue wouldn't come. Lucinder considered jumping out the window of his own volition. How easy it would be to save the world. And by doing so, he would perhaps save those planning a reckless attempt to rescue him.

There was something about the idea that made him feel every bit as courageous as the heroes of legend he so admired. One morning, he actually opened the window and started to climb onto the ledge. But fear of the dizzying drop caused his courage to wither and Sir Bertrom's promise of rescue gave him an excuse to back down. He returned to his room and shut the window. As he stood next to it, shuddering with guilt, his head searing with pain, there was another knock at his door.

The servant that came in with his breakfast barely spared him a glance. She left a platter laden with food. Lucinder stumbled over to it, intending to throw the food onto the ground in defiance. As he grabbed the edge of the platter, he felt something under it. A folded slip of paper.

Lucinder opened the paper and read the note inside, hope renewing within him.

> *Our plan is in motion. Watch the city at night.*
> *Fires will announce our arrival. Have courage*
> *and be sure to destroy this note – Knight*
> *Bertrom.*

Chapter Twenty Two
Sir Edge – Puppets

Edge and his companions followed Jhonate's trail to the northwest for two weeks without any major problems. They were fortunate that the weather remained fair, if a bit chilly. Deathclaw and Rufus never lost track of her scent for more than an hour or so before picking it back up.

Jhonate mainly kept to roads and thus far was traveling in the direction they assumed she would. One thing that did change was that the roads became more and more populated with travelers. Most of them were gray-clad pilgrims who were no trouble to the party, generally keeping their heads down and moving off of the road while Edge and his friends traveled past them. Unfortunately, their tracks made Jhonate's scent harder to distinguish.

The pace of their tracking became agonizingly slow for Edge's taste, but they gradually made up ground on their quarry. When they had left the spot of Vern's ambush, Jhonate and the thief had a full two days lead on them. By the time those two weeks had passed, they were only a day behind.

To Edge's relief, the Bash Brothers weren't much of a distraction. His main misgiving about hiring them on for the journey had been the possibility that the three huge orcs would slow the party down. Fortunately, that wasn't the case. The runes that were tattooed on their skin enhanced their bodies in many ways, including giving them increased stamina.

They were able to keep up with the pace of the tracking quite easily and when it came time to stop for the night, the

Bash Brothers were a great help. They did a fine job setting up a camp site. Delvin and Chester did most of the work, clearing brush, gathering wood, and digging a firepit while Evastus observed and called out encouragements.

The brothers were more genial than any orcs Edge had ever run across. They bantered with the rest of the party, shared jokes, and told stories of their mercenary adventures. Fist and Rufus hit it off with them right away and spent their evenings laughing with the orcs by the fire. Lenny and Deathclaw were more standoffish, but after a few days of complimenting Lenny's cooking at every meal, even the dwarf grudgingly began to enjoy their company.

Edge couldn't quite join the others in their enthusiasm. No matter how entertaining the three orcs' act was, he knew that it was an act. Evastus was alive, but something had happened to the souls of the other two. Squirrel called them dead, but Edge didn't think that was true. They didn't act like the kind of animated dead he had dealt with in the past.

Perhaps Delvin's and Chester's bodies were constructs of some kind. That would explain why his sword's power didn't work on them. Their souls could be inhabiting the minds of the bodies without filling them completely. This would have many benefits, such as allowing them to ignore pain or discomfort that would bring down other creatures.

He wasn't certain if they had done this to themselves on purpose or if someone had forced this situation on them, but he found it difficult to trust them. Until he could figure it out, Edge did his best to distance himself from the likeable orcs.

One night after dinner as the brothers sat around the campfire joking with Rufus and Lenny, Edge saw something that sparked his curiosity. Evastus had developed a facial tic. Each time one of his two brothers made a remark his right eyelid would flutter. This had never happened before that Edge had seen.

"The ground started rumbling like there was a quake or something!" Chester was saying, his wide smile displaying craggy teeth. "So we turned around and looked up and guess what we see rolling down the mountain towards us?"

"What?" asked Rufus eagerly, leaning towards them.

"A turtle!" the brothers said in unison and Evastus' eyelid twitched again.

"A huge rock turtle," Delvin added, spreading his arms as wide as they would go.

"Dag-gum!" said Lenny. "I done seen them things. Some of 'em are big as blasted hills!"

"This one was," Evastus agreed. "It was so big we thought the mountain was crashing down on us!"

"We didn't have much time to think," Chester said. "So me and Delvin picked up the merchant's wagon and carried it off of the trail."

"Just in time too," said Delvin and Evastus' eye twitched again. "The turtle nearly hit us. It still squished one of the horses."

Rufus hand went to his mouth. "Ouch!"

"Wonder what could get such a big thing tumblin' down the mountainside," Lenny mused.

The three brothers chuckled and Chester said, "We think it just stepped too close to a cliff and fell off. Wanna know why?"

"When it rolled past us, its big floppy head looked right at me," said Evastus. "And it looked so embarrassed!"

They all roared out in laughter and Evastus' eyelid quivered with each bellow.

Squirrel chose that moment to skitter swiftly up Edge's body and crouch on his shoulder. The creature might have been old for his kind, but he could still move swiftly when he wanted to. Fist was already asleep in his bedroll nearby, but Squirrel still managed to send his thoughts through the ogre's side of the bond. *Do you see that?*

I do, Edge replied mentally.

As do I, said Deathclaw, who was peering down from a tree overlooking the camp. He was uneasy, watching them with one hand on a throwing dagger, as if at any moment they might attack.

What do you think it means? Squirrel asked. No sooner had Squirrel asked the question, than the other two orc brothers began to exhibit a similar eyelid twitch, but from their left eyes.

Perhaps they are breaking, Deathclaw said. The twitching was done in concert, all three eyelids moving at the same time.

Squirrel nodded quickly. *Yes, that would make sense since the two bigger ones are already dead.*

Why do you keep saying that? Edge asked.

I can smell it, Squirrel said. *Like a body that's just starting to decay.*

I don't smell that, Deathclaw disagreed, confident that he couldn't possibly miss something like that. *They have an odor, but that is just the smell of unwashed orc.*

Maybe I have become more Deathclaw than you, Squirrel suggested smugly.

Perhaps it's time I talk to them about this, Edge replied. As he said this, a sudden chill breeze blew through the bond and Edge sensed that a pair of ice blue eyes were peering through his own.

How interesting, said Artemus' wizened voice within his mind.

Edge smiled. *Artemus!*

You are awake a bit earlier than usual, Deathclaw observed.

Indeed, the wizard said. *Since our last engagement, the elemental and I have come to an arrangement.*

Is that so? Edge said. He was unsure whether this was going to be good news. The last time Artemus had wakened, the old wizard had been unable to keep the Scralag completely at bay. *When we last spoke, you said that the time for you to use your powers solely to protect others had passed.*

Artemus took a moment to respond. *Yes. This is true. Our purpose will soon be at hand. The elemental knows this and has agreed to . . . work with me.*

He has? said Edge. *In what way?*

I have agreed to use him in battle and he has agreed to leave me be when I decide that his presence is not needed, said the ancient wizard.

Good! said Squirrel.

Edge was less enthusiastic. *Last time you used the Scralag's presence, you rushed into battle on your own.*

Artemus let out a sigh. *Yes, well, his ability to cooperate is a work in progress. I do believe it will get better.*

Does this mean you won't have to sleep for weeks every time you fight? Deathclaw asked.

I am not completely certain, the wizard replied. *The elemental will still need to rest to recharge our power, but perhaps I will be able to remain awake and present.*

I would like that, Edge said. Even if Artemus wasn't able to use his power, his presence within the bond was always a welcome one. The wizard often saw and understood things that passed the rest of them by.

Artemus shifted his attention back on the three twitching orcs. *I see you have a new companion.*

Three of them, Edge said and sent the wizard his memories of everything that he had noticed about the brothers through the bond. *I know that Delvin and Chester are somehow living without the use of their souls, and that they are all somehow connected but their exact nature eludes me.*

You don't see the spirit magic that connects them? Artemus asked.

I've looked for it before. Edge switched to spirit sight, but nothing about them particularly stood out.

Artemus let out an amused grunt. *It seems that my existence as a being of pure spirit has some advantages after all. There is a faint line of magic that leads from Evastus to the others. Perhaps if you get closer you will see it.*

I'll look too, said Squirrel. He hopped down from Edge's shoulder and scurried over to the three warwielders.

His curiosity piqued, Edge walked over to them. The twitching was even more obvious than before. Rufus hadn't noticed. He was laughing at some joke they had made, slapping the ground with a huge hand.

Lenny, however, was watching them with one bushy eyebrow raised. "You boys alright?" the dwarf asked them.

Delvin and Chester cocked their heads. "What do you mean?"

Lenny pointed. "Yer eyes are twitchin' somethin' fierce."

The three orcs raised their hands over the affected eyes. "Oh, that just means we're tired," they said in unison.

"You sure?" Lenny said. "Yer eyelids are flappin' like gad-flamed shutters in a windstorm."

"It'll be better in the morning," Evastus assured him and the other two brothers nodded.

While they were speaking, Edge walked around behind them. Artemus spoke encouragingly in his mind. *Look at the back of their necks. That seems to be the source of the magic.*

Oh! I see! Squirrel had climbed up to Chester's shoulder and was pointing directly to a cluster of runic tattoos on the back of his neck right at the base of his bald head. *Spirit runes.*

Interesting, said Artemus.

Edge leaned in closer, his eyes straining, and he was just able to make out a very faint line of silvery gray magic leaving the base of Evastus' head and entering the runes on the backs of his brothers' necks. Lenny saw Edge's close inspection and sent an odd look his way. Evastus noticed the dwarf's gaze shift and turned to look back over his shoulder, one hand still covering his twitching eye.

"What're you looking at, Friend Sir Edge?" he asked with a slight frown.

Edge gave him a disarming smile. "Oh, I was just appreciating your tattoos. Uh, I hadn't seen the one on the back of your necks before."

The three brothers reached up with their other hands and covered the back of their necks. Squirrel had to jump down to avoid being smashed by Chester's large hand.

"That's private," they said together and stood, disturbed looks on their faces. "We are going to sleep now."

They took a few steps away from the fire and lay down in their usual night time formation. The three of them laid on their backs in a row, shoulder-to-shoulder, and closed their eyes. They didn't sleep in bedrolls or even use a blanket. They didn't need to. Some of the runes on their skin kept the night's chill away and other runes made them tough enough that they didn't mind the odd rock or stick jabbing into their backs.

Lenny walked up to him and in a loud whisper said, "Touched a nerve there, Son."

"Ooh!" Rufus agreed and through the bond said. *They were mad.*

"I noticed," Edge said.

"Maybe some things ain't worth bein' curious 'bout," Lenny observed and patted Edge's arm before heading to his own bedroll.

Edge wasn't sure he agreed. Evidently the nature of the orcs' connection was something Evastus wanted to keep quiet, but he was paying them a lot of money. If he was going to depend on them in battle it would be best if he understood how the three of them worked in concert.

He went to sleep that night with concerns about the brothers still burning in his mind. The next day, the three orcs acted like nothing was wrong. Their eye twitch was gone, and they seemed to have forgiven Edge for prying into the nature of their runes. The day began as any other and the party was quickly back onto the scent of Jhonate and the thief.

They traveled for three more days, reaching the outer edge of Razbeck. The air grew more and more hot as they left the tree-filled countryside and passed into the rocky wildlands to the north. It was at this point that it became evident that their run of good weather had come to an end.

On their first afternoon in the wildlands, the wind picked up and dark clouds rushed across the western horizon towards them. They came to the top of a rise and Edge could see that torrential rain obscured the landscape ahead of them in a thick mist. Lightning sparkled through the oncoming storm followed seconds later by booming thunder.

"This is gonna be a gusher!" Lenny yelled. "We don't wanna be tryin' to track in the middle of that."

"Get over to those rocks." Fist said, pointing to a cluster of tall boulders just off of the road. "Rufus and I have a trick we've developed for just this sort of occasion."

"Ooh!" said Rufus in excitement.

The rogue horse stepped off of the roadway and Fist and Edge climbed down from his back. Then Rufus stood next to the rocks and began to grow in size. But he didn't grow proportionately this time. His arms and lion-like rear legs lengthened and while his body rose above everyone else, he also caused his torso and rear end to widen. His skin and bones stretched, his internal structure adapting to fit this new shape. Soon the black and tan rogue horse was nearly as wide as he was tall.

Lenny grimaced at the absurdity of it. "Yer turnin' Monkeyface into a gad-burned rain shelter?"

"He likes it," Fist assured the dwarf. Rufus' leonine tail was certainly wagging happily.

Trevor H. Cooley

The ogre then enacted a spell to go along with Rufus' transformation. He sent thick cords of earth magic up from the ground to travel up the rogue horse's thick arms and rear legs. Then he tied the cords of magic together and spread them in a net-like structure across Rufus' back to act as grounding wires to protect him and the rest of the party from lightning strikes.

When they were finished, the rogue horse's underside was nine feet off of the ground. There was just enough room for the entire party to huddle under him just as the storm hit. Everyone did so, even Lenny's horse, who took some coaxing to stand under this strange hairy shelter.

The land around them darkened with the approach of the water-laden clouds, and the storm struck with a roar of wind and falling rain. The rocks around them kept the worst of the wind away, but even Rufus' new form couldn't stop the rain that blew in sideways. Edge's legs and back were drenched, but fortunately the worst of the wind was soon over and they were left standing under a ridiculous torrent of water.

Rufus put his big head down to look at them, his wet hair clinging to face. He grinned widely at them, his face upside down as rain poured off of him in sheets. "I'm wet!" he huffed in his staccato voice.

"Dag-gum!" said Lenny, who was standing next to Albert, doing his best to keep the horse calm. "It smells like the world's biggest wet dog under here!"

"Not a dog!" Rufus protested with a frown.

"I didn't say you *was* a dog," Lenny replied. "I said you smelt like one, you hairy half ape!"

"Oh," said the rogue horse, feeling much better about the insult.

Lightning continued to crackle overhead and there was a strike not far away. The bolt hit the ground with a booming report that caused Albert to whinny nervously. Fist's magical protections weren't needed, but Edge was certainly glad they were in place.

The Bash Brothers were the ones standing closest to his face and they reached out to pat his upside-down head in approval. "You make a good shelter, Rufus," they said in unison.

The rogue horse's smile returned. "Yes! I'm wide."

Edge once again felt the chill presence of his great grandfather's thoughts through the bond. *I have been giving some thought to these Bash Brothers,* the wizard said. *I have a theory about them and it is a bit disturbing.*

Edge looked over at the three affable brothers who were continuing their conversation with Rufus. *Go ahead,* he sent, and he made sure the rest of his bonded were listening in.

Warwielders are rare among orcs. They are mostly found in the orc capitol in Khalpany, the ancient wizard began. *They are the apex of their race and are treated like royalty over there.*

Edge thought he could see where Artemus was going with this. *So it's strange that three of them would be wandering around as mercenaries.*

Indeed, it is. Why are they not commanders of orc armies or living a pampered life being tended to by human slaves? Artemus asked.

Perhaps they were banished for crimes in their city, Deathclaw suggested. The raptoid was crouched next to Edge. He wasn't happy about sheltering under Rufus, but he didn't wish to remain out in that heavy rain.

Or they chose to leave that life voluntarily, Artemus posited. *Whatever the reason may be, for the three of them to go through such an experience and stay together means that they are very close.*

That much is evident, Edge agreed.

In the memories you shared with me, Lenny told you he had heard that two of them had died, is that correct? Artemus said.

Yes, sent Fist. He wasn't as worried about the nature of the Bash Brothers as Edge was, but he was just as curious. *And from what we have learned about their spirits we can only assume that Evastus was the survivor.*

He is seemingly the youngest of them, added Deathclaw. *And he is definitely the smartest.*

Imagine his state of mind if his two older brothers were killed, said Artemus.

Fist gave the orcs a sympathetic glance. *He would have been devastated.*

Indeed, and I imagine that this grief-stricken warwielder brought his brothers' corpses to a powerful wizard, likely one that dabbled with the darker side of magic, Artemus continued.

Edge nodded. *We know that they have access to at least one powerful wizard. And even if it wasn't Ghazardblast, there are usually wizards of that nature in Khalpany.*

Whoever it was had to be extremely knowledgeable in spirit magic. And evil because what I believe the wizard agreed to do to them is stomach churning, Artemus said. *He managed to restore their bodies to health, and covered them with those intricate protective runes, but obviously it was too late to return their souls.*

The wizard let out a morbid chuckle. *I know that it sounds strange coming from an old soul that's living in his great grandson's chest, but dead is dead. Once a spirit leaves its body, it can't be returned.*

Then how are they breathing? Edge asked. He had already guessed much of what Artemus was suggesting, but this was a sticking point in his mind. The practice bodies that the Mage School wizards kept alive had to be constantly monitored and the spells that did the work were replaced daily. The bodies' organs would stop working otherwise.

The wizard bound the spirits of some kind of creatures to their bodies, Artemus explained. *They could have been cows*

269

or some other large beast. The creatures didn't have to be very intelligent, he wasn't intending to use their minds, just their life force to keep their blood pumping.

Using the souls of animals to keep bodies alive with binding magic . . . said Fist in awe. *It's unethical but I can see how it would work.*

Deathclaw hissed in disgust at the idea. *Then how do they talk and act like living orcs, even if they are stupid ones?*

I'm getting to that. Evastus would have wanted his brothers back as they had once been, but since the wizard couldn't do that, he was left with few options. Now I don't know if this was Evastus' suggestion or if he was tricked into it by the wizard but, and this is the most disturbing part, said Artemus. *What he did was insert magical devices inside them that connected their bodies to their younger brother. I've been puzzling over the runes at the base of their heads and that's what they tell me. Evastus' mind controls both of them.*

You mean he just uses them like . . . puppets? Edge said, aghast.

To his mind, their bodies are an extension of his, Artemus explained. *It likely took a long time for him to figure out how to move them independently. It requires him to split his reflexes in three directions.*

It sounds impossible, piped in Squirrel, who was warm and dry in his pouch at Fist's side.

Edge knew what kind of mental acrobatics it took to communicate to multiple people while keeping track of his own actions. It had been very difficult at first, but he had gotten used to it over the years and it came instinctually to him now. Nevertheless, trying something like what Evastus was doing would be a great stress on anyone's mind.

This explains why they often talk in unison, he sent. *And it explains the facial tic he got the other night.*

But for him to pretend that his brothers are alive? That is insanity, said Deathclaw.

Edge tried to put himself in Evastus' shoes. He was grief-stricken and lonely and now had control of his brother's bodies. He could see how tempting it would be to carry on conversations with them no matter how wrong it was. *Do you think he's still aware that this is what he's doing, or has he become completely crazy?*

From the way he acts, he has to be crazy at this point, Artemus said.

I'm not so certain, Fist said, watching the three orcs conversing with Rufus' upside-down face. *I think he tries to forget that they are dead, but there are times that you can tell he is aware of it.*

Like the other night when he got upset at me for looking at his runes, Edge said.

The main question you should ask yourself is can someone that is both this powerful and this unhinged be trusted? Artemus asked.

Edge wasn't sure and at this point neither were any of the others.

The Bash Brothers noticed that everyone was staring at them and instinctively covered the backs of their necks. "What? Are our eyes twitching again?"

"Naw," Lenny assured them. "Yer fine. I don't know what these goofuses are gawkin' at."

"We were just thinking," Fist said.

"About how all the tracks are messed up now?" Evastus asked.

"Yeah," said Edge and that was certainly a huge concern.

A rain this intense would destroy all evidence of scents or tracks. Unless they could pick up the trail again, the only thing they knew for certain was Jhonate's end goal. Hopefully the thief didn't have other plans.

The storm passed over them a short time later and the heat of the day returned with an intensity that filled the air with

271

mist as the water evaporated. Edge and the others walked out from under Rufus and while the rogue horse resumed his usual shape, they stepped out onto the misty road. For the moment, every depression in the landscape was filled with pools of water that would be quickly absorbed by the parched earth.

Soon the sun's rays banished the lingering mist and revealed that their party was not alone on the muddy road. Edge found himself looking at four drenched pilgrims of unlikely size. The dripping gray cloaks that they wore obscured their identities, but each of them was nearly seven feet tall and heavily muscled.

The pilgrims gasped when they saw him. "Sir Edge!" Cried one of them and his voice was strangely familiar. "What a surprise."

They threw back their hoods to reveal faces that were a seeming mishmash of different races, not one of them the same. One was part human with greenish skin, another part elf, but with sharp teeth. One of them was a female with beady red eyes. Other than their size, the only other thing they had in common was a slight sheen of slime that covered their skin.

The one who had spoken took a step closer to him. He appeared to be part human, but had light green hair and reptilian scales covered part of his face. His eyes were slitted and yellow. He smiled. "You do remember me, don't you, Sir Edge?"

Edge's eyes widened as he realized why he knew the voice. "Aldie?"

This was the last place he had expected to find trollkin.

Chapter Twenty Three
Sir Edge – Recollections

"Is that Sir Lance's boy?" asked Lenny, hurrying up to stand beside Edge.

Aldie smiled at the dwarf, exposing a set of teeth that were trollish and sharp up top, but human on the bottom. He shook the dwarf's hand with his large clawed hand. "Yes, Mr. Firegobbler, Sir. I didn't know if I'd ever see you again."

"Well hell, Son," Lenny said, patting the sopping-wet, part-reptile trollkin on the arm. "It's good to see you, too."

"Aldie!" said Fist as he and Deathclaw came over to join Edge and Lenny with the four trollkin. They knew Aldie fairly well.

Aldie had once been a human Battle Academy student before he had gone to Malaroo with Edge years ago. He had been swallowed by the Troll Mother, a god-like troll behemoth that lived under the swamps. She had rebirthed him as one of her trollkin, which were amalgamations of trolls and other beasts. The Troll Mother had swallowed and changed thousands of people and animals of different races before Edge and his companions had managed to destroy her.

The part-reptile trollkin greeted both of them warmly. "It's so rare that I get to see the friends I made before I became trollkin."

Rufus and the Bash Brothers walked up to join them. The orcs looked at the trollkin with curiosity. "What are these wet people?" they said in unison.

"They're called trollkin," Lenny said.

"What are they?" asked Aldie, looking back up at the brothers and their huge clubs with alarm.

"They're just orcs," Lenny assured him.

"Aldie, what are you four doing way up here in the wildlands?" Edge asked. They were a long way from the city of KhanzaRoo where the trollkin people lived.

Aldie looked a bit embarrassed as he answered. "Well, uh-." He gestured at the other trollkin. "Bernard and Ebner and Meg, and-uh me, are pilgrims now."

"We can see that by how yer dressed," Lenny pointed out. "Why?"

Aldie blinked at them as if the answer was self-evident. "To get our curses removed. Lots of us trollkin have joined the movement."

Edge frowned slightly. He wasn't a proponent of the pilgrim movement. He didn't feel that it was his place to judge, but the vast majority of the people who were traveling around were simply wasting years of their lives. Only a small number of the them had actual curses and of those, he doubted that any would find healing in this manner. Even if the holy sites had healing properties, the guardians that protected the sites didn't let random people through. These pilgrims just got as close to the sites as they could and then turned around.

Fist had similar thoughts. "But what you have isn't a regular kind of curse."

"What else would you call it?" Aldie said.

"Well, curses are generally caused by evil spirit magic," Fist said, and he gestured as he explained. "In your case, what happened is that the behemoth digested you. Then it mixed the very building blocks of your bodies with troll tissue, grew you a new body, and then put your soul back in it." He shrugged regretfully. "I'm sorry, but there isn't a curse to break. The Mage School has worked with your king and looked into every solution, but there is no cure. Your original bodies are . . . gone."

Lenny gave the ogre a dumbfounded look. "Dag-gum, Son. That's a cold way to put it."

Fist winced and glanced back at Aldie. "I apologize if I offended you. I just didn't want you to continue travelling all this way without knowing what you were up against."

If they were discouraged by the ogre's doubt, they didn't show it. "We understand what happened to us, and we're not looking for a cure," said Meg, the female trollkin. "We're looking for a miracle."

Aldie smiled at her and patted her shoulder. "When pilgrims first started showing up in Malaroo wanting to see the Jharro Grove, we heard their stories and realized that they had the only possible answer. Since no one else is able to fix our problem, why not seek out the Creator's help?"

Edge did his best not to grimace at the idea. The Creator didn't directly intervene in the lives of the races. He sent the prophets to do that. Of course, who was he to judge? Hadn't he just spent months listening to his rune and trying to follow the Creator's will? Wasn't his wife right now traveling to a holy site hoping to break her own curse?

He sighed. "Does your king approve of this?"

"It's not his favorite plan," admitted the half-elf trollkin that Aldie had referred to as Bernard.

Edge hadn't thought it would be. The Troll King was a good ruler. He wouldn't want them wasting their lives on false hope. He watched out for his people and knew that their condition wasn't something that could be fixed.

"But he knows about it. He said he wouldn't stop us," Aldie added, nudging Bernard with his elbow. "And the other pilgrims are really nice. They know what it's like to be cursed. They don't shun us for the way we look." He noted the lack of encouragement in Edge's eyes and gestured at the female trollkin. "And-and it's been working. Meg's slime has started to go away."

"It has!" said the trollkin with the beady red eyes. She stuck out her hand and slime dripped from her skin in long stringy ribbons. Meg looked at her hand and hurriedly put it down. "Oh, well it's like this right now, but it's been much better lately. E-ever since we stopped at the barrier."

Any reduction in her slime was likely due to dehydration, Artemus observed coolly. *The air out here is abysmally dry.*

"Have you been out to the barrier, Sir Edge?" Aldie asked.

"No," Edge began, but the trollkin cut him off in excitement.

"Oh! It's amazing," Bernard said.

Aldie nodded. "There's this place where the air just shimmers and when you reach out and touch it, your whole body just vibrates. It's a feeling that's so unique."

"It's a feelin' that's tellin' you that if you keep pushing on the barrier, it's gonna vibrate yer dag-blamed skin off!" Lenny said disapprovingly. "Folks should stay away from it."

Meg scoffed. "We're smart enough not to touch it for long. All pilgrims know that. We mainly go there in hopes of seeing one of the Khobareth."

"I don't know if I believe that part," said Bernard.

Deathclaw cocked his head in partial recognition of the word. It seemed to mean something to Artemus too, because he let out a contemplative hum.

Edge pursed his lips. As much as he liked seeing Aldie again, this conversation was getting them nowhere. "Well, we'll let you continue on your pilgrimage. We are in a hurry ourselves."

"Oh," said Aldie, looking a bit disappointed. "Are you trying to catch up with your wife?"

Edge froze. "You saw her? Where?"

Bernard's eyebrows rose in surprise at his reaction. He pointed up the road northward. "Uh, just on the far side of Hoolahan Crossing."

"Hoolahan Crossin'?" said Lenny. "Never heard of it. That a village or somethin'?"

"It's a pilgrim tent city," Aldie explained. He peered back the way he had come. "You can't see it from here because of all the steam, but it's huge. You can't miss it. Just stay on the road for a few miles and you'll get there. She was camped on the northern outskirts with another person. We wanted to stop and talk to her, but she was asleep when we went by and a man yelled at us and told us to leave."

"Are you certain it was her?" asked Deathclaw.

All four trollkin nodded in response. "We could never forget our king's favorite sister," said Meg.

"I saw her braids and green ribbons," Bernard added.

"Are they still there?" Edge pressed.

"I-I don't think so. We hung around a little while and saw them packing up to leave," Aldie said, taken aback by the intensity in his eyes. "Is she okay? Do you want us to go with you?"

Edge considered it. The trollkin were formidable allies. They were strong and the behemoth had given them regenerative abilities that allowed them to shrug off fearsome wounds. That could come in handy when they had to face the holy site's guardians.

Nevertheless, he shook his head. He couldn't ask them to put their lives on the line for his sake. "Thank you for offering, Aldie, but it's dangerous and I don't know how long this will take."

"Oh," said Aldie slowly. "Are you going into the Whitebridge?"

"I'm fairly certain we'll have to," Edge replied.

Aldie nodded. "At least let us give you something that could help." He held his hand out to the fourth trollkin, Ebner. The part-human gave him a surprised look. Aldie gestured urgently. "Come on. The orb."

Meg put a hand on Aldie's arm. "Are you sure?"

"It's been useful to us, but this is for the king's sister," Aldie said.

Meg licked her lips, but dropped her hand. "Give it to him, Ebner."

Blinking, Ebner reached within his cloak and pulled out an object that Edge recognized right away. It was a wooden ball, perfectly round and polished. There were no visible runes on its surface, but as it came into view, Edge could feel the bewitching magic radiating from it.

The three warwielders flinched as they felt it. "What is that?" asked Evastus.

"It's a talisman," said Aldie. "It repels insects and predators. It won't stop anything smart, but it will keep away much of the nastiness in the desert."

The prophet Matthew had made several of these items and had used them to protect a small village from the mindless aggression of trolls. During the war against the Troll Mother, Matthew had given Deathclaw one to help him travel through the swamps unmolested. Edge wondered if the Troll King knew that Aldie had taken this. "Are you certain you can part with this?"

"We were gonna use it to get through the desert ourselves so that we could stand before the stair to Alsarobeth," said Bernard. "But when we got there, uh."

Aldie cleared his throat. "We thought about it, but everyone says not to. It's really dangerous and really hot."

"And dry," added Meg. "Also, the orb won't chase away dragons."

Edge took it from Ebner reverently. "Thank you. All four of you. I'll tell Jhonate of your generosity."

Aldie smiled. "I hope you find her soon."

"Me too," said Meg.

"Good luck!" added Bernard.

The fourth trollkin gave him an encouraging gesture but said nothing. Perhaps it couldn't speak.

Edge gestured to the rest of the party and they continued down the road towards the sweltering rocky valley. The ground still steamed in places, but most of the puddles left by the rain storm had already evaporated, leaving the dirt surface of the landscape cracked.

Deathclaw lingered behind for a moment and approached Aldie. "You have been to the barrier at the edge of the Known Lands. How were you able to do this without crossing the desert?"

"Oh, there's many places where you can reach the barrier in this world," Aldie said.

Deathclaw gave him a dull look. Of course, he knew that. The barrier surrounded the Known Lands after all. The Trollkin had intimated that they had done so here in the north.

"We went around the Whitebridge," Meg explained. "If you reach the stream at the edge of the desert, you can follow it east until you almost get to the Wide River. Then there's a safe route north to the barrier. Most of the pilgrims go that way."

Deathclaw let out a disappointed hiss. Without saying another word, he moved past them and hurried to catch up with the others, leaving the trollkin standing there perplexed.

Now that Edge knew a place where Jhonate and the thief had last been seen, Edge was in no mood to tarry. He had Fist tell Rufus to grow so that he, Fist, and Deathclaw could ride him. Then he handed the orb to Deathclaw and the raptoid put it away in one of his bags.

"What're you doin, Son?" Lenny asked as he watched the rogue horse extending the length of his back so that Deathclaw could fit.

"We're going to rush ahead to the tent city," Edge explained. "If we get lucky, we might find someone who knows exactly where they were headed. You and the Bash Brothers can meet us there."

"Sure," said Lenny with a frown. "But why don't we just hurry there together?"

"Yeah. We can run really fast," Evastus assured him.

Edge let out a frustrated sigh. "Because with Fist's power we can get there faster. Every minute that goes by makes it less likely we'll find someone who saw them." He didn't bother to add the fact that if he didn't get there as quick as he could, his head might explode.

"There is no use trying to talk him out of it when he gets like this," Deathclaw said as he leapt up to perch on Rufus' leonine back end.

The dwarf's frown deepened into a scowl. "I hear you, but dag-blast it, what if you catch the trail and get too far ahead of us? We ain't the trackers in this group."

"Well, that's where your new connection with Edge will come in handy," said Fist, pointing to his temple. "You won't be able to lose track of us."

"It's a good test of the magic," Edge agreed and called out mentally for Rufus to run ahead.

"What's he talking about?" Chester asked the dwarf.

Lenny hurried over to Albert and climbed up into the saddle. "He's sayin' we'd better well get our dag-gum arses in gear so's we don't get left behind."

Rufus rushed down the road in a full-on gallop. The rogue horse's large size was the only thing that kept him from sliding on the road's still-muddy patches. Still, it was a rougher ride than usual. Deathclaw was forced to grab onto Fist's robes to keep his balance.

Alright, Fist, Edge said through the bond. *Now.*

Fist hesitated before using his power. *Are you sure you want me to do this?* he asked Edge through the bond. *If we use up too much of Rufus' energy he won't have it when we need it.*

It's just to get us to the city, Edge said. *I'm tired of being patient.*

The ogre grinned. *Then I suggest you hold on tight.*

Edge wisely grabbed a double fistful of the mane that ran down Rufus back.

Fist reached into his bond with the rogue horse and tapped into the vast well of power within him. Then he reached into his connection with his mace and its quickening power. *Are you ready, Rufus?*

"Ooh-ooh! Yes!" Rufus huffed. Fist connected the two magics and poured speed into the rogue horse.

Edge's stomach lurched as Rufus darted forward, his arms and rear legs a blur. The landscape passed quickly by them and he found himself laughing as they careened down the road. This is the kind of speed he had wanted to move in from the moment he had felt Jhonate's presence leave the ring on his finger.

Deathclaw wasn't quite as happy with the ride. Edge was sitting in the most stable place on Rufus' back, while the raptoid was crouched on the rogue horse's rear haunches. Deathclaw was bounced and jostled and he instinctually gripped into the tan fur of Rufus' rear with his talon-like claws.

"Ouch!" Rufus bellowed.

Sorry, Deathclaw replied, but he didn't dare loosen his grip. Fist sent his thoughts into Rufus' body and caused the skin on his back to thicken and toughen so that it no longer hurt.

In contrast to the frantic speed of the rogue horse, Artemus spoke coolly in Edge's mind. *While I slept, I remembered more about Alsarobeth. Edge, we do not want a servant of the Dark Prophet to reach that place.*

Edge's interest was piqued. He hadn't expected the wizard to have more knowledge about the holy site, but he shouldn't have been surprised. Despite regaining his sanity, spending two centuries as a frost elemental had caused Artemus to forget many things.

Hopefully we catch up to them before they get there, Edge said.

If we do, and the thief is exposed, will Jhonate still wish to go there?

I guarantee she will, Edge replied. She would still want to meet with Seer Rahan after all. *Why? What have you remembered?*

Sarine and I went there with John once, Artemus said.

Edge was intrigued, but not surprised by the development. Artemus had been one of the Prophet's companions before the Dark Prophet's priestess of war had killed him. *You saw it?*

No, said Artemus. *My memory of those events is fuzzy, but I do recall that John had us wait at the entrance while he went up to commune with his master.*

Is there anything else about it that you can remember? Edge asked.

The wizard grunted to himself. *I remember that John impressed upon us how important the site was. I . . .* His tone became frustrated. *There was more. I know there was! It is not a place one should approach lightly. I shall meditate on it more. Perhaps I can wring more from my dusty mind.*

Thank you, Great Grandfather, Edge replied.

There it is, said Rufus from within the bond. He sounded disappointed that the ride was coming to an end.

The tent city of Hoolahan Crossing spread across the rock-strewn horizon like a white blanket. If not for the hazy distortions caused by the heat, he might have thought it was snow.

"Huh," Edge said. He had seen larger encampments before, enormous armies awaiting battle. This one was impressive in a different way. These were people of every race and nationality, united for a purpose other than war. Perhaps he had been too dismissive of these pilgrims.

Fist released Rufus from his mace's magic as they drew near to the city and the three bonded slid down from the rogue horse's back. "A peaceful encampment," said Fist, echoing his thoughts. "Impressive."

"This is no proper encampment," Deathclaw replied, his upper lip curled.

Edge's rising level of respect for these people only lasted until they entered the city. Then he understood Deathclaw's distaste. The smell of the place was the first thing Edge's heightened senses picked up. It was foul.

In a military encampment, soldiers were ordered to dispose of their waste in proper fashion. In this city, there was little to no oversight in such things. He saw many children running around the city's outskirts and hoped dearly that their families wouldn't stay long before moving on. Disease was likely to run rampant.

"Stinks!" said Rufus with a shake of his head.

"These people need proper leadership," Fist said.

Edge agreed. The cause that kept these people together was too tenuous for such things. There was little order to this place until they entered the center of town and stepped into the bazaar. Now Edge understood the true reason this tent city existed.

The bustling center of the city was a merchant's paradise. Tents with colorful entrances lined the road. They could sell whatever they wanted, charge whatever they wanted, even swindle who they wished. There was no oversight here. There was no police force to enforce laws. There were only the mercenary guards standing at the entrances to the largest tents.

Between each merchant tent, lesser sellers hawked their wares, yelling out to passers-by. Edge wondered how long this place would be able to exist. Did the humble pilgrims that came through here have enough gold to make it worth their while?

Fist looked around at the vendors with curiosity, but Deathclaw hated the place more than Edge did. He never had liked being in such a tight press of people. Fortunately, the tight press of people managed to leave a gap between themselves and Edge's frightening bonded. Even the vendors took one look at their party and decided that it wasn't worth bothering them.

Let's continue to the north side of the city, Edge sent. He had intended to ask around and see if anyone had seen Jhonate passing through, but she wouldn't have lingered in this place. Even if she had decided to buy something, she wouldn't have revealed anything about herself.

When they made their way out of the bazaar area Edge felt a sense of relief. The northern side of the city was a more orderly place. The tents were spaced farther apart and it didn't stink as much as the southern side. He wasn't sure why there was such a delineation. Perhaps there was leadership in parts of the city.

They continued down the road looking for any evidence of a site that had been recently vacated. If they could determine where Jhonate had been, they'd have a better chance of finding someone who had spoken to her.

Edge's determination faded as the light of the day waned. He and Fist began to ask around at different campsites, but if anyone had seen her, they refused to talk. These pilgrims were protective of each other and Edge and Fist were obviously not part of their movement. He began to regret his decision to deny Aldie's offer of help. If they had brought the trollkin with them, not only would they have been able to find the right spot, but people might have been more willing to talk.

284

Without finding the actual site where Jhonate had stayed the night before, the close press of people kept Deathclaw and Rufus from picking up any scents. It grew obvious that their best bet was to get away from the city and try to find their trail once more. They decided to make camp just outside the city.

Lenny and the Bash Brothers caught up to them just before dark. All four of them looked weary. Evastus' eye was already starting to twitch.

"There you are, you arse-headed nose-lifter!" Lenny barked as soon as Albert drew close enough for Edge to hear. "You better've learned somethin' to make this rushin' 'round worth it!"

"Nope," said Rufus. Edge just gave him a dull look.

Shaking his head, Lenny climbed down from his horse and began to unload his things near the fireside so that he could start dinner. "Sorry to hear it, Son."

Edge sighed. "We'll make it a short night and keep moving down the road in the morning."

"At least, you found us okay," said Fist, heading over to help the dwarf with his preparations.

Lenny shrugged. "It weren't hard at all. I could feel where you was the whole time. To tell you the truth, I could even kinda tell it weren't goin' so well."

"Then why did you ride up acting so surprised?" Fist asked.

"I wanted to give you ignorant log heads a hard time, but yer dag-gum sad puppy faces took the fun out of it," the dwarf grumped.

Lenny made a quick stew of dried beef and spices and tossed in a special sort of rice that he had purchased in the tent city. It fluffed up quickly in the pot, absorbing the water almost instantly.

The Bash Brothers seemed to be in a funk. Rufus approached them wanting to joke or wrestle, but they waved him off. When dinner was ready, they walked up and ate their share, then went promptly to lie down.

"Are you three okay?" Edge asked.

"Just tired," they said in unison, then closed their eyes.

Chester and Delvin began to snore right away. Edge figured that it was best not to press the issue and returned to the fireside to refill his bowl. As usual, Lenny's cooking was both flavorful and filling. Edge had even grown to appreciate the heat from the added spices.

As Lenny ladled some of the meat and rice into his bowl, he said, "You know, Edge, I'm kinda gettin' used to the idear of this new bond we got."

"Really?" Edge asked.

"Yeah," Lenny said and picked up his own bowl. He took a bite and talked between chews. "I like that it lets me keep track of you without yer thoughts messin' 'round in my gall-durn mind."

"That is convenient," Edge agreed with a smile.

"Also it gives me a good excuse. You know, I love my life with my family and workin' the forge. Even dealin' with the Academy fer the Wobble dwarves ain't so bad most days." He hesitated and took another bite. "But there's times when I get restless and I just got to get out and stretch by gad-flamin' legs."

"I know," said Edge. "Everybody knows. It's just part of who you are. Even the other dwarves respect it."

Lenny blinked as if surprised by that remark. "Yeah, well Bettie gives me an ear full of hell every time I start thinkin' about getting' away fer a while."

"And yet she let you come with me here," Edge pointed out.

"That's just cause it's you and it's Jhonate," Lenny said. "But that's what makes this bond thing so good. I can head out with you more often without getting my con-sarned head bit off. But now any time I gotta head out, I can just say it's that bond again and you need me. She's bonded to Tollivar. She knows what it's like."

Edge chuckled. She was bonded to Tollivar, but Tollivar was the most laid-back bonding wizard Edge had met. Bettie and Willum both lived far away from him and he rarely asked them all to get together. He didn't point that out to Lenny though.

"Well, good," he said, patting the dwarf's shoulder. "I'm always happy to have you around and now you'll always know how to find me."

I'm not so certain, said Artemus' chill voice in Edge's mind. *The nature of your connection to the dwarf is puzzling. I don't believe it is a true permanent bond, though the way your magic keeps inspecting it, maybe it wants to be.*

Maybe it will grow stronger, Edge said. *At first, Lenny could sense me but I couldn't sense him back. Now I'm getting a sense of what direction he's in. That tells me it's strengthening. I don't know why this happened when I healed him, but I think it's a good thing.*

It may be, said Artemus. *Unfortunately, such things are not up to you. The Creator chooses the bonded. If you were meant to bond with Lenui Firegobbler, it would have happened already. I'm not trying to discourage you. I just want to make sure that you're not too surprised if you wake up one morning to realize that his bond has faded.*

Yeah. Thanks, Edge said irritably. He liked the idea of Lenny joining the bonded family.

When Edge went to sleep that night, his dreams were troubled. He dreamt that he spent days and days following Jhonate's tracks, but he never got any closer. When Edge woke up to Artemus' excited voice in his mind it felt as if he had been chasing after her for ages.

I remembered something else about Alsarobeth! the wizard said. *And it is crucial information.*

Edge rolled over in his bedroll, still groggy as the dreams slowly faded from his thoughts. It was early. The stars were just beginning to fade. He let out a soft groan. *Good. What is it?*

Because of Alsarobeth's importance to our world, it was given two separate sets of guardians to protect it, Artemus said.

Head Wizard Valtrek told us that much, Edge replied with a sigh. He tried to blink the sleep from his eyes. He was still so tired. His limbs felt leaden. *Do you remember what they were like?*

The guardians closest to the site are hungry relentless monsters and they assault you mentally as they attack, the wizard said. *Even though Sarine and I did not pass the perimeter of their domain, we could hear them in our minds. It was quite an unpleasant day.*

They sounded like the guardians Hilt had run into at the top of the mountain where he had met Beth. But that had been far away in Dremaldria. *Is there anything else you can remember about them? Were you able to catch a glimpse of them?*

The wizard thought. *Uh . . . I'm not completely certain. I vaguely remember seeing shapes in cave entrances all around the stone stairs. Their mental calls tormented us mercilessly, but they quieted when John came down.*

Okay. Edge forced himself to sit up. *What can you tell me about the other guardians between us and the site? Valtrek described them as merciless guardians that 'bite, sting, and kill with unending thirst.'*

My memories about them are less clear, but I believe they are part of the nature of the Whitebridge Desert itself, Artemus replied.

Edge stretched and rotated his shoulders. *What do you mean by that?*

You should ask Deathclaw, Artemus said. *He was one of them.*

Now Edge was wide awake. *What?*

Before the wizard could reply they were interrupted by Deathclaw himself. The raptoid ran into the camp, his thoughts alarmed. "The Bash Brothers are gone!"

Everyone stirred at his exclamation and Lenny barked, "What do you mean gone?"

"They left the camp," Deathclaw said. "I followed their tracks and they ended at a pile of crumbled bricks." He tossed a chunk of broken brick onto the ground in front of Edge. The surface of it was covered in darkened runes.

Chapter Twenty Four
Sir Edge – The Whitebridge

The party stood around the pile of crumbling bricks in a mix of frustration and concern.

"Dag-blasted, dirt-headed, snaggle-toothed . . ." Lenny sputtered, his lips moving but unable to form more curses. He kicked the pile of bricks smashing some of them to powder. He swung around to face Deathclaw. "How come you didn't notice them leavin'?"

"I too must sleep sometimes," the raptoid protested. He folded his arms. "Yet, you are right to question this. I keep my senses aware even as I slumber and the orcs are loud. I do not know why I wasn't wakened by their leaving."

Neither was I, remarked Squirrel, who was standing on Fist's shoulder. His arms were folded in front of him and he shook his tiny head.

"Me neither," Rufus huffed with a pout, feeling guilty that he too had been asleep during the brother's departure. He and Deathclaw needed the least amount of sleep in the group and until this night they had done an excellent job keeping watch.

"The fact that all of us were caught unawares makes me think that their departure was cloaked by a spell," Fist said.

Lenny grunted and gave Deathclaw an apologetic nod. "So whaddya think this means, Edge?"

Edge stood pondering the situation, one hand stroking his chin. His immediate reaction had been a deep feeling of betrayal. He had reached out to the power of Peace and was letting the sword drain away his emotions so that he could think through events clearly.

Before he replied, Deathclaw voiced similar thoughts to his own. "Either they have betrayed us or they were taken against their will."

I can think of no other reason, Artemus agreed.

"Whatever the Bash Brothers' reasons for leaving, there is nothing we can do about it at the moment," Edge decided. There was no reasonable way for them to track the brick portal to its source. "What concerns me the most is that the wizard was able to come here and leave without our detection. If he had wished to attack tonight, his mercenaries could have killed a few of us before we were ready to fight back. We have to be more diligent from here on out."

"This will not happen again," Deathclaw swore. "Rufus and I will make sure that one of us is awake and alert at all times." The rogue horse huffed in agreement.

"It was my fault," Edge said, placing a hand on his chest. "Rufus would not have been so tired if I hadn't insisted on using Fist's magic to speed him up."

"You couldn't have known," Fist said.

Edge shook his head. "You were right to warn me before using the magic. I should not have let my eagerness for speed put us in danger. What we should learn from tonight is that we need to keep possible attack in mind at all times. Be sure to remind me of this should I lose my wits again."

Fist put a comforting hand on Edge's shoulder, but Edge didn't need the comfort at the moment. The sword was sucking away all his guilt. Only the facts were left in his mind.

"We should go," he said, looking to the slowly brightening sky. "The Whitebridge isn't far away from here. I want to use every minute of daylight we can."

"Well," Lenny said before kicking the bricks one more time. "Least there's one good thing outta this. You ain't gotta pay those dirt-licker's a single silver!"

"Jhonate will be glad of that," Deathclaw agreed.

Edge couldn't deny that was a relief. He hadn't looked forward to telling her how much he was paying the orcs. Then again, he'd rather pay it than have to face them again in battle. Not only were they extremely dangerous, but he'd come to like them. It would be a shame to have to kill them.

They returned to the campsite and packed up quickly. They were heading north on the road before the sun peeked over the rocky hills. A few hours later, they topped a rise and caught their first good glimpse of the Alsarobeth's snow-capped peak on the far horizon. Lying before it was a shimmering while line of sand.

Edge's mind was awhirl with thoughts and concerns, but he kept his sword's magic at work to keep any anxiety at bay. Their destination was in sight. He could only hope they would manage to catch up to Jhonate before they reached it.

Artemus, he sent through the bond. *What was it you were trying to tell me earlier? You said something about Deathclaw and the desert?*

I suppose you had better have everyone listen in, Artemus said. Edge nodded and made sure the wizard's voice was carried to all of them.

What is it? Deathclaw asked.

As I was telling Edge earlier, I have uncovered more memories about my visit to the Whitebridge Desert over 200 years ago. It is no coincidence that the Whitebridge Desert stands between the rest of the world and Alsarobeth. John told Sarine and I that the desert itself was part of Alsarobeth's creation, Artemus began. *It was designed to keep people away. The creatures that live in the desert are all essentially guardians. They fight and breed and feed on each other, but their main purpose is to stop interlopers.*

I have no memory of this being the case, Deathclaw replied.

Have you ever wondered why raptoids are not found outside of this place? Artemus asked.

No, said Deathclaw. He had always just taken the existence of raptoids in the desert as a matter of fact.

The blood magic of dragons allows them to adapt their bodies to any environment, Fist guessed. *Raptoids are simply the product of centuries of adaptation to the desert.*

This is true in part, said Artemus. *But there are more than one type of dragon in the desert.*

There are many, Deathclaw agreed. *Huge red dragons that breathe fire. Worm-like dragons that burrow beneath the dunes and spring out to eat any living creature that comes too close.*

And all of those species are unique to the Whitebridge, Artemus said. *The creatures born in the desert become guardians and are unable to leave of their own free will.*

Deathclaw hissed. *I left. And it was my decision to do so.*

I have a theory about that, the wizard replied. *When Ewzad Vriil used the power of the Rings of Stardeon on you, he severed your ties to the desert.*

Deathclaw pondered the possibility. It was true that he had never felt an inclination to leave the desert before Ewzad had changed him. He had tried to stay with his kind, but the moment that he had been changed, the other raptoids had shamed him. Had they sensed that he was no longer one of them in more ways than just his appearance?

Edge quoted the words on Valtrek's map. '*Merciless guardians that 'bite, sting, and kill with unending thirst.*' *That describes the memories of the desert that you have shown me.*

Perhaps, Deathclaw admitted. *But will this give me any advantage while we are there? Is there anything about being a guardian of this place that remains within me?*

I can't say, Artemus replied. *But I thought it would be good for all of you to know this as you enter. The Whitebridge was built to keep you out. Every thing in it is hostile to invaders. You must take care.*

We will, said Edge. In his mind this new information had changed their plan very little. *It's Jhonate I'm worried about. She's entering the desert and the only person she has with her is this thief.*

Seer Rahan told her that she needed to be named and carry her holy artifact, said Fist. *She followed those requirements.*

He also said that she would need to make sacrifices, Edge said. *Those words have troubled me from the start of our journey.*

"Hey!" said Lenny. The dwarf had turned in his saddle and was staring back at the pensive looks on all their faces. "I can feel that yer talkin' 'bout somethin' important. Y'all gonna tell me?"

Later that day, Rufus picked up Jhonate's trail once again. She and the thief had stopped for the night just off the road and Edge was dismayed to find that they had lost ground. The thunderstorm and the time they had spent in the city had slowed them. Jhonate's scent was once again more than a day old.

It took every bit of Edge's self-restraint not to ask Fist to have Rufus charge ahead again. Nevertheless, he asked Deathclaw and Rufus to quicken the pace as much as they dared without losing the trail.

They tracked until past dark before setting camp. He asked Fist to go around the perimeter of their camp and set up wards that would alert him if any magic was used nearby. In addition, the ogre added additional earth magic wards that would signal him if any creature approached. Then they set the wooden orb out in the open and let it keep animals and insects away. He had done some testing over the last few days and as long as it was left uncovered, the orb's magic seemed to extend about 100 yards in every direction. That wizard wasn't going to sneak up on them again, no matter how clever his spells were.

They kept their sleep as brief as they dared and left before dawn again the next day. The scope of the desert grew before them as they traveled. The daytime heat of the Wildlands was already hot enough, but as he watched rippling dunes ahead of him being distorted by waves of heat rising from the sand, he felt a deep sense of foreboding.

Edge kept his mind immersed in the power of his sword as he went over his plans. They had spent a good deal of time over the past weeks going over their strategy for traversing the desert. They had brought extra water skins along for the journey and if needed, Fist could use his magic to pull water up from deep within the earth.

As for the other dangers of the desert, Deathclaw was certain that he could use his senses and experience to divert them past most of them. And now that they had the wooden orb, they were even more secure. Their largest concern would be if some of the desert's smarter denizens caught their scent.

When they finally arrived at the small stream that bordered the desert, they filled their water bags and prepared themselves for the trials ahead. From where they stood, the white sands of the desert started not far from the stream's banks. A small stretch of brown grass was all that stood between them and the first dune.

"Huh," said Lenny as he stopped to splash water on his face. "It ain't as hot as I thought it'd be out here."

It will get worse, Artemus warned in Edge's mind.

"He is right," said Deathclaw.

Lenny turned to face Edge. "What? Did yer granddaddy say somethin' else?"

"He says it gets hotter," Edge said.

The dwarf snorted. "I know that! It's just that the place looks hotter than the forge. I was expectin' my skin to be burnin' already."

"It can be that hot in parts of the desert. You fear such heat?" Deathclaw asked.

Lenny laughed and slapped his knee. "Son, I'm a dwarf smith! My daddy started me jugglin' live coals when I was six. I been stokin' flames that'd melt a bandham's balls since I was ten. Some days when I stop for lunch I just fry an egg on my own damn forearm!" He spat. "Me fear heat? It's y'all's tender arses I'm worried 'bout."

Deathclaw let out a rare hissing laugh of his own. This was one occurrence when the dwarf's humor mirrored his own. "I agree. I too fear they may die! But not from the heat. From monsters."

His own merriment fading, Lenny walked over to Albert. "Alright, boy. It's time to gear you up fer this part."

Lenny reached for the horse's saddlebags and pulled out four curved pieces of hardened leather. The pieces were heavily runed and glowed blue and gold to Edge's mage sight. The dwarf crouched next to the horse and laced one of the leather pieces around each of Albert's ankles.

The dwarf then led Albert to the stream where the horse began drinking thirstily as if aware of the journey ahead. Lenny glanced over at Edge. "His saddle will keep his core temperature from gettin' too high, but these things'll keep his feet and ankles from burnin' on the hot sand."

"Very smart," said Fist. He glanced at Rufus. "How about you? Will you be okay on the hot sand?"

"Ooh!" Rufus held his hand out in front of his face and his skin thickened and darkened from dark silver to black. He pounded his fist on his chest. "Tough!" Then he looked at the way Albert was still drinking and rushed over to stand in the stream.

The rogue horse grew to four times his normal size and bent down to gulp in as much water as he could. The stream actually stopped flowing for a few moments before he stopped and turned around to face them with a smile, muddy water dripping from his chin. Satisfied with himself, Rufus shrunk back to his normal size.

"Hey, what the hell happened to the water when you shrank back down?" Lenny asked.

Rufus shrugged.

"Best not to think 'bout it," Lenny said with a shake of his head and motioned to Edge. "Check this out. I made somethin' while we was travelin' today." Lenny mounted up onto Albert's back and lifted a length of leather cord that was dangling from the saddle horn.

Edge had indeed seen the dwarf cutting leather into strips and braiding it together, but he hadn't given it much thought. Lenny always did things like this while traveling on horseback. Albert generally followed Rufus without much input, so Lenny was free to mend clothes or bags or make little things.

"You got that magic wood sphere?" Lenny asked.

Edge retrieved it from his bag and handed it over. The dwarf tied some leather loops around the orb and tied it around Albert's neck.

"This way it's out in the open and none of us'll have to carry it all the time," Lenny explained. "I'd have put it on Rufus, but it ain't magic like his saddle. The first time he grew big it'd snap."

"Good thinking," Edge said, but there wasn't much enthusiasm in his voice. His eyes were once more trained on the desert in front of them and the mountain beyond. "It's time we get going."

They crossed the stream and the moment they did so, the heat increased. There was a well-trod trail from the stream up to the edge of the sand. Someone had posted a sign there that read, *"Only for the hopeless."* Piled next to the sign were dozens of empty boots.

"Dag-gum," said Lenny with a grimace. "Who do you think left that sign?"

"It's for the pilgrims," said Edge.

Fist shook his head. "A sad sentiment for sure."

Deathclaw approached the boots and briefly looked them over then crouched low at the trail's end and looked out into the desert. "Jhonate entered here less than a day ago." A gust of wind blew by carrying a cloud of sand with it. He turned back to face Edge. "It will be harder to track them once we enter. Wind covers tracks quickly in this place."

"Then we'd best get started," Edge said.

The entered in the agreed-upon formation. Deathclaw went first, determining the best trail, followed by Albert and Lenny, with Rufus bringing up the rear, Edge and Fist on his back.

In the beginning, the going wasn't so hard. The path into the dunes was covered by sand in some places, but bare in others. It wasn't until about a mile in that the dunes rose in height and footing became difficult. The sun beat down on them relentlessly, but each of them had their own ways to shield themselves.

For Edge, the heat wasn't so bad. Ever since bonding with Artemus and receiving the frost-covered scar on his chest, he had discovered that he didn't burn. He wasn't foolish enough to test it too boldly, but the frost elemental's mere presence seemed to shield him. Of course, each gust of wind brought hot sands that struck exposed skin like stinging bees.

The others had their own protections. Though Deathclaw had been born in this place and had spent decades of his life in the hot sands, he had acclimated to life outside the desert. It took some time for the magic in his body to adjust to the heat, but he bore it stoically. Fist had brought a cloak with runes sewn into it that kept him cool and Squirrel stayed in his temperature-controlled pouch.

Oddly enough, Lenny, despite his boasting, had the worst of it. His leather armor had been runed to regulate his temperature much in the same way that the horse's saddle did, but a few hours into the desert, his armor's magic failed. He began to sweat profusely, but he bore the discomfort with another dwarf tool. Cursing.

"Dag-blasted heat's nothin'! I once snorted hot kiln dust on a dare!" he shouted.

"You alright, Lenny?" Fist asked.

"Like I said, it's nothin'!" A gust of wind carried stinging sand into his open mouth and he hacked and spat. "I was-. Quenchin' blades with-. With my own gad-flamed, garl-friggin', dag-burned . . ."

He continued the string of curses in a continuous stream. He didn't stop until a few minutes later when they passed their first dead pilgrim. The man was half buried in the sand and desiccated. Much of his flesh had been eaten away by insects, though there were none presently on his body. Perhaps the orb's power had driven them away from their feasting.

Deathclaw declared that the body was two days dead and suggested that they move along quickly. The insects exuded a chemical that kept the body from stinking, allowing them to eat undisturbed, but now that they were gone the smell would bring bigger scavengers. Some of them were smart enough that the orb's power might not work.

The party quickly moved on and continued into the late afternoon hours, passing the bodies of three more partially submerged pilgrims along the way. These ones were little more than skeletons, their flesh eaten away. The last one still had a creature feeding on it, clinging to the inside of the skeleton's ribcage. It was a small black thing with leathery skin and no noticeable eyes. Deathclaw warned them to keep their distance. Such creatures were known to latch onto larger creatures with sucker-like mouths and were difficult to dislodge and even more difficult to kill.

Edge couldn't help but wonder how many more bodies they had passed, unseen, covered by the sand. Though his sword pulled away the dread that built within him, he knew that Jhonate was passing through the same conditions that these pilgrims had. She was an experienced survivor and in many ways was stronger than he was, but she didn't have an orb to drive away stinging bugs or poisonous snakes or leathery creatures with sucking mouths.

As the sun faded, the heat of the day was replaced by chilling night air. Deathclaw searched for a place for them to stop and rest for the night. Finally, he pointed them towards a craggy rock formation that jutted from the sand. The rock was pitted and worn by centuries of sand and wind. There were a series of caves in the side of the formation and he was able to find one that was just large enough for all of them to huddle inside. Luckily, it was unoccupied.

Fist set wards in the area outside the cave and they placed the orb in the center of the floor. Without wood to build a fire, they collapsed against the cave walls and ate cold rations, the small cave lit only by a small glow orb. While they ate, Deathclaw left for a brief scouting mission, and Fist sent his magic into the rock floor of the cave, searching for an underground water source he could tap into and replenish their stores.

"Gall-durn it!" Lenny growled.

He had pulled off his leather armor and was searching for the problem that had caused its cooling magic to falter. He fingered a gash in the leather. When Vern had struck him in the side with his axe, some of the runes had been damaged. The magic hadn't failed right away, but white sand had gotten into the gash and disrupted the runes.

"Is it fixable?" Edge asked.

"If'n I can get all the sand out I might be able to put some sealer in. If I'm lucky the magic'll work again, If not, well it still does ever'thin' else it's 'posed to," he said and walked over to his bags to get his leather repair equipment out.

"Edge," said Fist. The ogre had both hands placed against the floor. "I can't find any water."

"Then we will have to look elsewhere tomorrow," Edge replied. "We brought enough water with us to last another day."

You may not find any, Artemus said. *Remember, this place was designed to stop people from reaching the mountain. That includes wizards with earth and water magic.*

Edge sighed. *What did you do for water when you came?*

I was with the Prophet, Artemus reminded him. *He could wring water from a rock if he needed to.*

"Right," he said. "Fist, can you generate water any other way?"

"The air's so dry," Fist said and scratched his head. "I will try some things." *What about you, Artemus? Can you help?*

Like you said, the air here is dry, Artemus replied. *Without a water source below or clouds in the air to expand upon, it will take an immense spell to generate enough water for just Albert and Rufus alone.*

What about this? Squirrel asked and everyone turned their heads. He was standing in the center of the cave next to the wooden orb and he was balancing a quivering sphere of water almost as big as he was over one hand. *Is this water enough to expand upon?*

I felt that he was up to something with my magic, Fist sent. Squirrel had long ago learned how to pull threads of magic from Fist's side of the bond and manipulate them himself. Years of practice and experimentation, only some of which Fist knew about, had led him to creating some unique spells. "Squirrel, how did you do that?"

301

I killed a big viper, he said with a yawn. *It was in a hole in the back of the cave. It was trying to get away but had nowhere to go.*

Fist wasn't surprised about the dead snake side of his story. "But what about the water?"

I extracted it from its body, Squirrel said. *I was hoping for more, but this was all I could get.*

"That's . . . snake water?" Edge asked.

It's just water, Squirrel replied patiently and directed his next thoughts to Fist. *Can you do that one spell to expand this water?*

Fist reached out his hand and Squirrel lobbed the sphere of water over to him. Fist's magic caught the water and he sent energies into it, causing it to triple in volume. "That's about as far as I can make it stretch."

Impressive, Artemus said. *Using the excess energy in the water's basic structure to cause it to increase in volume.*

"Wizard Locksher taught me that trick. But the excess energy is used up now," Fist said. "I can't make any more out of it."

"Is there anything wrong with the water after you do that?" Edge asked.

"It's perfectly drinkable, just useless for working magic with," Fist replied. He lifted his water bag, which was mostly empty, and caused the water to funnel down into it. "All the life in it's gone. It also tastes . . . flat. Perhaps bland is a better word for it. Or insipid?"

"Is there any reason you can't do that with the rest of our water?" Edge said. "Make it stretch?"

"I suppose so," Fist said. "But I was serious when I called it bland."

I can always just find more things to kill along the way, Squirrel suggested.

Deathclaw's thoughts rushed into the bond. He was a good distance away in the dunes and there was worry in his mind. *We have trouble. This area we are in is surrounded by scent markings. We are in the midst of several territories.*

What kinds of territories? Edge asked.

Raptoids, Deathclaw hissed. *Large packs.*

"Ooh," said Rufus, perking up with excitement. "Scary."

"Huh?" said Lenny, looking up from his patch job. "What's scary?"

"We've got raptoid packs out there," Edge told him. *What are our options?*

We can backtrack a few miles and try to find another way through, but I can't predict how far out of our way we will have to travel-.

Or? Edge pressed. He did not like the thought of delaying.

Or we can chance travel through the territories, Deathclaw said and his thoughts were uneasy as he considered it. *Packs this big will have large areas to roam. If we are fortunate, we could get through without them noticing.*

How likely is that scenario? Fist asked.

Our group has a large scent footprint, Deathclaw said. *Between you and Rufus and the horse . . . If we had a sense of where the packs were, I might be able to keep us downwind from any of them, but we would have to be fortunate.*

Edge felt a surge of anxiety, but forced himself to consider all angles of the situation. *Alright, Deathclaw. Jhonate is somewhere out in this desert, maybe travelling through these same territories. Knowing that, what would you suggest we do?*

Knowing that she is in this desert has no bearing on the decision, Deathclaw said. *We do not know where she is. Therefore, we have no way of rescuing her or guiding her out of danger. Considering the size of this desert the possibility that we could run into her at this point is very remote.*

He makes a good point, Artemus agreed.

Edge wanted to shout out that they were both wrong, but he realized that he had once more lost his objectivity. He grasped Peace's magic again and it was obvious that Deathclaw's logic was right. *Very well. What do you recommend?*

If our goal is to catch up to Jhonate, we have no choice but to assume that she is going to make it to the mountain unscathed. Our best course of action is to arrive there before she does, Deathclaw said to Edge's surprise. *We cannot afford to delay. Therefore, I suggest we travel through the territories, doing our best to avoid detection. If we are fortunate, we will get through without a fight. If not? We will have to win.*

Well thought out, Artemus said.

I concur, said Fist.

Me to, Squirrel said.

Lenny was watching Edge's facial expression, his eyes squinting. "It feels like you've made a decision. What're we doin?"

Chapter Twenty Five
The Big and Little People Tribe – Packs

The next morning, Deathclaw left the cave early and climbed to the top of the rock formation to see if he could get a better idea of the lay of the land. From his vantage point atop the craggy spire, he could see a large swath of the desert in the rising light. He knew that this land contained parts of four different raptoid territories.

He couldn't tell which part of the land belonged to which territory from here, but he did see to his dismay that one pack was nearby, running along the dunes. He doubted he would be seen from this distance, but he focused on his scales and caused them to shift color and blend in with the rock. There were a dozen raptoids in this pack, a group dangerous enough that he wasn't sure his tribe could handle them.

These raptoids were about the height and weight of large humans. Their heads were like that of a reptile, with two hawk-like eyes on either side, and a large mouth filled with razor sharp teeth. Their legs were longer and more muscular than their arms and each limb ended in a set of nasty claws. They had a long thick tail that ended in a cruel barb and ran hunched forward with the tail reaching straight behind them for balance.

He noted that their formation was a focused one. Their leader knew where it was headed, which meant that they had caught a scent. He felt an old and mostly forgotten feeling swell in him, and he remembered what it had been like to be the leader of the pack, the deathclaw. To run along the dunes with a prey's scent in his nostrils and to chirp out a command for his powerful pack members to follow in perfect concert . . .

The deathclaw was a concept in the mind of every raptoid. He was the one who directed the pack. He was also the one to strike the killing blow. They didn't have a word for this concept, just a tone of voice. There was a hierarchy to be established within the pack, but once it had been established, only the true deathclaw could chirp at the others with that tone. For as long as he could remember, this had been his identity.

Deathclaw had once been the leader of the largest pack in this desert. It had been over two dozen strong until he had taken on stronger prey than mere raptoids could handle. In his hubris he had taken on a pair of red dragons, enormous monsters. His pack had been destroyed, cut down to five. He had been in the midst of rebuilding it when Ewzad Vrill had changed his body into what he was today.

As he watched the raptoid pack run into the distance, he felt a call within him. It was a subtle thing, but real. The desert remembered him. It had rejected him once before when he had been something changed and new. The magic that tied this place to the holy site of Alsarobeth sensed the strength within him. There was room in the desert for a new deathclaw.

He rejected the call. He was Deathclaw. He had carried the concept away from this desert with him and had made it his own. He was part of something greater than a raptoid pack with their instinctual hierarchies. It had taken him many years to understand this, but he was now part of the Big and Little People Tribe, where every member had their own unique importance that was greater than any position in a pack.

We must go to the northeast, he sent to Edge and included mental images of the surrounding geography. *If we can manage to stay at the borders between territories, they may not discover us.*

Alright, come back down and we will set out, Edge said. He shared Deathclaw's information with the others and they began to get ready to leave.

Lenny, who was frustrated as he put his leather armor back on, saw everyone moving and asked, "What're we doin'?"

"We're leaving," Edge replied. "Deathclaw thinks he has a route picked out for us to take." He noted the way that the dwarf tugged at his armor and asked, "Did your repairs work?"

"Seems to be fer now, but it ain't the best patch job. Don't think I got every grit of sand out. Dag-blamed thing's liable to stop workin' on me when we get out there."

Edge nodded in concern. "Let me know if it fails."

"You'll hear me hollerin'," he grumbled.

Edge turned to head towards the cave entrance, but paused and turned back to the dwarf. "Actually, I'd rather you didn't holler. I'll need you to follow my directions, but don't speak. If we are going to get past these raptoids without being noticed, we must keep silent every step of the way."

"How in the gall-durn hell am I 'posed to know what you want me to do if'n we can't talk 'bout it?" Lenny complained.

"This isn't your first stealth mission, Lenny," Fist said.

"'Course it ain't, you eight-foot nostril farmer!" the dwarf snapped. "I know how to be quiet when I wanna be."

Edge glanced at Fist. *Don't take it personally. He's having a bad morning.* The ogre shrugged and began tying his bedroll to Rufus' saddle. Edge returned his attention to the dwarf. "You and Albert ride behind Rufus this time. Just keep your eyes on me as we move. I'll signal to you."

Lenny scowled, his eyes darting between Edge and Fist. "All y'all can do this mental thing, but I'm the only one who don't friggin' know what's goin' on. It didn't bother me much before, but now that I can just kinda hear it at the edges of my mind, it's startin' to piss me off!" He shook his head at the helpless expression on Edge's face. "Turds. Don't know how Jhonate put up with this fer sixteen dag-gum years."

Edge blinked. "Wait a minute." He laughed at his own stupidity. Jhonate had also felt left out of the group at first, but she had found a simple solution.

Lenny narrowed his eyes at Edge's mirth. "Har har. I get it. I'm a grown blasted dwarf, not some-."

"That's not it, Lenny," Edge told him. He pulled his Jharro bow off of his back. "I really don't know why I didn't think of this before." He grabbed the side of the bow and twisted, pulling a soft piece of gray wood free. The wood transformed in his fingers, forming a narrow ring. He held it out to Lenny and solemnly said, "Will you marry me?"

The dwarf raised a bushy eyebrow. "That ain't funny."

Edge chuckled. "I'm sorry. I was laughing at myself. I hadn't considered giving you a piece of my bow before, because I figured your blood magic would interfere, but since we already have that partial bond it might work."

Lenny grunted in curiosity and took it from him. He looked at his hands and considered which finger to put it on. The only ring he wore was on his left hand and it was the one Bettie had made for his wedding band. It was made of gold and silver intertwined. He placed the Jharro ring on the forefinger of his right hand, It didn't want to go on at first, but it grew to fit.

"Don't feel nothin' different," he said.

And now? said Edge in his mind.

Lenny jumped and a gap-toothed grin spread his face. "Holy hell, I hear you." He tried sending his thoughts through the ring. *CAN YOU HEAR ME?*

Everyone winced.

"Ouch!" said Rufus, putting a hand to his head.

Perhaps this isn't such a good idea, Artemus remarked.

Deathclaw appeared at the cave entrance and sent a mental hiss through the connection. *You don't have to think so loudly, Dwarf!*

"Alright! Alright," Lenny said, feeling embarrassed. *Dag-gum! Is this better?*

It is still loud, but it doesn't make my head hurt, Squirrel remarked from his perch on Fist's shoulder.

The dwarf smiled again, *Is that Squirrel I hear? Ain't never heard you before. You sound smarter than I thought you would.*

Squirrel put his hand on his hips. *Is that supposed to be a compliment?*

"Uh, sorry," said Lenny. *Sorry.*

Now that we have that settled, Edge sent as he replaced his bow on his back. *It's time we move.*

The party left the cave and set back out, Deathclaw leading them. Lenny and Albert kept to the rear with the wooden orb hanging from the horse's neck. Squirrel, feeling chipper this morning despite his age, climbed to the top of Rufus' head and perched there to get a better view of the sands around them.

They kept in the shade of the rock formation, using it for cover as long as they could, then headed into the open desert. Deathclaw stayed a short distance ahead of them, extending his senses, keeping track of every territory marking.

Raptoid packs kept their territories marked with pungent internal scent glands that mixed pheromones with their urine. The scent penetrated into the sand and stayed in place fairly well, but it did fade over time as the wind changed the desert landscape. If raptoids weren't hunting, they often patrolled the edges of their territory, re-marking places where the scent had faded.

Deathclaw did his best to keep his tribe on the side of the territory line with the strongest scent in the hopes that the pack wouldn't soon return. The morning went by without major incident, the tribe working together quietly and efficiently. Lenny was enjoying his new ability to speak with everyone mentally through the ring. He spent time talking with

Squirrel and had even started a spirited discussion with Artemus about great smiths of the ages.

As they traversed the sands, the mountain on the horizon loomed larger and larger. The snow-frosted slopes looked so tempting to the parched tribe. Just looking at it was a cruel reminder of the ridiculous heat that raged around them, kept at bay only by the magics protecting them.

The closer they came to the mountain, the easier it was to see the barrier that spread to either side of it. The barrier at the edge of the Known Lands had a faint shimmer to it that gave the air an ominous green tint. Edge realized that the desert sands extended beyond the barrier to the opposite sides.

Artemus, does the desert encircle the mountain entirely? Edge asked.

I asked John the same thing, the wizard replied. *He said that it did, but would not say much more on the subject. He was more secretive than usual when it came to Alsarobeth. But Sarine and I speculated and felt that this place was likely a holy site for both sides of the barrier.*

What does that mean fer us? Lenny asked curiously. *Do we got a reason to want to be at Alsarobeth besides helpin' Jhonate and getting' the dark dagger back from that thief?*

I would think not, Fist said. *If the Prophet wants everyone to stay away from this site so badly that he would create such a deadly defense around it, I can think of no reason to-.*

Dag-blast it! Lenny swore loudly into the bond.

What happened? Edge asked, looking over his shoulder at the dwarf.

Lenny sat slumped in his saddle, a sour expression on his face. *Dag-gum armor failed again.*

The dwarf got more and more miserable in the heat of late afternoon and Edge began to regret giving him the ring. It was one thing to hear a string of complaints aloud. It was another, to hear them loudly in your mind.

Edge, sent Deathclaw in a part of the bond where only he could hear. *Can you make him quieter?*

I could cut off connection with the ring, but that would be mean. He would notice it right away.

Then order him to be quiet, the raptoid replied. *I cannot concentrate while he yells like this.*

Why don't you do it? Edge said. *He would expect it coming from you.*

Deathclaw hissed, then sent to Lenny, *Dwarf-*!

Len-wee! Shut UP! cried Rufus through the bond. *My head hurts*!

The dwarf's eyebrows rose. *Dag-gum. What? Was I loud?*

Yes! said everyone.

Lenny became uncharacteristically silent. He sat in the saddle, sweating, his handlebar mustache in constant motion as he mumbled to himself. He took something round out of his pouch and began tinkering with it. Edge felt guilty, but the silence was actually kind of nice. Besides, they were in too dangerous a position to allow distractions.

As the sun set, they still weren't out of the raptoid territories. Fortunately, Deathclaw found a place for them to wait out the night. He led them to a field of strange cacti that rose from the dunes like a forest of prickly trees.

They had many branches almost like a pine tree, but they weren't very wide. Just tall. They were anchored in the dirt floor underneath the desert and some of them rose 12 feet in the air above the highest dunes.

What are them things? Lenny wondered.

They are not real cactuses, Deathclaw said. *They are the tongues of monsters that live under the earth below. They are very sensitive and if any creature touches their needles, they wrap around it and drag them into the ground to be eaten.*

Watch, Deathclaw said and ran a good distance away from the rest of them until he was near the outer edge of the wooden orb's power. Then he picked up a rock and threw it at one of the cactus trees. The tall structure immediately coiled around the place where the rock had struck it and sunk into the sand. *Raptoids know to avoid fields of tongues like these. They won't come in here after us.*

Lenny shook his head. *Ain't no gall-durn way I'm sleepin' near one of them.*

The orb will protect us from the creatures below just as it did in the swamps of Malaroo, Deathclaw assured him and returned to their side. He picked up another rock out of the sand and threw it at a nearby cactus tree. It quivered with the impact, but didn't move. *I still would not suggest you touch them. The needles are sharp.*

Lenny grimaced as the others carefully made their way into the field of cacti to find a clear spot of ground to sleep in. Fist edged his way between them and Rufus wisely shrank down to the size of a dog before entering.

Maybe we can just ride on through the night? He asked hopefully. *The moon should be out.* Although no one was looking back at him, he pointed towards the mountain. *We can't be that far from the edge of this blasted place.*

Come on in, said Edge. *Be careful leading Albert.*

"I know to take care of my own damn horse, dag-blast it!" Lenny grumbled to himself, then followed after them. "Nasty dag-burned tongue forest."

They found a reasonably-sized area clear of cacti where they could stop for the night. Though the cactus field would protect them from raptoids, the field was sparse enough that they didn't make a fire or use a light orb. Deathclaw also recommended they keep all conversations mental because of how well the sound would carry.

Lenny glumly passed out rations and they drank some of the bland water Fist had produced. He hadn't been exaggerating. There was something very unsatisfying about drinking it. He assured them that it would hydrate their bodies, but it did very little to quench their thirst.

Lenny was right about one thing, Edge said. *We are getting close to the base of that mountain.*

I was right 'bout lots of things, Lenny corrected.

How far do you think we are from the edge of the desert? Fist asked.

It is hard to gauge, Deathclaw replied. *But I would say perhaps ten miles. We could be there tomorrow afternoon if we have no delays.*

Then why'd y'all ignore me when I said we should keep goin? Lenny asked.

To avoid delays, Deathclaw replied. *It is much more difficult to navigate the dunes at night. We could walk right into a raptoid pack . . .* He cocked his head, his thoughts focused.

A chirping sound echoed through the night. A few seconds later a chorus of other chirps replied. Edge knew right away that these were no birds. Deathclaw sometimes made chirps like this when talking to his sister.

It is a pack, Deathclaw said. He stuck out his hand. *No one move. Just listen.*

Edge closed his eyes and focused on his ears, intensifying his sense of hearing. He could hear them now, striding around the exterior of the cactus fields, their feet scattering the sand.

Another chirp echoed out, followed by a hiss.

They know we're in here, Deathclaw sent. *They've found our tracks and are trying to decide what to do about us.*

Would you like me to go out and kill them? Squirrel asked.

No! said Fist.

They all sat in silence for several minutes before the raptoids chirped again. Some stayed by the place where the party had entered. Others began to pace around the cactus field, looking to make sure they had not exited somewhere else.

This is quite the predicament, Artemus observed.

Do you recommend we stand and fight? Edge asked Deathclaw.

Yes! said Squirrel.

We should wait them out, Deathclaw said. *If we make no noise, they may assume that the beasts under the sand ate us. That is if there is no breeze to give us away.*

Or if the horse doesn't snort, Artemus pointed out.

I can cast a spell of silence, Fist said. *They will hear nothing, even if Lenny snores.*

Hey, Rufus snores just as loud as me, Lenny complained. *If you do this spell, will it still let sound in so we can hear 'em?*

Yes, said Fist and he was already enacting the spell as he said it. A dome of golden magic rose over the group. *It should be fine now.*

If it's alright to y'all, I'd still rather not talk out loud, Lenny said.

They waited for almost an hour before trying to sleep, but the raptoids didn't let up on their patrols around the field. Eventually, Edge urged them all to try and push their worries aside and rest. Deathclaw and Rufus could take turns at watch. They would decide what to do in the morning.

Squirrel waited until Fist had fallen into fitful slumber before exiting his pouch, one cheek bulging. He was wearing the intricate scalemail vest that Bettie had made for him. The inside of the vest was stamped with protective runes and the metal scales on the outside were polished to a high shine.

On his head, he wore a helmet that she had made him to go along with it. It wasn't magical, but it was in a fearsome

314

dragon design with wicked metal teeth. Bettie had thought it was cute and had made it for him never intending for him to use it in battle. Squirrel felt it made him look formidable.

As he snuck silently away from the others his back was a little stiff, his hip sore. He knew he was old for a squirrel, but he refused to be like other squirrels. He wasn't a mere rodent. He wasn't just Fist's pet as most people believed.

Squirrel was part of the Big and Little People Tribe, a founding member, and even though he was little, he had learned to be something more. He had spent time speaking with Deathclaw and when the raptoid wasn't paying attention, he had stealthily picked through the raptoid's memories. He had learned about the raptoid packs of Deathclaw's past. He had learned of roles within packs and had come to understand something important. There was no room for weak members in a pack.

The Big and Little People Tribe were strong, but they had one flaw. They were made up of groups of individuals with different agendas. Many members of the tribe were scattered across the Known Lands. Often times even Fist and Edge lived many days of travel apart from each other.

Fist's only bonded were Squirrel and Rufus. He needed a deathclaw. Even if Fist was scared to let him fight, even if he was old, Squirrel was determined to prove that he could still fill that role. And he had a secret weapon to help him do so.

Once he was out of sight of the other tribe members, he stopped and reached into his cheek pouch. He pulled out a green olive. It glowed black to his mage sight, proof of its potency. It was a Khalpan Olive, grown in the fertile homeland soil of the Pruball Elves, the most concentrated form of elf magic possible outside of drinking their blood directly. Just having it in his cheek pouch had left him abuzz with energy.

Squirrel had stolen it from Mistress Dianne's stash. These olives were the secret to her youthful looks at the ripe age of 200. He hoped to extend his life at least another ten years, maybe longer.

He wasn't sure how much was the correct amount to eat. He had bitten a tiny piece a few days ago and had felt better than he had in years. What would happen if he ate the whole thing? He shook his head. Better to try a few bites first.

The flesh of the olive was bitter and vinegary, but the moment that he swallowed, a flood of energy filled him. It was a feeling similar to when Fist healed him but a great deal stronger. His aches and pains fled.

He stopped after just a few bites, eating only a quarter of the olive before stuffing it back in his pouch. He felt strong enough to fight an army of raptoids, which was essentially what he was about to do.

He reached into his bond with Fist and withdrew strands of air magic, then formed the complex spell that turned him invisible. A second air spell muffled the sounds of his footsteps in the sand. He had practiced these spells so often that they came second nature to him now. Fist wouldn't be able to feel the drain on his power. One advantage to being small is that it didn't take a lot of magic to hide him.

Squirrel skittered between the branches of the deadly cactuses, careful not to touch any of the needles, and headed towards the chirping sounds of the raptoids. Deathclaw thought there were at least a dozen. He counted the sounds of ten different creatures pacing around outside the cactus field.

He drew closer until he saw them. The raptoids were just as he had seen in Deathclaw's memories, lean and vicious looking, every part of their body a weapon. He had often considered how he would go about killing one of these creatures. It was time to find out if his ideas worked.

Squirrel watched them carefully, trying to determine which one was the leader. It wasn't easy for him to pick out at first, but then he noticed one of them that was slightly larger than the others. It had gray scales that gleamed in the moonlight and when it was stalking outside the cactus field, sniffing at the tribe's tracks, the other raptoids watched.

This was his target. Squirrel felt an eagerness rise within him. He adjusted his invisible helmet with his invisible hands, then reached his thoughts back into the bond. He pulled out several more threads of air, then touched Fist's connection with his mace.

Squirrel darted towards the raptoid leader at a speed twice what he was normally capable. His steps were silent, the only signs of his passing small puffs of sand. The raptoid was so intent on the tracks, he didn't sense Squirrel coming. He ran up the raptoid's body, blades of air extending from his claws.

The raptoid pack cocked their heads in confusion as blood sprayed from the joints on their leader's left leg, then up his back. The leader screeched and collapsed as its leg gave out. Before it hit the ground, a final slash opened its throat.

Squirrel sprung away from the dying raptoid, narrowly avoiding the convulsing slices of its claws as its lifeblood soaked into the sand. The pack took a wary step back as their leader writhed in his death throes. They looked around for the attacker, focusing on the cactus trees that they already knew were dangerous.

Thrilled by the efficiency of his first kill, Squirrel didn't let up. He headed towards the next largest raptoid and ran between its legs. He slashed out with another blade of air and cut off its foot at the ankle joint.

The surprised raptoid didn't know what had happened to it at first. It felt a sting in its foot and stumbled. Then its other foot came off and it hit the sand, looking with confused eyes at the stumps at the end of its legs.

The raptoids around their wounded packmate cocked their heads as another blade of air slashed its belly open. Other kinds of animals might have scattered after two such gruesome attacks, but raptoids lived in the most dangerous environment in the Known Lands. There were hundreds of dangerous enemies that could attack in various ways. Instead of panicking, they looked carefully to see where the attack was coming from.

Squirrel came to a sudden stop, avoiding a raptoid's tail that slashed through the air in front of him. The creature's sharp barb could have torn him in two. Instead, he lashed out and the severed barb rolled across the sand.

He realized that he had made a mistake killing two raptoids that had been standing so close to each other. The rest of the pack converged on his position, their claws slashing at the sand as they looked for the invisible attacker. Their nostrils flared. They had caught his scent now. Squirrel needed to change his strategy. He formed another spell.

One of them lunged forward, his toothy mouth converging on Squirrel's position. Its mouth closed on a ball of lightning. It screeched and fell jittering, smoke rising from its burnt palate.

Squirrel ran, pulling more speed from Fist's mace. He swung another blade of air and opened the stunned raptoid's abdomen on the way. As its entrails uncoiled, the others followed the path of the attack. They ran after him, noticing the scattering sand under his soundless feet. The raptoids had lost three of their number but now had a way to smell him and to track him.

He was still faster than them, though. Squirrel led them on a pursuit along the edge of the cactus field, making sure that he was outside the radius of the wooden orb's magic. He let up on his speed to be certain they were all following, then when they were almost on him, turned abruptly and darted into the cactuses hoping they would be foolish enough to follow.

Most of them stopped before entering the field. Only one went inside and it instantly realized its mistake. It stopped and tried to back out, but the edge of its tail struck the side of the cactus. The cactus' needles pierced through the raptoid's scales and the tall trunk of the cactus bent toward it reflexively, coiling around the creature. The raptoid screeched in pain and horror as it was dragged under the sand.

Squirrel's friends heard the commotion and Fist's panicked thoughts came to him through the bond. *Squirrel, what are you doing?*

Killing raptoids, he said. *Four are dead so far.*

Holy hell, thought Lenny.

Stop! Come back to us! Fist said, then let out a slow breath and forced the fear and anger out of his thoughts. *I am proud of you. I'm sure you've scared them. Now please come back before you get hurt.*

Squirrel shook his head as he circled back around behind the raptoid pack. *You think I am too frail to fight. But you should trust me by now.*

It's not about whether I trust you or not, Fist argued.

Deathclaw's thoughts cut in. *How many are left? I counted twelve different chirps.*

I saw ten, Squirrel said, then he saw two more come in from the desert to join the others and changed his assessment. *No you were right. There were twelve. Now there are eight. I killed their deathclaw.*

Impressive, Deathclaw said. *It will not take long for a new one to be chosen, though. Be wary.*

Should we go out there and help him? Lenny asked.

Squirrel, come back in and we'll all fight them together, Fist said.

Squirrel darted out from a cluster of cacti behind the raptoids and sent a gust of wind out from the bottoms of his feet, launching him into the air. *They'll all be dead before you arrive.*

He arced towards the shoulders of the rearmost raptoid and prepared two long blades of air as he went. He slashed out with the blades as he landed and they neatly severed its spine at the base of its head. The creature jerked and fell.

As Squirrel let go of the blades and jumped off of its body, a raptoid lashed out at him with its tail. By pure reflex,

Squirrel brought up a shield of air in a solid sphere around him, but the weight of the tail hit the shield and sent him hurtling towards the cacti.

He struck one of the cactus trees and bounced off, striking another one before hitting the ground. The cactus trees were under the orb's power and didn't attack, but each impact slammed Squirrel against the inside of the shield. He felt something crack within him and, as he struck the ground, the shield dissipated. He tasted blood in his mouth and looked down. A long cactus needle was protruding from his belly. It must have penetrated his shield.

Fist felt the impacts. *Squirrel!*

Immediately, the ogre's mind dove through the bond to assess Squirrel's wounds. *Why did you do this?*

I'm sorry, Fist, he sent weakly.

Fist saw right away that the right side of Squirrel's body was badly bruised. He had several broken ribs and one of them had pierced his lung. The cactus needle had pierced through his abdominal wall but hadn't struck any vital organs.

He set to work on Squirrel's worst injuries first, using his magic to mend the ribs and heal the hole in his lung. He was surprised how easy the repairs were and realized that Squirrel's body was coursing with elf magic.

How did you-? Fist sighed. *You have to remember that you are small and-and if you died . . . I couldn't . . .*

I suppose I don't make a good deathclaw after all, then, Squirrel said bitterly.

Fist started to repair the hole in his abdomen. *What are you talking about? You, a squirrel, killed five raptoids tonight. You've killed ogres, trolls, even a giant. I know you can fight.*

Then why must you always tell me not to? Squirrel asked.

How many times over the years have we had this discussion? the ogre said. *I don't need you to be my deathclaw.*

I can fight. Rufus can fight. Isn't it enough that you're my best friend?

Squirrel felt Fist finish his healing. He sat up without the slightest twinge in his body and picked up the long cactus needle. It still had a smear of blood on it. *I will always be your friend. But I am getting old. I want to fight while I still can.*

But you always have to fight things strong enough to kill you in one hit! Fist argued. He felt Edge's hand on his shoulder.

In a private part of the bond where Squirrel could not hear, Edge said, *Both of you are right. There has to be a way for you to meet in the middle on this.*

Fist nodded. *But now isn't the time to figure it out.* He stood and turned to face the others. Aloud he said, "We need to kill the rest of those raptoids."

"We must do it and fast," Deathclaw agreed. "We are straddling the line between two territories and the noise of this battle will have been heard."

"I got an idea how to do that," Lenny said. He held out the round thing he had been fiddling with earlier. It was the paralyzing orb that the mercenaries had tried to use on them. "Somebody kicked it during the fight and there was a dent put in it, but I got the runes all lined up. All it needs is to be charged with magic."

"That does take some of the fun out of it," Fist said as he took the device in his hand and began pouring energies into it.

"That sounds fine to me," said Edge. "Right now I just want to get out of this place."

All seven remaining raptoids were waiting as the tribe exited the cactus field. Their new leader chirped out a command and the pack spread out, waiting for their prey to try and run. Edge lobbed the orb into the midst of them. A buzzing sound filled the air and the raptoids froze in place.

Fist turned to look at Squirrel, who had exited the field next to them. He looked dejected and was holding his little helmet in his hands. The ogre rested his heavy mace on his shoulder and said, "Well, Squirrel? Do you want to help me finish what you started?"

Squirrel perked up. He placed the helmet on his head. *I will kill the three on the right.*

Chapter Twenty Six

The Big and Little People Tribe – Alsarobeth

The desert was a torturous experience for Jhonate. She and Nod had weighted themselves down with water, but the way that the sun beat down on them from the moment they stepped onto the sand, she had known it wouldn't be enough.

Nod pulled out the hand drawn map he had received from the wizard and imp pilgrims he had met at the tent city. Jhonate had known right away that it would be of little use. The map was very basic. The mountain was at the top of the map and their starting point at the bottom, but though there was a route drawn with a dotted line, there was no legend to give a sense of scale or distance. A few squiggly lines were drawn in to give an impression of dunes, but at the edge of the map was a warning that said dunes constantly shift with the wind.

The only things that were helpful were a few circled danger spots marked with numbers. One read, "Hot spot. Searing Sands." Another read, "Not cactus field. Actually monster tongues!"

"Perhaps we should return to the city and come back better prepared," she suggested.

"Naw, that won't be necessary, Sar!" Nod assured her with a smile, sweat dripping from his lip. "You read our letters from the Seer. All you need is your name and your artifact. Wif' me here to help guide you, you'll get there right as rain!" He winced up at the clear bright sky. "Could use some rain."

Hours later, she was certain Nod was wrong. They had passed the bodies of dead pilgrims, large fearsome insects feasting on their carcasses, and came upon their first monster. A huge worm-like creature rose from the dune in front of them. It was covered in glittering scales and its circular maw was big enough to envelop both of them in one bite.

She had gotten in a defensive stance, her Jharro staff at the ready. But Nod had cowered behind her and shouted out for her to use her talisman. When the creature reared above them, she had drawn Tulos, her naming weapon. The dagger had gleamed a purer white than the sands around them and the red rubies on its hilt had pulsed with a power she didn't understand. The monster veered away from them and dug its long body under another dune.

"See, Sar!" Nod had cried. "The seer was right!"

As they continued through the hot sands, Jhonate realized that as long as she had her dagger out of its sheath and held aloft, creatures would leave her alone. She didn't like carrying it unsheathed because it meant she couldn't use her staff effectively in case she did have to fight something off. Nod offered to carry it for her, but Jhonate thought of a better solution.

She caused the end of her staff to open up. She then slid the handle of Tulos inside and had the Jharro wood tighten around it. Her two weapons had now become one, a de facto spear.

They soon discovered that the protection given her by the dagger's presence didn't also apply to Nod.

A giant scorpion-like creature with a single large eye and two sets of pincers skittered over a dune and lunged at him. He managed to swing his leg out of the way of its pincers but its tail stinger plunged into his horse's side and pumped it full of poison. The horse screamed and tried to run away, but the thing's pinchers had latched onto its legs.

Nod had the presence of mind to grab his pack and a back of water before he jumped down. Jhonate tried to rescue

324

the horse and a few swipes of her new spear caused the scorpion thing to back away, but it was two late. The horse collapsed and wouldn't get back up.

Nod walked at her side for a while, but it soon became evident that if Nod took more than a couple steps away from her, the monsters would circle around to attack. Unfortunately, this meant that he had to ride behind her.

Jhonate had thus far escaped being in such close proximity to the man, but she had no choice. Every time something moved in the sands nearby, he would cling to her. It happened more often than she deemed necessary and she sometimes had to clout the man to get him to let go. He claimed that he hadn't meant anything by it, and she understood that it was reasonable for him to fear for his life, but she had seen Nod in battle before. This was not a man who quavered in dangerous situations.

When night came, she planted the end of her staff in the ground and the two of them huddled around it, swaddled in blankets. During those long hours, Nod didn't make any overt moves that would have caused her to eject him onto the sand, but he was constantly brushing up against her. Once again, she had to warn him to keep his hands, crippled and non-crippled alike, to himself.

As their water supplies dwindled, she took to an old Roo-Tan technique and began chewing certain herbs that she had brought along with her. They were often used as a cure for poison, but they also had the side effect of keeping thirst at bay. In the filthy swamplands of Malaroo, such things could often times save a warrior's life and in this desert she was fairly certain it saved hers. While Nod ran out of water on the morning of the third day, she was able to make hers stretch.

They did their best to keep to Nod's poorly drawn map, but it caused them to meander a bit from the straight line to the mountain that Jhonate so wanted to follow. The only time they were certain that the map had any accuracy was when they saw the field of cactus tongues in the distance on the afternoon of their third day. Using the field as a reference point, they reoriented themselves and made good time the rest of the day.

Just before they stopped for the night, Jhonate's horse collapsed of heat exhaustion and died. They rescued what supplies they could from it and set camp. In the morning, just as they set off on foot, they heard chirping noises in the sands. Soon they were surrounded by creatures Jhonate recognized right away. A pack of raptoids encircled them, watching with curious eyes.

Jhonate feared that the power of her dagger wouldn't be enough this time, but when they didn't attack right away, she walked slowly towards them, Nod clinging to her cloak. They didn't move until she was mere paces away. Then, slowly, they gave her space to walk between them. As they walked by, one of the creatures swiped its claws at Nod and he threw his arms around her.

She pointed her spear at the raptoid and it backed away. "Nod, if you do not relocate your hands right now, I will throw you to them," she growled.

"I ain't gonna try and fondle you at a time like this, Sar!" Nod protested, but he moved his hands down to her waist.

They made their way through the crowd of raptoids, but the pack followed behind them the rest of the morning, as if waiting for Nod to take two steps away from her. The raptoids didn't leave until they took their first steps out of the desert sands and arrived at the base of the mountain at midday.

The air grew steadily cooler with each step they made away from the desert and soon, they had to bundle up to ward off a chill. They came upon a pathway that wove through the foothills and as they turned a corner, their goal came into view. Ascending the mountain, winding up the steep slopes was an ancient stone staircase.

"There they are," said Nod excitedly. "The stone stairs of Alsarobeth!"

At the base of the stairs was a small waterfall and both of them rushed over to drink their fill of ice-cold water and refill their water bags. The water was so refreshing. Jhonate was reminded that she hadn't been able to bathe in weeks. If Nod hadn't been there, Jhonate would have stripped down and washed off under that waterfall, no matter how cold it was.

"So what do ya 'fink, Sar?" Nod asked, peering up at the stair. "Should we rest here and camp for the night or start up?"

Jhonate stretched and rotated her shoulders as she looked up at the long climb ahead of them. "I have no desire for this journey to last one day longer than it has to."

She didn't see it, but the smile Nod sent her way had a sense of menace to it. "You won't get no arguin' from me."

Jhonate started up, but before Nod joined her, he stopped to take something out of his pack. It was a rectangular brick covered in complex runes. He sat it down not far from the stair and climbed up after her.

"What was that thing you left down there?" she asked.

"That was part of the deal I made with that wizard pilgrim fella back at the tent city. He gave me his worthless map, and I told him I'd leave his brick at the stairs of Alsarobeth. It's a tradition for the man. He leaves one of those bricks at every holy site he can."

"Why a brick?" Jhonate wondered as she resumed her climb.

"I asked him the same 'fing," Nod replied. "Say's it's from his childhood home. He does it in memory his old dad. His story warmed my heart, I must say. I told him I'd be happy to do it."

"I do not understand why a brick would remind a man of his-," she began before a chorus of voices invaded her mind.

"Named one." "So hungry." "The seer . . ." "That dagger . . ."

The voices were loud, and she was certain she heard them in her ears as well as in her mind. The voices were full of emotion. Some were angry or ravenous, others were curious, wistful, or even reverent. "Do you hear that, Nod?" she asked.

"*Feed us!*" "*Come closer.*" "*EAT YOU!*" "*Defender of the Grove . . .*"

"Don't listen to 'em!" Nod snapped. His crippled had was clutched protectively against his chest and he had drawn his sword with the other. "They lie!"

"Do not let the voices get to you," she warned. "They are not talking about you. They are the guardians of this place."

"Maybe you're hearin' some'fing different than me, Sar. It sounds very personal," Nod replied.

"*HATE!*" "*Dance with us . . .*" "*Hungry.*" "*Mother . . .*"

The last one sent a shiver up her spine and as she looked up the mountainside, she saw a series of caves pockmarked the slopes. Strange figures were emerging from them. Suddenly, perching on a rock not far from her, she saw a bizarre creature.

It had the torso of a bear and stood on two hairly legs that ended in bird-like talons. Its arms were long and hairless with short fingernails and its head was that of a huge rat. In the middle of its broad chest, spreading nearly from arm-to-arm was an enormous mouth that opened to show sharp fangs.

* * *

Edge and his friends hurried through the desert, hoping to get as much distance between them and the cactus fields before the heat of the day overtook them. They hadn't gone far before they heard the alarmed chirps of a second raptoid pack inspecting the bodies of the twelve that Fist and Squirrel had killed.

Will they come after us? Edge asked through the bond.

Deathclaw replied with a mental hiss. *Yes. Though if we are fortunate, they will be careful. Any prey that can take down a pack like we did is one to be respected.*

Lenny, who was taking up the rear on Albert, kept looking back over his shoulder. *You sayin' careful like, 'Daggum, we better not mess with them folks,' or careful like, 'We'd better kill them sons of dogs 'fore they come after us?'*

Careful as in they will decide how best to kill us after watching us awhile, Deathclaw replied.

Indeed, the signs that they were being followed continued into the early light of dawn. The raptoids didn't show their faces, but their chirps were heard continuously. Some of them were questioning, others sounded like orders.

What are they saying? Fist asked.

They are wondering how creatures that smell like us were able to kill so many of their kind, Deathclaw replied.

Edge wasn't thinking about what was behind them. His eyes were on the mountain looming ahead. At the pace they were going it couldn't be more than a half a day's ride away.

As the morning hours wore on, the heat grew until it was miserable even for those with protections. Lenny was once again hit the worst. For a while, he joked about removing Albert's saddle and wearing it himself. Rufus was even complaining.

Hot! Ooh! So hot! he moaned. The rogue horse was slowing down, his tongue lolling from his mouth.

Artemus, Edge asked through the bond. *Is there anything you can do for him?*

The wizard gave it some brief thought. *He is Fist's bonded, and not directly connected with me, but if Fist will allow my magic entrance, I should be able to cool him.* He sent complex threads of air and water magic into the rogue horse and Rufus shivered.

"Ooh ooooh," he said, sighing in relief.

Got anythin' fer me? Lenny hoped.

The kind of bond that the Jharro ring gives isn't strong enough for me to pass a spell through, Artemus said apologetically. Then a thought occurred to him. *Actually, there may be one thing we could try. Edge, can you give him Whisper?*

Edge perked up in his saddle. He drew his great grandfather's naming dagger from its sheath at his waist. The blue ice that filled the crack in the naming rune steamed in the hot air. He held it out to Lenny and as soon as the dwarf grabbed the handle, he gasped as the wizard's magic rolled over him.

Frost came out of his mouth and he smiled widely. "Well, dag-gum! Ain't never been so happy to be cold."

It will only work as long as you hold the handle, Artemus told him.

Ain't never lettin' go, the dwarf promised.

The mountain loomed closer and closer and as the end of the desert was in sight, the chirps behind them grew in urgency. *They're coming,* Deathclaw declared.

Edge ordered that they pick up the pace. Deathclaw jumped up onto Rufus' back and they started to run. While they did so, Edge turned around to face the oncoming pack and drew his bow.

How many? he asked.

I tried to keep track but it was difficult, Deathclaw replied. *Larger than the other pack.*

I have twenty arrows, Edge replied. He strung the bow in one quick motion and drew an arrow from his quiver. *I just have to keep them off of us until we reach the mountain. I don't think they'll follow us out of the desert.*

Deathclaw didn't disagree. *They'll run on either side of us and try to box us in. They're faster than us. Rufus might be able to outrun them, but Albert is too hampered by this loose sand.*

When the first raptoid appeared behind them, Edge was ready. The Jharro bow flexed as he fired, and the arrow darted faster than any normal bow could shoot. The arrow struck the running raptoid between the eyes and passed through its skull, continuing into the desert air beyond.

The animal tumbled dead to the ground and Edge drew another arrow, searching for his next target. Deathclaw pointed to their right where two more raptoids ran, flanking them. Edge lined up his shot on the larger of the two and put this arrow through its heart.

Lenny whistled. "Nice dag-gum shot!"

Edge drew another arrow, ready to fire again, but a chirp echoed out. The raptoids fell back. Evidently, they had decided that this particular prey wasn't worth it.

No other major threats faced them as they approached the mountain. Nevertheless, when Albert and Rufus stepped out of the sand and stepped onto hard rock, everyone let out a sigh of relief.

"It's already cooler," Fist said with a smile and with every step, that fact was more evident.

"Now the question is where to start climbin'," Lenny said, looking up at the steep slopes and sheer cliffs with trepidation. He had climbed mountains before, but it wasn't the part of adventuring he was fond of.

"I can do it!" Rufus declared, looking at those same cliffs with delight.

The guardians would disagree. Artemus said through the bond. *We must find the stairway. It is where Jhonate would have gone.*

"Stairs," said Lenny more cheerfully.

"We still may have to fight our way up them," Edge warned.

"Perhaps not," said Deathclaw. He was crouched next to a trailhead that led into the hills. "I found Jhonate's scent. She was here recently. Not more than two hours ago."

Edge's heart leapt into his chest. So close! "Let's hurry. We still may be able to catch her before they start their climb."

They started up the path at a jog. With the trail this fresh, Deathclaw was able to follow her scent easily. The path moved up and down, but meandered very little and Edge soon caught a glimpse of the stairway that Artemus had spoken of in the distance. It wound its way up into the snow-covered slopes.

Edge focused his vision, hoping to perhaps catch a glimpse of his wife, and noticed that there were caves dotting the mountainside all around the stairs. Strange misshapen figures moved about on the slopes. "I see the guardians moving around up there."

Someone has stirred them up, Artemus said.

Hurrying forward, they turned a corner in the path and the bottom of the stairway appeared. Standing in front of it was a glowing brick portal and several familiar figures. The Bash Brothers stood next to the Wizard Ghazardblast and the armored imp. The only unfamiliar person was a lanky seven-foot-tall gnome warrior with a shaved head The number three was tattooed onto the side of his skull and he carried short swords in each hand. In front of all of them standing with feet widely planted, was Lenny's nemesis.

"Hey, Lenui!" shouted Vern. The dwarf was once again dressed in full platemail, but he was wearing a different helmet this time. It was covered in runes and painted red instead of the Earthpeeler family crest, the forehead was simply embossed with the letter 'V'. He was holding Lenny's throwing hammer in one hand.

"I got somethin' to return to you!" Vern snarled and threw the hammer as hard as he could. The hammer left his hand and the magic took control, rocketing the weapon forward at incredible speed.

The head of the hammer struck Lenny square in the chest.

*   *   *

"Killer!" "EAT YOU." "Dance . . ." "The seer!"

The mental calls of the guardians were incessant. However, the power of her dagger still seemed to keep them at bay. They prowled the mountainside and lined the trails, but none attacked. A few reached for Nod, but once again he stayed close enough to her to avoid them, keeping his good hand on her hip.

The guardians were a bizarre group of beasts. Actually, they were more of a mishmash of beasts. No one was the same as the other. Some had the heads of birds, some reptiles, others mammals of some kind. Their arms, legs, and torsos were just as diverse. The only similarities between them were the mindless expressions on their faces and the enormous toothy mouths in their torsos.

"I find it hard to fathom," she said. "With those mouths in their chests, where are their hearts or lungs?"

"I doubt they have 'em, Sar," answered Nod with a shaky laugh. "Can't kill a guardian without a heart, can ya?"

"The Grove . . ." "Chew you!" "EAT!" "Named one." "So hungryyy . . ."

The disturbing mental calls bothered her less and less as they climbed. They had become repetitive. The only ones that actually bothered her were related to the fact that she wanted to be a mother. She still had nightmares about the day that her baby had been taken from her, killed in her womb. But she was able to brush the attacks aside. She was doing something about that. Soon she would reach the top. Soon her curse would be gone.

Nod didn't take the mental barrage as well as she did. He became more and more on edge as they went and sometimes he mumbled to himself. Because of the guardian's voices it was hard to make out, but she was pretty sure he was just saying "Almost there" over and over.

The slopes around them were now coated in a thick layer of snow, but none of it was on the stairway. Each step was clean and dry and Jhonate wondered if there was magic that kept the stairs clear or if these monstrous guardians cleaned it themselves.

The climb continued as the afternoon passed and Jhonate continued to put one foot before the other, careful to keep her spear tip held aloft as the guardians lined the way ahead, waiting for a misstep. Her legs went numb, her hands trembled. She lost track of how long she had been climbing and then, suddenly, the stairway came to an end.

She found herself standing atop the mountain on a shelf so flat it was as if the tip of the peak had been sheared off by an immense blade. The edges of the shelf fell away into sheer cliffs on all sides, and running through the rear third of it was the barrier. It shimmered with a slightly greenish tint, blurring the details of the world on the other side.

In front of the barrier was a marble archway made of four curving stones. At the center of each stone was a seal that looked to be made of clay. One seal was white, one black, and the other two were gray. In front of the archway, in the center of the mountaintop shelf, was a large stone altar.

Sitting on the edge of the altar was an old man wearing a gray robe. The man's dark skin was wrinkled, his hair white, and in his hands he held a folded piece of paper. He tucked the paper into his robes when he saw her.

"Seer Rahan?" she asked and was careful to make sure that she still felt Nod's hand on her hip.

He gave her a resigned smile and slid down from the altar. He swayed on unsteady feet and took two steps towards her. "Ah, child. You came. What name did the Bowl give you?"

Jhonate blinked and showed him the rune on the back of her right hand. "I am Sar Zahara. I received your letter."

"Zahara?" said the seer with a smile. "Ah yes. Very appropriate. An ancient name with many meanings. Trainer?

334

Yes. Teacher? Yes. Commander? Yes. Did you know it also could mean mother?"

There was no mocking tone is his voice. Still, after the calls of the guardians, she winced. "Seer Rahan. I have come too far to be patronized."

She felt a sting in her hip and Nod's hand was gone.

"I meant no offense," Rahan assured her.

"No, I think you were mockin' the lady," Nod said, appearing behind the seer. The old man jerked and Jhonate saw the pilgrim's sword sprout from the center of his chest. Nod sneered and whispered into his ear, "Bet you didn't see that comin'."

"Nod!" Jhonate shouted in disbelief. She stumbled and had to hold on to her staff to keep her feet.

The seer turned his head to look at the man. "Oh, but I did. I foresaw your destruction in this place, Nod. Or should I say, Zeston? Your kind always meets a tormented end." Nod's eyes widened, and the seer gave his killer a wan smile. "Haven't the voices in your head told you? You poor boy."

With a snarl, Nod wrenched his sword to the side.

Before Rahan went limp, his eyes shifted to Jhonate. Their gazes connected, and a jolt went through her. She wasn't sure what had just happened, but it was as if something important had been given to her.

Chapter Twenty Seven
The Big and Little People Tribe – Mercenary

The throwing hammer struck the center of Lenny's chest with a loud crack. Then it bounced to the ground. Grinning with relief, Lenny bent to pick it up. He kissed the head of it. "I'm glad to see you, Buster Junior One! I thought I'd lost you fer good."

"Dag-blast it!" Vern swore.

The imp sneered in response. "You underestimated his armor again. I told you, it's runed to repel impact. We went over this in preparation."

"Shut yer trap, needle-mouth," Vern growled, his glare focused on Lenny. "Shoulda thrown it at yer ugly face, Firegobbler!"

Grinning, Lenny pointed the throwing hammer at the dwarf. "I dunno how you got here, Vern, but I'll tell you what. Since you was so kind as to return my hammer to me, I'll give y'all a chance to turn yer gall-durn, ugly, corn-lickin', arse-faces outta the way."

"Please don't make us kill you," Fist added, his gaze focused on the Bash Brothers.

"That's right," said Lenny and he let out a tired laugh. "We just wanna get up the damn mountain."

Vern scowled at the party and bellowed, "This is as far as you go!" With a confident sneer, he added, "What you see before you is a crew hand-picked to exploit yer every weakness. Either you turn around and head back into that desert or-."

"Enough of this nonsense," Edge said, stepping towards him with a look of smoldering anger. "Look, I don't have time for your posturing. I'm tired. We're all tired. We know you're not gonna back down. Let's get this fight over with so that I can go find my wife."

Vern snorted in disappointment. "Fine. If yer in a hurry. Ghazardblast!"

The wizard signaled, and the mercenaries rushed towards their targets. The imp darted at Fist with a burst of speed, the gnome warrior ran at Deathclaw, and Vern strolled towards Lenny. Edge watched the wizard, preparing himself to defend against a magical attack.

The wizard noted Edge's attention and thrust his staff into the air. He pointed his finger. Power pulsed from the staff and surged across his torso and down his arm. A complex weave of fire and air erupted from the wizard's fingers, but instead of surging towards Edge, it moved out in a large grid-like pattern.

Walls of intense fire sprang from the ground, rising twenty feet in the air. Edge shook his head at the attempt for further delay. Ghazardblast had separated the combatants.

Edge turned around and saw that he and Rufus had been left alone in a wide quadrant with the Bash Brothers. He cracked his knuckles.

Deathclaw watched the gnome warrior's approach with interest. The best fighter he had ever fought against was a gnome warrior named Cletus. When it came to fighting, Cletus was an unparalleled genius. When it came to anything else, he was as Lenny would say, dumb as rocks. Of course, gnome warriors were known for their low intelligence.

"What is your name, gnome?" Deathclaw asked as he drew Star from the sheath on his back.

The seven-foot-tall gnome didn't reply, but rotated his bald head on his neck with a series of cracking noises. He twirled his swords in his hands.

"Can you not speak?" the raptoid hissed and wondered why the gnome had the number 3 tattooed on the side of his head. Was he the third in a series of mute gnomes?

The gnome lifted a short sword in each hand and bared his teeth at him. "I'm not paid to talk."

Deathclaw cocked his head. Perhaps this bald gnome wasn't as stupid as other gnome warriors. "Do you know a gnome warrior named Cletus?"

"I'm not paid to know Cletus," the warrior replied and Deathclaw realized that he was stupid after all.

Then the gnome came at him and Deathclaw's questions about the warrior ceased. There was only the fight.

"Alright, you gad-flamin' moon-head," Lenui said as Vern drew closer. "Why you gotta make me prove my point again? Yer just not good 'nough. I'll admit that the Earthpeeler family's got some good eggs in it, but none of 'em are you."

Vern hefted his double-bladed battle axe. "I'm tired of yer insults and constant belittlin'. Ever'body knows yer just a loud-mouth who likes to strut around and think yer better than the rest of us."

"I only think I'm better than you when yer around," Lenui said. Actually, he kind of felt bad for Vern. "Listen here. I know it couldn't've been easy to be an Earthpeeler in Corntown raised in the shadow of us Firegobblers. I can also see that it would've been hard to find yerself matched up against me at every turn. But dag-blast it, you fiddle-head, some of it was yer own fault."

Vern guffawed. "It's my fault that ever'where I went all I heard about was the great Lenui Firegobbler? The great new talent?"

"No, it's yer fault that you couldn't leave me the hell alone!" Lenui said. "I got no reason to try and keep 'nother dwarf down, but ever'where I went, you was there tryin' to stub my dag-blamed toe! When I'd set up shop, you'd come in on the same blasted street. When I had my eye on a lady, you'd tell her nasty things 'bout me."

"Never needed to do that," Vern said. "Any lady with any smarts could smell you comin'!"

Lenui narrowed his eyes. "You told Adelaid Hillstomper that I shaved my own arse."

Vern blinked. "That weren't me. That was yer cousin Beveau."

"Beveau? That saddle-sniffin'-." He sighed. "Look, it don't matter. What I'm tryin' to tell you here, Vern, is that this is gonna stop. Now. Today. My toe's sore 'nough. If'n you leave and never make trouble fer me again, I'll swear never to piss on yer name again. We leave each other be."

Vern's axe lowered a bit and for a moment Lenui thought he would see reason. Then he hawked and spat. Some of the spit left the face hole of his helmet, but most of it didn't and dangled from the bottom of the mouth guard in a long stringy glob.

"I see. Yer scared now, ain't you? Spendin' days in that desert's got you worn down." Vern chuckled. "But that's too bad. I got you dead to rights. I done fixed my armor and I'm ready fer all yer tricks and weapons." He rapped on his helmet with the side of his axe and it didn't move a bit. "When I'm done killin' you, I'm gonna make sure yer friends are dead. Then I'm headin' to Reneul and introducin' myself to yer widow. She's gonna need a good strong dwarf in her sad life."

Lenui sucked at his teeth and nodded to himself. Then he threw Buster Junior One at the dwarf's steel-shod right boot. The weapon left his fingers, the magic engaged, and the hammer rocketed forward to cave in the toe of the boot with double impact.

Vern howled and hopped on his other leg and Lenui surged forward. He grabbed the hilt of Artemus' dagger. *Hope you don't mind doin' some cuttin' fer me,* he sent and stabbed the tip of the dagger right through Vern's faceplate and into his skull.

The dwarf collapsed to the ground in a crash of metal and ice sprouted around the fatal wound. "Sorry, Vern. Guess you didn't know all my tricks'n weapons after all."

Fist barely brought Quickening down in time to block the strike of the imp's flame-colored sword. Heat blazed from the weapon and the imp snarled at him with a mouth full of sharp yellow teeth.

"Our fight was cut short before, Master Fist," it said.

"How are you so strong and fast?" Fist asked. The imp could only have been five and a half feet tall at the most and was most likely a quarter his weight.

I bet it's his armor, said Squirrel. He had exited his pouch and was watching from a rock nearby, still wearing his scalemail vest and polished helmet.

"When Ghazardblast and I prepare for a job, I make certain I have the abilities needed," Belfae said, then pushed Fist back and swung his sword down at the ogre's legs.

Pulling on Quickening's speed, Fist jumped back and swung the mace in a fierce strike at the imp's head. Belfae ducked.

Yep, it's the armor, Squirrel said, taking a bite of an olive he had pulled from his cheek pouch. *But the runes are on the inside. When he moves real fast, I can sometime catch glimpses of them. You need an air shield.*

Fist had no time to wonder where Squirrel had gotten an olive. The imp was slashing again with his fire sword and the ogre was barely able to avoid it. Then Belfae took a step back and thrust out his hand and a plume of fire shot from his palm.

Thanks to Squirrel's warning, Fist was already raising his left arm. He sent threads out to form a large shield of golden magic that sprouted from his forearm to deflect the flames.

Try shock, Squirrel suggested,

"I know," Fist said aloud. He sent vibrating strands of air and earth magic along his mace's length and when the imp raised his sword to block it, electricity jolted through the metal.

The imp winced but didn't falter. "I was expecting you to try shock, war wizard. This armor is grounded."

He's not wearing a helmet, Squirrel pointed out.

The problem is hitting it, Fist replied as he traded blows with the imp. *He's good.*

Can I help? Squirrel said, putting the partially eaten olive back in his cheek.

Fist's instincts were to say no, but after the morning's events he had realized that things needed to change. He couldn't keep treating Squirrel like an animal. He had evolved past that.

Fist raised his air shield to block another fire attack. *Just bide your time. Watch for an opening.*

Squirrel was already standing between the imp's legs. He touched the ground and a sharp spike of rock erupted from the earth.

Edge approached the Bash Brothers with a look of grim disappointment. They gave him bland looks, each hefting their magically enhanced clubs.

"What are you three doing here with these mercenaries?" Edge asked.

"Ooh! Yeah, friends!" Rufus said, beating his chest with one fist. "What you doing?"

The three warwielders looked at each other. "It's a job," Delvin said reluctantly.

Edge folded his arms. "Fighting us?"

"We don't want to fight," Chester said, rubbing his bald head with a reluctant hand.

"We told Ghazard we won't kill anybody," Evastus said, crossed his arms over his yellow vest. "So he says our job is just to delay you."

"Want to play cards?" Delvin asked hopefully.

Edge shook his head. "That's not good enough. I hired you to help me find my wife. What you're doing right now is putting her in danger."

"We'll still help you later," Chester assured him. "After this part's over."

Edge glared at Evastus, ignoring his puppet brothers. "What part? The part where Fist and Lenny and Deathclaw are forced to fight for their lives? The part where Jhonate climbs up that mountain not knowing she's with a servant of the Dark Prophet? You said that you would fight anyone who threatened us, even Ghazardblast."

"Yeah!" said Rufus angrily. He grew a few inches larger in size just to show he was serious.

Evastus wouldn't meet Edge's eyes. "We kind of owe him, though."

"He betrayed you," Edge reminded them. "Abandoned you and ran away."

"He was gonna come back," Chester replied.

Delvin stuck his chest out. "It was just a tactical retreat."

Again, Edge didn't acknowledge them. He advanced on Evastus. "We have a contract. You and me. What do you owe this wizard? Is he the one that helped you when your brothers died?"

Chester and Delvin looked at each other and laughed. "That's crazy talk!" They said and though Evastus didn't speak, his lips moved along with them.

"They got . . . hurt," Evastus corrected. "Ghazard healed them."

"And gave you the connection to them?" Edge asked. "How much did he charge you?"

"We owe him . . . favors," Evastus replied.

"Do you have a contract with him?" Edge asked.

"We owe him," said Chester and Delvin.

Edge pointed at Evastus. "You are a mercenary. What happens when word gets out that you betray your clients?"

Evastus frowned and said slowly, "I told you that we will still honor our deal."

"You're breaking it right now," Edge growled.

Chester loomed over him. "We will do our favor for Ghazard first! Work for you later!"

Edge wasn't going to play Evastus' game anymore. He reached out to the power of Rage. His right sword had absorbed Edge's worry and anxiety for weeks and was buzzing with the power it had gained. He pulled that power through the bond and into the sword's connection with the naming rune on the back of his right hand.

Chester leaned in close to him. "Hey. You listening to me, Sir Edge?"

Edge backhanded the puppet across the face. The moment the rune touched the orc's skin, he released a third of the sword's stored energy in an explosion of force that sent the eight-foot-tall warwielder hurtling end over end to collide with the rocky mountainside behind him.

"Chester!" Delvin and Evastus cried.

"Oh!" said Rufus, putting a surprised hand to his head.

Edge jabbed a finger at Evastus. "You are talking to me. Don't hide behind the corpses of your brothers!"

The orc finally looked at him, his eyes full of anger. His hand gripped his club. "They're not dead! Ghazard fixed them."

As he spoke, Chester stood and shook his head. He tried to open and close his mouth but seemed to be having some trouble. The protections on him were as strong as Edge had figured. All that blow had done was dislocate his jaw.

"He's okay!" Rufus declared.

"You're a liar," Edge told Evastus. "You lie to yourself and you lied to me when you broke our contract."

Evastus swallowed. "I didn't . . . We don't break contracts."

"I'm done talking to you," Edge said. He turned away from the orcs and walked towards the wall of fire. He drew his swords. "I'm leaving. If you try to stop me, Evastus, I'll kill you. What will happen to your brothers then?"

Without waiting for a response, Edge called out, "Artemus!"

Mist flowed from his chest and a cold pale hand soon rested on his shoulder. The wizard stood two feet taller than him with red eyes and a beard made of ice. "The fire?"

"If you would," Edge replied.

The elemental flowed over to the barrier and as he neared it, the flames simply ceased to be. The entire barrier evaporated.

Ghazardblast, who had been sitting on a rock and humming as he waited for the fighting to end jumped in surprise. He stood with his staff at the ready, but when he saw Artemus standing there, he swallowed.

"We are ending this fight!" Edge announced, but he soon saw that two of the battles were already over. Both the imp and Vern lay dead on the ground. Lenny was standing next to the dwarf, counting coins that he had found in Vern's coin purse.

Squirrel was doing something similar, rooting around in the dead imp's armor. Fist's cheeks colored as he saw Edge looking on. "Oh, I was about to dispel the fire myself," he claimed.

Only Deathclaw and the gnome warrior still danced around each other. Each of them was a blur. The raptoid's skin was bleeding in several places, but the wounds were minor. The gnome warrior, however, appeared untouched.

Edge could see that the two of them were incredibly well-matched, but if he had to give an advantage to one over the other, the gnome had an edge. The gnome was quicker and likely had centuries of fighting experience. Deathclaw's innate control of his body and ability to take damage kept him in the fight.

Edge turned to face Ghazardblast. "This is over. Call off your gnome."

The wizard turned a scowl on the Bash Brothers. Chester had returned to his brothers' sides and was rubbing at his jaw. "What are you doing, Evastus? Why aren't you fighting? They killed Belfae!"

"We're not fighting because we had a contract with Sir Edge and his tribe," Evastus replied and the three huge warwielders walked towards the wizard. "No matter what you say, we don't break deals."

"Besides, we never liked Belfae," said Delvin. "He cheated at cards."

"Call off the gnome!" Edge repeated.

"Fine," the old wizard said with bared teeth. "Three! Your task is over. Come back."

The gnome took one last swipe at Deathclaw. When the raptoid dodged, the gnome flipped backwards, landed on his feet, sheathed his swords, and without further emotion, ran to the wizard's side.

"Hey!" Deathclaw shouted and started to run after him.

Stop, Edge said. *Let him go. We have enough challenges ahead.*

Deathclaw hissed and glared at the gnome.

Three didn't care about the raptoid's frustration. He addressed the wizard. "I want full pay."

"Half," the wizard replied. "This mess got cut short."

The gnome nodded and walked through the portal. The wizard motioned to the Bash Brothers. "You coming?" Evastus hesitated and the wizard pressed, "I'm not coming back for you. If you don't come with us now you can walk back to Khalpany."

Evastus looked to Edge. "If you want us to leave, we'll only charge you the basic fee."

"You mean you'll prorate it," Lenny said firmly. "You was only with us fer three gall-durned weeks."

"No," Edge said, looking up at the milling hordes of guardians crowding the slopes. "Stay and help us fight our way up this mountain, Evastus. If we survive, I'll pay you for the full two months we agreed upon."

Evastus looked to his two brothers. They shrugged back at him. "We did have a contract."

"Might as well keep it," Chester said, though with his jaw dislocated it came out as a mumble.

"Alright, fine," said Evastus. "We'll fight with the Big and Little People Tribe."

Ghazardblast craned his neck to see the foes above them and shook his head. "Yeah, doubt I'll see you again," he said and walked through the brick portal. The moment he stepped inside, it crumbled to the ground

Are you ready? Edge asked his bonded. They nodded in the affirmative. *Artemus?*

"The elemental craves this fight," he said, his voice a chilling rasp.

"Then it's time to climb," Edge said, and he drew his swords.

Chapter Twenty Eight
The Big and Little People Tribe – Guardians

Nod let the seer's body slide to the ground and turned his attention to Jhonate. "Don't run, love."

"Run?" Jhonate thrust her spear at him. He dodged to the side and the sudden movement caused her to stumble. He smiled. He could see that her legs were failing her. The poison dart he had stabbed into her hip was taking effect.

Nod laughed and stumbled a bit himself. He really wished he hadn't needed to expend so much energy just to get to this place. The stairs combined with the constant mental barrage had worn him down. At least he didn't have to simper around the awful woman anymore.

He winced and stretched out his previously crippled left hand, his fingers stretching wide. "Ya got no idea how much it hurt to keep me hand all scrunched like that for days on end."

She leaned on her spear once more, trying to get her unruly legs under control. "Why did you pretend to be crippled? I would have believed another type of curse."

"Mayhap," he said. "But ya woulda' been right curious about this glove of mine." Grinning he removed the glove and showed her the back of his hand. "Would've given me right away, now wouldn't it?"

Her shoulders slumped as she saw the black spirit magic rune that marked him as a warrior in the service of the Dark Prophet. "Of course. The Dark Bowl." She gave him a stony look. "Why did you bring me all the way here? Was it just to kill the seer?"

"That was a nice side benefit, I'll give ya that," he said. "Rahan's been on the Dark Prophet's kill list for a long time. His prophecies could be somewhat . . . frustratin' to the cause. But in truth, what I needed was that dagger of yours."

"This?" she said, shaking the staff. "Why did you not just kill me and take it. You had plenty of opportunities."

"Well, I was thinkin' about it. At first. But then ya went and used it to get yourself named and that changed things, dinnit? If ya kill a named warrior, the weapon breaks. Poof! Done. I've seen it a'fore."

She slumped further, grasping her spear, barely able to keep from falling over as the poison worked. "So what is your plan now? We are here. If you want my dagger, you still cannot kill me."

"I don't gotta tell ya every'fing, love," he said.

"I am not your love," she said.

"Ya know, that's right!" He laughed ruefully. "I dragged your highness all the way across the damned world, puttin' up with your high and mighty act, me hand aching all day and night. And me having to pretend to have a curse on me noodle when some'fing lookin' like you's across the fire? I hate ya now. I hope ya understand why."

"I hate you, too," she said with a bleary scowl. "I have loathed you since the second day of our journey." She shook her head and blinked her striking green eyes. "I still do not know what you want."

"I'm waitin' for ya to drop so I can take the dagger," he said with a smile. "Won't need it long."

"Is that all?" She tossed the spear to him. "Take it."

Out of reflex, he reached out with his right hand and snatched the Jharro spear out of the air. The moment his hand grasped the warm wood, he knew he had made a mistake. Spikes sprouted from the wood, piercing the flesh of his hand.

Cursing, he tried to let go, but the spikes hadn't grown straight. They had curved through his flesh, entrapping him.

Jhonate stood straight, the tired expression leaving her face. "It is an old Roo-Tan trick. Make your enemy trap himself."

Nod grimaced, clutching his arm. The spikes were still growing. Even worse the staff was seven feet long and dragging it like this was unwieldy. He knew he might have to cut off the hand. How infuriating. He had avoided losing a limb thus far, unlike most of the past Zestons. He eyed the four seals near the barrier. The staff still had the dagger attached to it. His mission could still be a success.

He grunted and edged his way towards the arch, dragging the spear across the ground, leaving a trail of his blood on the ground. "You're lookin' awful chipper all the sudden."

"I have spent the last four days chewing a cure for poison," she said, keeping pace with him. "Do you remember? I offered and you said you did not want any."

"Oh, those leaves," he said bitterly. Stupid coincidence. A general cure. If he had chosen a different poison, it might have still worked.

Jhonate seemed to notice that he was trying to get close to the archway, because she hurried to cut him off. Oh well, change of plan. He winced. "Tell me, Sar. What do I gotta do to get this rig off me arm, huh? Obviously you've won. I can't run off with this think hangin' on me now, can I?"

He lifted it and held it out to her, scooting the spear closer so that she could grab it. Keeping her distance, she crouched down and reached for the staff. As she did so he whipped his left arm forward, throwing his wicked short sword towards her belly.

It was a carefully targeted throw. If it hit too close to her most important organs, the magic in the sword could liquify them. If she died quick, he'd lose the dagger.

Jhonate saw the attack at the last moment and tried to dodge. The sword struck her side instead of her belly. The magic in the leather breastplate she wore fought against the sword, but there was a reason Nod liked that sword so much. The breastplate only deflected part of the magic. The blade bit into her side with destructive power. It only slid in an inch, but that was all he needed.

She cried out in pain. Nod pulled away from her, still intending to drag the dagger with him, but Jhonate had the staff open up and release it to the floor with a clatter. She picked it up and faced him with the dagger in one hand. Her other hand clenched her side. Blood flowed from the wound.

"Well, we both got an owwie now, don't we, Sar?" Nod said with a laugh.

"What do you still want Tulos for?" Jhonate pressed, her teeth bared. "Do you think it can be turned back to the Dark Prophet's uses?"

He snorted and moved his left hand behind his back to the throwing dagger he had hidden. "Not bloody likely."

Jhonate saw him grabbing for something and rotated around him, causing him to turn to follow her. As he did so, the shaft of the Jharro staff lost its rigidity and went limp. The rope-like wood curled around his leg and before Nod could react, it hardened again.

Yelping, he stumbled and tripped and as he reached out to stop his fall, the woman stabbed the back of his left hand with her white dagger. The moment that the blade cut through the rune, Nod screamed. A rushing sound filled his ears and, as he watched, the black rune on his hand evaporated.

He blinked with a mix of horror and amazement. "Y-you cut my connection to the Dark Prophet?" He laughed. "Why would you want to free me?"

"Free you?" She arched an eyebrow. "Yes, I want to free you."

Jhonate jerked the dagger out of his hand, then bashed him between the eyes with the handle's bulbous base. Nod saw flashes of light and he nearly passed out. Shaken, he barely noticed as she caused the staff to untangle from his legs and straighten once again. She grasped the shaft of her staff and used it as leverage to make him climb to his feet.

Nod stumbled blearily, feeling the pain of the injuries to his hands, but knocked loopy. She pulled him along the flat surface of the mountain top and he tottered along with her, trying to blink away the dizziness. Then, grunting with the strain and the pain of her own injury she swung him towards the edge.

As he stumbled off into the emptiness, she had the wooden spikes withdraw back into the staff. Bewildered, Nod plummeted towards the rocks far below.

"Be free," Jhonate said.

The satisfaction she felt at her victory was brief as pain lanced through her wound. Her side continued to bleed profusely, and she had seen the kinds of wounds that Nod's sword made. A wave of weakness came over her and it wasn't just loss of blood. The leaves she had chewed counteracted some types of poisons, but only weakened others.

Leaning heavily on her staff, she made her way to the altar where Seer Rahan had been sitting when they arrived. Groaning, she sat on the corner of the marble slab. She knew that she needed to remove her breastplate and bandage the wound, but first she needed to lie back for just a moment.

As she did so, her blood pooling on the altar beneath her, the pain fled. She looked up into the clear sky and realized that it wasn't even cold up here. It was pleasant in fact.

Suddenly, though there was still plenty daylight left, she could see the stars. But it was more than just stars. Light filled her eyes and she saw everything.

* * *

"Twice named!" "EAT!" "Soft ones . . ." "Dwarf meat."
"Puppetmaster!"

The guardians called out in a cacophony of mental attack as Edge and his companions fought their way up the meandering stone stairway. Usually, the bond was an effective shield against spirit magic attacks, but there was something about these guardians that allowed them to get through the bond's protection. Edge didn't know if it was because their power was holy in some way or if they just weren't using a traditional spirit magic attack, but whatever it was, their mental assault was effective.

"Slow!" "DEVOUR YOU." "Snake." "Frail thing . . ."
"I'm hurt." "Help me!"

The guardians called into each mind, pinpointing fears and weaknesses, all amidst the non-stop physical assault. They poured from the caves continuously. Each one was a different mutated conglomeration and the more that came, the sloppier their construction seemed. Some had three heads, some none. The size or lack of brain didn't seem to matter. Others had two left arms or multiple legs. Edge saw one dragging itself along without any legs at all.

The thing they had in common was the wide toothy mouth in their chests. This seemed to be the only truly vital part of them. Edge had quickly discovered that the swiftest way to dispatch them was to slash at the sides of their mouths and sever their jaws. Without a way to bite, the beast would collapse lifelessly.

He and Deathclaw worked as a unit on the right side of the stairway. The raptoid whirled and slashed with sword and tail while Edge cut beasts apart with Peace and blasted them to the side with Rage. Body parts littered the mountainside and faded from view.

When a guardian was felled, its body simply sunk into the earth and disappeared. Edge didn't know where they went. The only certain thing was that more kept coming.

"Short one!" "Dwarf King?" "Deserter . . ." "EAT you!"

"It's like there's a garl-friggin' army of demented toddlers under the mountain assemblin' these things from random body parts!" Lenny yelled, blasting aside a scaled beast with four arms and an insectoid head. Another creature rose up to meet him, this one a wide beast without skin, just exposed muscle and sinew.

There are theories about this, Artemus said as his elemental form flowed slowly up the path at the forefront of the group. He froze large swaths of them with his magic, then shattered them with thrown javelins of ice.

"Dead!" "Old one!" "Ghost." "Freeze me!"

Some say that when this world was created, there were many unused parts and that the power of the holy site pulls them from there, said Artemus. *Others say that these are the assembled bodies of creatures long buried or forgotten. I for one think that perhaps what we see is not real at all. Perhaps they are just mental representations of beasts and that the defense of the holy site is an entirely mental one.*

They seem real enough to me! Fist said as one bit into his leg. He sent a shock through the thing and it fell smoking.

"An ogre . . ?" "MEAT." "Master." "So soft . . ." "MY FRIEND" "Wizard"

Fist and his bonded fought together on the left side in a tight group. He and Squirrel buzzed around with magically induced speed, the ogre pulping guardians with swings of his mace and Squirrel cutting them to pieces with blades of air. Rufus, grown huge, smashed guardians with his enormous fists or threw them down the mountainside. Sometimes, if he was bitten, he'd bite back, tearing them in two and spitting them out with a grimace.

The rogue horse was perhaps the most susceptible to the mental attacks. He didn't take well to being mocked and fought with tears rolling down his black cheeks. Despite Fist's and Squirrel's encouragement, he started to slow.

The only ones completely unaffected by the attacks seemed to be the Bash Brothers. They kept to the rear and smashed aside guardians with their long magical clubs, sending broken bodies off of the stair with ruthless efficiency. They were a consistent force keeping the party from being overwhelmed from below.

"Bonding wizard." "Worthless magic." "She's dead." *"DEAD."*

The fighting wore on and though they made steady progress, the way was long and the enemy was endless.

Despite his weariness being sucked away by Peace's magic, Edge knew he was growing weaker. So were the others. No matter how powerful, everyone had limits.

Artemus had reached his. He exhausted his magic with a final freezing blast. With an apologetic sigh, he said, *Any more and I lose all cohesion. Survive, Edge. I must rest.* The elemental crumpled in a pile of icy snow and retreated to his home within Edge's chest.

"Crap!" shouted Lenny, seeing the wizard's retreat.

Edge moved to take Artemus' place and waved his sword, blasting apart a slew of frozen guardians with explosive magic, and looked up the slopes. They were only halfway there. Had he doomed everyone?

"Dying" "Soon now!" "We will feast!" "Twice-named . . ."

Edge! shouted an excited voice through the bond. *Edge! Edge! Edge!*

A new source flooded through the bond, perking everyone up and Edge saw a shape descending the mountain towards him. The beast was a blur, ignoring the stair and bounding down the slopes with cat-like grace, scattering misshaped guardians along the way.

It was large, perhaps ten feet at the shoulders, and it ran on all fours. Its head was that of a lizard and scales covered its clawed legs and lower half of its body. A long thick tail whipped out behind it, knocking creatures aside as it went. Its back was covered in a short pelt of fur and there was a strangely shaped leather saddle strapped to it. Horse-like ears stood at the top of its shaggy mane.

Edge! she cried and her joy filled the bond. *My tribe! I am here*!

Joy bloomed within Edge's heart and he didn't let the sword steal it away. "Gwyrtha!"

*   *   *

As the lights faded from Jhonate's vision, the things that she had seen started to fade from her mind. She tried to grasp hold of them but there was too much of it. More than her waking mind could grasp.

She tried to sit up, but the pain that stabbed through her side was so great that it made her cry out. Grimacing, she rolled over and swung her legs down from the altar. She pushed herself into a standing position and grabbed her staff and dagger, still trying to remember some of what she had seen. These were important things.

She placed her dagger back into the end of her staff and nearly stumbled over the body of Seer Rahan. The old man was slumped at the base of the altar. She winced as she saw that some of her blood had dripped off to intermingle with his.

"Poor man," she mumbled. How long had he been up in this place waiting? What did he eat up here?

Jhonate blinked and shook her head, realizing that she was still loopy. She was supposed to be bandaging herself, not looking around. Nevertheless, her eyes moved to the barrier and the archway that was attached to it.

To her surprise, there was movement on the other side. With one hand clutching her spear and the other clutching her side, she approached the barrier for a closer look. The thing that had moved on the other side came closer too, and she could make out a blurry figure. It gestured to her urgently, beckoning her closer.

Jhonate did so, entranced. She couldn't make out what the figure looked like, but it was humanoid in shape.

The figure's gesturing became more urgent and, as she watched, it pressed itself against the barrier. Doing this seemed to cause it pain, and she could make out the shape of a mouth opening with a cry.

"Do not!" she urged, holding out her hand pleadingly. "You will hurt yourself!"

The figure backed off somewhat and pointed towards the archway. Jhonate's eyes focused on the four seals. Two were gray and one was white. The other one was black. It radiated evil. Instantly, she knew that she could destroy it with her dagger. That must be what the figure on the other side of the barrier was trying to tell her.

Her eyes bleary, her mind still fuzzy from the effects of poison and loss of blood, this made sense to her. The seal was evil. Her dagger destroyed evil. She moved towards the seal and lifted her spear to strike.

"Stop!" commanded a voice with such power and authority that the tip of Jhonate's dagger came to a quivering stop inches from the seal.

She turned her head and saw a man that she recognized. His hair was brown and he wore a short beard and he was as familiar to her as a brother. Yet she knew that the moment she looked away she wouldn't be able to remember what his face looked like. Except for those eyes. Those kind eyes. "John?"

"Sar Zahara," the Prophet said. "Please don't destroy that seal. It would be very bad."

"O-oh," she said and pulled the spear away from the archway.

John walked over to Seer Rahan's fallen form and crouched next to him. With a sad sigh, he closed the old man's eyes and reached within his robes to withdraw the folded paper that Jhonate had seen Rahan put away. The edge of the paper was bloodstained, but that didn't seem to bother the Prophet as he opened it up and read.

"But . . . John, this seal is evil. There was a person standing there, wanting me to destroy it," she said, but when she pointed at the barrier, there was no one there.

John looked away from the letter to the place where she had pointed, his brow furrowed with a look of anger. "I would suggest not paying any heed to people on that side of the barrier. If you had destroyed that seal, the sacrifices of many good people would have been for naught." He looked back at the letter.

"But . . . Why is something evil allowed in this place?" she asked him.

"To erect this barrier required a balance. The combined power of all four prophets keeps the Known Lands separated from the rest of the world," John replied.

"Then the black seal came from the Dark Prophet," she realized, and blinked. "You said four prophets?"

"Yes," he said, one hand stroking his short beard as he reread parts of the letter. "One of us stayed on the other side. But please don't ask me any more questions about her. There are some things this world doesn't need to know."

Jhonate turned to approach him, but when she did so she winced and clutched at her side. Blood was once again running from the wound. "I think . . . this is a fatal wound, John."

"No it isn't," the Prophet said absently and as he said so, the pain eased. He closed the letter and gave Seer Rahan a sad smile, then came to her side. "But it will need to be healed." He held the letter out to her. "Most of what he says is for you."

When she took the letter from him, his fingers brushed hers and the cloudiness that the poison had left in her mind faded. She stood a little straighter and gave him a grateful nod, then began to read. The letter began in much the way that the first letter had, with a few notable changes.

> *To Jhonate bin Leeths of the Big and Little*
> *People Tribe, Defender of the Grove, Daughter*
> *of Xedrion Bin Leeths, Wife of Sir Edge,*
> *Academy Graduate, Named Warrior, Seeress,*
> *Mother of Arriana and possible mother of many*
> *more,*

Stunned, she looked back to John. "Seeress?"

"Well, a seeress in training, perhaps," he said. "Keep reading."

> *I am writing this letter in hopes that you will*
> *find it after my death. I am sorry that I will not*
> *be able to tell you these things in person. I am*
> *also sorry to tell you that your curse is not*
> *something that a simple seer like myself can*
> *break. However, the mere fact that you have*
> *come all this way and made the sacrifices*
> *needed tells me that you have the power and*
> *determination to see it done.*
>
> *If you wish to have another child, you should*
> *know that the sacrifices you have made thus far*
> *are small ones compared to what will come.*
> *Many of those closest to you, and to your*
> *husband, will die. The conditions are very*
> *specific . . .*

As she read on, her expression filled with horror and she looked to John. "Does this have to be? I-I take it back. I can live with the curse."

The Prophet's kind eyes were sympathetic. "I am afraid that events have already been set in motion.

359

Please don't think that this is your fault, though. If you hadn't come here it still would have happened eventually. But thanks to what happened today, the time is upon us."

Feeling a deep sense of guilt, she returned to the letter.

> *Take heart. Though this new burden you have been given means you will face some of these trials alone, the man you have married and the tribe you have joined will be there to support you along the way. Don't fear to depend on them. They are as crucial to this world's survival as you are.*
>
> *May you be blessed,*
>
> *Rahan*
>
> *One last thing. John, I know you will be reading this. Please don't bother to bury my body. I promised the guardians they could eat me after I died. Don't worry. I won't be needing it anymore.*

She frowned at the weight of the responsibility that was now on her shoulders.

"He's right," John assured her. "Though the burden may feel like something you have to bear alone, it's not. You've surrounded yourself with good people. Use them."

Jhonate nodded, then cocked her head. "How did you get up here?"

"Oh, I prefer the side route to the top. The front feels so much steeper," he said.

She looked around. "Do you not have Gwyrtha with you?"

"Oh, she's run down the mountain to join your husband. She has missed him, and you, very deeply and has decided that my time with her is over." John rubbed his chin. "I suppose I should go back to the valley to choose another rogue horse. It is a pity. There are so few left."

"Wait," she said. "Edge is here?"

"Sir Edge and his bonded are currently fighting their way through guardians trying to reach you," John replied.

Jhonate's eyes widened in alarm. "He is fighting his way through those things? You are letting him?"

"Gwyrtha is having so much fun, and the guardians rarely get the chance to fight," he said. "But I have just ordered them to stand down. Shall we go down and meet him? You should have Fist tend to that wound properly. My blessing magic only does so much."

*   *   *

Gwyrtha plowed through a throng of misshapen enemies to get to Edge's side, but there was no time for embraces or affection. The fight raged on. Gwyrtha ran around the perimeter of the party, slashing and biting the guardians and bringing relief to each group.

"Geertha!" Rufus took heart at her presence and attacked with renewed vigor, banishing the emotional weight of the guardian's attacks.

Where did you come from? Edge asked her through the bond.

Me and John came to the top and I came down! she said happily as she whipped her head from side to side, shaking a snake-like monstrosity to pieces.

The Prophet is here? Edge said. *Is he with Jhonate? Is she okay*?

I don't know, she replied. *He told me you were here and I went.*

Gradually, the fighting eased. The guardians seemed to lose their enthusiasm for the battle. Even their mental attacks faded into disappointment.

"*Still hungry . . .*" "*Sad.*" "*There is nothing . . .*" "*Home . . .*"

The crowd around them dissipated and soon they were alone on the mountainside. The party collapsed.

"Dag-gum," said Lenny, dropping to the stair, sweat dripping from him. "Did we win?"

"The Prophet is here somewhere on the mountain above. I think he might be with Jhonate."

"Oh, that's the best news I've heard in weeks," Lenny said before being bowled over by a half reptile monster.

Lenny! Missed you! Gwyrtha pinned the dwarf down and covered him in big lapping kisses with her wide tongue, leaving him wet and sputtering. She moved on to the rest of the group, avoiding the Bash Brothers, and assaulted them all, leaving them wet and knowing they were loved.

"This is not the part I missed," Deathclaw hissed, wiping slobber from his face.

Finally, she came to Edge and he wrapped his arms around her huge head. "I missed you so much, Girl."

I'm staying with you now, she promised him. *I'm not leaving again. John will find a different ride.*

"That makes me very happy," he said. *Will you take me up to Jhonate?*

Yes! Ride, she said and shrunk down until she was back to her normal size, her shoulders level with his.

"You can rest here," he told everyone else. "Gwyrtha's taking me up." Edge reached into his bond with her and pulled energy from her blazing core. Then, feeling rejuvenated, he climbed into her saddle.

Rogue horses were designed to be ridden by bonding wizards and there was nothing in the world Gwyrtha liked to do more than run with Edge on her back. She ran up the mountainside, sometimes using the stair, but most often sprinting up the steep slopes. She was in her element and Edge was too. He clung to her back with practiced ease and reveled in her joy, his worry for Jhonate fading with the knowledge that John was with her. That worry returned in full force when she came into view.

Jhonate and the Prophet were a short distance from the top when he saw her. She was descending the rough-hewn stairway gingerly, one hand gripping her staff, the other one clutching John's arm. She was pale and her side was caked with blood.

"Jhonate!" Edge yelled and urged Gwyrtha to pick up speed.

She saw him coming and a smile brightened her face. He felt her presence return to the Jharro ring on his finger and she spoke to him. *Justan, my love!*

Are you okay? he asked.

Gwyrtha finally reached them and Edge leapt from the saddle and rushed to her side. He wanted to embrace her, crush her against him, but he didn't dare. He reached out to cup her chin. "You're injured."

"John says it is not fatal," she assured him.

"I was taking her to Fist so that she can be healed," John said. "Can you ask him to join us?"

"No. Edge can do it," Jhonate said.

Edge frowned. "Are you sure?"

She placed her hand on his arm, "We have much to tell each other. Heal me. It is the fastest way."

Edge nodded and drew Peace. He flipped the sword around so that the dagger-like point on the bottom of the handle was extended toward her. She pierced her hand on the tip.

Edge's mind was drawn into hers. He saw what she had gone through over the past few months as he had been gone searching for the Prophet. She had missed him and during those lonely nights had agonized over their lost child and childless future. When the letter from Seer Rahan had come it had been a chance for her to stop waiting and mourning and do something about it.

He experienced her meeting with Nod and saw her journey play before him. He felt her agony and frustration, and most strongly, her sense of purpose. He saw her trials in the desert and her mountain climb and Nod's betrayal and their fight. But when she laid on the altar, his mind was pushed from hers. Edge knew that there was something there that he was not meant to see. He began working on her wound.

While he had been living her memories, she had done the same with his and as he healed her, he felt her love for him fill his mind.

You went through so much for me.

Everyone did, he said as he carefully worked to stitch together the torn tissues in her side. It was delicate work. The magic of Nod's sword had done severe damage. If it had pierced her any deeper, she would not have survived.

I will show all of them my gratitude, she promised. Her thoughts became troubled. *I saw things, Justan. When I laid on the altar . . . Horrible things.*

I could not see them, Edge said. *The power of this holy place didn't let me.*

Many of them have faded from my mind as well, she said. *But after what the seer told me . . . I am afraid.*

He frowned. Jhonate never admitted to being afraid. *What could there possibly be that would make Jhonate bin Leeths afraid?*

It is Sar Zahara now, she said somewhat bitterly. She still wasn't used to it and the connotations that came from the things Rahan had told her about it made her uneasy. A great deal of new responsibility had been added to her life.

Edge understood what that was like. *Oh, is that what you want me to start calling you now?* he teased.

Only when we are in front of others, she replied, but she wasn't amused for long. *Justan, the thing that makes me fearful is what must be done before my curse is broken.*

Stop saying that. It's our curse, Edge said. *You don't bear this burden alone.*

You do not understand, she said. *This is not some selfish fear. Hear me. Seer Rahan left me another letter and in it he told me that before the curse is broken, people that we know and love, people in our tribe, will die.*

Edge felt a stirring of dread. *Do you know who?*

I do not.

He let out a stubborn grunt. *Well, I refuse to believe that such things are inevitable. We will have to be certain to do everything we can to make sure that doesn't happen.*

We may have no choice, she replied.

There is always a choice. If anyone can do this, it's us. Finally finished with the healing, Edge removed her hand from his sword and embraced her, kissing her soundly.

He turned to John who had politely stepped away and was brushing Gwyrtha's mane. "John, did you get the dark dagger back? Celos? The one that Nod stole from the Mage School?"

"No," said the Prophet. "He didn't have it with him."

"He may have passed it on to someone in Filgren," Jhonate said. "I saw him delivering packages there."

"Packages?" Edge said.

"Unfortunately, yes," John said. "He stole the Rings of Stardeon."

Edge swallowed. "How can that be? I gave them to you. I hoped you would destroy them."

John gave him a patient look. "I told you I could not do that. I stored them in the vault at the Mage School and he took them at the same time he was taking the dagger."

"Alright." Edge sighed. "So we need to retrieve the Rings of Stardeon. Great. That's never been hard before."

We can do it! Gwyrtha assured him.

"Unfortunately, neither the rings nor the dagger are our largest problem right now," John said. "David has beaten me today, outsmarted me."

"But . . . we stopped him," Jhonate said with a frown. "The seals weren't broken. The barrier stands."

"The barrier breaking is just one of two calamities that I have long known were coming to this world. Both of them are inevitable," he said. "I have heard my master's thoughts on this and he had told me that they are coming.

"Nevertheless, I have managed to delay them for two centuries. Through my efforts and the efforts of bonding wizards and those named by the Bowl of Souls, generations of good people have been able to live full lives without seeing the horrors that are to come."

"You say two calamities," Jhonate said. Her brow creased in a frown as she thought of the Seer's final letter. "Is one of them the Dark Prophet's return?"

"It is," John said. "You two have helped me stop him before. But David is clever and he never enacts one plan without having several other backup plans in the wings. Recently, I discovered that many of his attempts to return were decoys, ruses to keep me occupied through the years while his true designs went by undetected. Today, those designs came to fruition."

That feeling of dread within Edge swelled. "What did he do?"

"He made me choose between those two great calamities," John said with a tired sigh. "My choices were to come here and save Alsarobeth and you from destruction, or go

366

to Khalpany and save a child to prevent David' return. He knew that I couldn't be in both places at once. And he knew which choice I would make."

Edge swallowed. "This isn't the first time you've faced a hard decision, John. You always seem to make the right one."

The Prophet placed a hand over his heart. "That is kind of you, but I often find it hard to believe." He shook his head. "The results of those choices are my burden to bear. Usually when I have to make a decision between options this horrible, I have servants in the area, people I can trust to fight without me."

"And this time?" Edge asked.

"I have good people there. People that have helped me stop David before. I trust them, but . . ." He put his hand on Edge's shoulder and there was deep sorrow in his eyes. "This time I fear they are not enough."

Edge swallowed. "What are you saying?"

"If my people are defeated tonight, dark times are coming, Edge."

Chapter Twenty Nine
Lucinder – Escape

Lucinder looked out his window, his headache forgotten. He watched with rapt excitement as the fires in the city blossomed. This was the signal. Tonight was the night of his escape.

For the past two weeks he had watched and waited, worried that Bertrom's attack would be too late and that the guards would come and drag him to the dungeons. But finally, the time had come.

He had so many plans for what he wanted to do once he got out of here. First, he would enter the Training School so that he could join the Academy. Then, he would kiss a girl. His interest was equally pulled in both those directions.

The fires raged and shouts filled the streets. Palace guards rushed out to help, something that Lucinder was certain was part of Bertrom's plan. During the distraction, his people would sneak into the dungeons and begin freeing prisoners. Then, somehow, they would create the impression that they were going after the Dark Bowl. While Priestress Sren and Warwielder Ghat gathered their forces, Bertrom would use the opportunity to come up and take Lucinder away.

The prince wasn't certain if the named warrior would appear at his window again or come to the door. Either way had its advantages, but he thought the fastest way would be to leave via the window. Lucinder still wasn't sure how Bertrom managed to jump from that high window without being hurt, but he trusted that the warrior would have a way for both of them to do it.

The only part he was nervous about was when it came time to cut off his toe. He knew it was necessary because of the tracking spell, but he wondered if there was a way to do it without it hurting too badly. Of course, compared to his horrendous headaches it couldn't be so bad.

He tried not to think too hard on the headaches. Maybe Sir Bertrom's friends would have a way to ease them. Or more likely, they would just go away. Lucinder had a suspicion that his headaches had something to do with this palace. Priestess Sren hadn't tried to do more than torment him when she had come to help. Maybe his parents had something to do with them. The pain could be a way of keeping him from trying to leave. It was hard to conduct an escape plan when you didn't want to leave your bed.

Lucinder's mind continued to go wild, bubbling from one fantasy to the next as he watched the flurry of activity outside. Then an hour passed. Some of the fires were extinguished. Another hour passed and there were no flames to be seen at all. Just smoke.

Fear built within him. It had grown quiet outside and Sir Bertrom had not come. Then he saw something that caused a chill to rise within him. He caught a glimpse of Priestess Sren passing through the courtyard below. She was entering his wing of the palace.

Lucinder swallowed. Something had gone wrong. His palms began to sweat. His headache throbbed back to full life.

Slowly he stepped up onto the window ledge. It was time to make a choice. He could hear loud footsteps coming down the hall. Sren was coming. He closed his eyes and let go of the sides of the window. He swayed for several long seconds and could feel death yawning before him. That was one type of escape.

There was a loud knock on his door, and he was so startled he almost fell then and there. He stumbled back inside, his heart pounding.

"Prince Lucinder!" shouted Sren's voice.

Lucinder cocked his head. There was something strange about her tone. "What is it?"

"Come. Open the door. There is something you must see!" she cried and there was joy in her voice.

Lucinder blinked. Joy? Priestess Sren? He began to wonder if this wasn't a trick. Could it be that this wasn't Sren at all? Was this a ruse?

"Open, Lucinder," she pressed, but there was no anger in her tone.

"Don't you have a key?" he asked. Thinking back, she had never knocked before. A grin appeared on his face. Was this someone sent by Sir Bertrom? It was a wild idea, a fanciful one, but he found himself moving towards the door.

"I didn't bring it with me," she said and this time there was irritation in her voice. "Come."

Hesitantly, he reached out and disengaged the lock. The door opened and Priestess Sren strode inside. He stepped back, realizing his theory was a false one. If this wasn't her, this was a very good disguise. It was her same beautiful face, blond hair, black lips, and the rune-marked armor was unmistakable.

The only thing that kept him from running and flinging himself out the window at that moment was the smile on her face. It was transcendent, changing her look from one of deadly beauty to true radiance.

"Wh-what are you so happy about?" he asked.

"Because it's time, Lucinder!" she said and laughed. It was a full-throated laugh, not a snicker or cackle.

He found himself laughing along with her. She grasped his hand and pulled him out of the room with her and his steps didn't falter. Alarms rose somewhere in the back of his mind, but she was so convincing. Surely someone as steeped in evil as Sren didn't have this level of joy inside them. If this really wasn't one of Bertrom's friends in disguise than something must have happened to the priestess.

She led him down the hallway, her hand grasped in his and she began to skip girlishly. The alarms in Lucinder's mind grew louder. This was beyond joy. This was the behavior of someone that was either mad or they had fallen in love. At least that was how people in love acted in the books he read. Then again, when people acted this way in the books it was usually a prelude to tragedy.

He swallowed. Madness was a more likely reason for her behavior. "Uh, you said it's time. It's time for what?"

She didn't answer, but continued to lead him, humming to herself. Then she took a turn and he realized that she was leading him into the section of the palace that was inside the cliff face. This wasn't the usual route that the guards took him, but a few more turns and she could be leading him to the dungeons.

He licked his lips, realizing what was happening. It was the obvious thing, after all. He had been so close to escape, and yet here he was like he had always been, the lamb letting himself be taken to slaughter.

"So, what happened tonight?" he asked. "I saw the fires in the city. Everyone was running around."

"Oh, that," she said cheerfully. "Those were just fools. Fools trying to stop the inevitable."

His body went numb. He wasn't sure how he was still moving. "Wh-what's going to happen to me?"

"Only the best thing ever. You, Lucinder, get to become the king of the world. The Known Lands. The Unknown Lands. All of it. You have the lineage. You have the power. All you need is the soul."

Lucinder wanted to run then. He wanted to pull away. But for some reason he couldn't. Despite his instincts telling him to run, he let her lead him into rough-hewn corridors and now-familiar passages. He was in the dungeons now and a short time later she pulled him into that familiar room.

There at the center of the depression was the Dark Bowl. Next to it were his parents. Tears were streaming down his mother's face and he noticed without emotion that she was now wearing a glove on her left hand. It was much like the glove his father wore to cover his shriveled finger, only it was white instead of black.

Sren gestured and Warwielder Ghat appeared. He was wearing his full set of armor, but one of his hands was missing. In its place was a three pronged hook. Ghat grabbed Lucinder's arm in his gauntleted hand and pulled hum further into the room. Lucinder now saw the wall that had been obscured by the doorway and a cry escaped his lips.

Sir Bertrom was chained to the wall. He was spread-eagled, his face bruised and bloodied, and his shirt had been torn away, exposing a torso that was covered in lacerations. The gaze he turned Lucinder's way was mournful.

"I'm sorry, kid. Didn't go as planned." He said, with a wheeze. He smiled through split lips. "Hey, at least Dagger got away. And your nurse."

Lucinder's head throbbed, the ache rekindling with a vengeance.

"And they will soon be caught," Sren said with a chuckle. She snapped her fingers and a orc servant in a black hood hurried forward and held out a long slender box of black wood. In the center of the lid was a jade stone and when she opened it a feeling of horror and anguish filled the room.

The dagger that lay within the box was long and curved and black. Its blade was stained brown with what looked like rust. The handle was a beautiful thing though and set in the pommel was a cluster of jade stones. Evil radiated from the thing with an insistent fury.

Sren laughed and once again it was a beautiful and open-throated laugh. Lucinder couldn't believe that this was the kind of thing that could bring anyone such joy. "Today comes the first of many sacrifices for the Dark Prophet's return. That's why I brought you here tonight, Lucinder." She turned to face Bertrom.

"Wait," said Lucinder. He head hurt more than ever. The dagger's power made him feel as if his brain would simply explode. "Don't kill him."

"Oh, this isn't my doing," she said with a smile. "This is all because of you. You brought him here tonight. You and your simple innocence made this possible."

Still grinning, she lunged forward and thrust the dagger into Bertrom's chest.

"No!" cried Lucinder in horror and as he reached out towards the warrior, something inside his mind broke.

An odd thing happened. The room went silent. A pulse of energy left his mind, glowing in colors of blue, red, black, gold, white, and gray. The pulse left his fingertips and struck Sir Bertrom. The power of it knocked Priestess Sren sprawling, the dagger still clutched in her hands.

Instantly, Bertrom's wounds faded. His face and chest were undamaged, and his eyes were wide and fill of vitality and energy. Lucinder's jaw dropped open in shock.

Then the moment ended. Priestess Sren laughed and climbed to her feet and her smile was wider than ever. Her eyes sparkled. "It worked! Lucinder, you finally had your awakening!"

"I'm so sorry, my son!" wailed Queen Elise and Lucinder realized she was sobbing.

"She's sorry." Sren shook her head good-naturedly. "Your mother chose this path long ago and we are all grateful for it."

Bertrom jerked at his chains, trying to get free, but his restraints were firmly planted in the wall. "It's not too late, kid," he shouted. "Get free! Go!"

But Lucinder couldn't go. Ghat was strong and he was frozen in the orc's grasp.

"Oh, be silent," Sren said and she stabbed Bertrom in the chest again. This time there was no burst of power. No miraculous healing. Instead, a swirl of black mist began to leech from the hilt. Bertrom screamed, pulling at his restraints as the darkness slowly gathered. Then he slumped, the life leaving his eyes.

Sren walked to the Dark Bowl and lifted the black orb that had long rested inside. She brought it over to him and gestured. Lucinder couldn't move. She reached out with the dagger and made a slashing motion. The prince felt no pain. He looked down and watched as she took the black orb and slid it into the hole she had just cut in his chest.

Lucinder's vision went black. He floated in emptiness. At least his head no longer hurt.

A familiar voice spoke to him. **You did it, Lucinder. I thank you.**

What happens now? Lucinder asked.

To you? The dark voice was almost kind as it said, **You rest here. It's time for me to return.**

The prince's eyes opened. He looked down and saw the faint scar on his chest where the black moonrat eye had been planted. He pulled his hand free from the warwielder's grasp.

"I live," he said and smiled. It amused him that the voice that came out of his mouth was the voice of a fifteen-year-old boy.

"David, it's you!" Sren said with a beautiful beaming smile. "Finally, you escape the world of death!"

David took a deep breath, reveling in the feeling of having a corporeal body again. This body was so very young. And so weary. Tendrils of the boy's headache still remained. He rotated his head, enjoying even the feeling of that fading pain.

Smiling, he turned to face the king and queen. He nodded to them. "Mother. Father. Come. There is much to do before this world can be mine."

Thus concludes Sir Edge

The Bowl of Souls series will continue with:
The Dark Prophet Saga Book Two: Halfbreeds

If this was your first Bowl of Souls novel and you would like to learn where the characters of Sir Edge and his bonded began, start from the beginning with Eye of the Moonrat, part one of the Moonrat Saga. The full list continues below.

If you are caught up with the Bowl of Souls, check out **The Wizard of Mysteries Series**, an urban fantasy series about Master Tallow, the Wizard of Mysteries who trained Locksher.

Tallow has come to modern day Atlanta, Georgia to help with a missing persons case and becomes embroiled in the dangerous case of a dark wizard who is bringing in magical objects and creatures from the world of the Bowl of Souls. Please read it and give it a try.

If you love Sir Edge, you are going to adore Master Tallow

The Bowl of Souls series:
THE MOONRAT SAGA
Book One: Eye of the Moonrat
Book 1.5: Hilt's Pride
Book Two: Messenger of the Dark Prophet
Book Three: Hunt of the Bandham
Book Four: The War of Stardeon
Book Five: Mother of the Moonrat

THE JHARRO GROVE SAGA
Book Six: Tarah Woodblade
Book Seven: Protector of the Grove
Book Eight: The Ogre Apprentice
Book Nine: The Troll King
Book Ten: Priestess of War

Book Eleven: Behemoth

THE DARK PROPHET SAGA
12. Sir Edge
13. Halfbreeds (2019)

The Wizard of Mysteries Series
Tallow Jones: Wizard Detective
Tallow Jones: Blood Trail

Also, try Noose Jumpers: A Mythological Western

Like Trevor H. Cooley on Facebook:
https://www.facebook.com/EyeOfTheMoonrat
Follow him on Twitter @Edgewriter
Or on his website http://trevorhcooley.com/
Book reviews are always welcome!

If you wish to become a Patron and become part of the creation of this world, you can join at
https://www.patreon.com/trevorhcooley

I would like to give special thanks to Patreon supporters and alpha readers:
Stephen Quinlan, Vincent Miles, Randy Stiltner, Justin Porter, Ethan Nicolle, Derek Morgan, Adam Masias, Aglaia Greenberg, Brian Layman, Brian Every, Michael R. Clay, Amanda, Alexander Arn, Keith E. Scott, Madisen Dunn, Rebecca Smith, Jay Williams, Elliott Williams, Dave King, Michael Schober, Honor Raconteur, Neil Davis, Kami and Jacob Jenkins, and Morgan Raines.

Also, thank you to all of you active supporters on Facebook, Discord, Twitter, and everyone who leaves reviews.

Please spread the word. The Bowl of Souls needs your help.

Made in the USA
Columbia, SC
12 December 2018